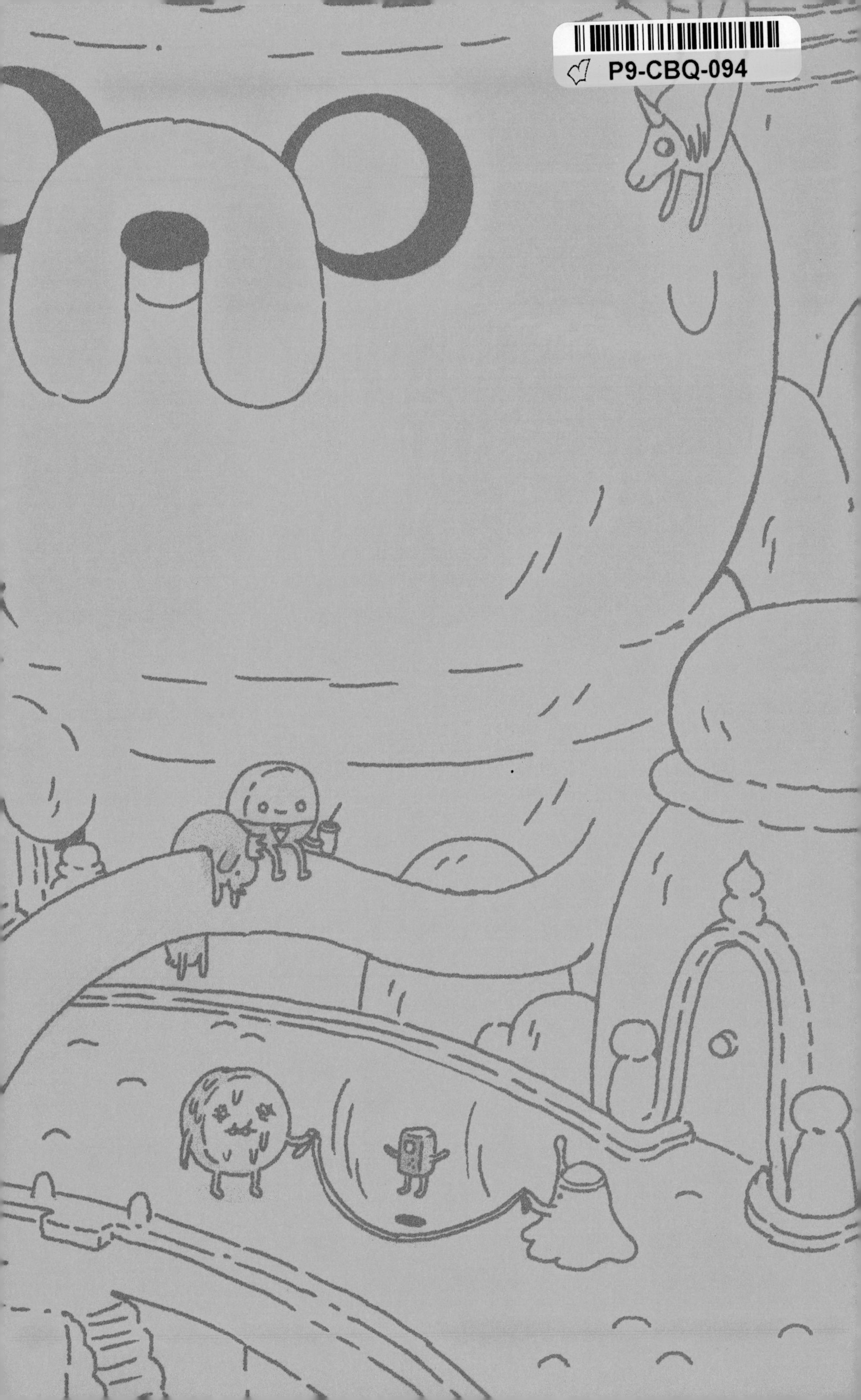

PUBLISHED BY KaBOOM!

ROSS RICHIE ~ CEO & Founder

MATT GAGNON ~ Editor-in-Chief

FILIP SABLIK ~ VP-Publishing & Marketing

LANCE KREITER ~ VP-Licensing & Merchandising

MATT NISSENBAUM ~ Senior Director of Sales & Marketing

PHIL BARBARO ~ Director of Finance

BRYCE CARLSON ~ Managing Editor

DAFNA PLEBAN ~ Editor

SHANNON WATTERS ~ Editor

ERIC HARBURN ~ Editor

CHRIS ROSA ~ Assistant Editor

ALEX GALER ~ Assistant Editor

WHITNEY LEOPARD ~ Assistant Editor

JASMINE AMIRI ~ Assistant Editor

STEPHANIE GONZAGA ~ Graphic Designer

MIKE LOPEZ ~ Production Designer

DEVIN FUNCHES ~ E-Commerce & Inventory Coordinator

VINCE FREDERICK ~ Event Coordinator

BRIANNA HART ~ Executive Assistant

AARON FERRARA ~ Operations Assistant

ADVENTURE TIME: SUGARY SHORTS
Volume One — October 2013. Published by
KaBOOM!, a division of Boom Entertainment, Inc.
ADVENTURE TIME, CARTOON NETWORK, the
logos, and all related characters and elements
are trademarks of and © Cartoon Network.
(S13) All rights reserved. Originally published
in single magazine form as ADVENTURE TIME
1-14. © Cartoon Network. (S13) KaBOOM!™
and the KaBOOM! logo are trademarks of
Boom Entertainment, Inc., registered in various
countries and categories. All characters, events,
and institutions depicted herein are fictional. Any
similarity between any of the names, characters,
persons, events, and/or institutions in this
publication to actual names, characters, and
persons, whether living or dead, events, and/or
institutions is unintended and purely coincidental.
KaBOOM! does not read or accept unsolicited
submissions of ideas, stories, or artwork.

A catalog record of this book is available from
OCLC and from the KaBOOM! website, www.
kaboom-studios.com, on the Librarians Page.

BOOM! Studios, 5670 Wilshire Boulevard, Suite
450, Los Angeles, CA 90036-5679.

Printed in China. First Printing.

ISBN: 978-1-60886-333-4

ADVENTURE TIME™

SUGARY SHORTS
Volume One

kaboom!™
CARTOON NETWORK
FREDERATOR

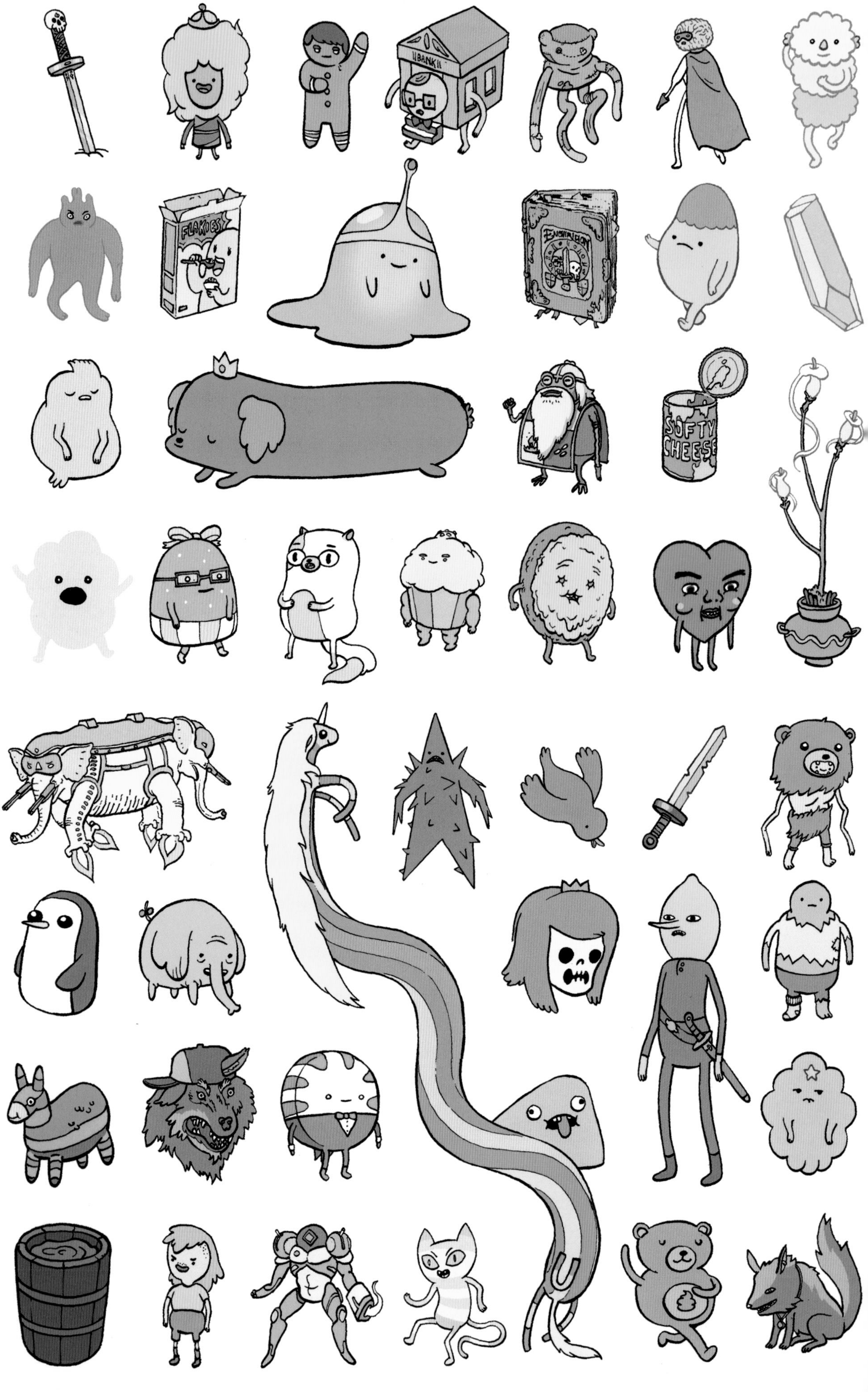
BANK
FLAKIES
SOFTY CHEESE

CREATED BY
Pendleton Ward

"MY CIDER THE MOUNTAIN"
WRITTEN AND ILLUSTRATED BY
Aaron Renier

"LAUNDROMARCELINE"
WRITTEN AND ILLUSTRATED BY
Lucy Knisley

"AFTER THE SHOW"
WRITTEN AND ILLUSTRATED BY
Zac Gorman

"BACON FIELDS"
WRITTEN AND ILLUSTRATED BY
Michael DeForge

"THE RIDE OF SIR SLICER"
WRITTEN AND ILLUSTRATED BY
Zac Gorman

"THE ULTIMATE PARTY DIP"
WRITTEN AND ILLUSTRATED BY
Chris "Elio" Eliopoulos
COLORS BY JOEY WEISER

"EMIT ERUTNEVDA"
WRITTEN AND ILLUSTRATED BY
Paul Pope
COLORS BY NOLAN WOODARD
AND ZAC GORMAN

"ICE KINGDUMB"
WRITTEN BY
Georgia & Chris Roberson
ILLUSTRATED BY
Lucy Knisley

"LEVEL 99"
WRITTEN AND ILLUSTRATED BY
Anthony Clark

"TIME WAITS FOR NO ONE"
WRITTEN AND ILLUSTRATED BY
Shannon Wheeler

"LUMPY SPACE DRAMA"

WRITTEN AND ILLUSTRATED BY

Zac Gorman

"HAPPY BIRTHDAY HOTDOG PRINCESS"

WRITTEN AND ILLUSTRATED BY

Frank Gibson & Becky Dreistadt

"FISHLING"

WRITTEN AND ILLUSTRATED BY

Shane & Chris Houghton

COLORS BY JOSH ULRICH

"HOT DEALS IN ICE KINGDOM"

WRITTEN BY

Jon M. Gibson

ILLUSTRATED BY

Jim Rugg

"THE MEANING OF BRAVERY"

WRITTEN AND ILLUSTRATED BY

Zack Giallongo

COLORS BY LISA MOORE

"THE ICE KING AND HIS MAGICAL MATCHMAKING MINI-COMIC"

WRITTEN BY

Alexis Frederick-Frost

ILLUSTRATED BY

Andrew Arnold

"THE DEVILISH DEVOURER OF DELICIOUS DELICACIES"

WRITTEN AND ILLUSTRATED BY

Josh Lesnick

"PRINCESS OF RAD HATS"

WRITTEN AND ILLUSTRATED BY

Chris Schweizer

ASSISTANT EDITOR
Whitney Leopard

EDITOR
Shannon Watters

TRADE AND COVER DESIGN
Stephanie Gonzaga
WITH Justine Andrade

NEW YORK COMIC CON EXCLUSIVE COVER BY
Dustin Nguyen

With special thanks to
Marisa Marionakis, Rick Blanco, Curtis Lelash, Laurie Halal-Ono, Keith Mack, Kelly Crews
and the wonderful folks at Cartoon Network.

MY CIDER THE MOUNTAIN

ANNAPOLIS COMIC-CON ISSUE ONE EXCLUSIVE COVER
SANFORD GREENE

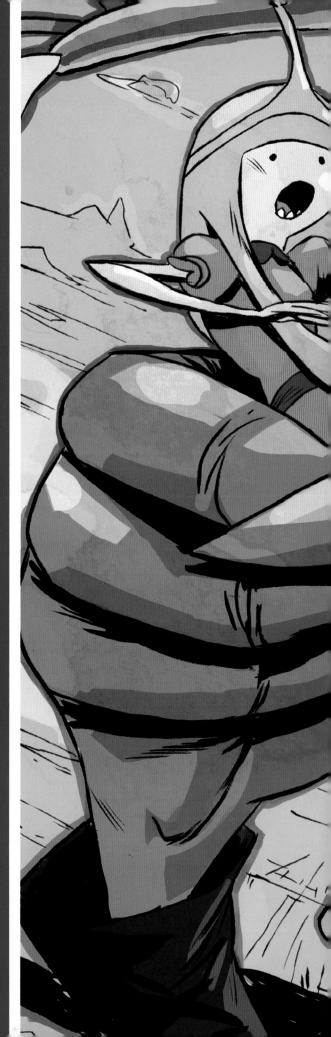

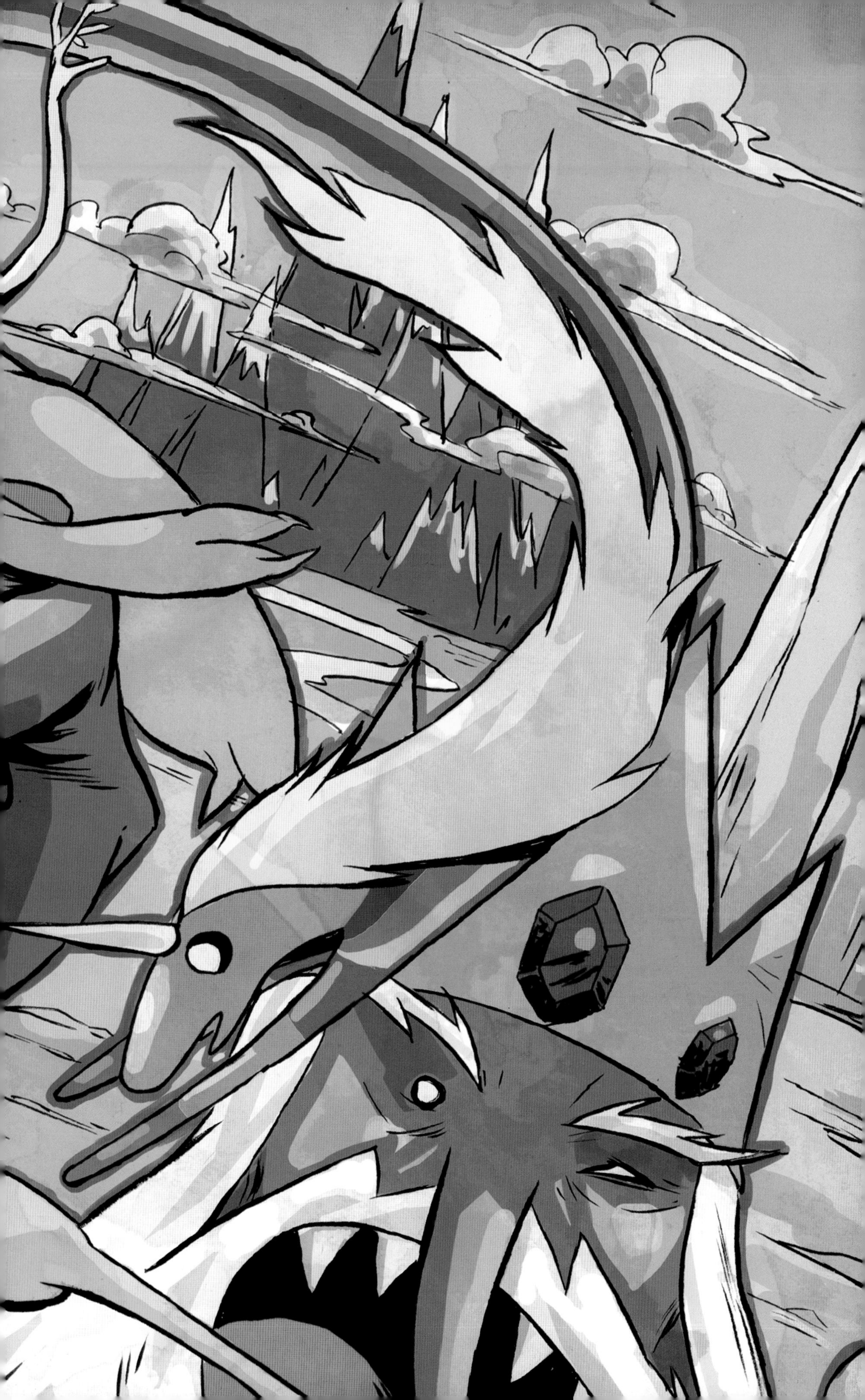

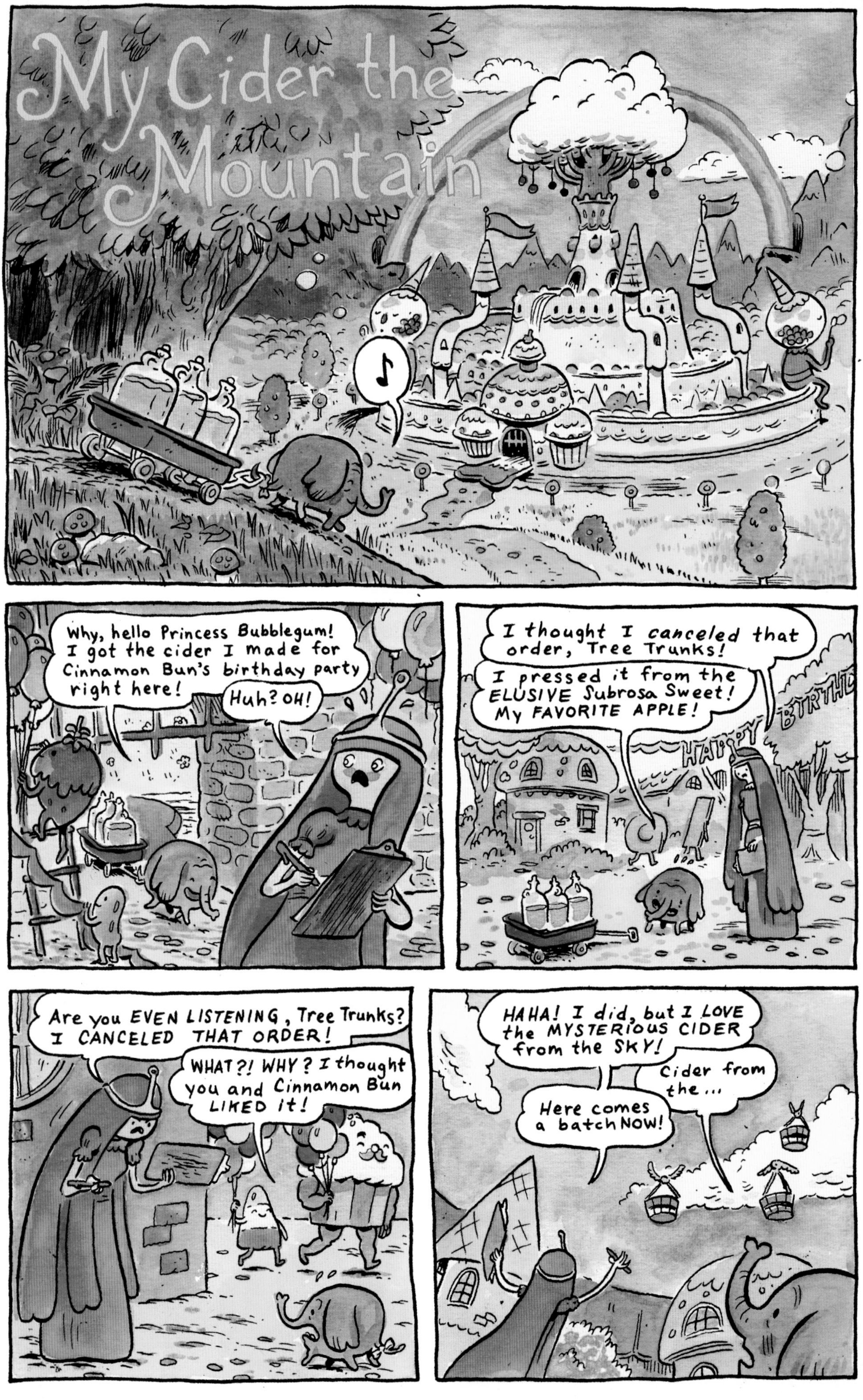
My Cider the Mountain
Why, hello Princess Bubblegum! I got the cider I made for Cinnamon Bun's birthday party right here!
Huh? OH!
I thought I canceled that order, Tree Trunks!
I pressed it from the ELUSIVE Subrosa Sweet! My FAVORITE APPLE!
HAPPY BIRTHD
Are you EVEN LISTENING, Tree Trunks? I CANCELED THAT ORDER!
WHAT?! WHY? I thought you and Cinnamon Bun LIKED it!
HAHA! I did, but I LOVE the MYSTERIOUS CIDER from the SKY!
Cider from the...
Here comes a batch NOW!

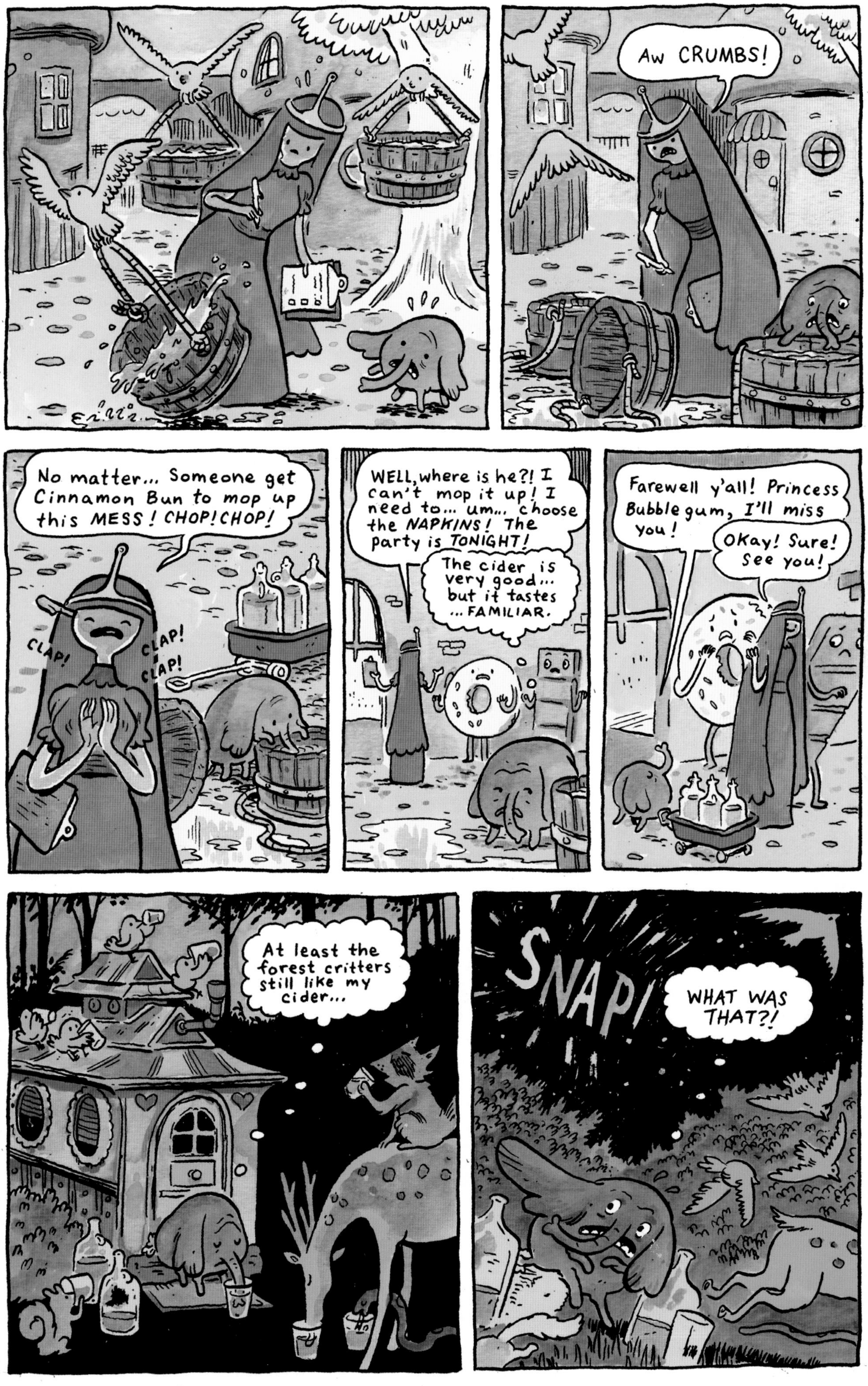
Aw CRUMBS!
No matter... Someone get Cinnamon Bun to mop up this MESS! CHOP! CHOP!
CLAP!
CLAP!
CLAP!
WELL, where is he?! I can't mop it up! I need to... um... choose the NAPKINS! The party is TONIGHT!
The cider is very good... but it tastes ...FAMILIAR.
Farewell y'all! Princess Bubblegum, I'll miss you!
OKay! Sure! See you!
At least the forest critters still like my cider...
SNAP!
WHAT WAS THAT?!

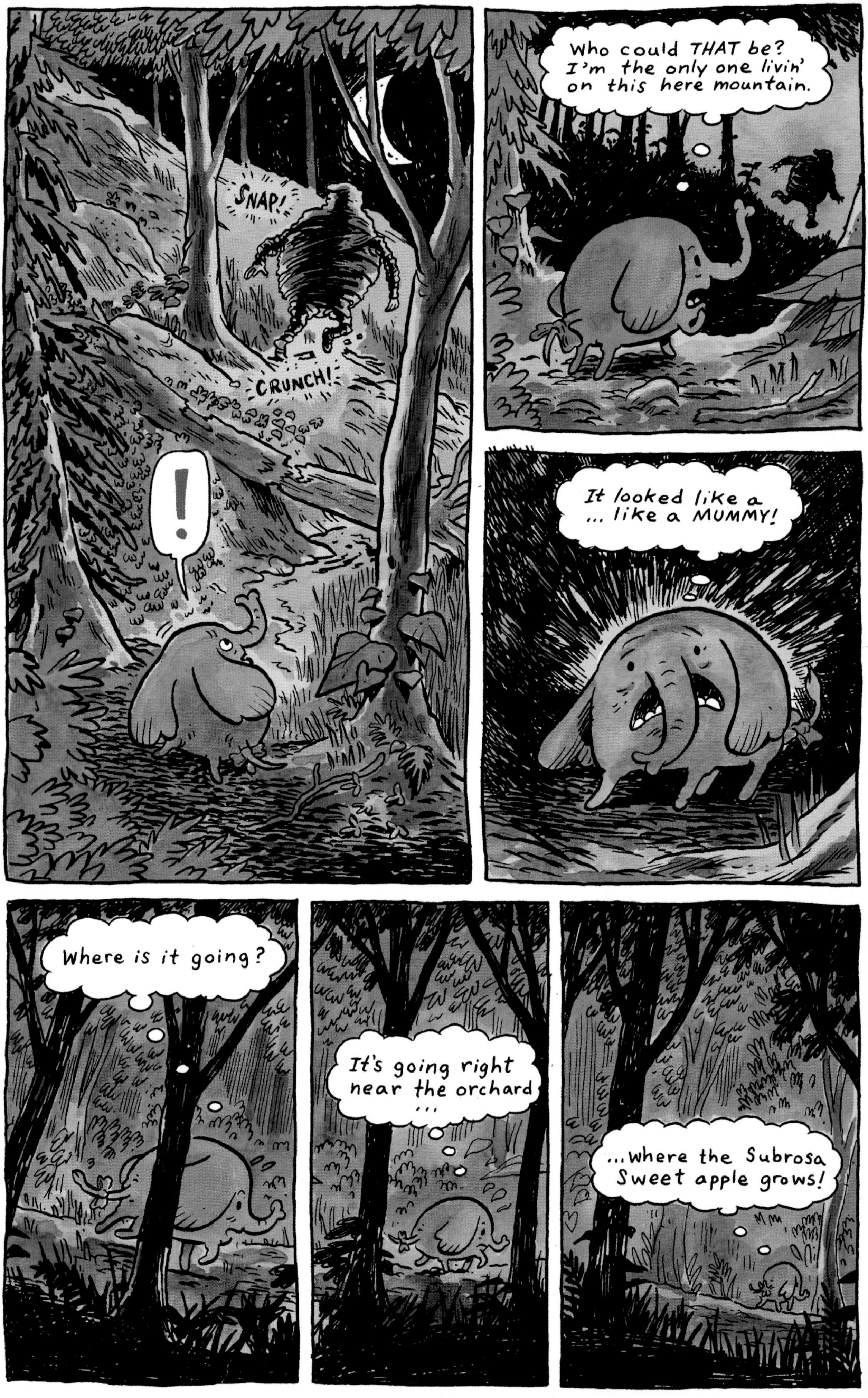
SNAP!
CRUNCH!
!
Who could THAT be? I'm the only one livin' on this here mountain.
It looked like a ... like a MUMMY!
Where is it going?
It's going right near the orchard ...
...where the Subrosa Sweet apple grows!

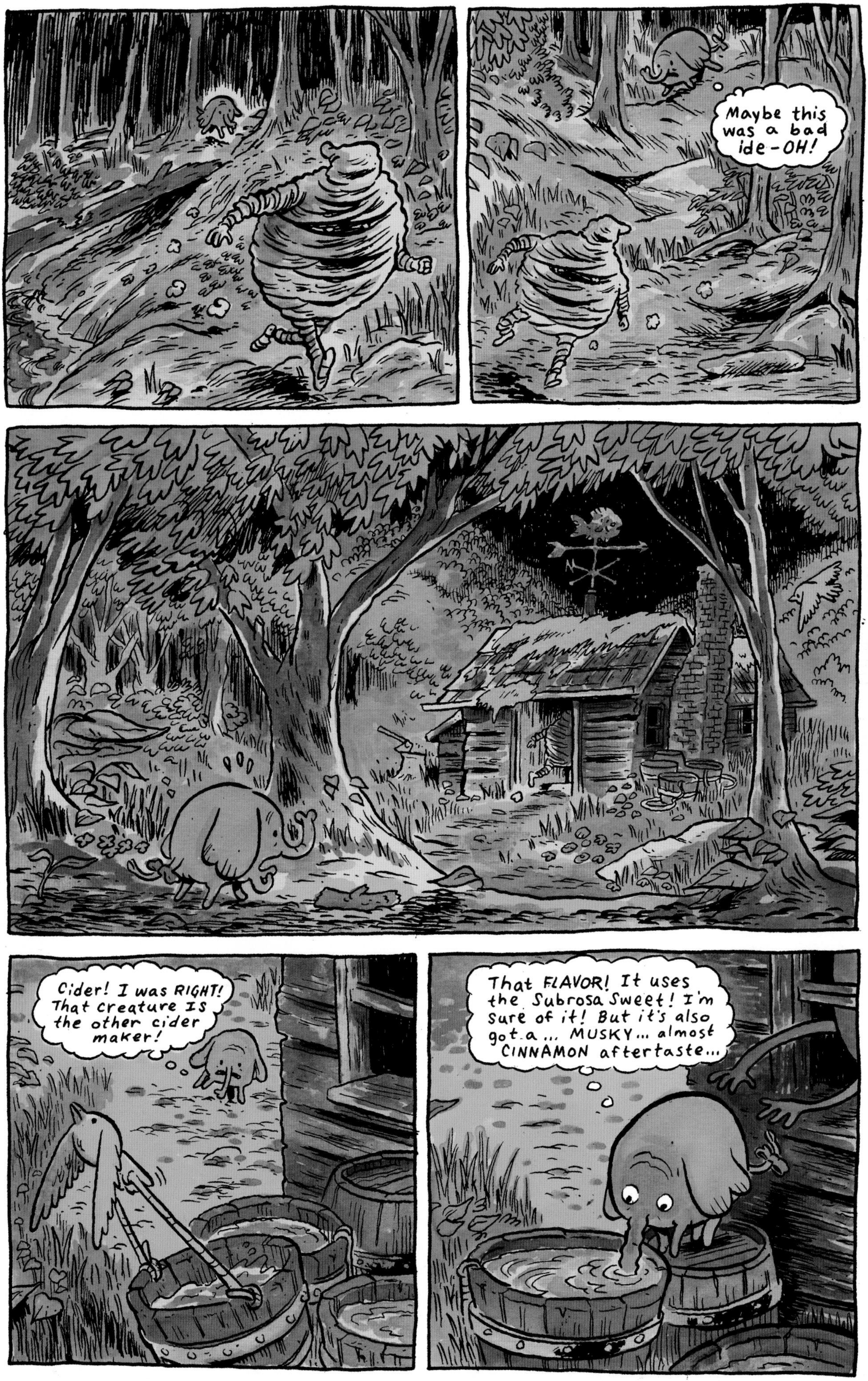
Maybe this was a bad ide-OH!
Cider! I was RIGHT! That creature IS the other cider maker!
That FLAVOR! It uses the Subrosa Sweet! I'm sure of it! But it's also got a... MUSKY... almost CINNAMON aftertaste...

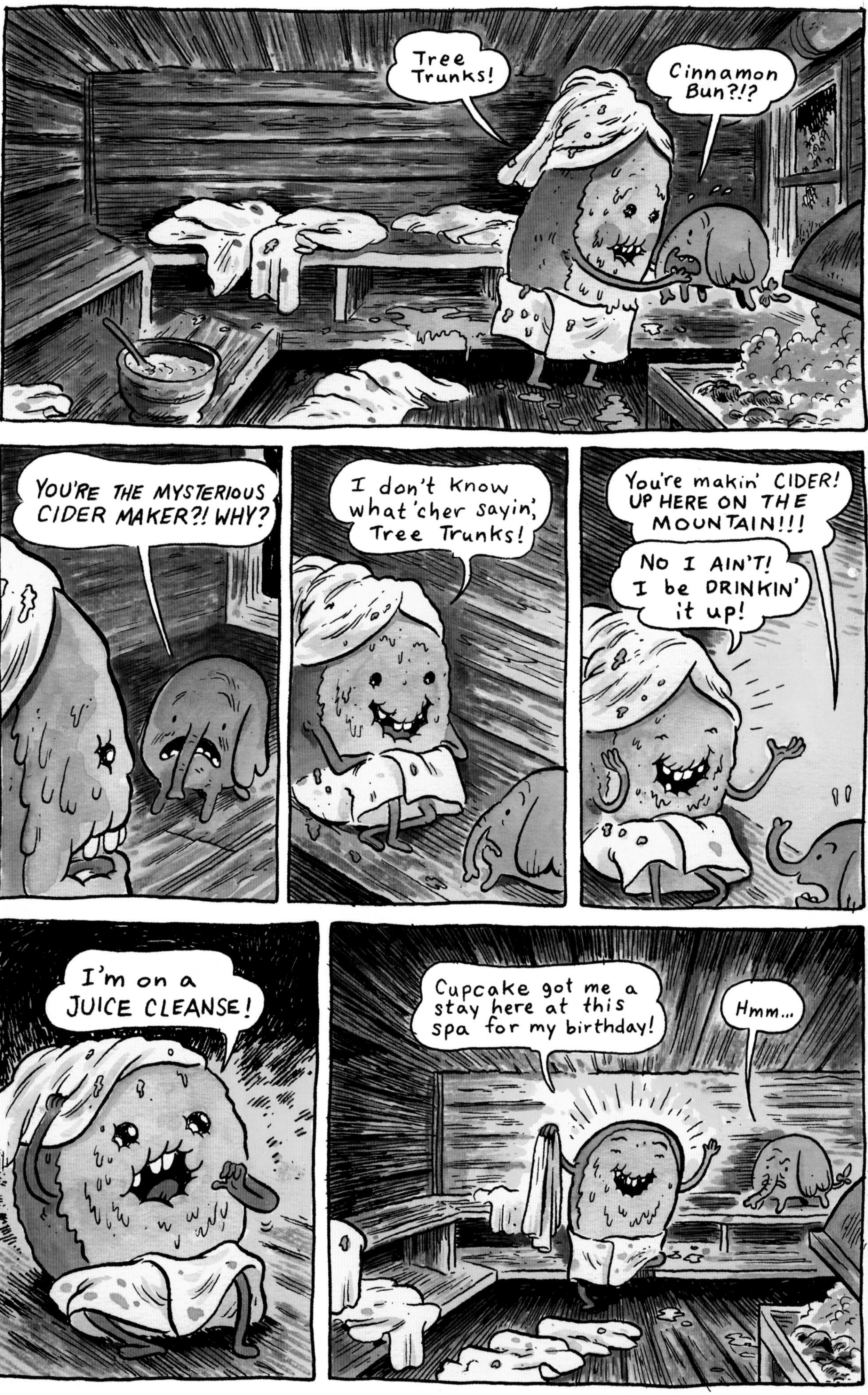
Tree Trunks!
Cinnamon Bun?!?
YOU'RE THE MYSTERIOUS CIDER MAKER?! WHY?
I don't know what'cher sayin', Tree Trunks!
You're makin' CIDER! UP HERE ON THE MOUNTAIN!!!
NO I AIN'T! I be DRINKIN' it up!
I'm on a JUICE CLEANSE!
Cupcake got me a stay here at this spa for my birthday!
Hmm...

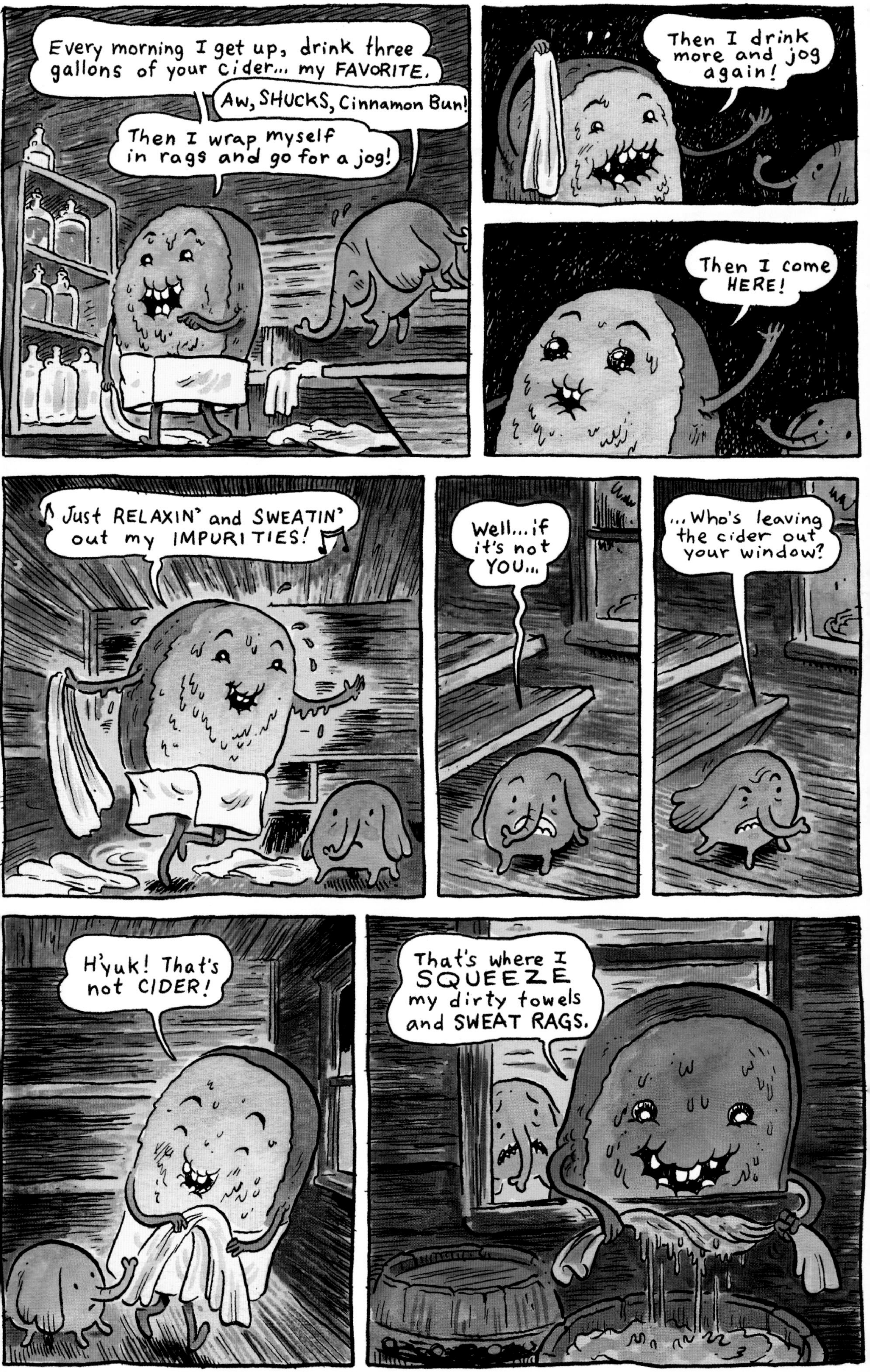
Every morning I get up, drink three gallons of your cider... my FAVORITE.
Aw, SHUCKS, Cinnamon Bun!
Then I wrap myself in rags and go for a jog!
Then I drink more and jog again!
Then I come HERE!
Just RELAXIN' and SWEATIN' out my IMPURITIES!
Well... if it's not YOU...
...Who's leaving the cider out your window?
H'yuk! That's not CIDER!
That's where I SQUEEZE my dirty towels and SWEAT RAGS.

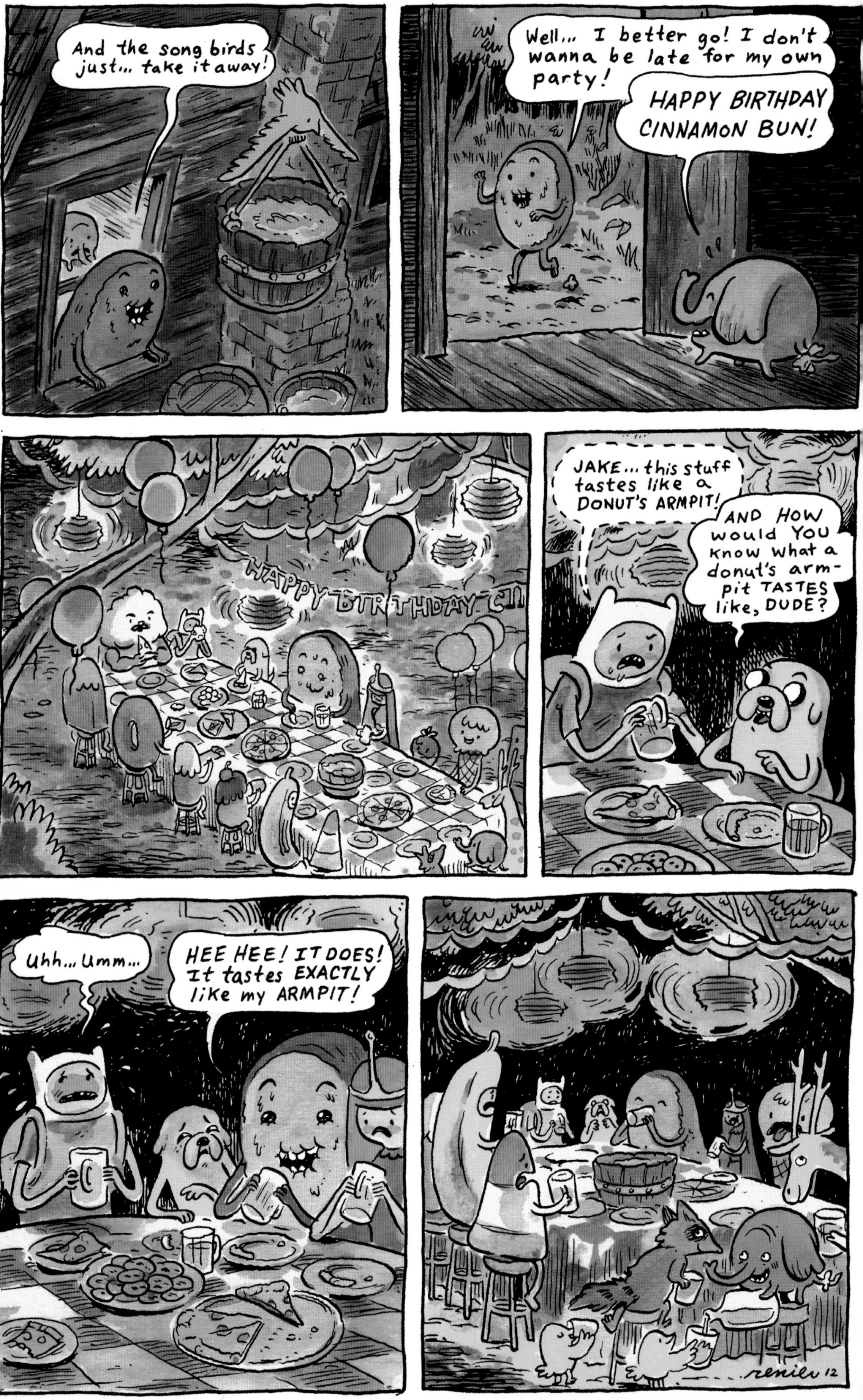
And the song birds just... take it away!
Well... I better go! I don't wanna be late for my own party!
HAPPY BIRTHDAY CINNAMON BUN!
HAPPY BIRTHDAY CI
JAKE... this stuff tastes like a DONUT'S ARMPIT!
AND HOW would YOU know what a donut's arm-pit TASTES like, DUDE?
Uhh... Umm...
HEE HEE! IT DOES! It tastes EXACTLY like my ARMPIT!
renier 12

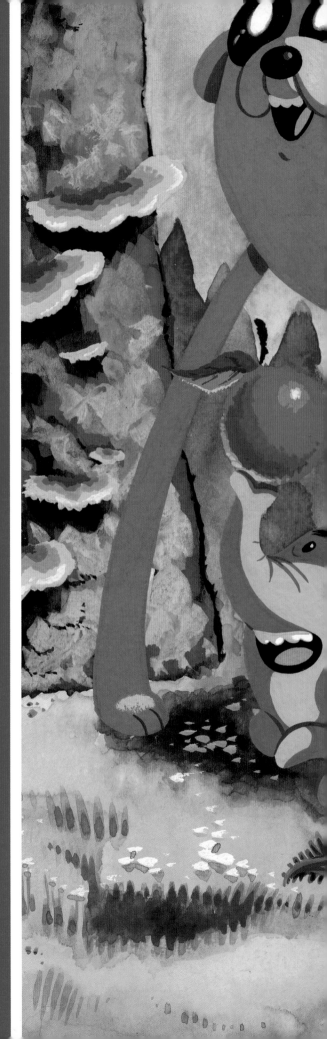

LAUNDROMARCELINE

ISSUE TWO, COVER D
FRANK AND BECKY

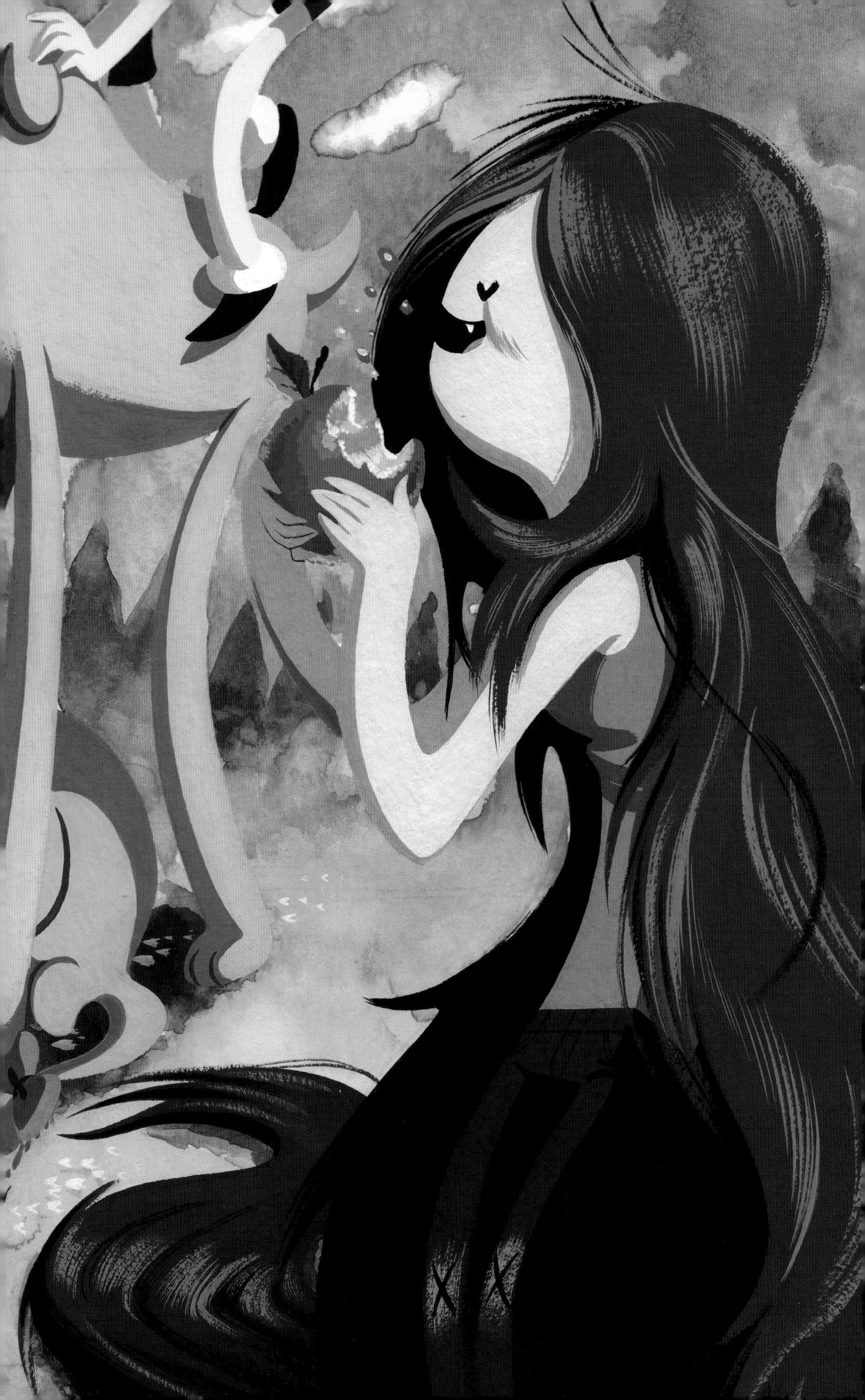

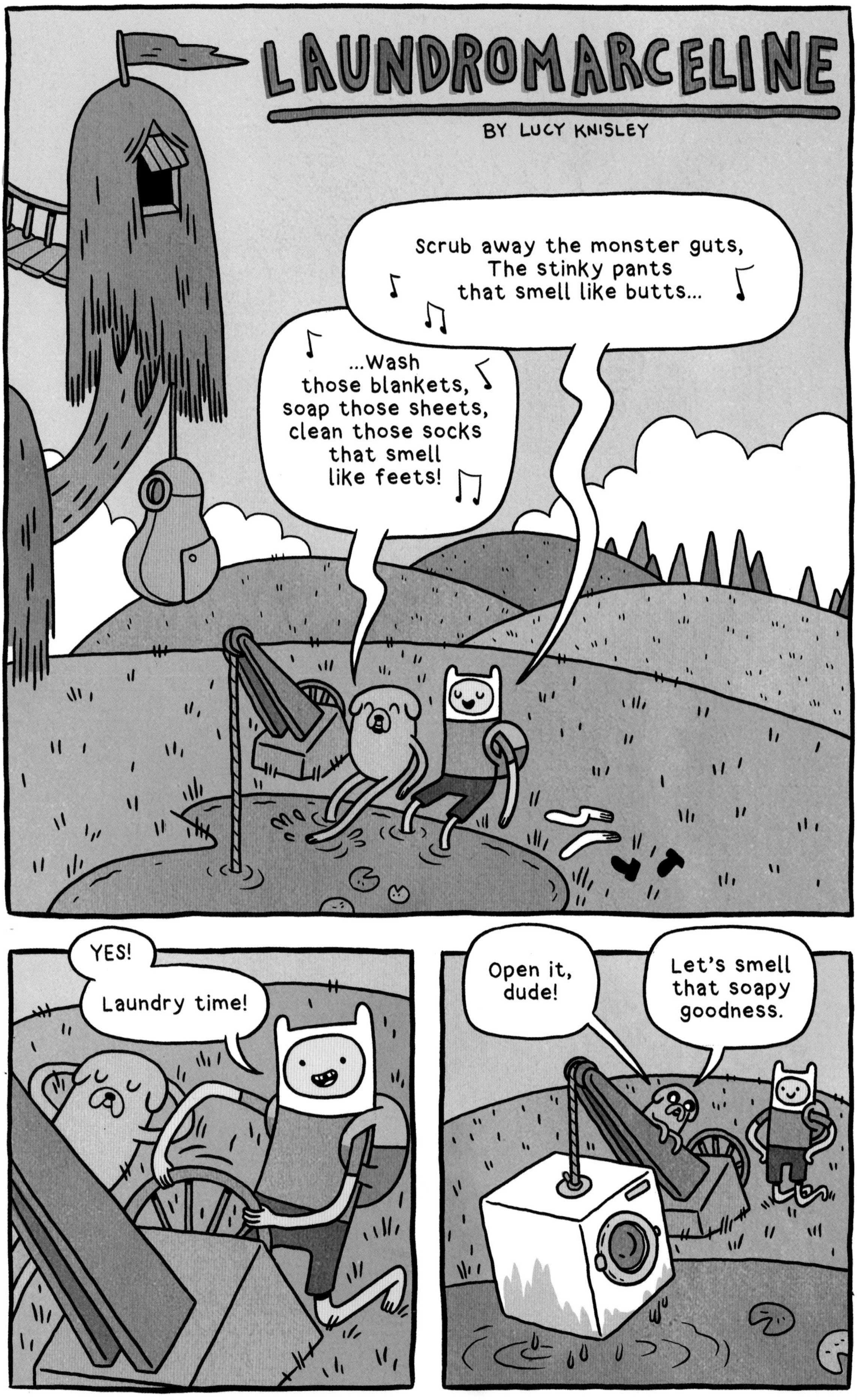
LAUNDROMARCELINE
BY LUCY KNISLEY
Scrub away the monster guts, The stinky pants that smell like butts...
...Wash those blankets, soap those sheets, clean those socks that smell like feets!
YES!
Laundry time!
Open it, dude!
Let's smell that soapy goodness.

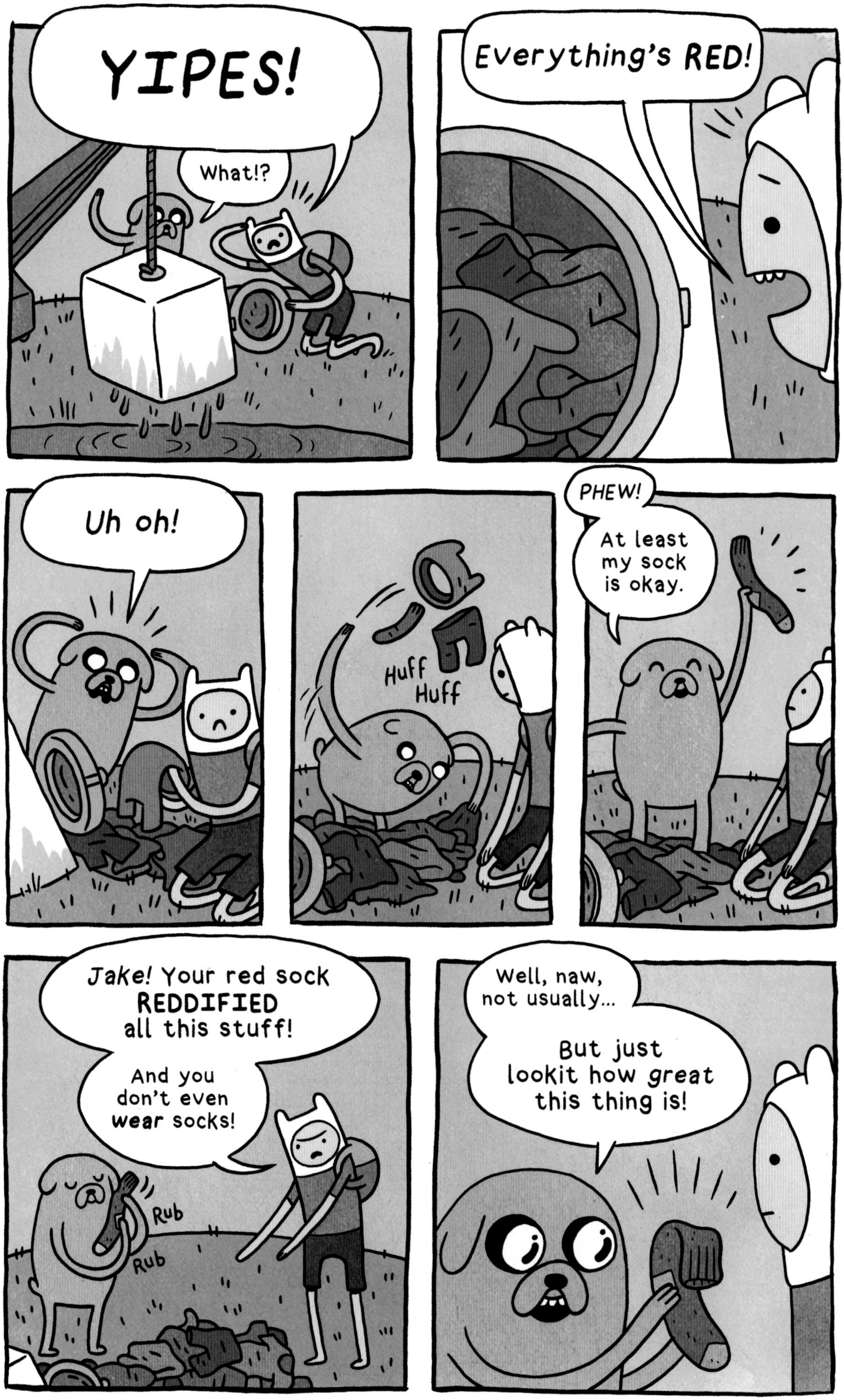
YIPES!
What!?
Everything's RED!
Uh oh!
Huff
Huff
PHEW!
At least my sock is okay.
Jake! Your red sock REDDIFIED all this stuff!
And you don't even wear socks!
Rub
Rub
Well, naw, not usually...
But just lookit how great this thing is!

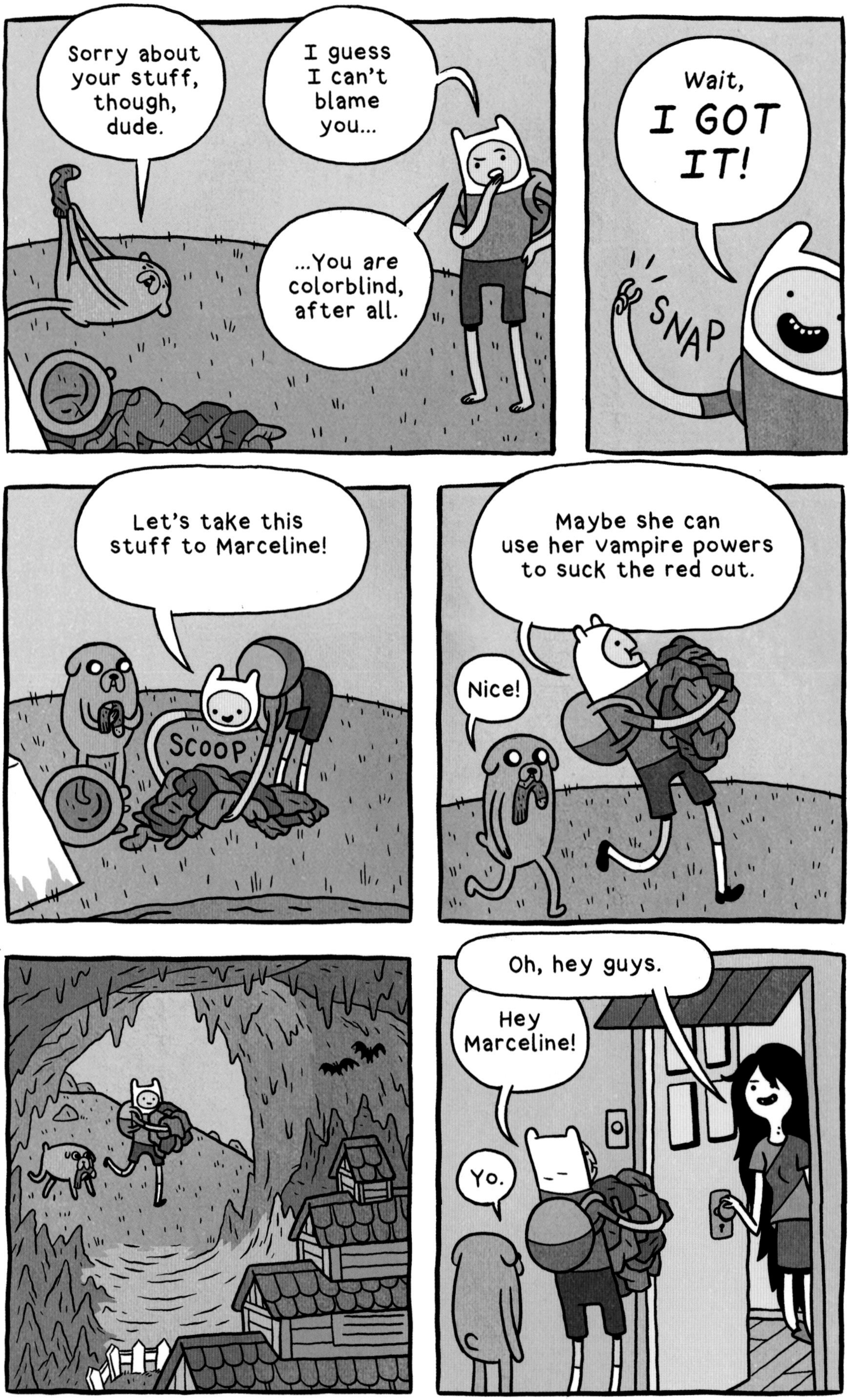
Sorry about your stuff, though, dude.
I guess I can't blame you...
...You are colorblind, after all.
Wait, I GOT IT!
SNAP
Let's take this stuff to Marceline!
SCOOP
Maybe she can use her vampire powers to suck the red out.
Nice!
Oh, hey guys.
Hey Marceline!
Yo.

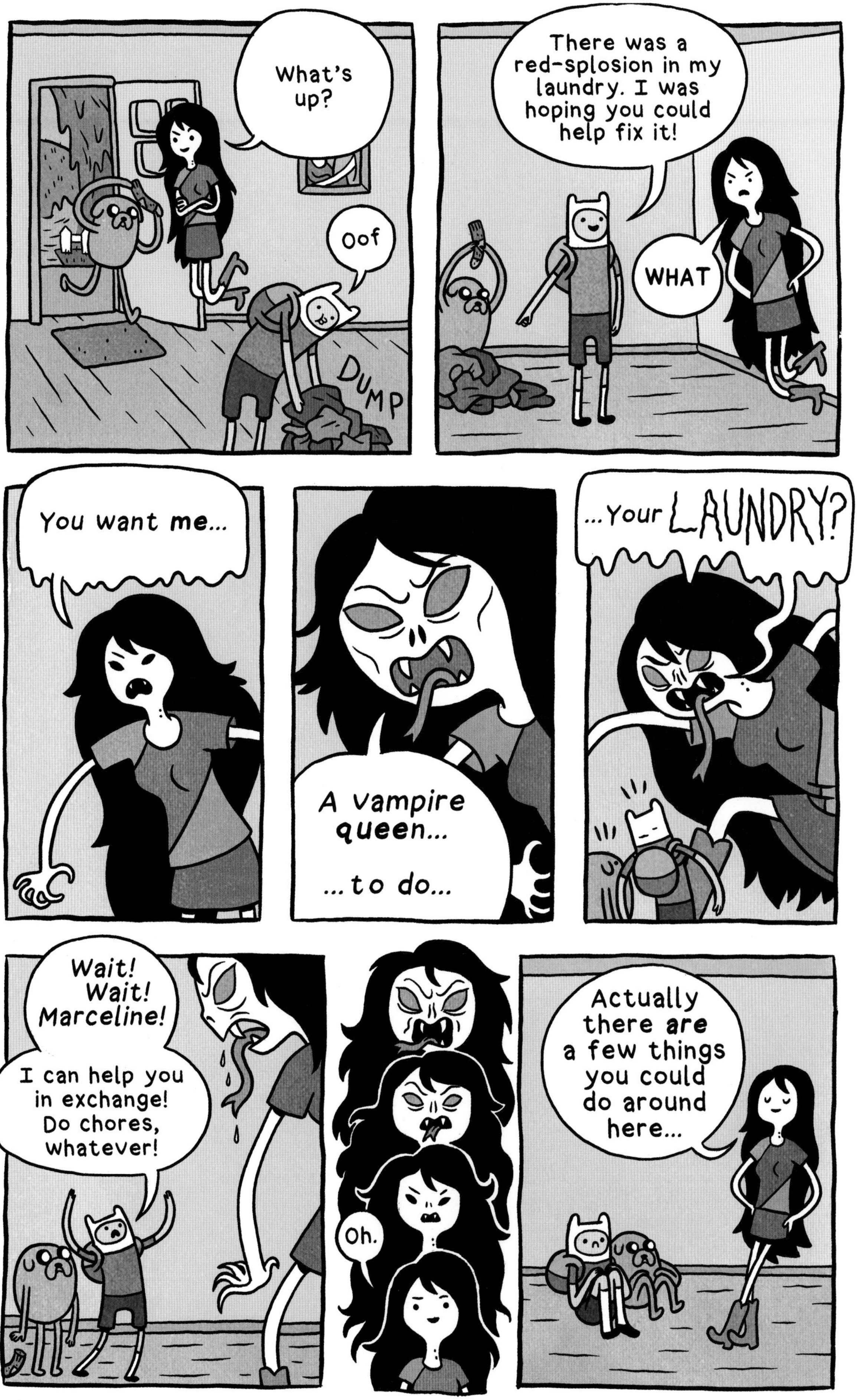
What's up?
Oof
DUMP
There was a red-splosion in my laundry. I was hoping you could help fix it!
WHAT
You want me...
A vampire queen...
...to do...
...Your LAUNDRY?
Wait! Wait! Marceline!
I can help you in exchange! Do chores, whatever!
Oh.
Actually there are a few things you could do around here...

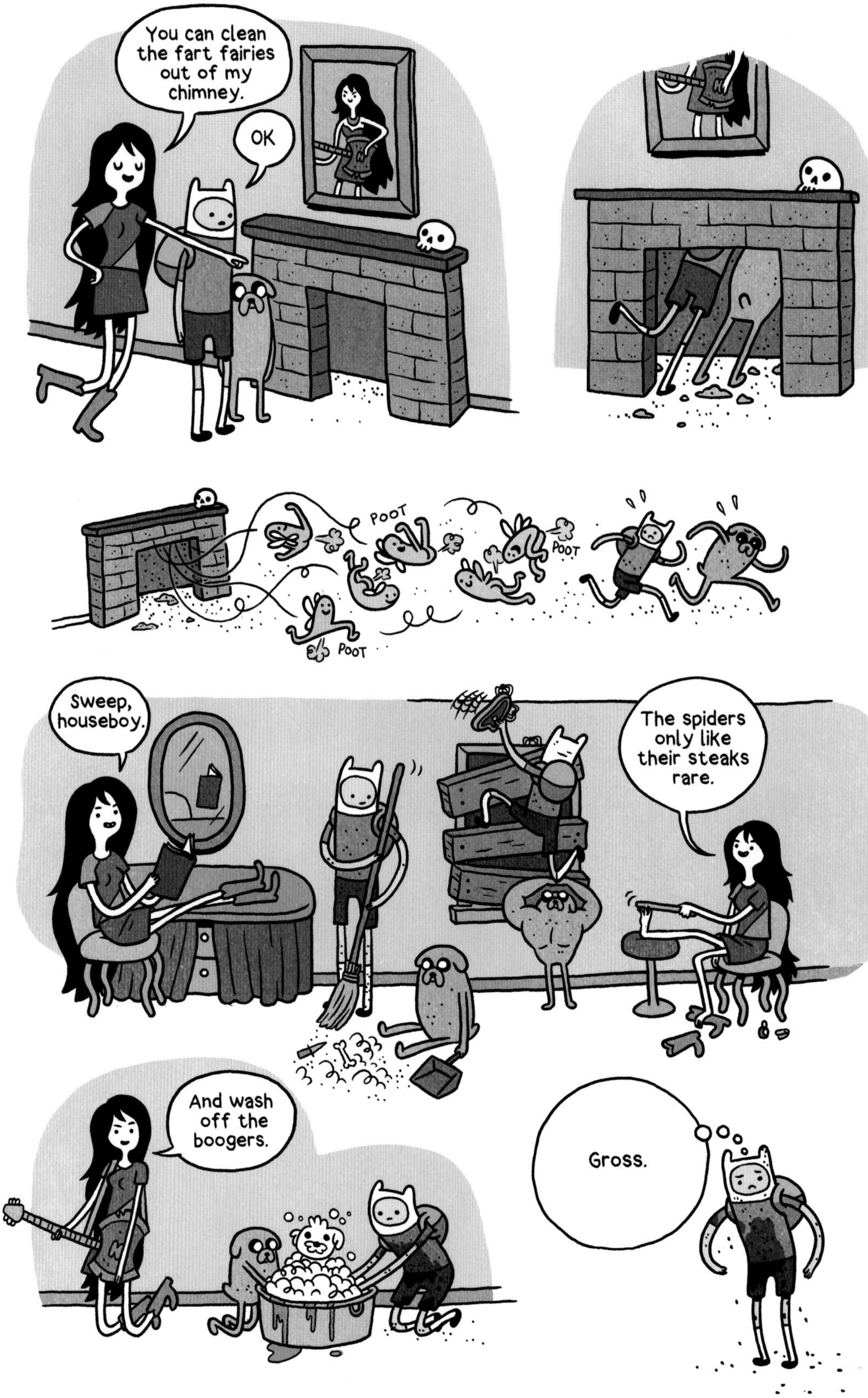
You can clean the fart fairies out of my chimney.
OK
POOT
POOT
POOT
Sweep, houseboy.
The spiders only like their steaks rare.
And wash off the boogers.
Gross.

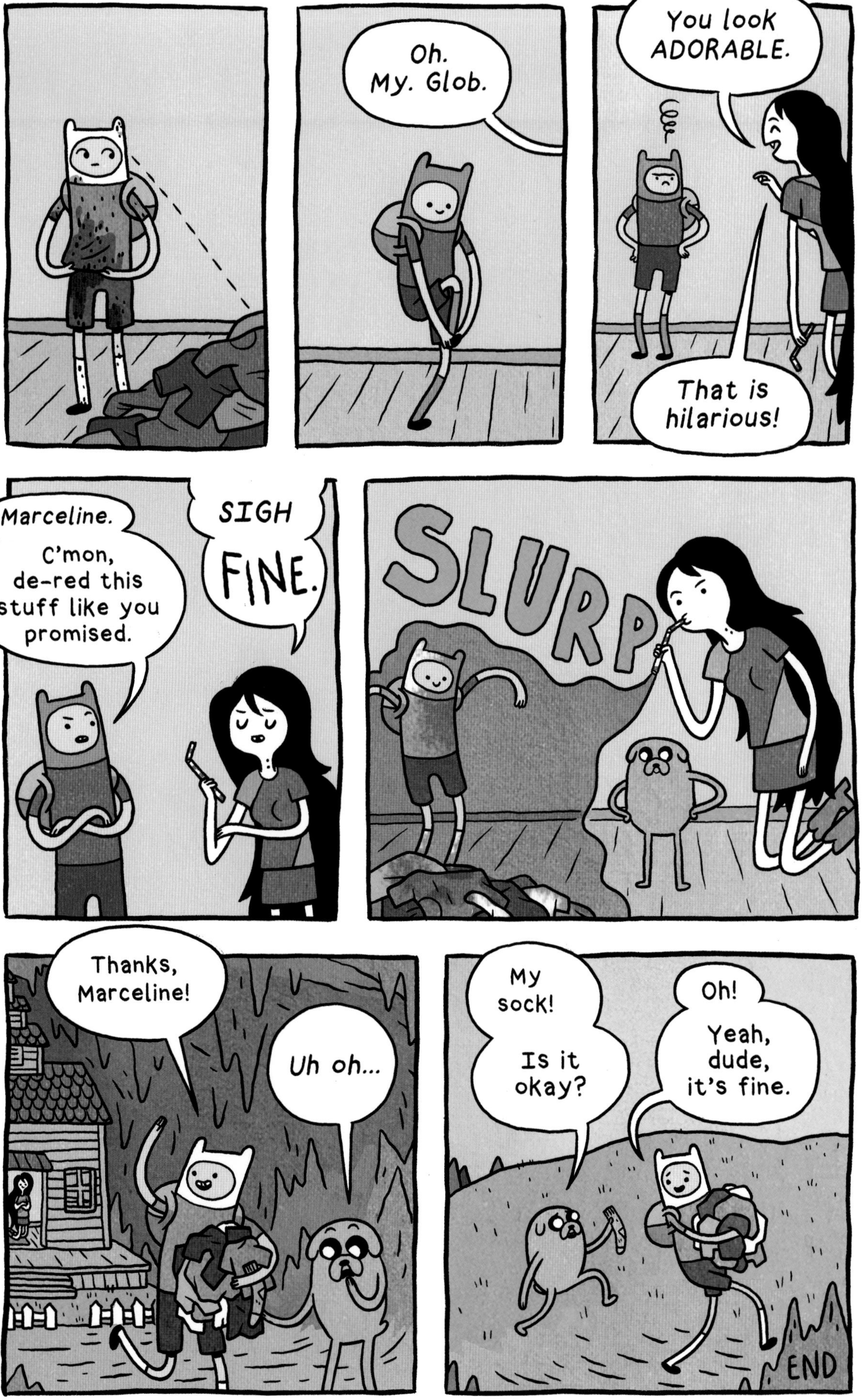
Oh.
My. Glob.
You look ADORABLE.
That is hilarious!
Marceline.
C'mon, de-red this stuff like you promised.
SIGH
FINE.
SLURP
Thanks, Marceline!
Uh oh...
My sock!
Is it okay?
Oh!
Yeah, dude, it's fine.
END

AFTER THE SHOW

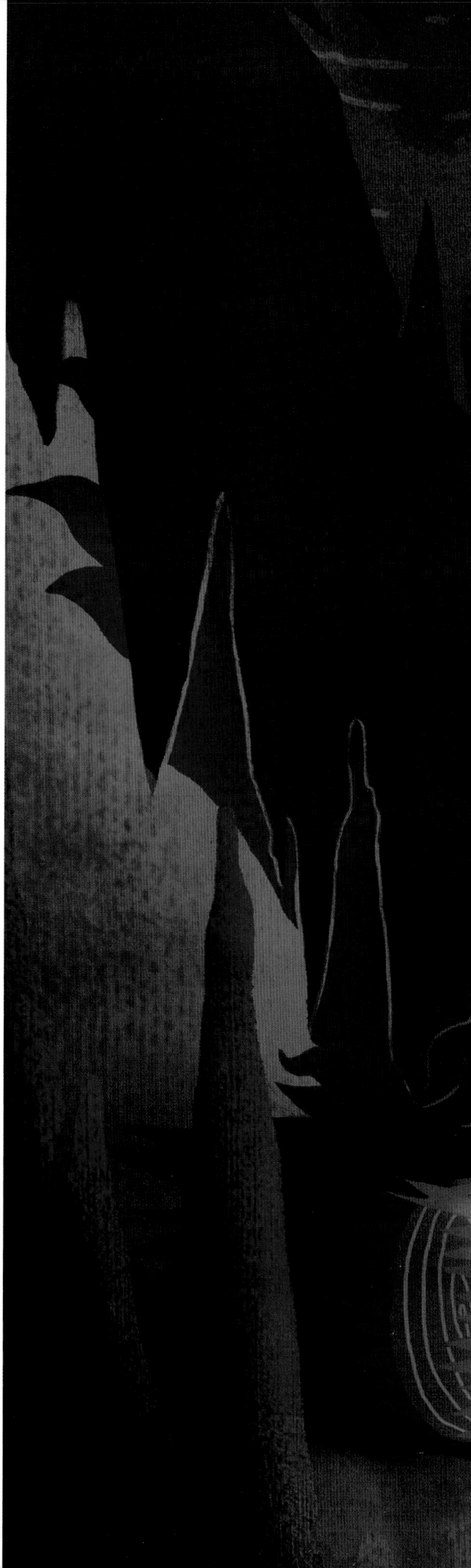

ISSUE TWO, COVER C
EMILY CARROLL

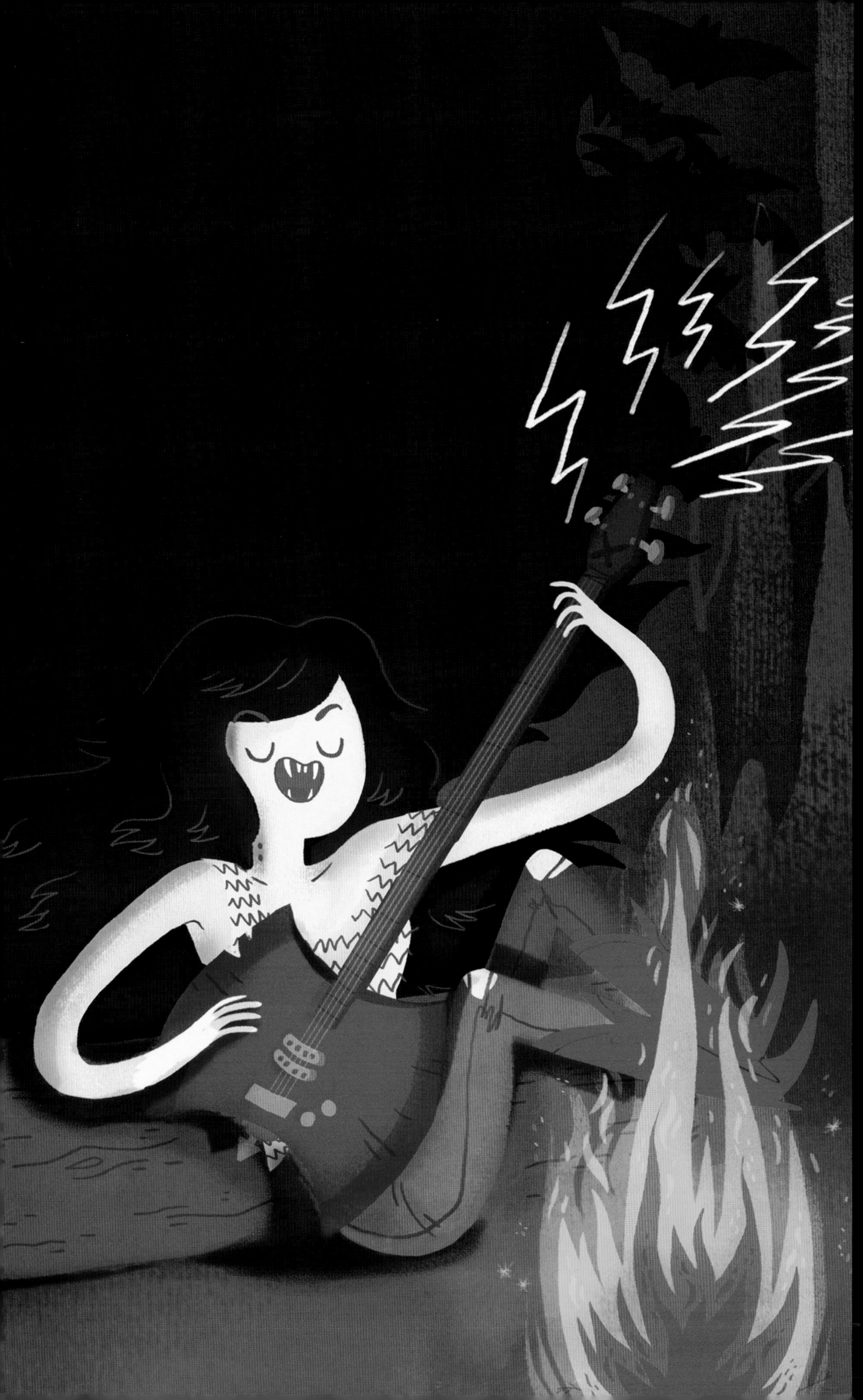

After the Show

–ZAC GORMAN

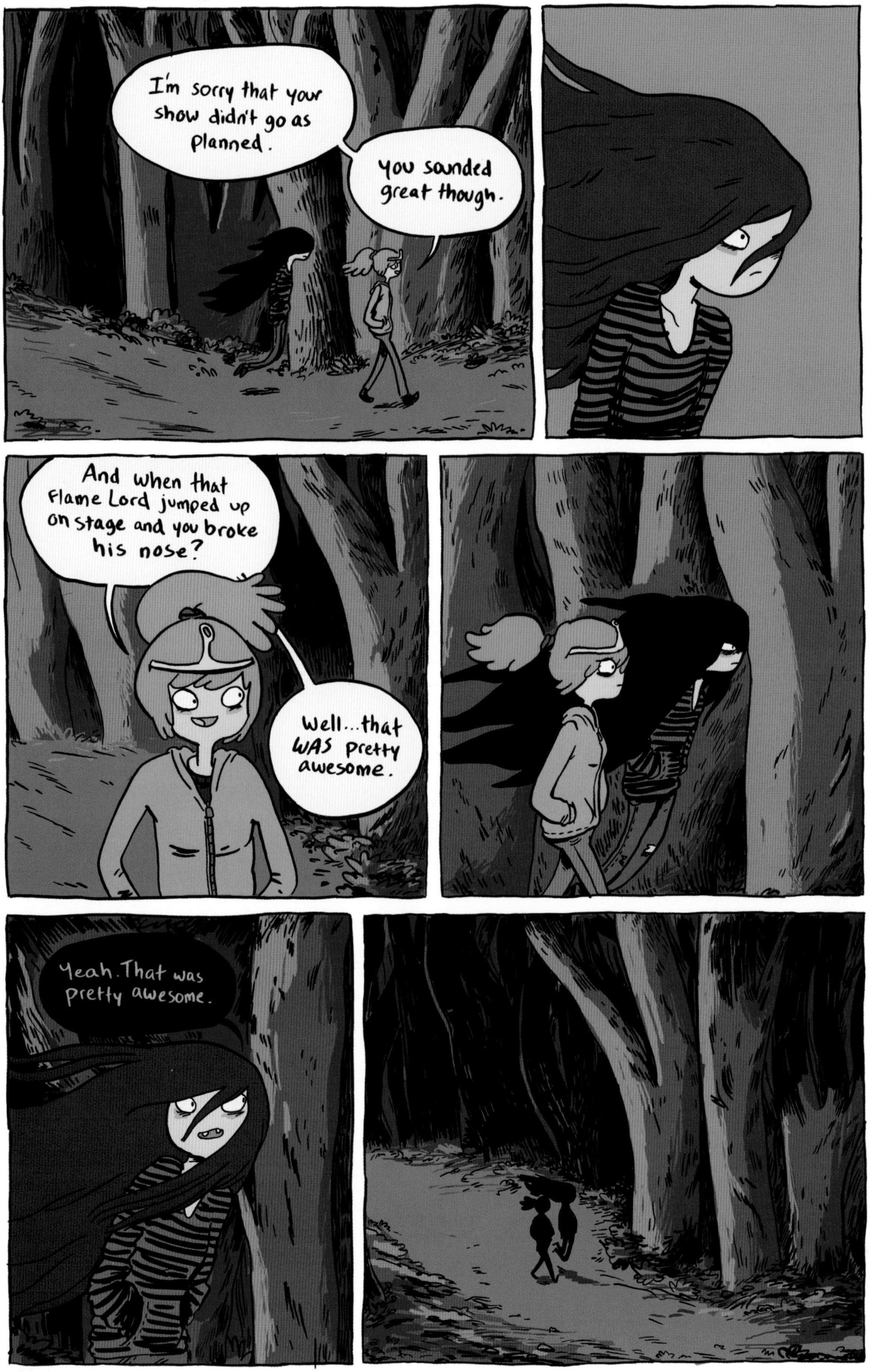
I'm sorry that your show didn't go as planned.
You sounded great though.
And when that Flame Lord jumped up on stage and you broke his nose?
Well... that WAS pretty awesome.
Yeah. That was pretty awesome.

END

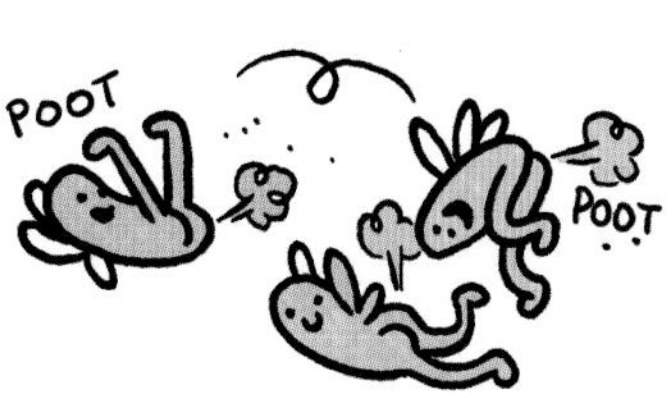
POOT
POOT

BACON FIELDS

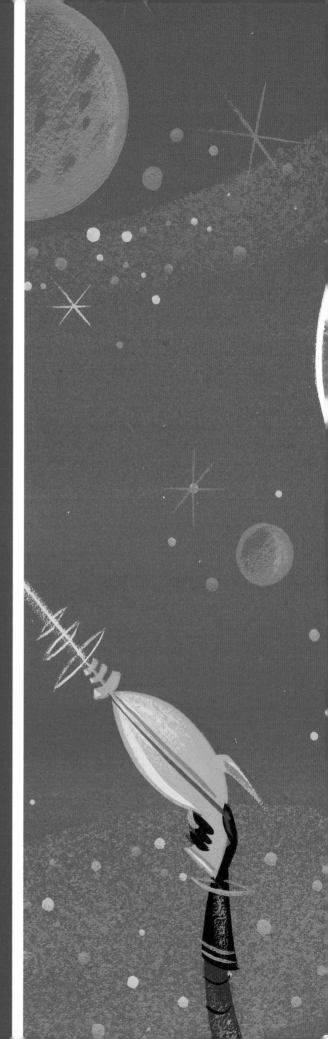

ISSUE THREE, COVER D
STEPHANIE BUSCEMA

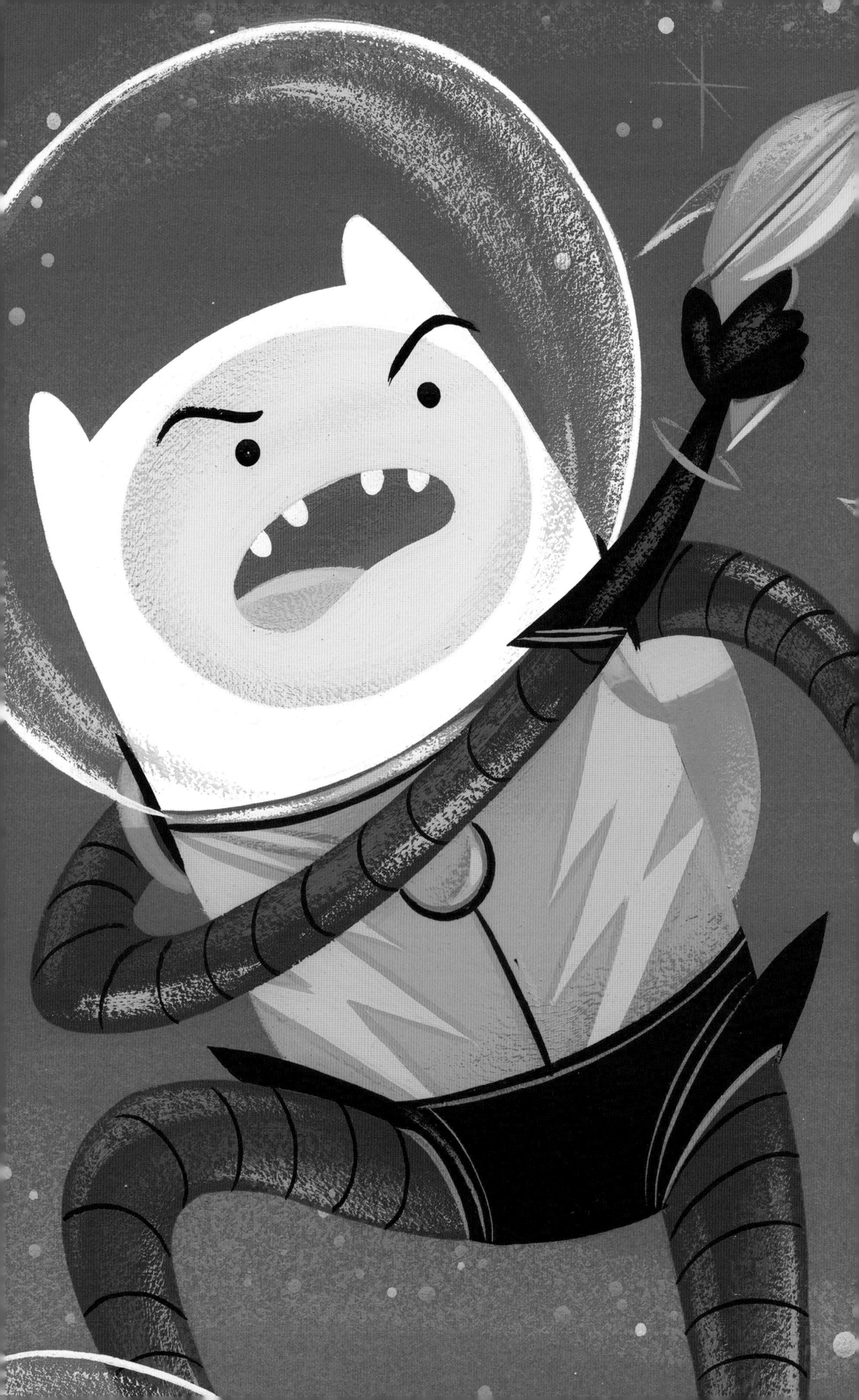

BACON FIELDS

BY MICHAEL DEFORGE

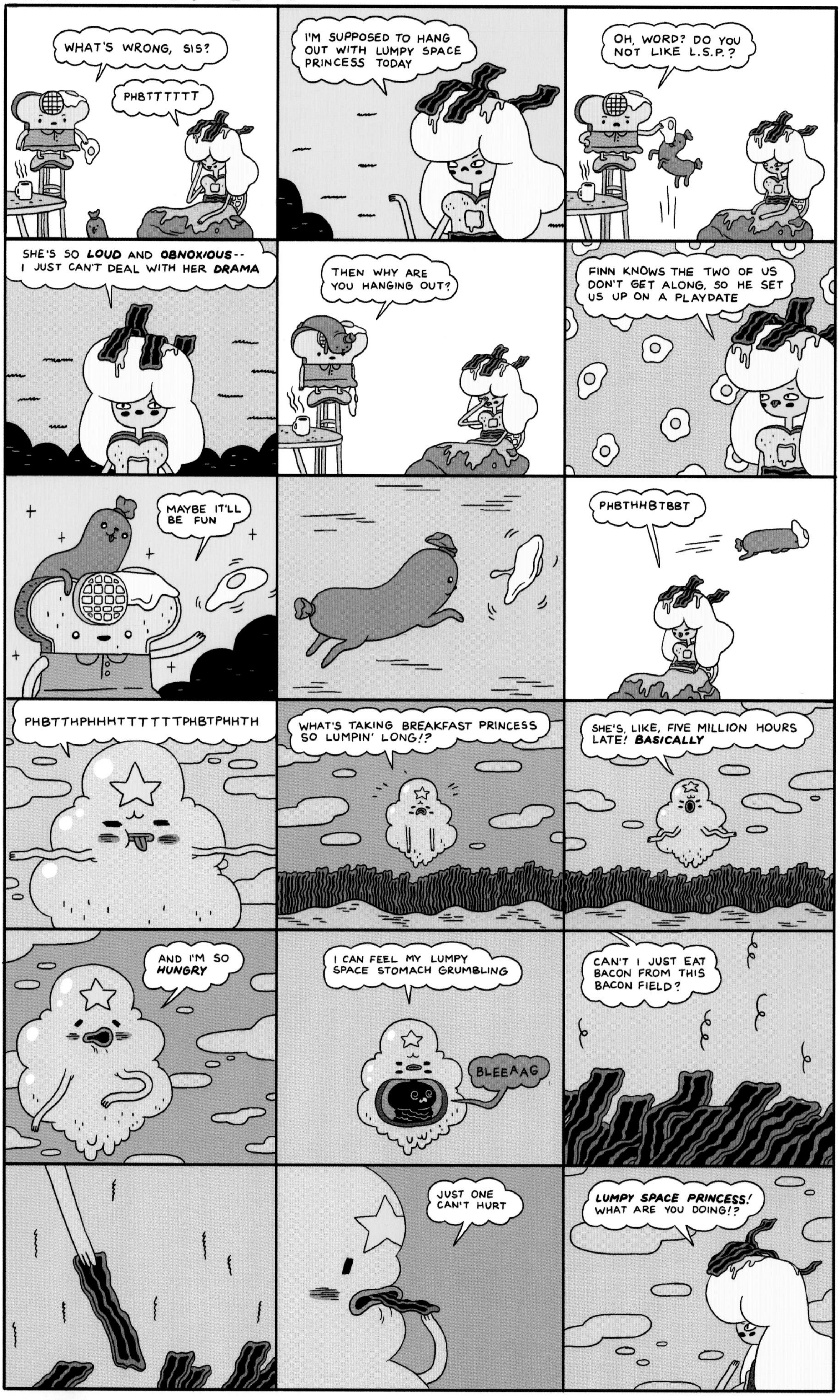
WHAT'S WRONG, SIS?
PHBTTTTTT
I'M SUPPOSED TO HANG OUT WITH LUMPY SPACE PRINCESS TODAY
OH, WORD? DO YOU NOT LIKE L.S.P.?
SHE'S SO **LOUD** AND **OBNOXIOUS**-- I JUST CAN'T DEAL WITH HER **DRAMA**
THEN WHY ARE YOU HANGING OUT?
FINN KNOWS THE TWO OF US DON'T GET ALONG, SO HE SET US UP ON A PLAYDATE
MAYBE IT'LL BE FUN
PHBTHHBTBBT
PHBTTHPHHHTTTTTTPHBTPHHTH
WHAT'S TAKING BREAKFAST PRINCESS SO LUMPIN' LONG!?
SHE'S, LIKE, FIVE MILLION HOURS LATE! **BASICALLY**
AND I'M SO **HUNGRY**
I CAN FEEL MY LUMPY SPACE STOMACH GRUMBLING
BLEEAAG
CAN'T I JUST EAT BACON FROM THIS BACON FIELD?
JUST ONE CAN'T HURT
LUMPY SPACE PRINCESS! WHAT ARE YOU DOING!?

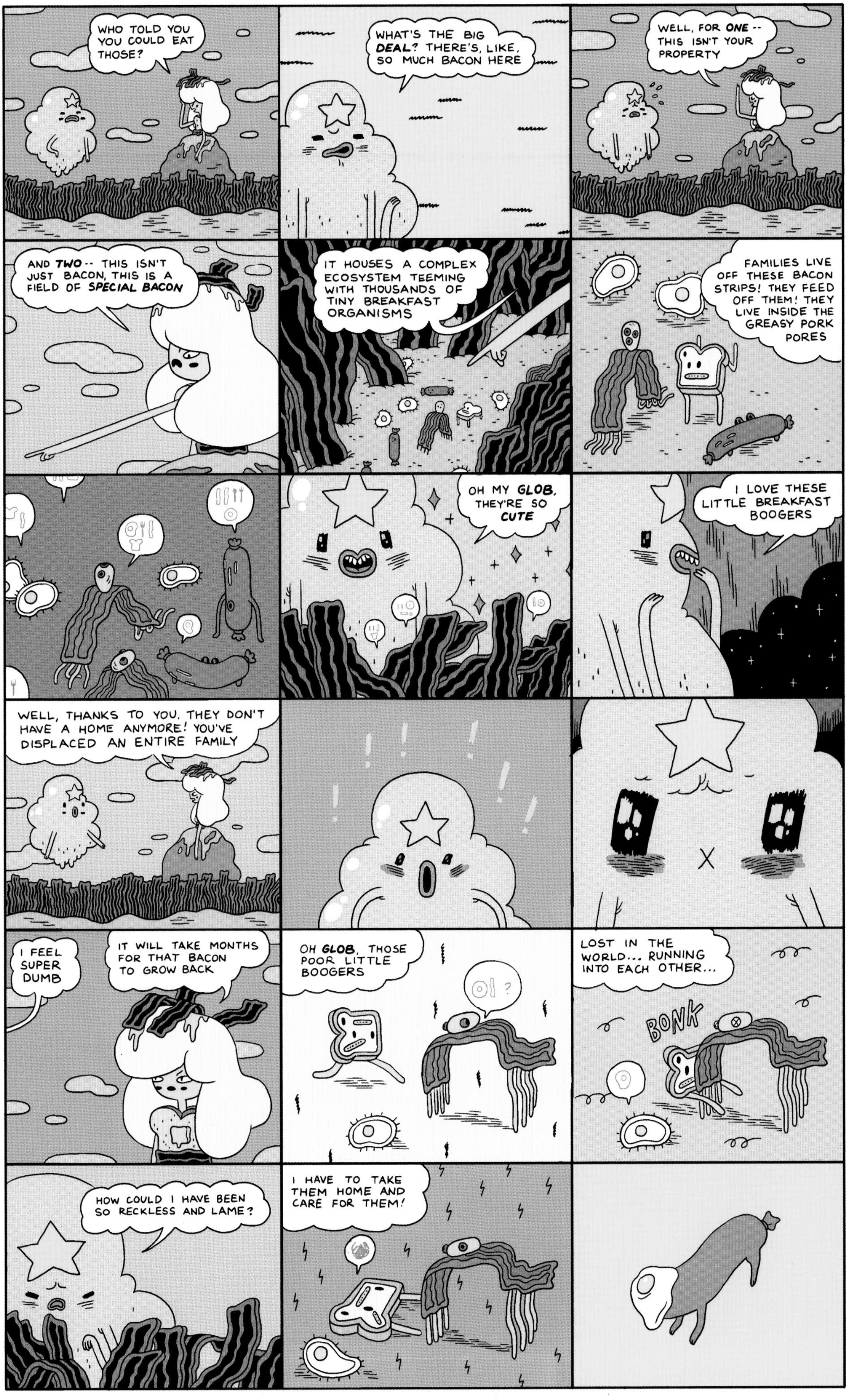
WHO TOLD YOU YOU COULD EAT THOSE?
WHAT'S THE BIG DEAL? THERE'S, LIKE, SO MUCH BACON HERE
WELL, FOR ONE -- THIS ISN'T YOUR PROPERTY
AND TWO -- THIS ISN'T JUST BACON, THIS IS A FIELD OF SPECIAL BACON
IT HOUSES A COMPLEX ECOSYSTEM TEEMING WITH THOUSANDS OF TINY BREAKFAST ORGANISMS
FAMILIES LIVE OFF THESE BACON STRIPS! THEY FEED OFF THEM! THEY LIVE INSIDE THE GREASY PORK PORES
OH MY GLOB, THEY'RE SO CUTE
I LOVE THESE LITTLE BREAKFAST BOOGERS
WELL, THANKS TO YOU, THEY DON'T HAVE A HOME ANYMORE! YOU'VE DISPLACED AN ENTIRE FAMILY
I FEEL SUPER DUMB
IT WILL TAKE MONTHS FOR THAT BACON TO GROW BACK
OH GLOB, THOSE POOR LITTLE BOOGERS
LOST IN THE WORLD... RUNNING INTO EACH OTHER...
BONK
HOW COULD I HAVE BEEN SO RECKLESS AND LAME?
I HAVE TO TAKE THEM HOME AND CARE FOR THEM!

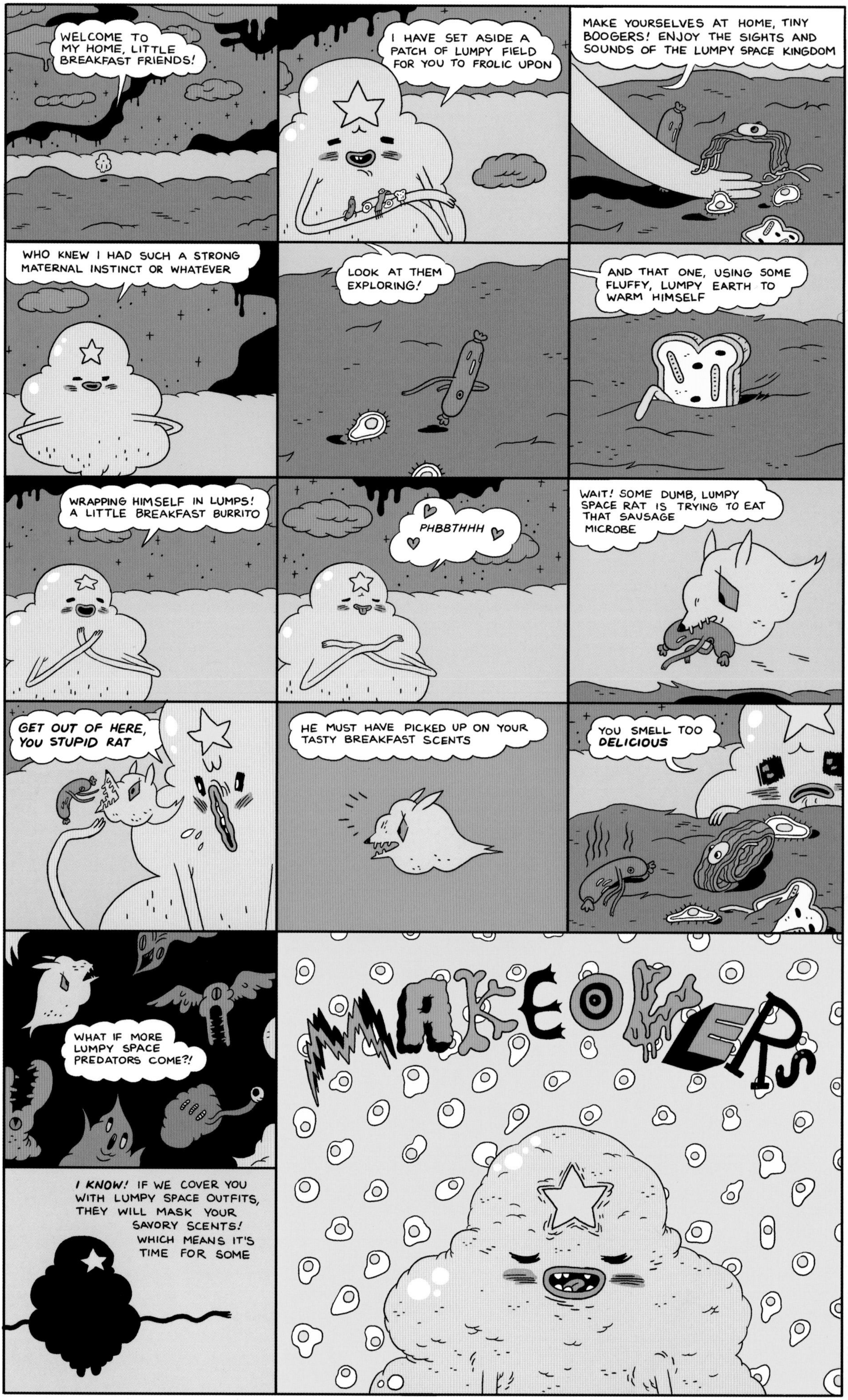
WELCOME TO MY HOME, LITTLE BREAKFAST FRIENDS!
I HAVE SET ASIDE A PATCH OF LUMPY FIELD FOR YOU TO FROLIC UPON
MAKE YOURSELVES AT HOME, TINY BOOGERS! ENJOY THE SIGHTS AND SOUNDS OF THE LUMPY SPACE KINGDOM
WHO KNEW I HAD SUCH A STRONG MATERNAL INSTINCT OR WHATEVER
LOOK AT THEM EXPLORING!
AND THAT ONE, USING SOME FLUFFY, LUMPY EARTH TO WARM HIMSELF
WRAPPING HIMSELF IN LUMPS! A LITTLE BREAKFAST BURRITO
PHBBTHHH
WAIT! SOME DUMB, LUMPY SPACE RAT IS TRYING TO EAT THAT SAUSAGE MICROBE
GET OUT OF HERE, YOU STUPID RAT
HE MUST HAVE PICKED UP ON YOUR TASTY BREAKFAST SCENTS
YOU SMELL TOO DELICIOUS
WHAT IF MORE LUMPY SPACE PREDATORS COME?!
I KNOW! IF WE COVER YOU WITH LUMPY SPACE OUTFITS, THEY WILL MASK YOUR SAVORY SCENTS!
WHICH MEANS IT'S TIME FOR SOME
MAKEOVERS

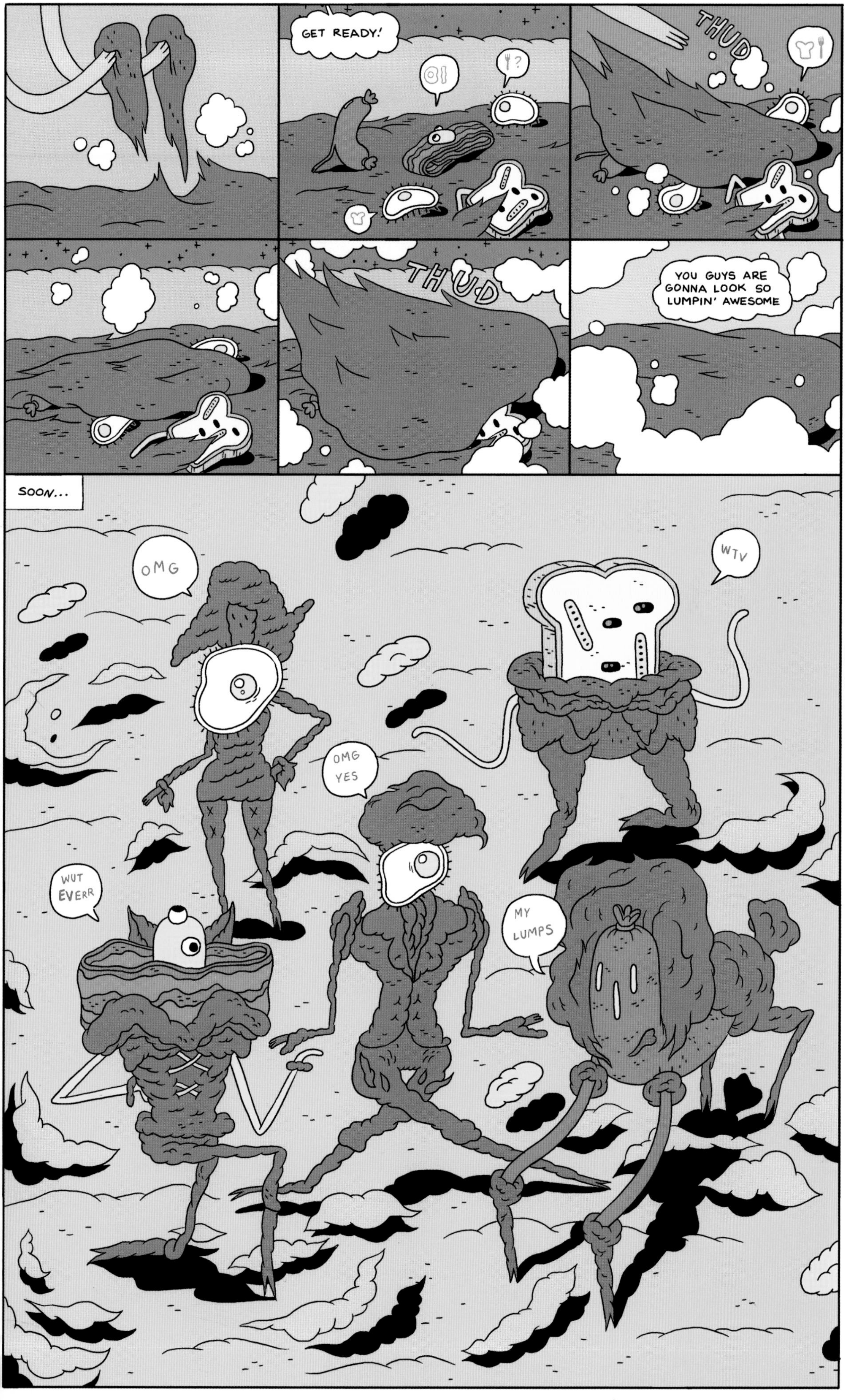
GET READY!
THUD
THUD
YOU GUYS ARE GONNA LOOK SO LUMPIN' AWESOME
SOON...
OMG
WTV
OMG YES
WUT EVERR
MY LUMPS

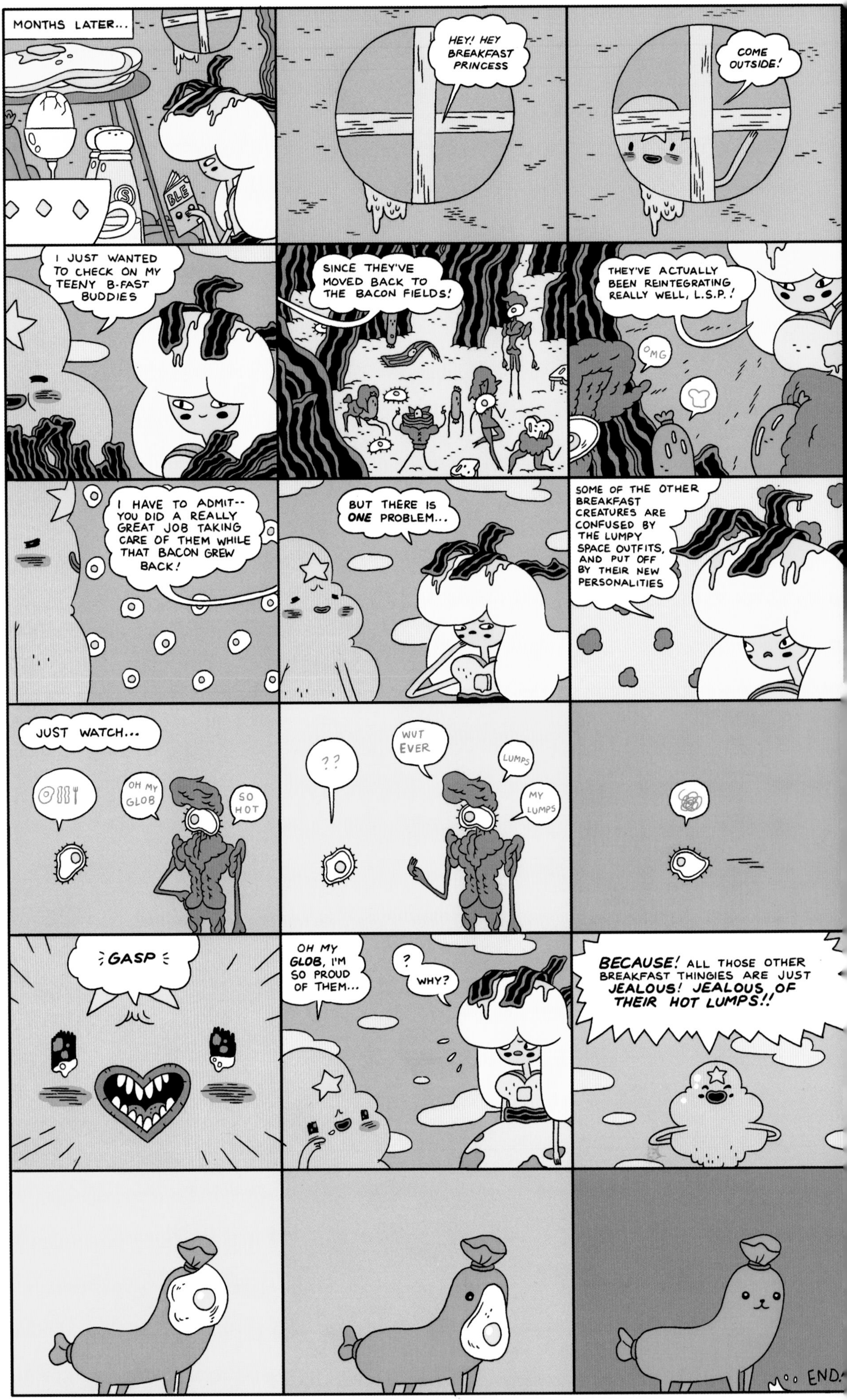
MONTHS LATER...
BLE
HEY! HEY BREAKFAST PRINCESS
COME OUTSIDE!
I JUST WANTED TO CHECK ON MY TEENY B-FAST BUDDIES
SINCE THEY'VE MOVED BACK TO THE BACON FIELDS!
THEY'VE ACTUALLY BEEN REINTEGRATING REALLY WELL, L.S.P.!
OMG
I HAVE TO ADMIT-- YOU DID A REALLY GREAT JOB TAKING CARE OF THEM WHILE THAT BACON GREW BACK!
BUT THERE IS ONE PROBLEM...
SOME OF THE OTHER BREAKFAST CREATURES ARE CONFUSED BY THE LUMPY SPACE OUTFITS, AND PUT OFF BY THEIR NEW PERSONALITIES
JUST WATCH...
OH MY GLOB
SO HOT
??
WUT EVER
LUMPS
MY LUMPS
GASP
OH MY GLOB, I'M SO PROUD OF THEM...
?
WHY?
BECAUSE! ALL THOSE OTHER BREAKFAST THINGIES ARE JUST JEALOUS! JEALOUS OF THEIR HOT LUMPS!!
END.

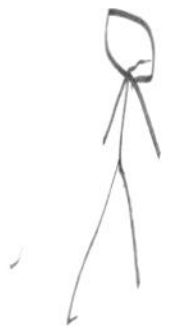

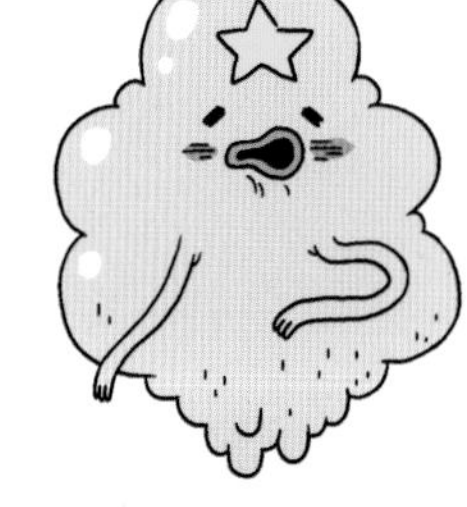

THE RIDE OF SIR SLICER

ISSUE FOUR, COVER B
KASSANDRA HELLER

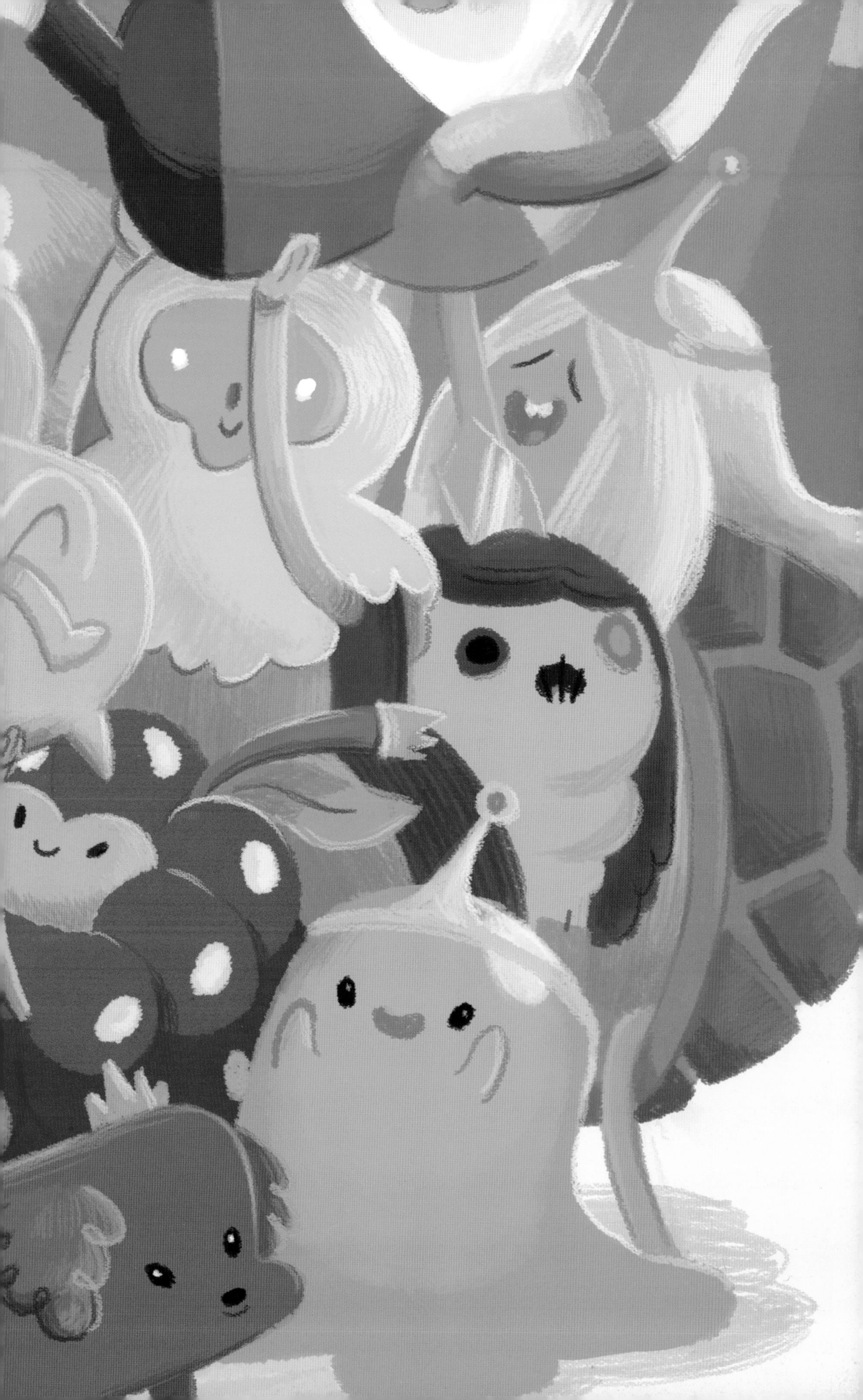

The Ride of Sir Slicer

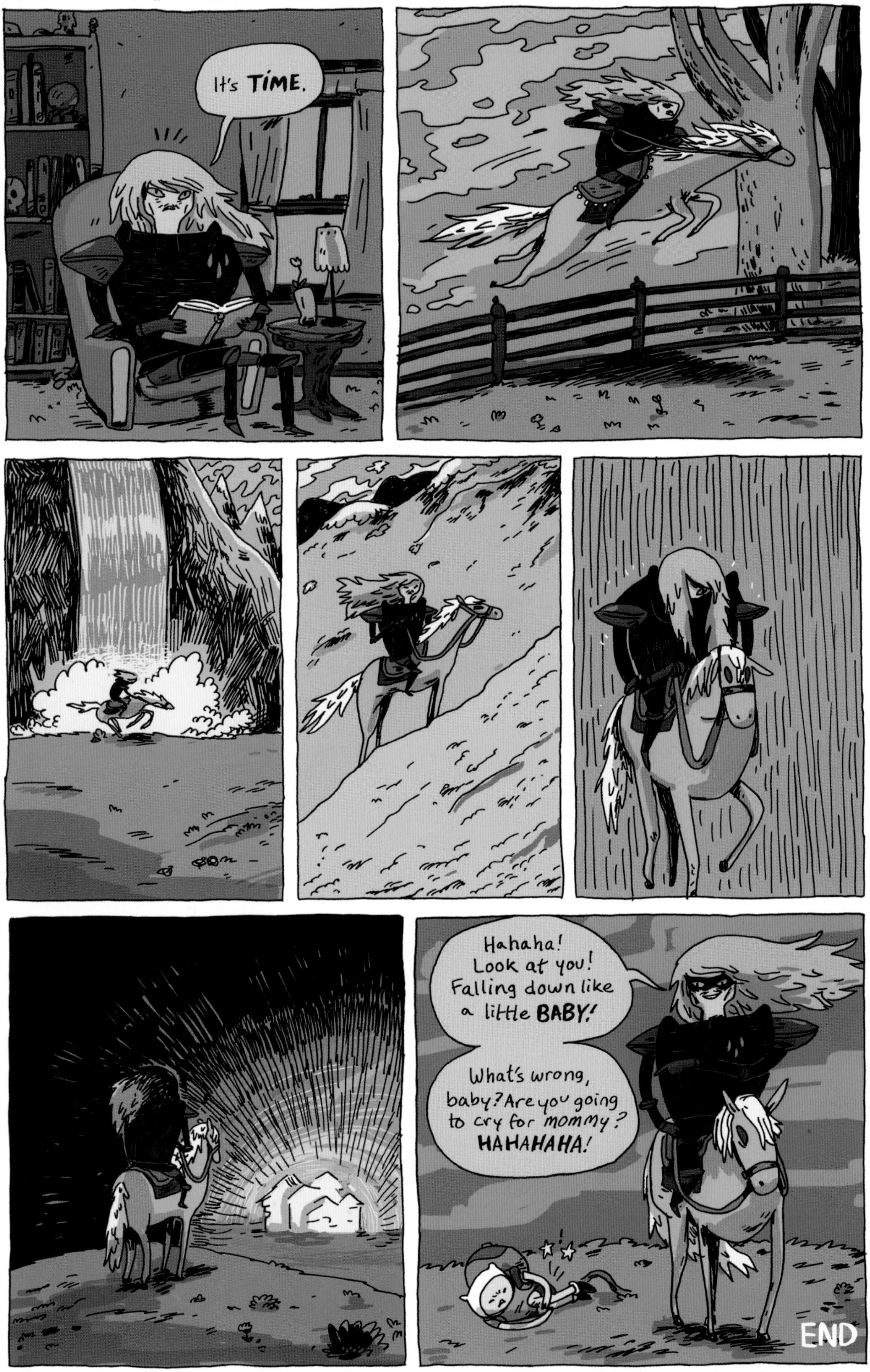

It's TIME.
Hahaha! Look at you! Falling down like a little BABY!
What's wrong, baby? Are you going to cry for mommy? HAHAHAHA!
END

-ZAC GORMAN

THE ULTIMATE PARTY DIP

ISSUE FOUR, COVER C
SCOTT C.

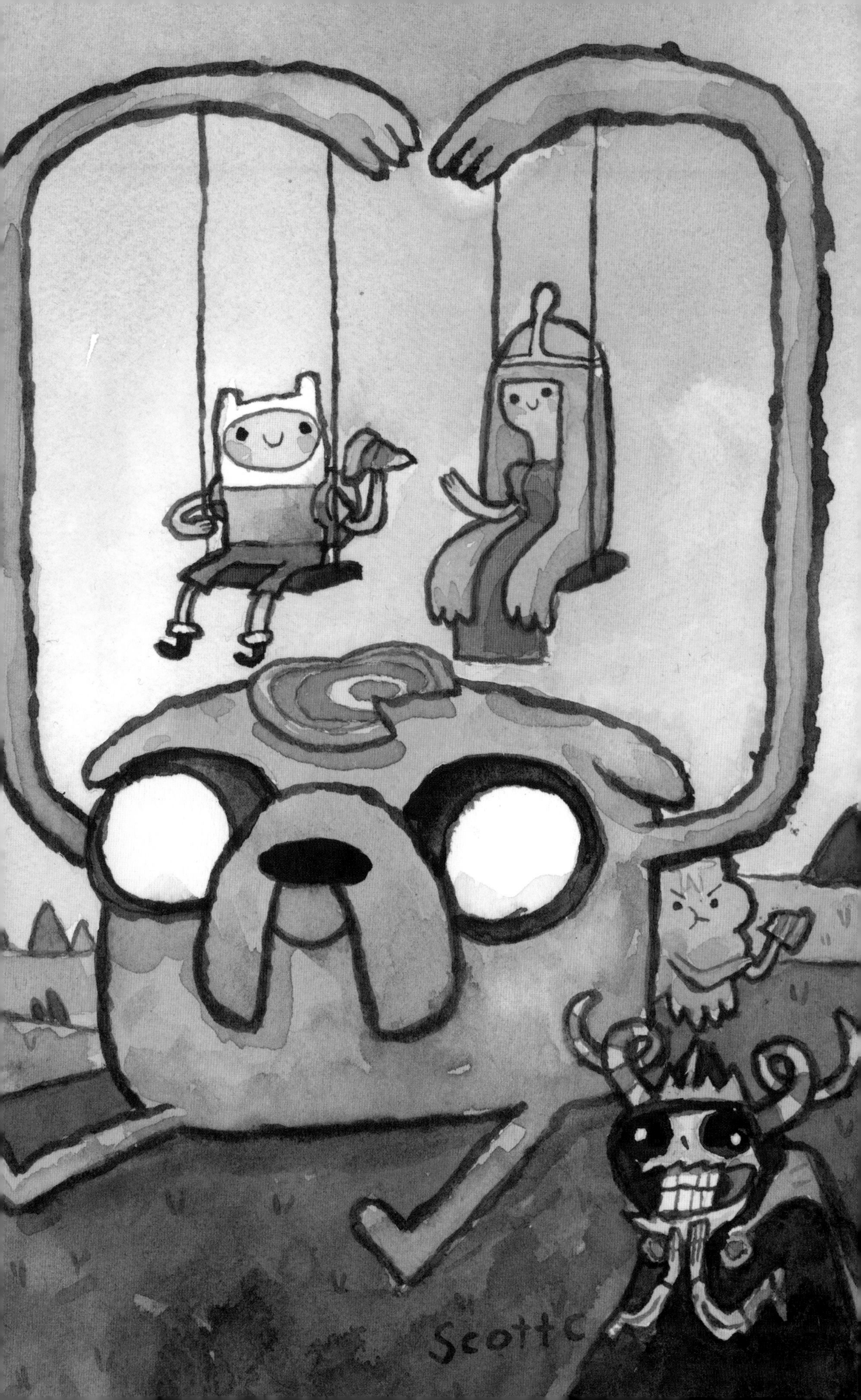
Scott C

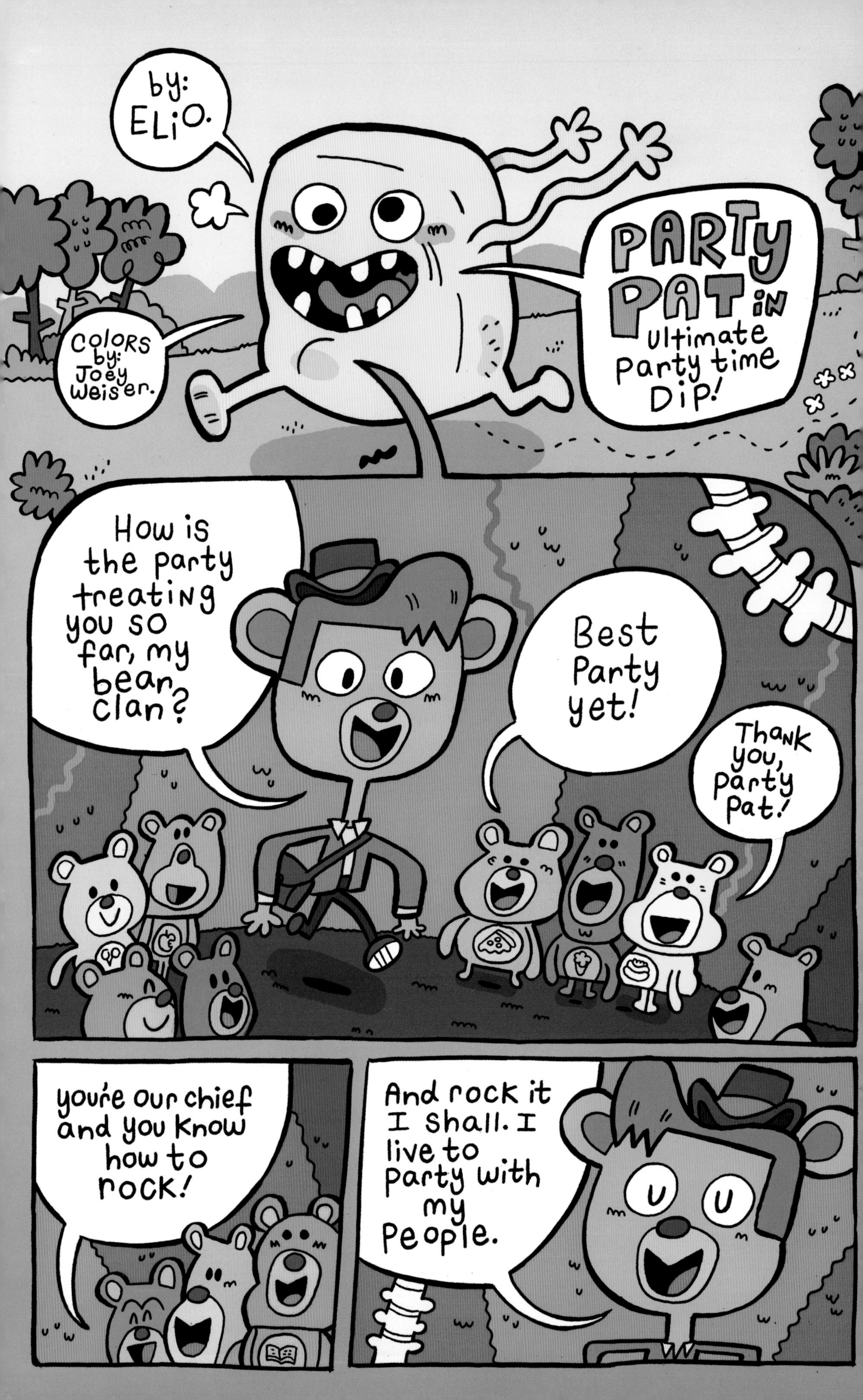
by: ELiO.
PARTy PAT iN Ultimate Party time Dip!
COLORS by: Joey Weiser.
How is the party treating you so far, my bear clan?
Best Party yet!
Thank you, party pat!
you're our chief and you know how to rock!
And rock it I shall. I live to party with my People.

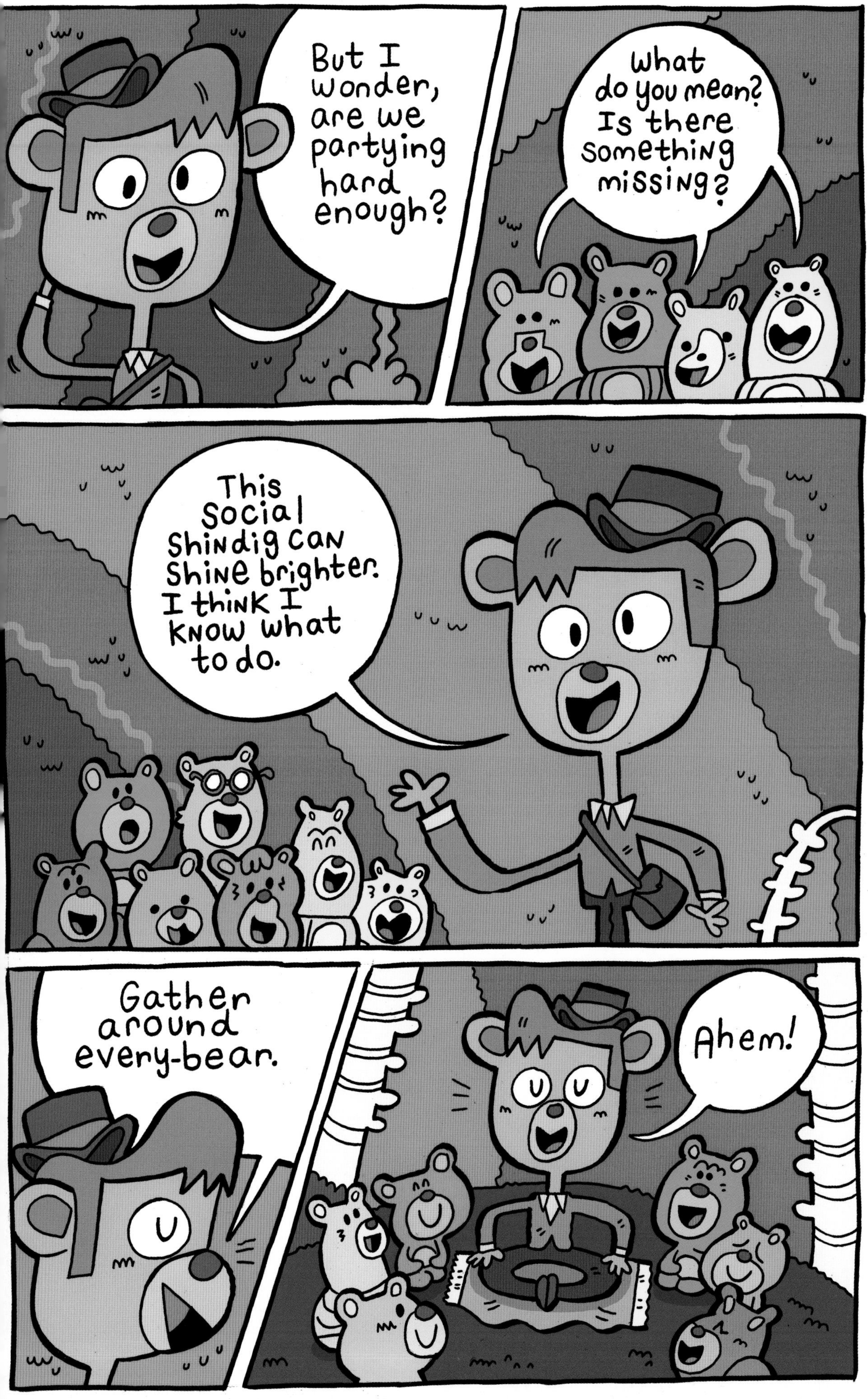
But I wonder, are we partying hard enough?
What do you mean? Is there something missing?
This social shindig can shine brighter. I think I know what to do.
Gather around every-bear.
Ahem!

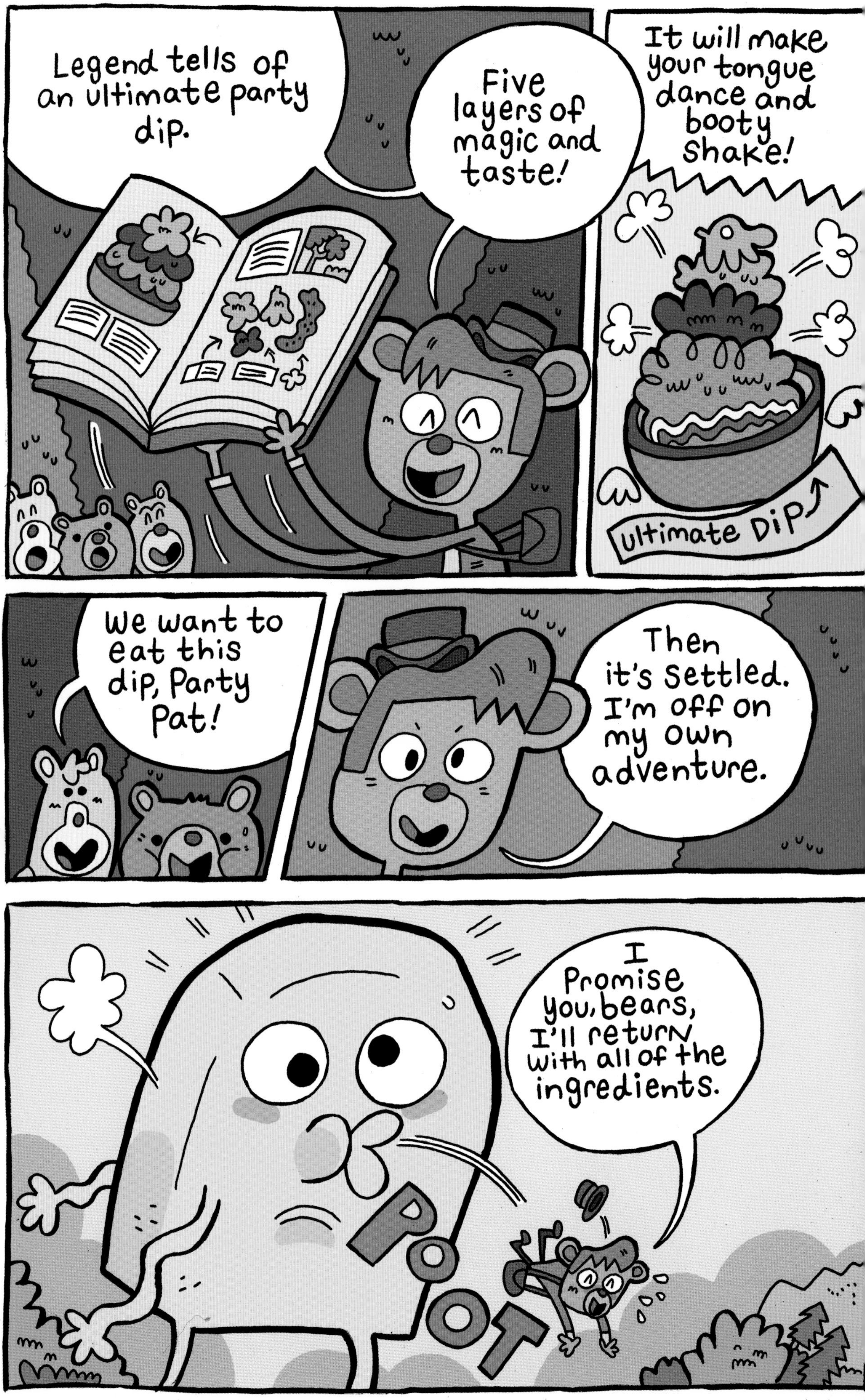

Legend tells of an ultimate party dip.
Five layers of magic and taste!
It will make your tongue dance and booty shake!
Ultimate DiP
We want to eat this dip, Party Pat!
Then it's settled. I'm off on my own adventure.
I Promise you, bears, I'll return with all of the ingredients.
POOT

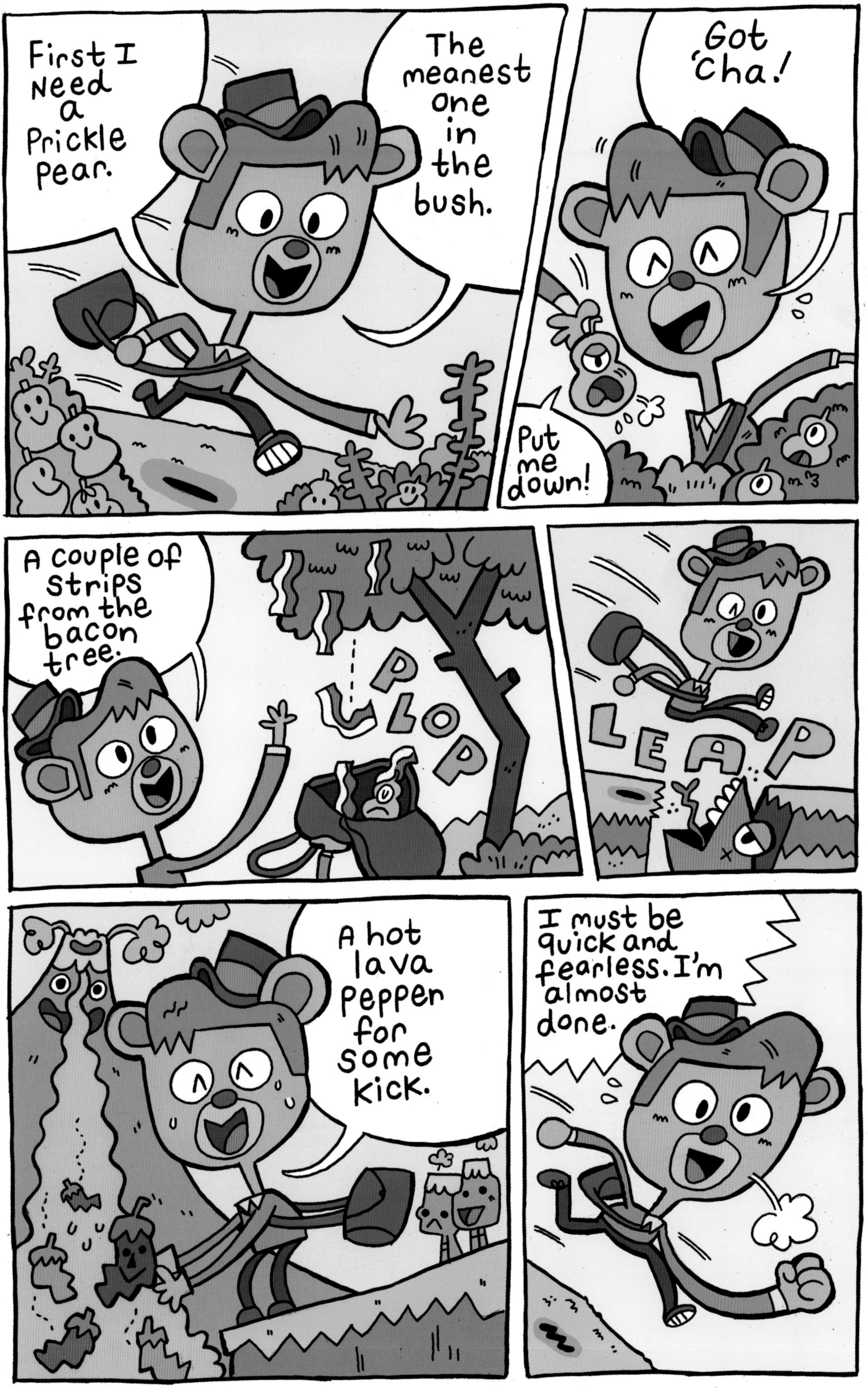
First I Need a Prickle Pear.
The meanest one in the bush.
Got 'Cha!
Put me down!
A couple of strips from the bacon tree.
PLOP
LEAP
A hot lava pepper for some kick.
I must be quick and fearless. I'm almost done.

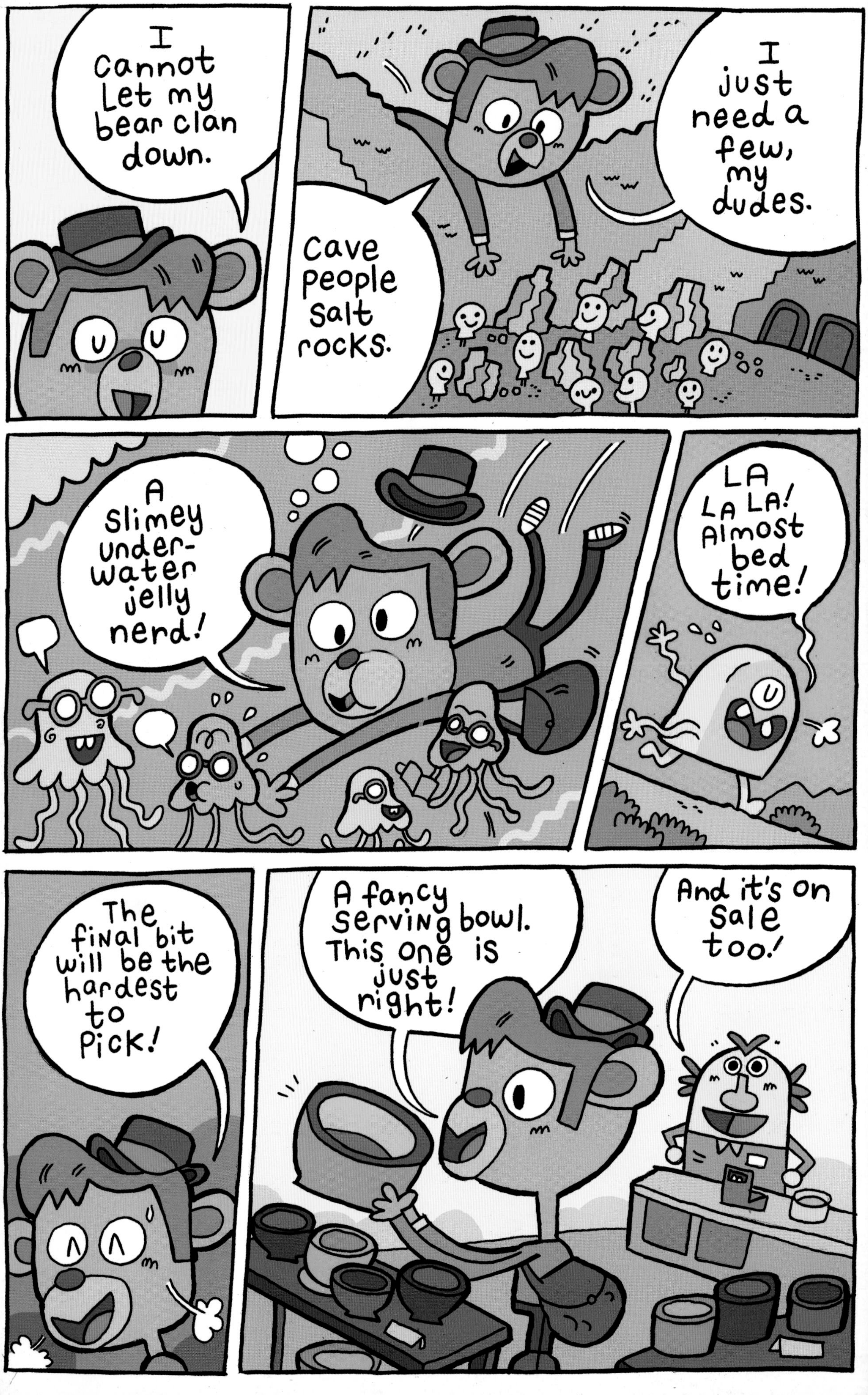
I cannot let my bear clan down.
Cave people salt rocks.
I just need a few, my dudes.
A slimey under-water jelly nerd!
LA LA LA! Almost bed time!
The final bit will be the hardest to pick!
A fancy serving bowl. This one is just right!
And it's on sale too!

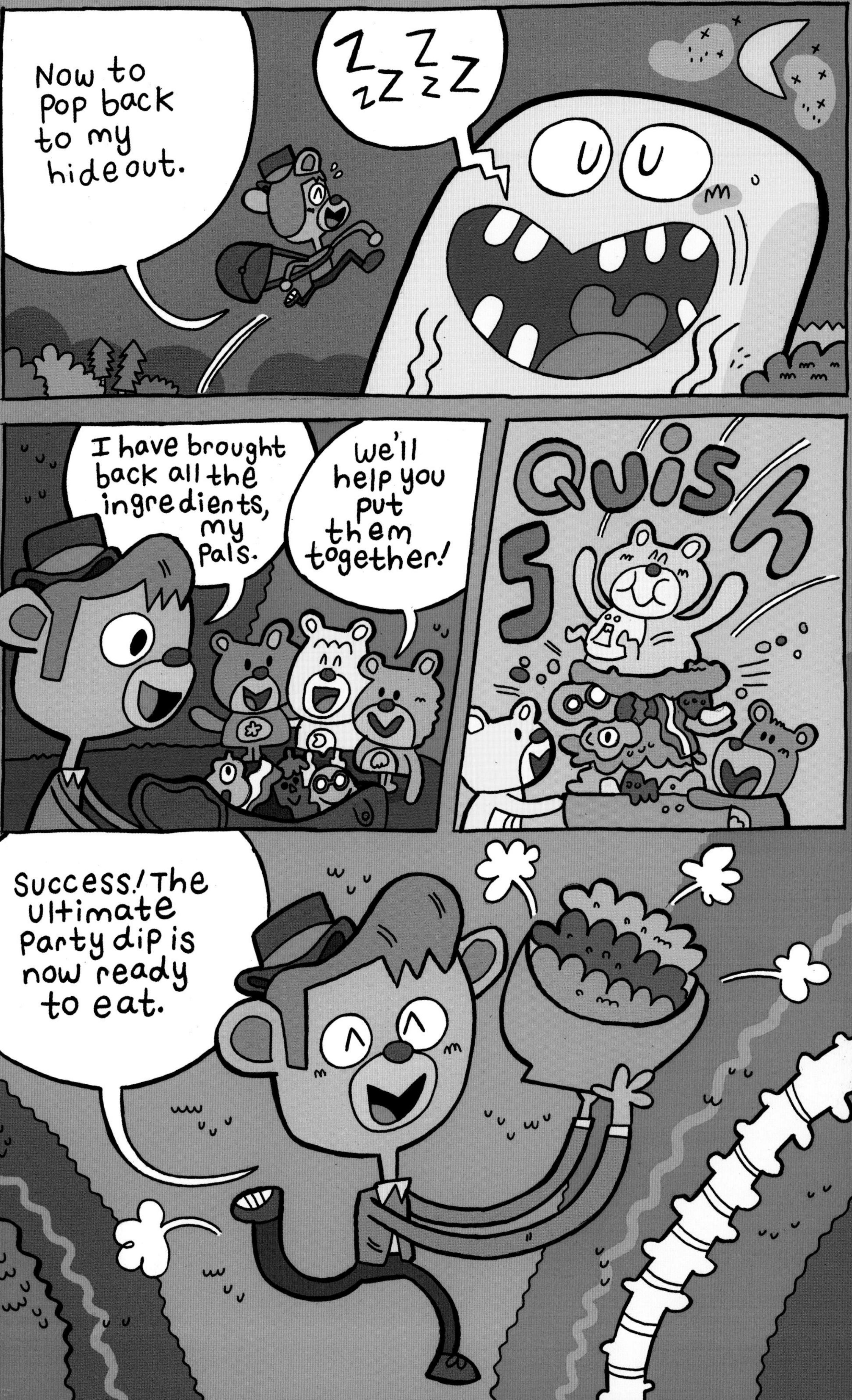
Now to pop back to my hideout.
ZZZZZZ
I have brought back all the ingredients, my pals.
We'll help you put them together!
SQUISH
Success! The ultimate party dip is now ready to eat.

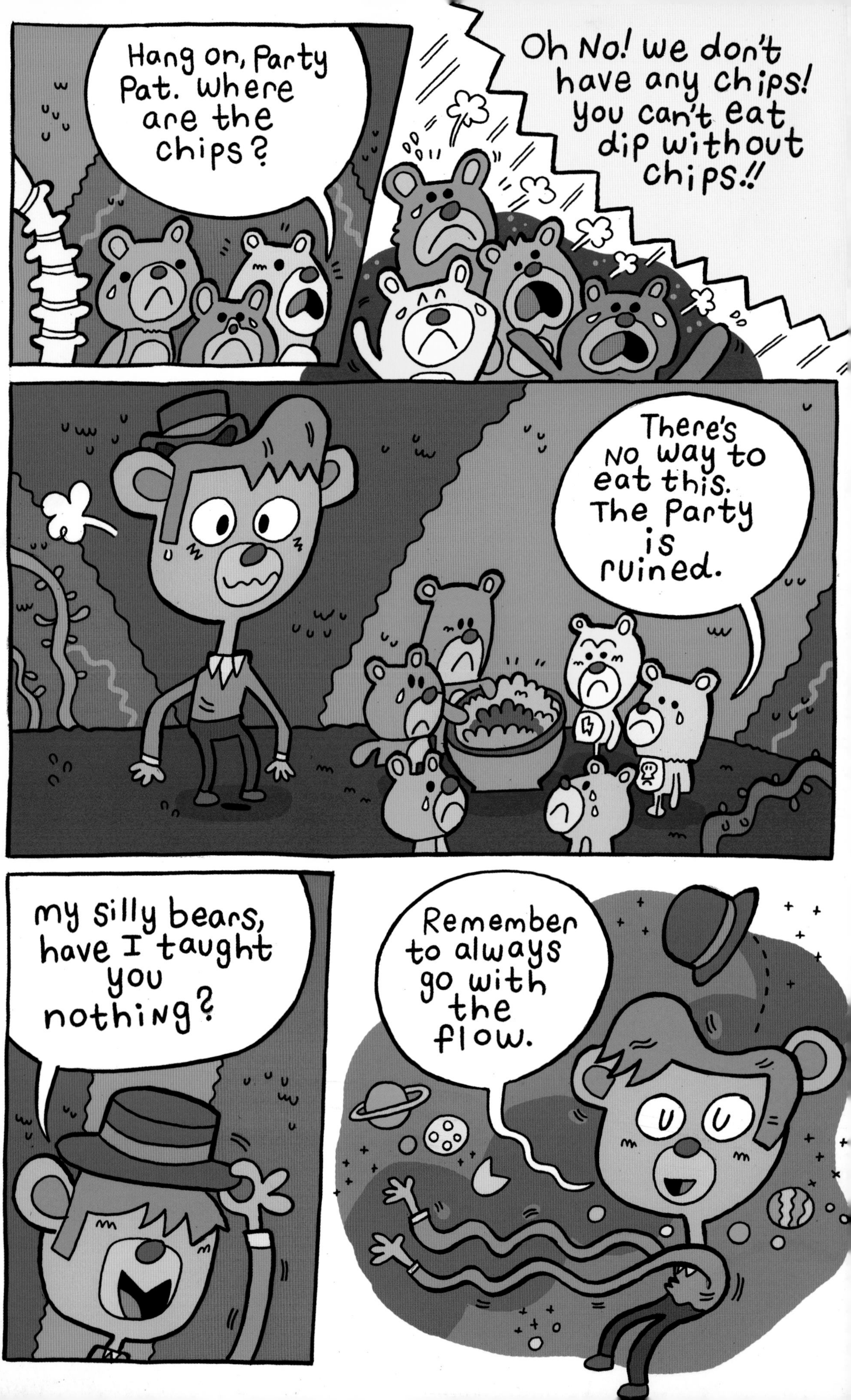

Hang on, Party Pat. Where are the chips?
Oh No! we don't have any chips! you can't eat dip without chips!!
There's No way to eat this. The Party is ruined.
my silly bears, have I taught you nothing?
Remember to always go with the flow.

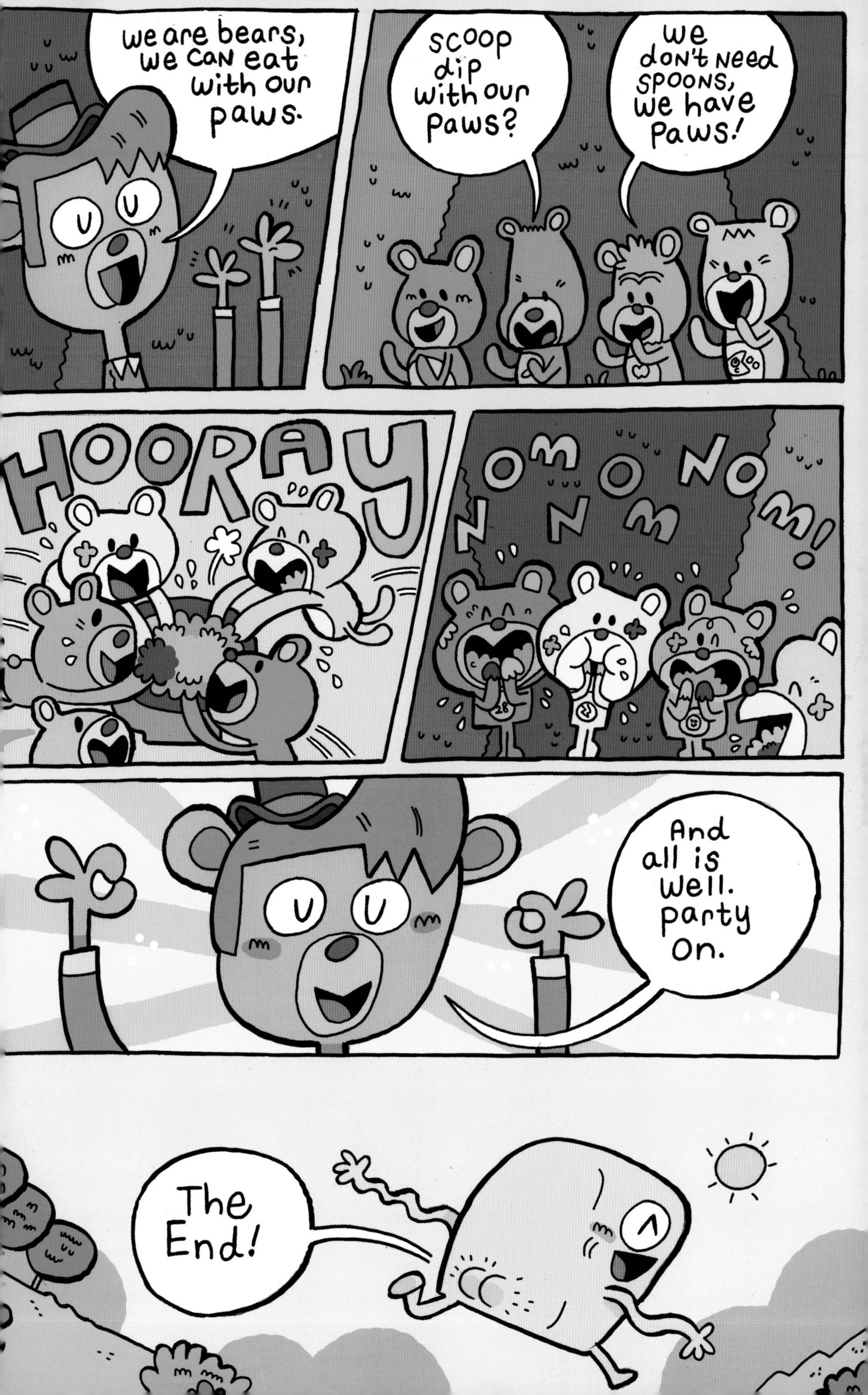
we are bears, we can eat with our paws.
scoop dip with our paws?
we don't need spoons, we have paws!
HOORAY
NOM NOM NOM NOM!
And all is well. party on.
The End!

EMIT ERUTNEVDA

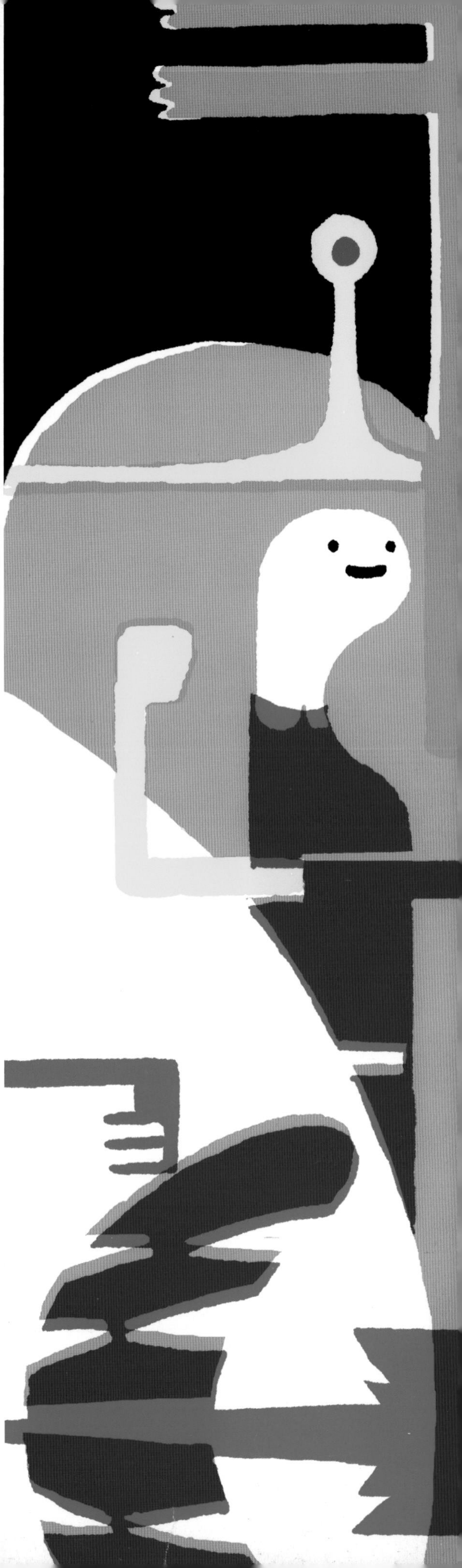

ISSUE FIVE, COVER B
ELEANOR DAVIS

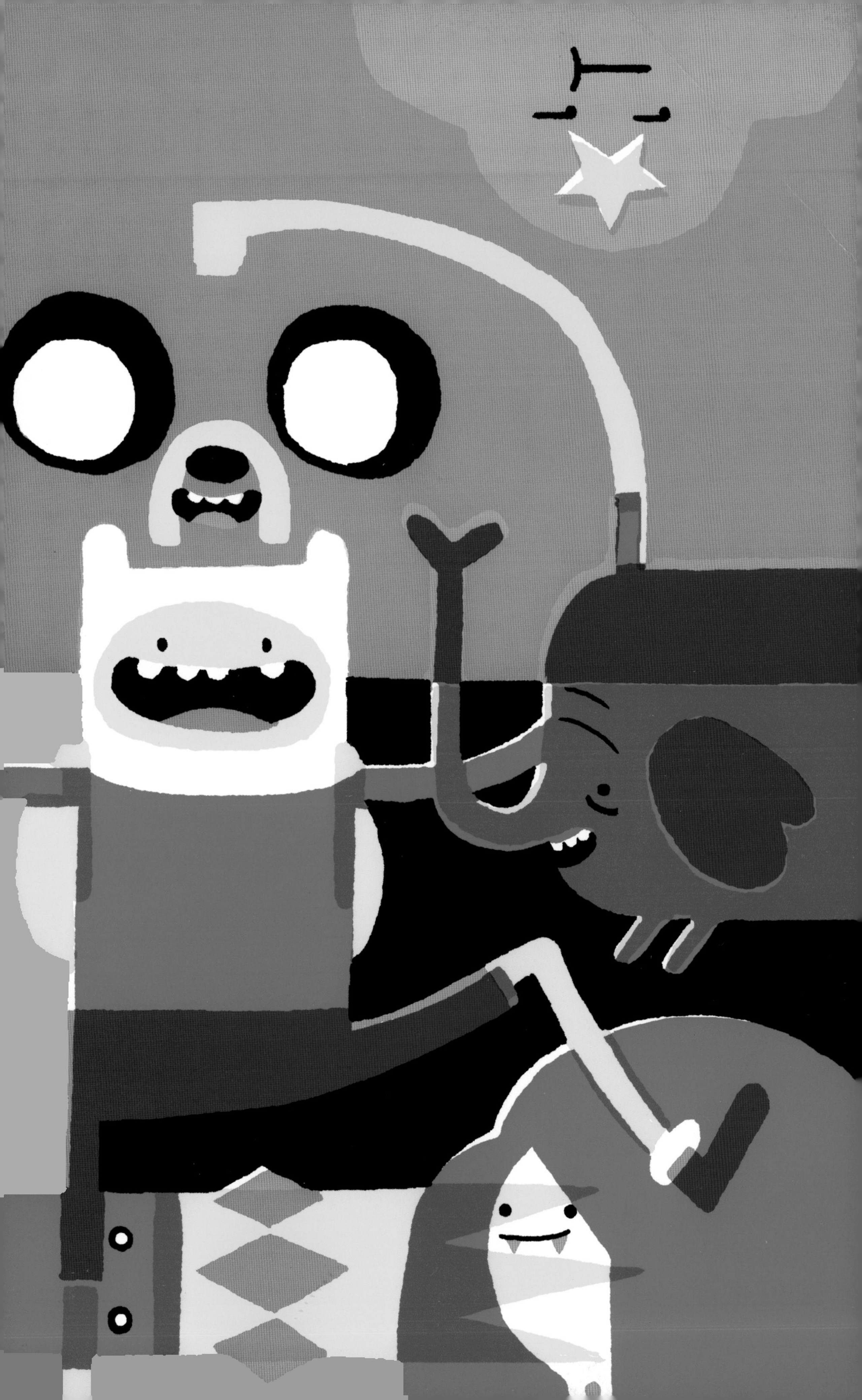

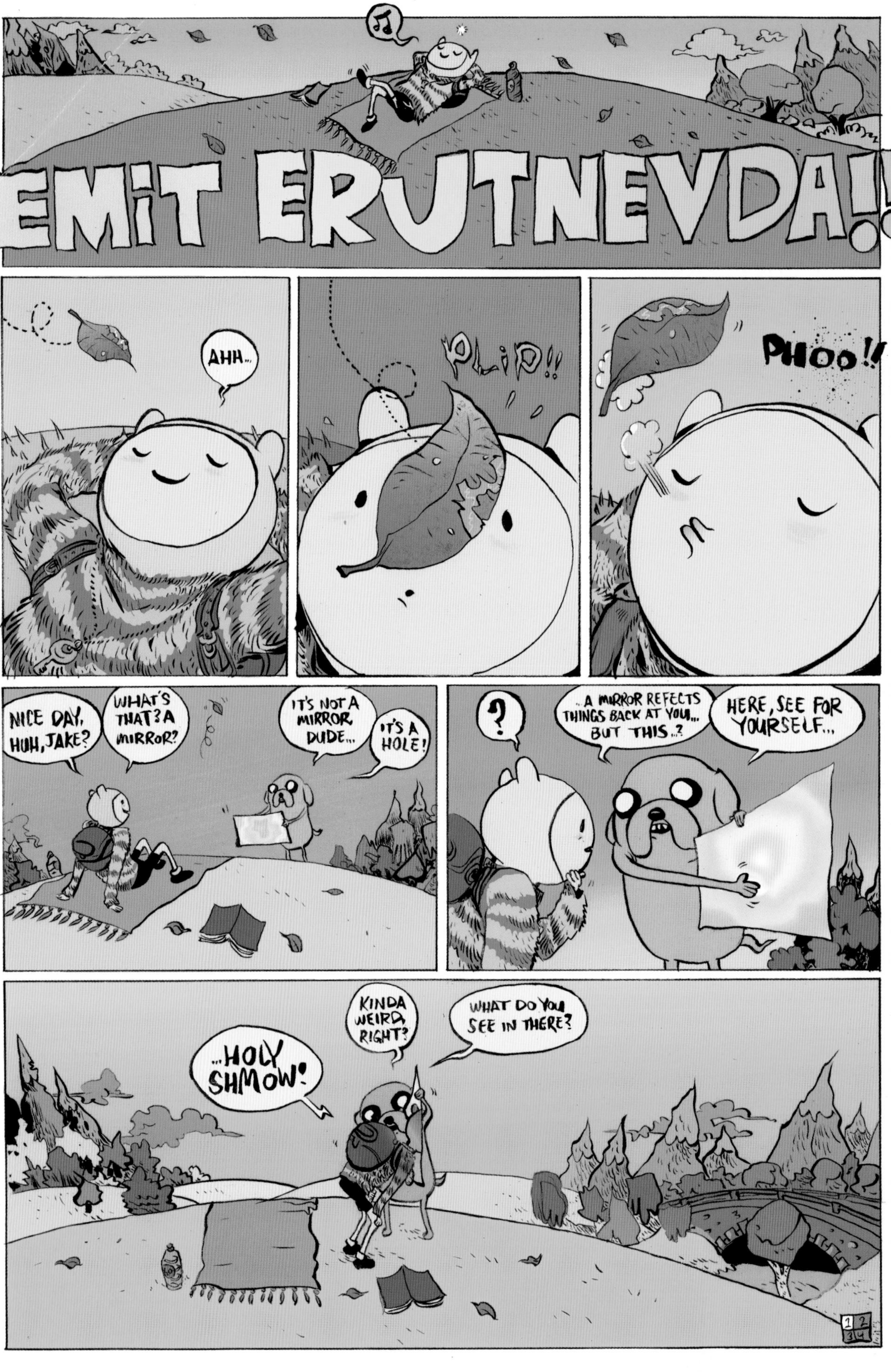
EMIT ERUTNEVDA!!
AHH...
PLIP!!
PHOO!!
NICE DAY, HUH, JAKE?
WHAT'S THAT? A MIRROR?
IT'S NOT A MIRROR DUDE...
IT'S A HOLE!
?
...A MIRROR REFECTS THINGS BACK AT YOU... BUT THIS...?
HERE, SEE FOR YOURSELF...
KINDA WEIRD, RIGHT?
WHAT DO YOU SEE IN THERE?
...HOLY SHMOW!

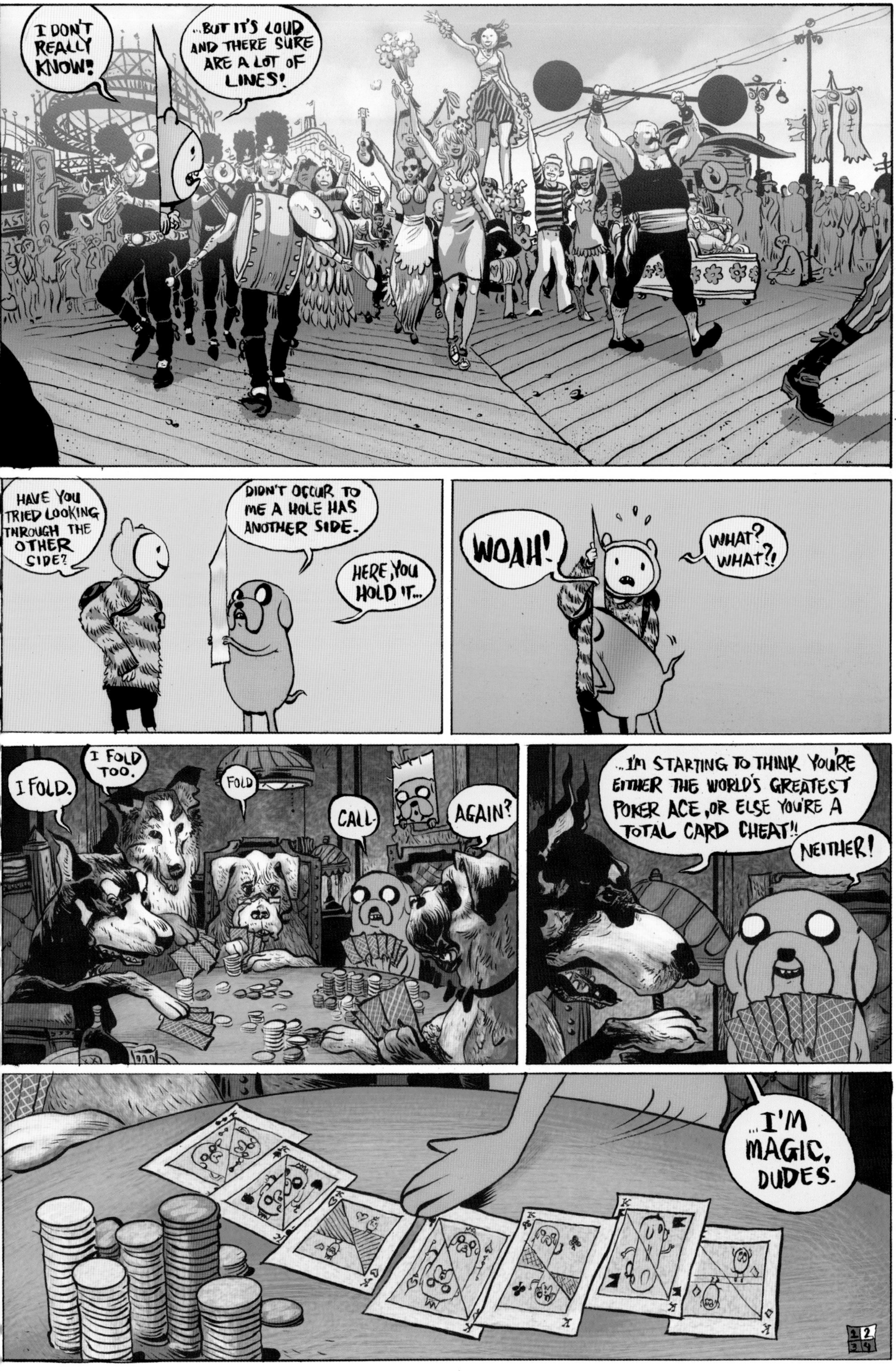
I DON'T REALLY KNOW!
...BUT IT'S LOUD AND THERE SURE ARE A LOT OF LINES!
HAVE YOU TRIED LOOKING THROUGH THE OTHER SIDE?
DIDN'T OCCUR TO ME A HOLE HAS ANOTHER SIDE.
HERE, YOU HOLD IT...
WOAH!
WHAT? WHAT?!
I FOLD.
I FOLD TOO.
FOLD
CALL.
AGAIN?
...I'M STARTING TO THINK YOU'RE EITHER THE WORLD'S GREATEST POKER ACE, OR ELSE YOU'RE A TOTAL CARD CHEAT!!
NEITHER!
...I'M MAGIC, DUDES.

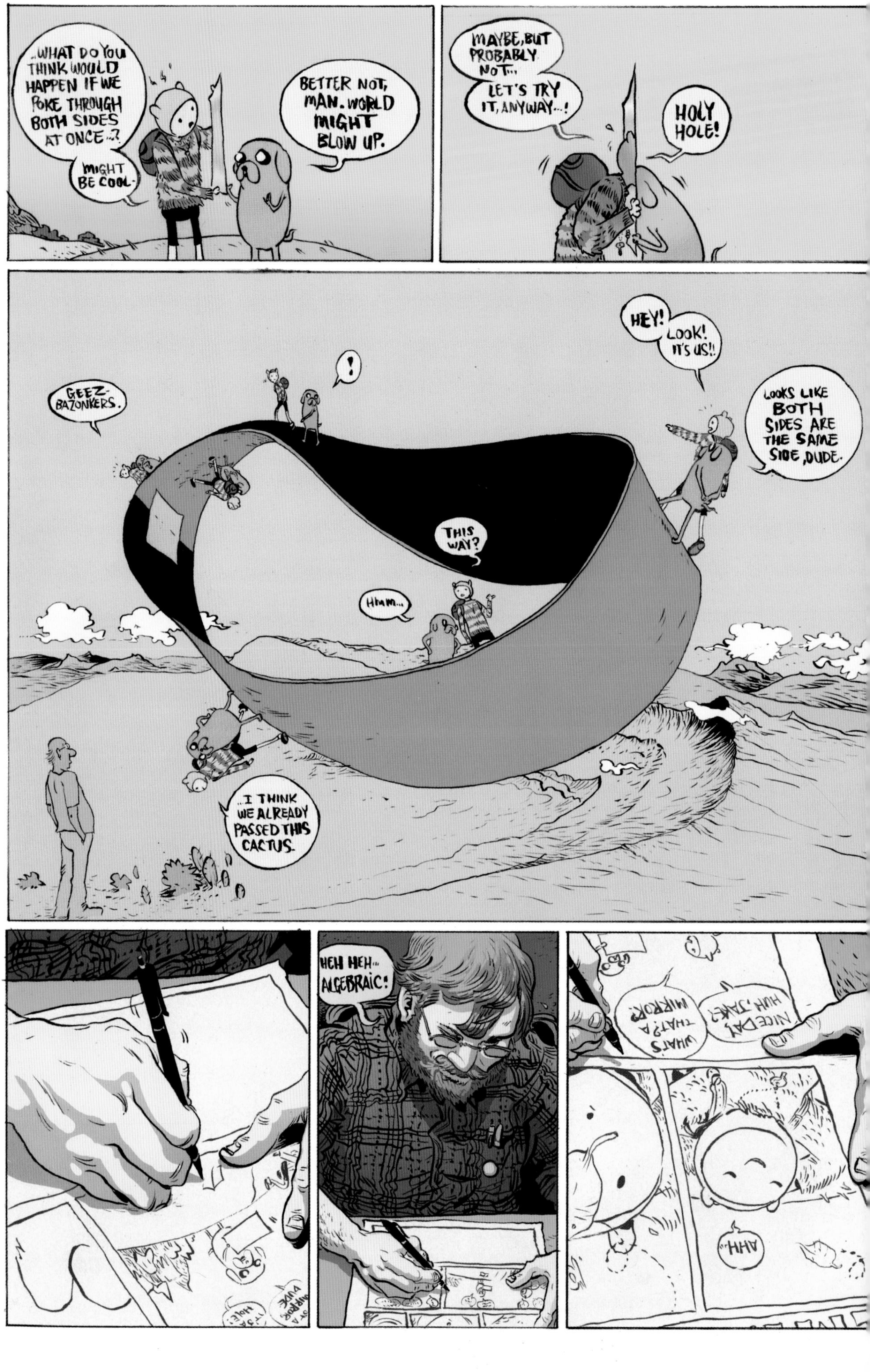
...WHAT DO YOU THINK WOULD HAPPEN IF WE POKE THROUGH BOTH SIDES AT ONCE...?
MIGHT BE COOL.
BETTER NOT, MAN. WORLD MIGHT BLOW UP.
MAYBE, BUT PROBABLY NOT...
LET'S TRY IT, ANYWAY...!
HOLY HOLE!
GEEZ-BAZONKERS.
!
HEY!
LOOK! IT'S US!!
LOOKS LIKE BOTH SIDES ARE THE SAME SIDE, DUDE.
THIS WAY?
Hmm...
...I THINK WE ALREADY PASSED THIS CACTUS.
HEH HEH... ALGEBRAIC!
WHAT'S THAT? A MIRROR?
NICE DAY, HUH, JAKE?
AHH...

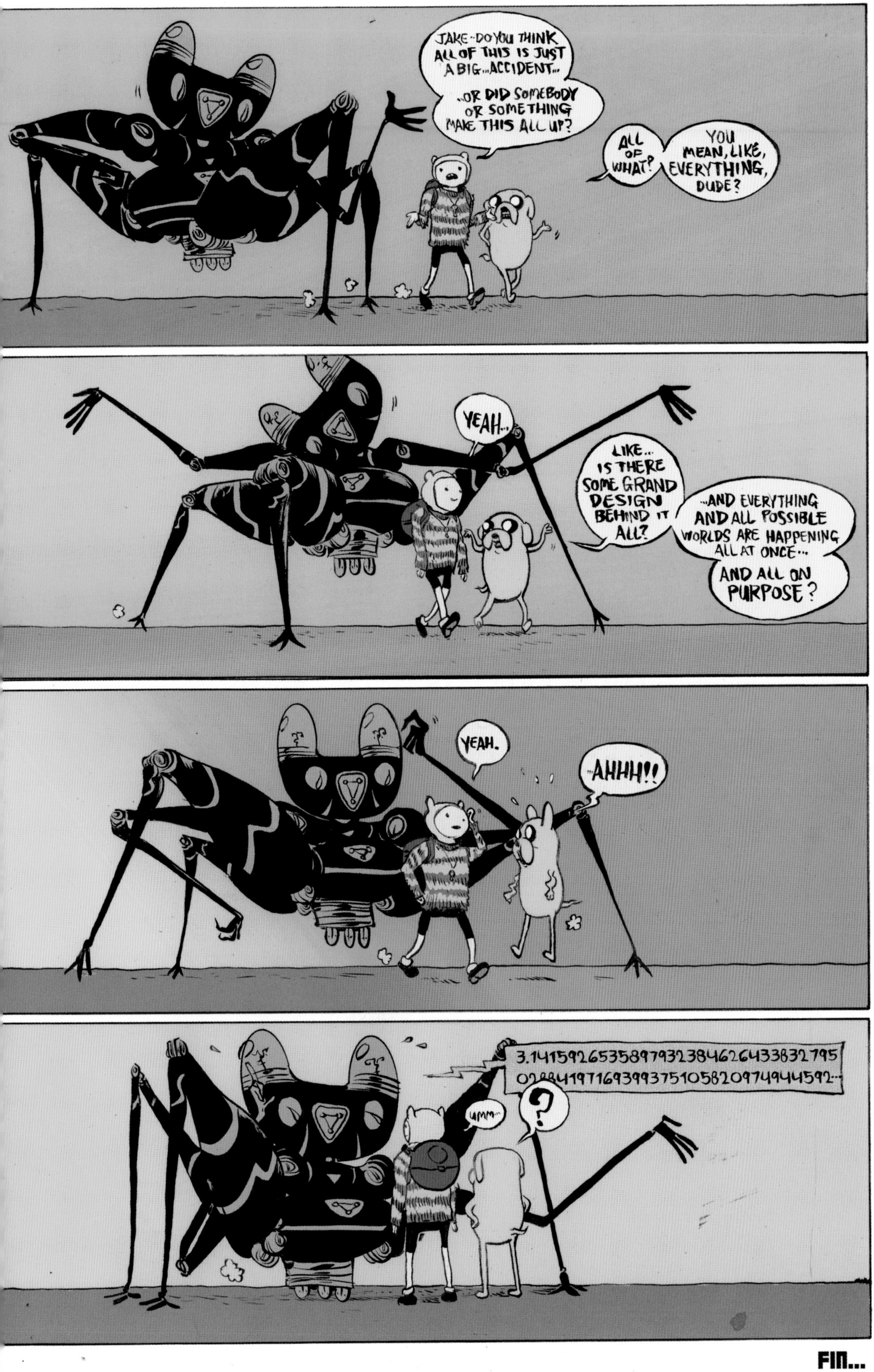
JAKE--DO YOU THINK ALL OF THIS IS JUST A BIG...ACCIDENT...
...OR DID SOMEBODY OR SOMETHING MAKE THIS ALL UP?
ALL OF WHAT?
YOU MEAN, LIKE, EVERYTHING, DUDE?
YEAH...
LIKE... IS THERE SOME GRAND DESIGN BEHIND IT ALL?
...AND EVERYTHING AND ALL POSSIBLE WORLDS ARE HAPPENING ALL AT ONCE...
AND ALL ON PURPOSE?
YEAH.
AHHH!!
3.1415926535897932384626433832795
02884197169399375105820974944592...
UMM...
?

FIN...

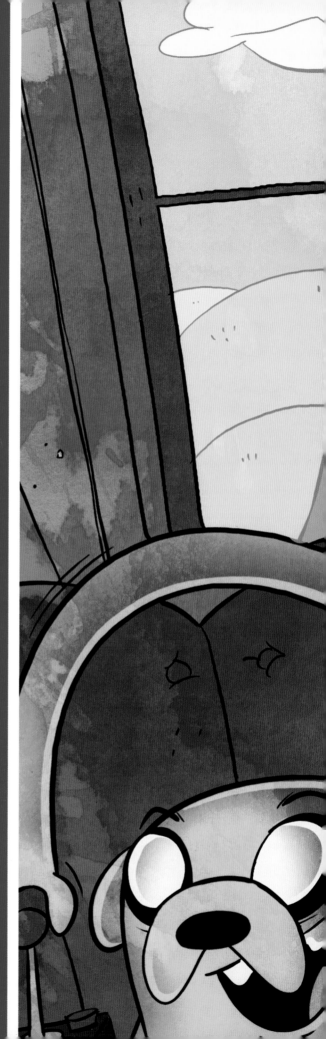

ICE KINGDUMB

ISSUE FIVE, COVER D
MIKE "GABE" KRAHULIK

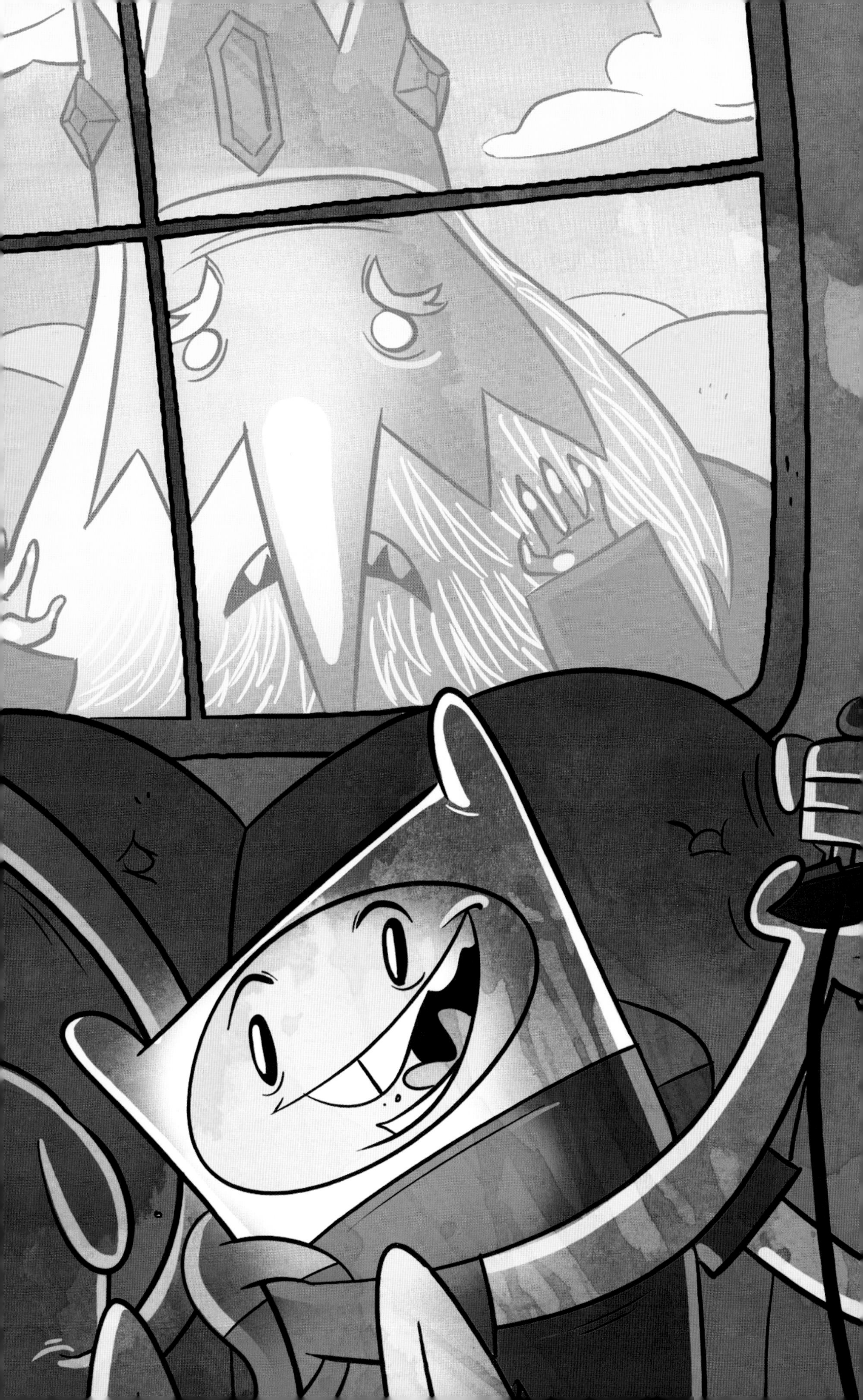

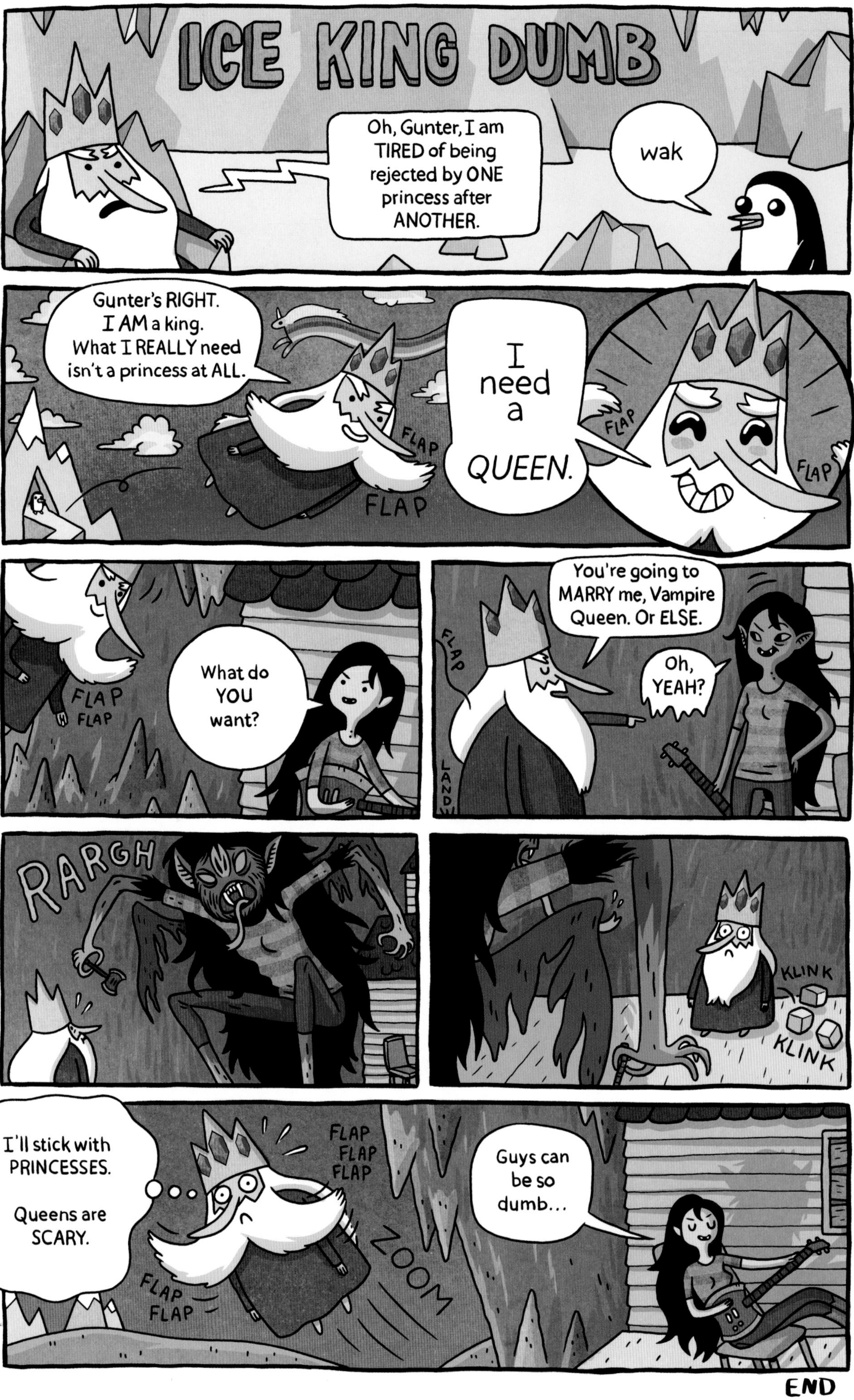
ICE KING DUMB
Oh, Gunter, I am TIRED of being rejected by ONE princess after ANOTHER.
wak
Gunter's RIGHT. I AM a king. What I REALLY need isn't a princess at ALL.
FLAP
FLAP
I need a QUEEN.
FLAP
FLAP
FLAP
FLAP
What do YOU want?
FLAP
LANDS
You're going to MARRY me, Vampire Queen. Or ELSE.
Oh, YEAH?
RARGH
KLINK
KLINK
I'll stick with PRINCESSES.
Queens are SCARY.
FLAP
FLAP
FLAP
ZOOM
FLAP
FLAP
Guys can be so dumb...

Writers: Chris Roberson & Georgia Roberson (Age 8) Artist: Lucy Knisley

END

LEVEL 99

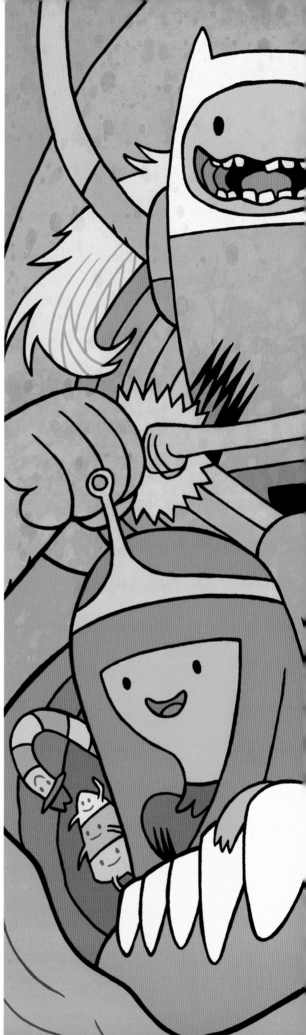

ISSUE SIX, COVER C
DAN HIPP

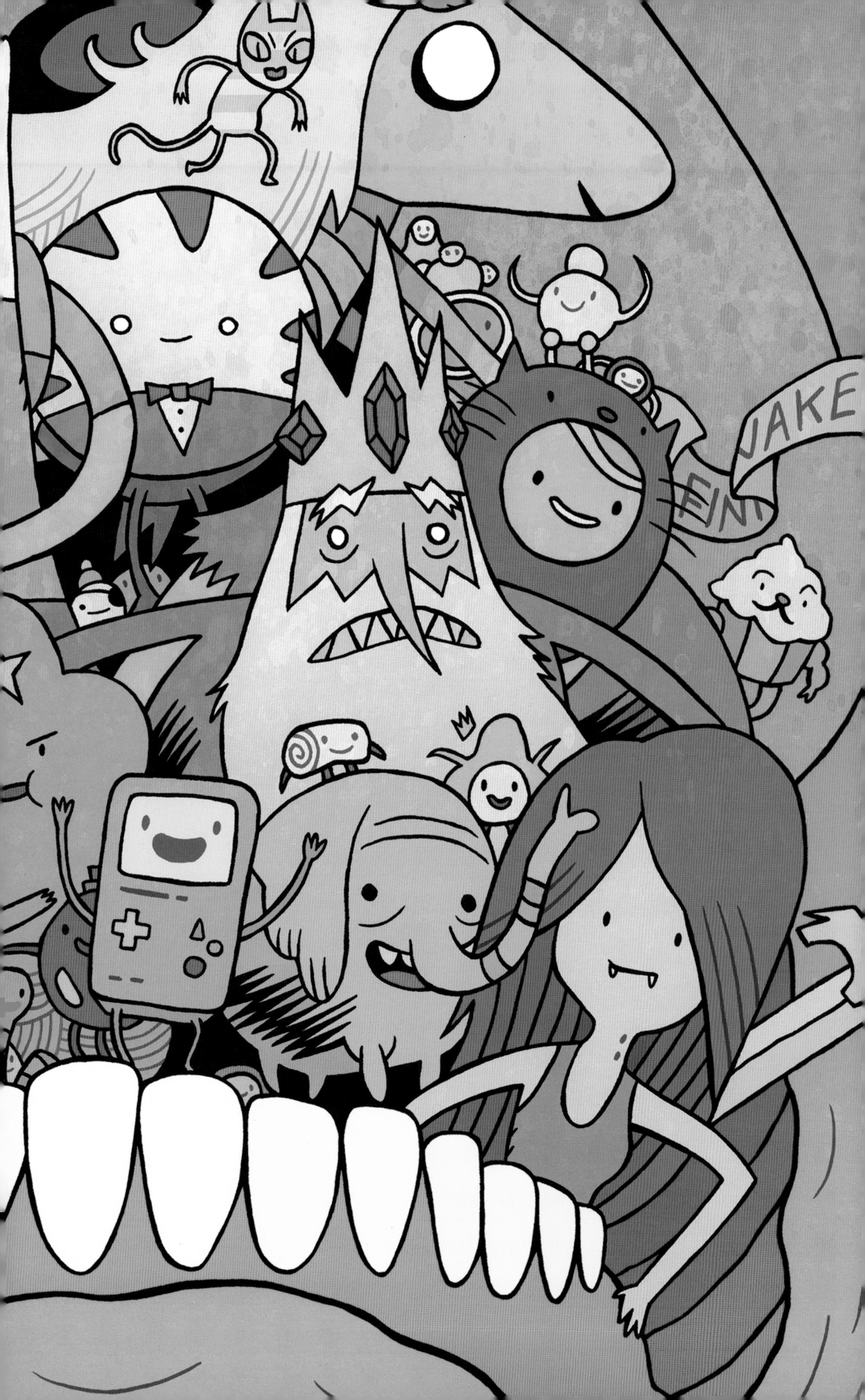
JAKE

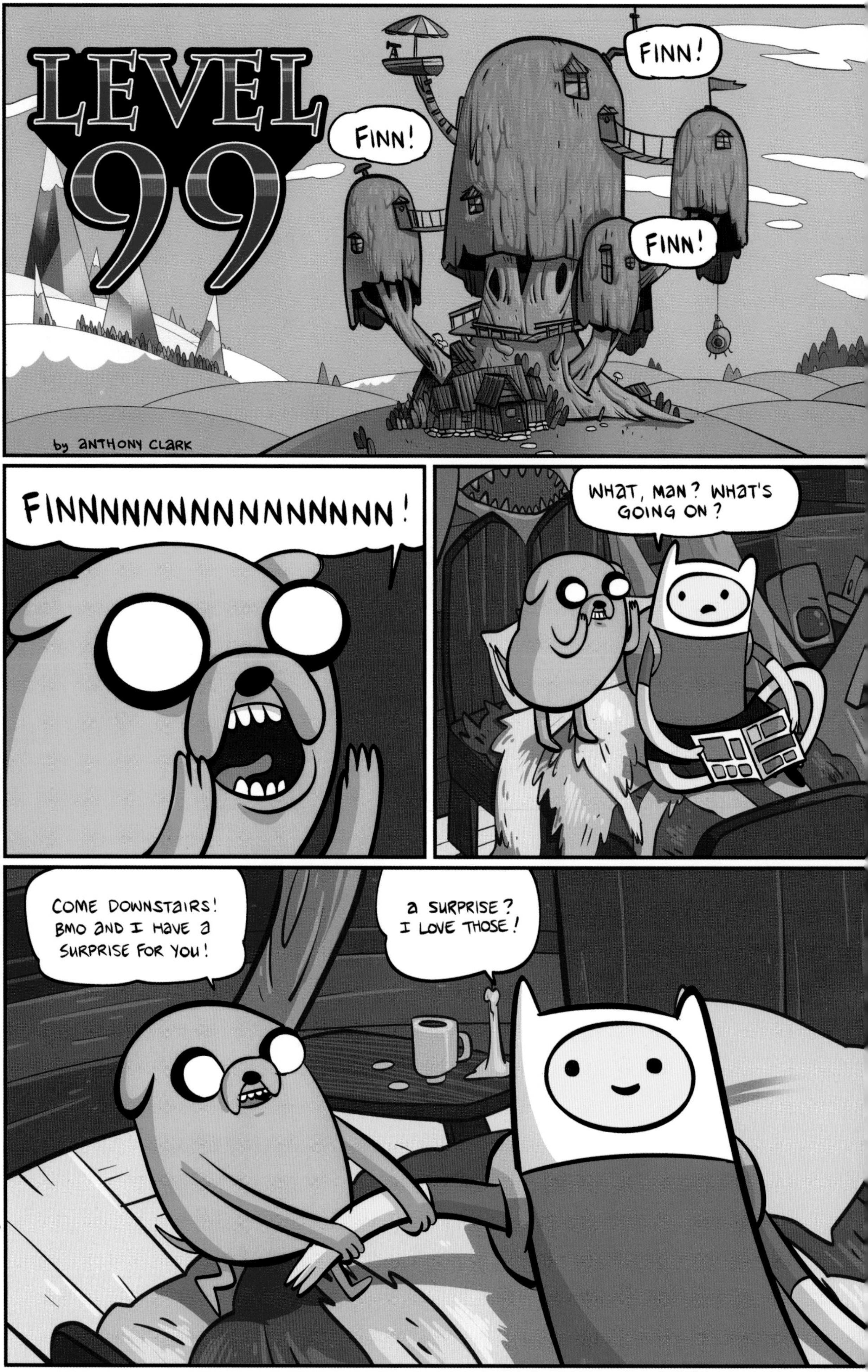
LEVEL 99
FINN!
FINN!
FINN!
by ANTHONY CLARK
FINNNNNNNNNNNNNNN!
WHAT, MAN? WHAT'S GOING ON?
COME DOWNSTAIRS! BMO AND I HAVE A SURPRISE FOR YOU!
A SURPRISE? I LOVE THOSE!

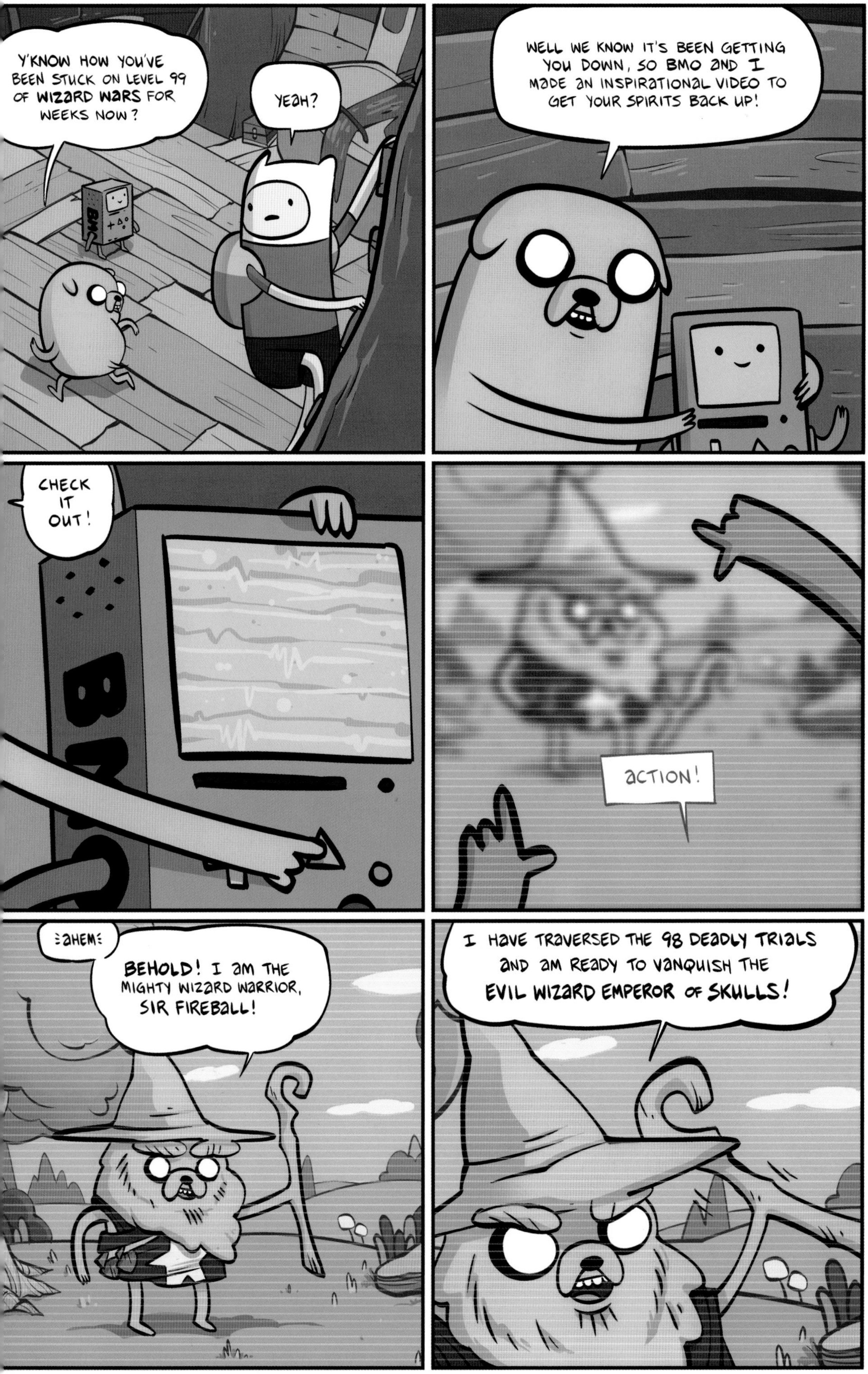
Y'KNOW HOW YOU'VE BEEN STUCK ON LEVEL 99 OF WIZARD WARS FOR WEEKS NOW?
YEAH?
WELL WE KNOW IT'S BEEN GETTING YOU DOWN, SO BMO AND I MADE AN INSPIRATIONAL VIDEO TO GET YOUR SPIRITS BACK UP!
CHECK IT OUT!
ACTION!
AHEM
BEHOLD! I AM THE MIGHTY WIZARD WARRIOR, SIR FIREBALL!
I HAVE TRAVERSED THE 98 DEADLY TRIALS AND AM READY TO VANQUISH THE EVIL WIZARD EMPEROR OF SKULLS!

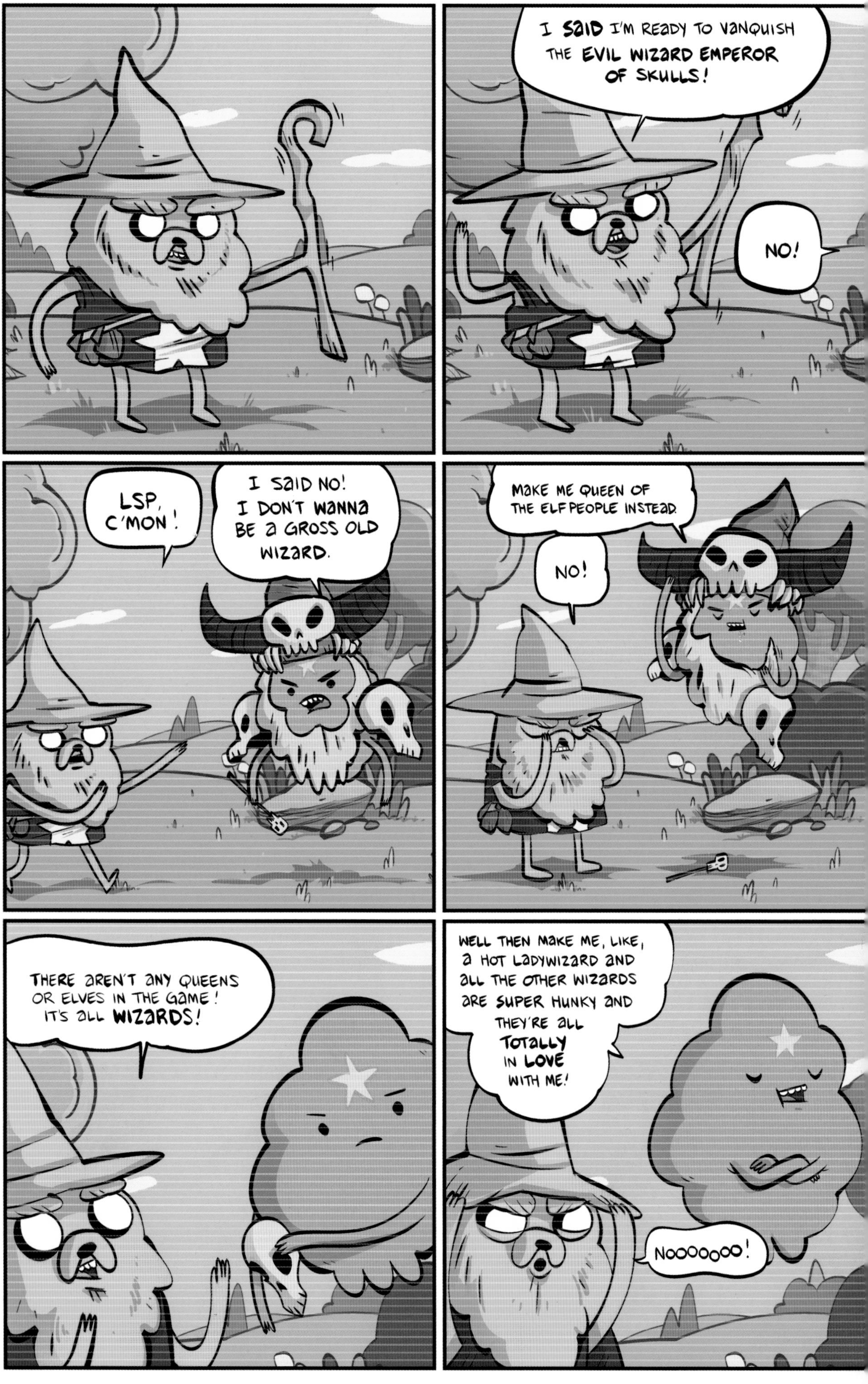
I SAID I'M READY TO VANQUISH THE EVIL WIZARD EMPEROR OF SKULLS!
NO!
LSP, C'MON!
I SAID NO! I DON'T WANNA BE A GROSS OLD WIZARD.
MAKE ME QUEEN OF THE ELF PEOPLE INSTEAD.
NO!
THERE AREN'T ANY QUEENS OR ELVES IN THE GAME! IT'S ALL WIZARDS!
WELL THEN MAKE ME, LIKE, A HOT LADYWIZARD AND ALL THE OTHER WIZARDS ARE SUPER HUNKY AND THEY'RE ALL TOTALLY IN LOVE WITH ME!
NOOOOOOO!

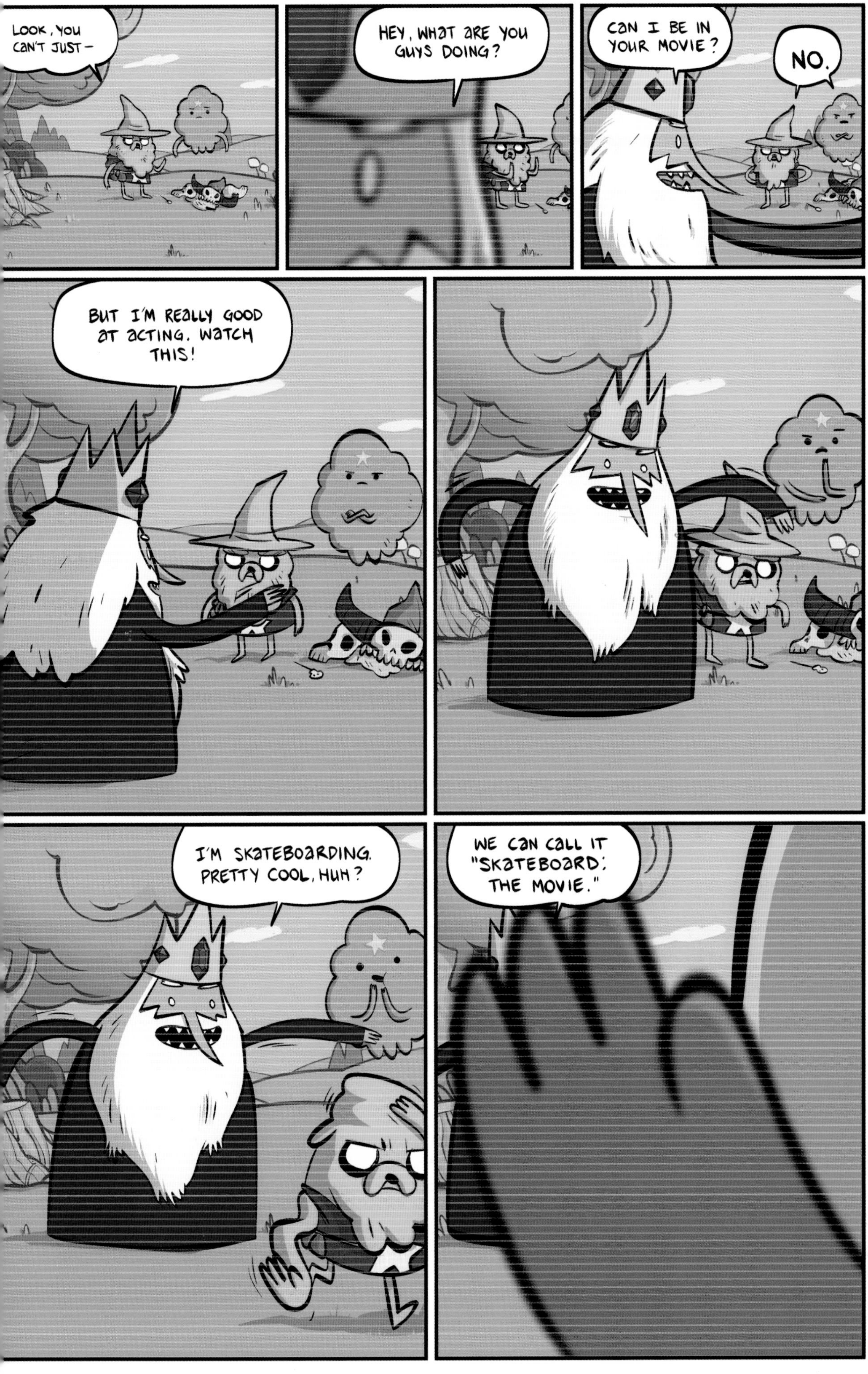
LOOK, YOU CAN'T JUST—
HEY, WHAT ARE YOU GUYS DOING?
CAN I BE IN YOUR MOVIE?
NO.
BUT I'M REALLY GOOD AT ACTING. WATCH THIS!
I'M SKATEBOARDING. PRETTY COOL, HUH?
WE CAN CALL IT "SKATEBOARD: THE MOVIE."

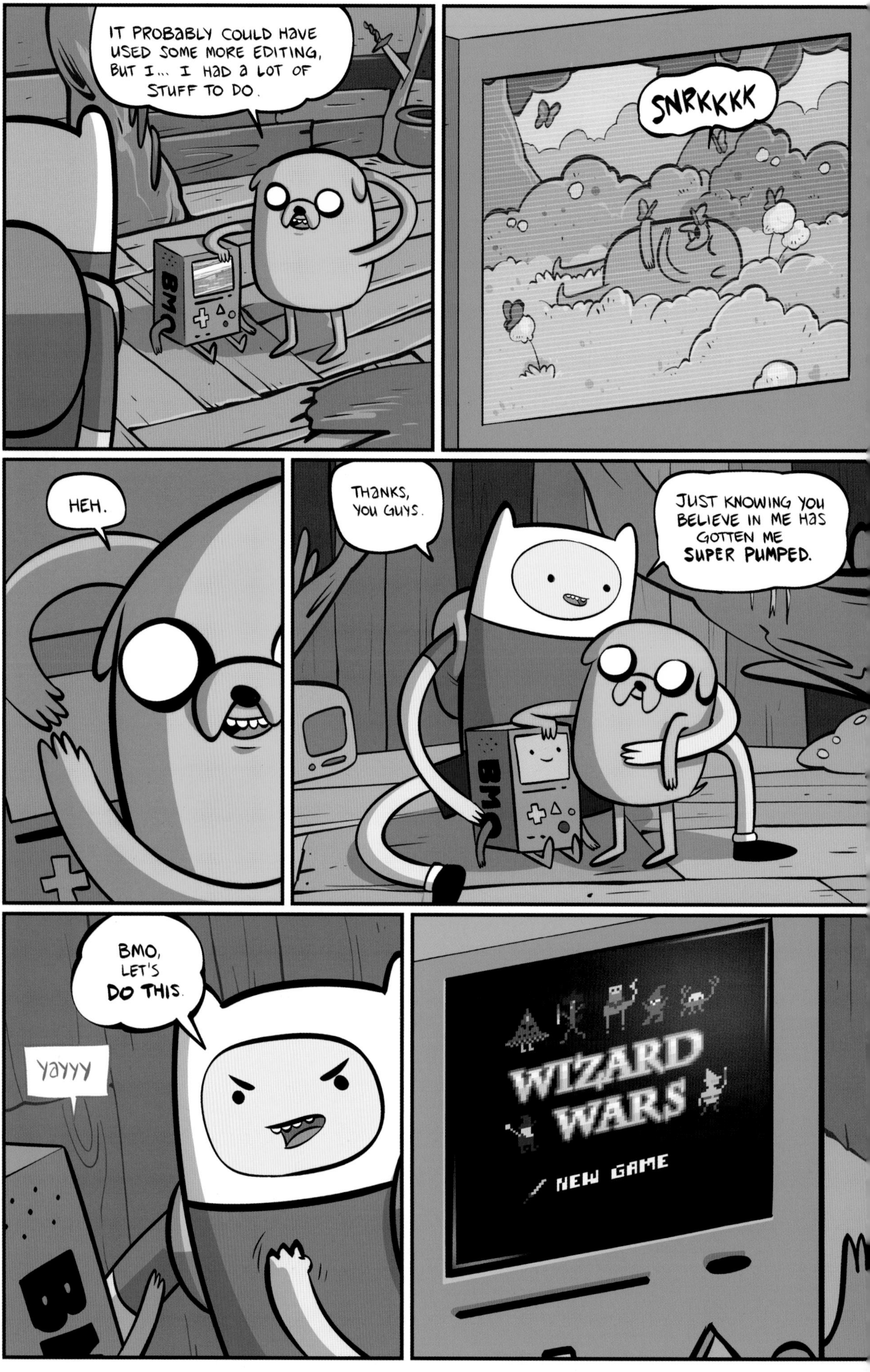
IT PROBABLY COULD HAVE USED SOME MORE EDITING, BUT I... I HAD A LOT OF STUFF TO DO.
BMO
SNRKKKK
HEH.
THANKS, YOU GUYS.
JUST KNOWING YOU BELIEVE IN ME HAS GOTTEN ME SUPER PUMPED.
BMO
BMO, LET'S DO THIS.
yayyy
WIZARD WARS
NEW GAME

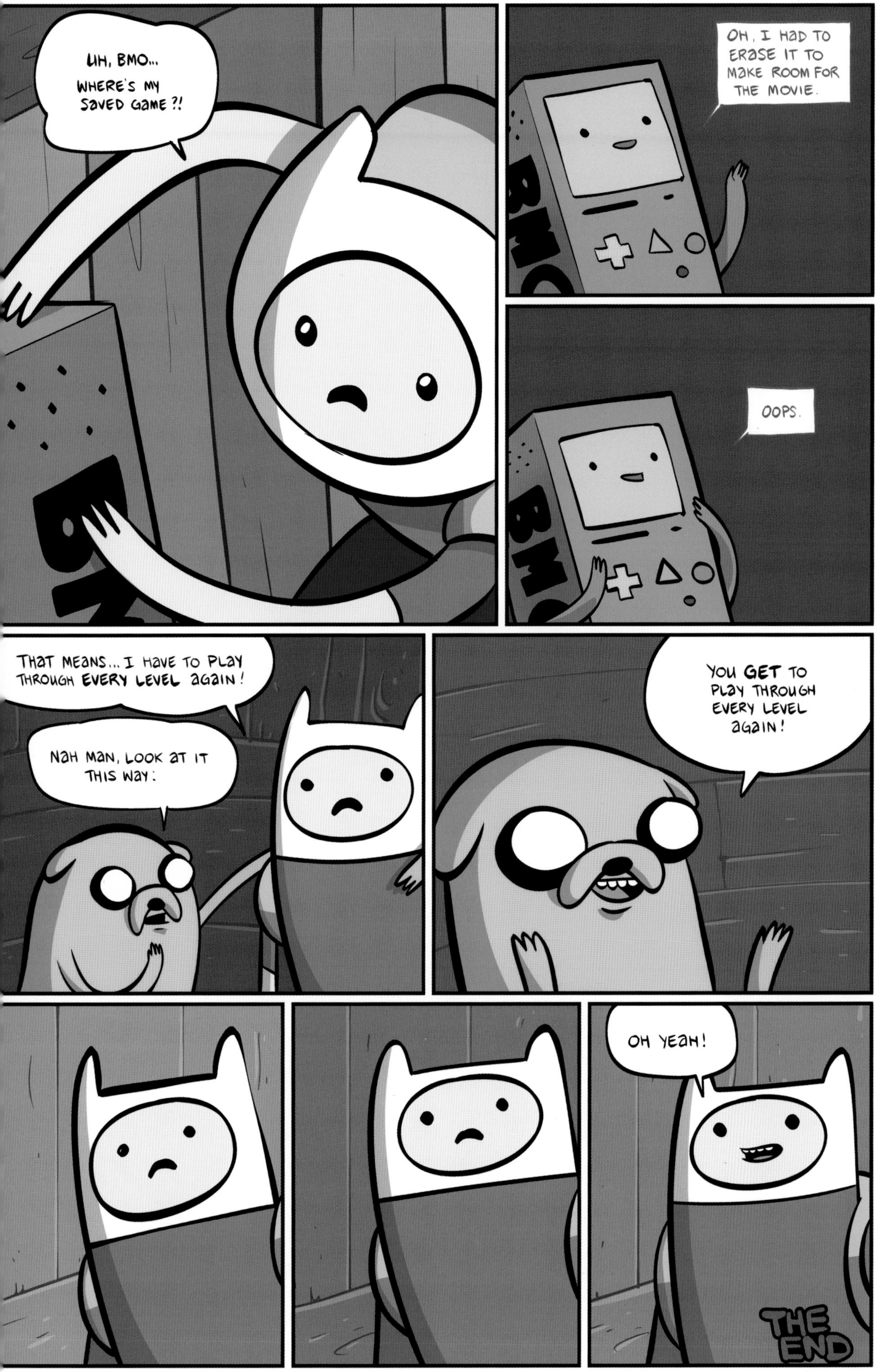
UH, BMO...
WHERE'S MY SAVED GAME ?!
OH, I HAD TO ERASE IT TO MAKE ROOM FOR THE MOVIE.
OOPS.
THAT MEANS... I HAVE TO PLAY THROUGH EVERY LEVEL AGAIN!
NAH MAN, LOOK AT IT THIS WAY:
YOU GET TO PLAY THROUGH EVERY LEVEL AGAIN!
OH YEAH!
THE END

TIME WAITS FOR NO ONE

ISSUE SEVEN, COVER C
GRAHAM ANNABEL

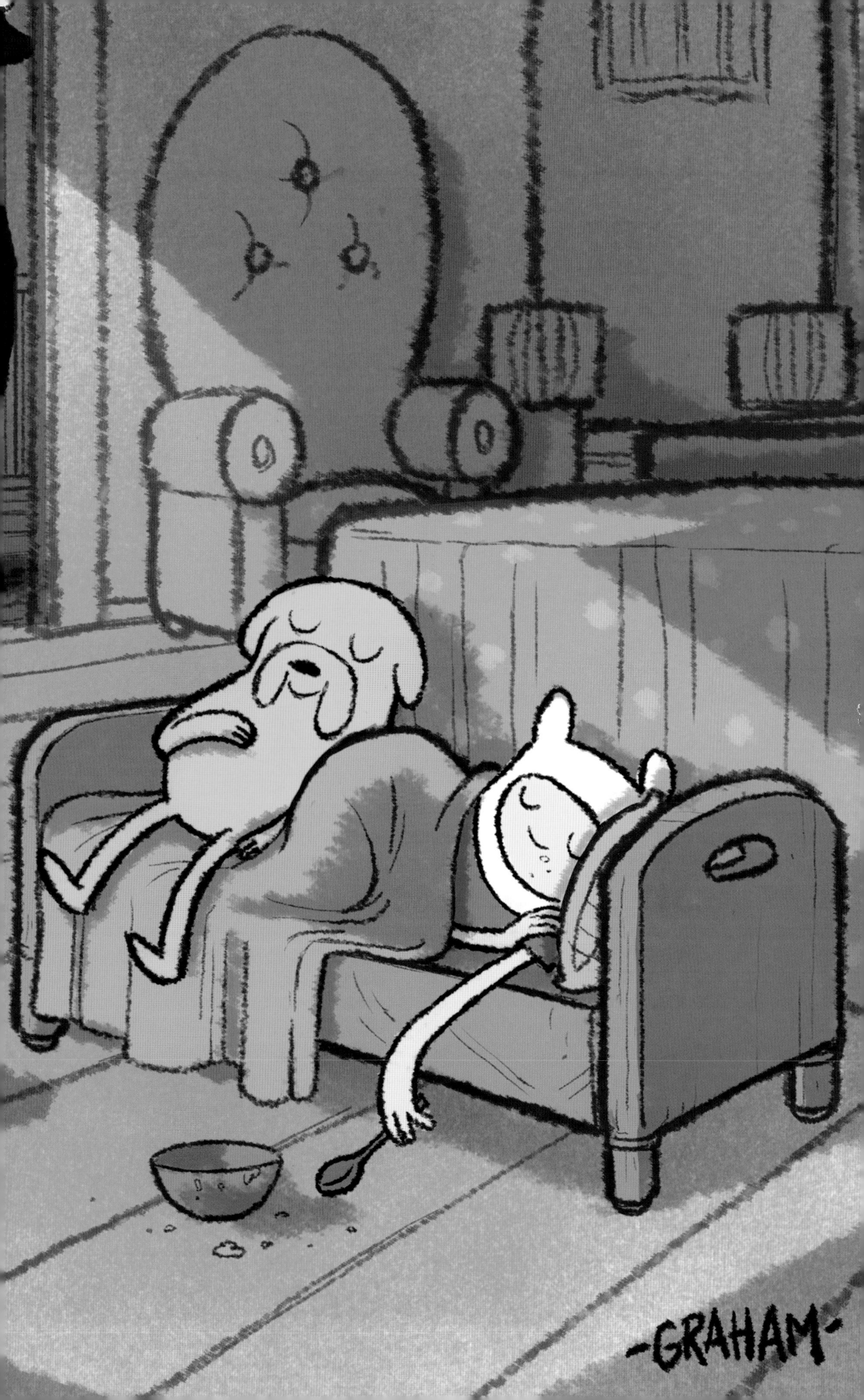
-GRAHAM-

TIME WAITS FOR NO ONE
WRITTEN AND DRAWN BY SHANNON WHEELER

I WANT TO MAKE A *TIME MACHINE.*

I DO TOO, BUT WE HAVE TO BE *CAREFUL.*

WHY?

NOT A LOT IS KNOWN ABOUT *TIME TRAVEL.*

ONE *THEORY* SAYS THAT TIME IS AN *ILLUSION.*

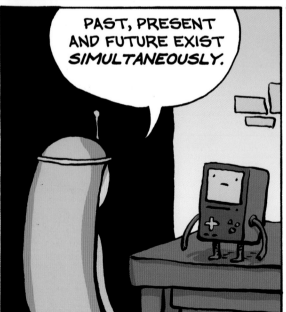

PAST, PRESENT AND FUTURE EXIST *SIMULTANEOUSLY.*

TIME IS A ROAD WE *THINK* WE'RE WALKING DOWN. IF WE WERE MORE *EVOLVED* WE'D *STEP OFF* THE ROAD AND SEE *EVERYTHING* AT ONCE.

WOW.

APOLOGIES TO KURT VONNEGUT

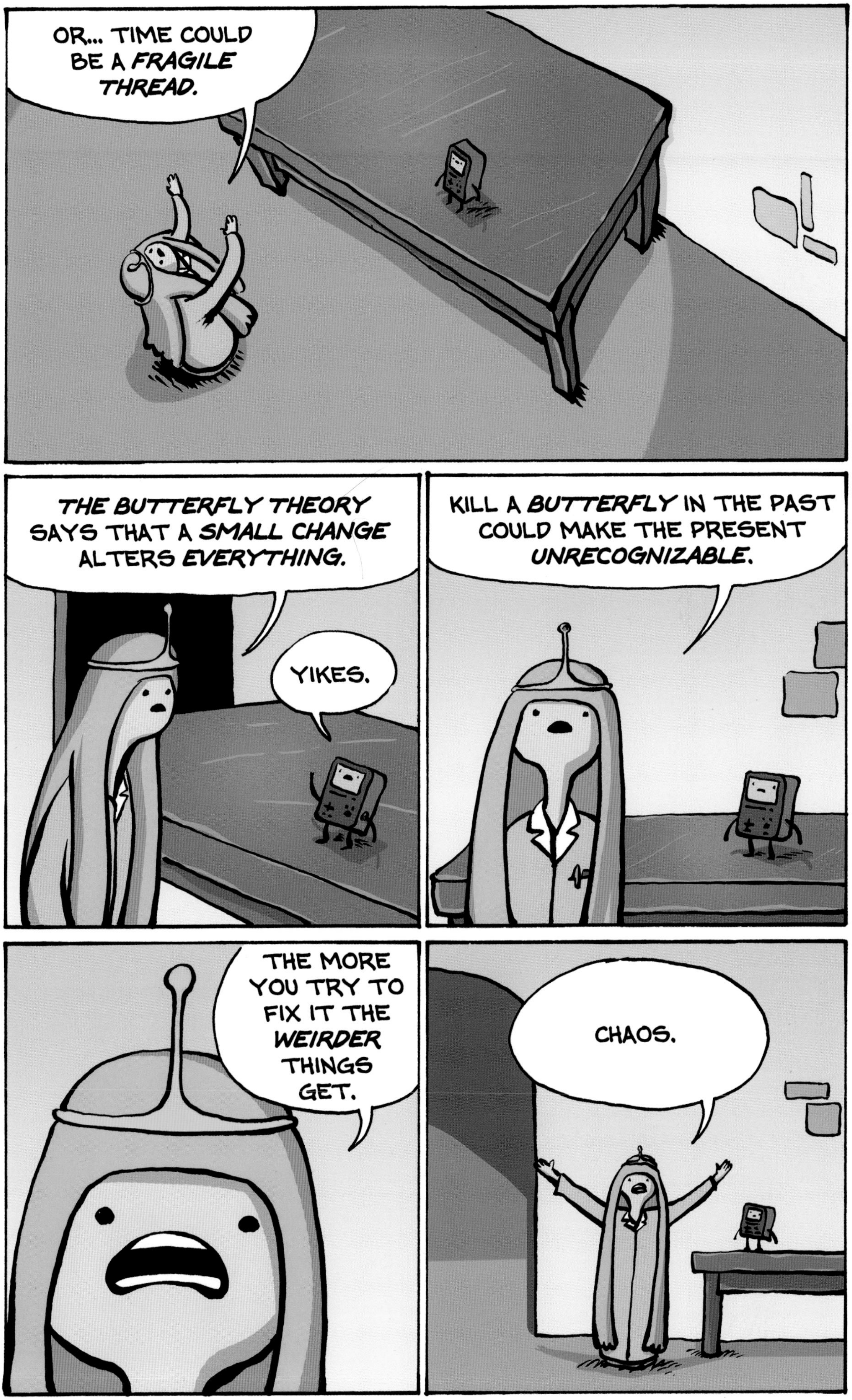
OR... TIME COULD BE A *FRAGILE THREAD.*
THE BUTTERFLY THEORY SAYS THAT A *SMALL CHANGE* ALTERS *EVERYTHING.*
YIKES.
KILL A *BUTTERFLY* IN THE PAST COULD MAKE THE PRESENT *UNRECOGNIZABLE.*
THE MORE YOU TRY TO FIX IT THE *WEIRDER* THINGS GET.
CHAOS.

APOLOGIES TO RAY BRADBURY

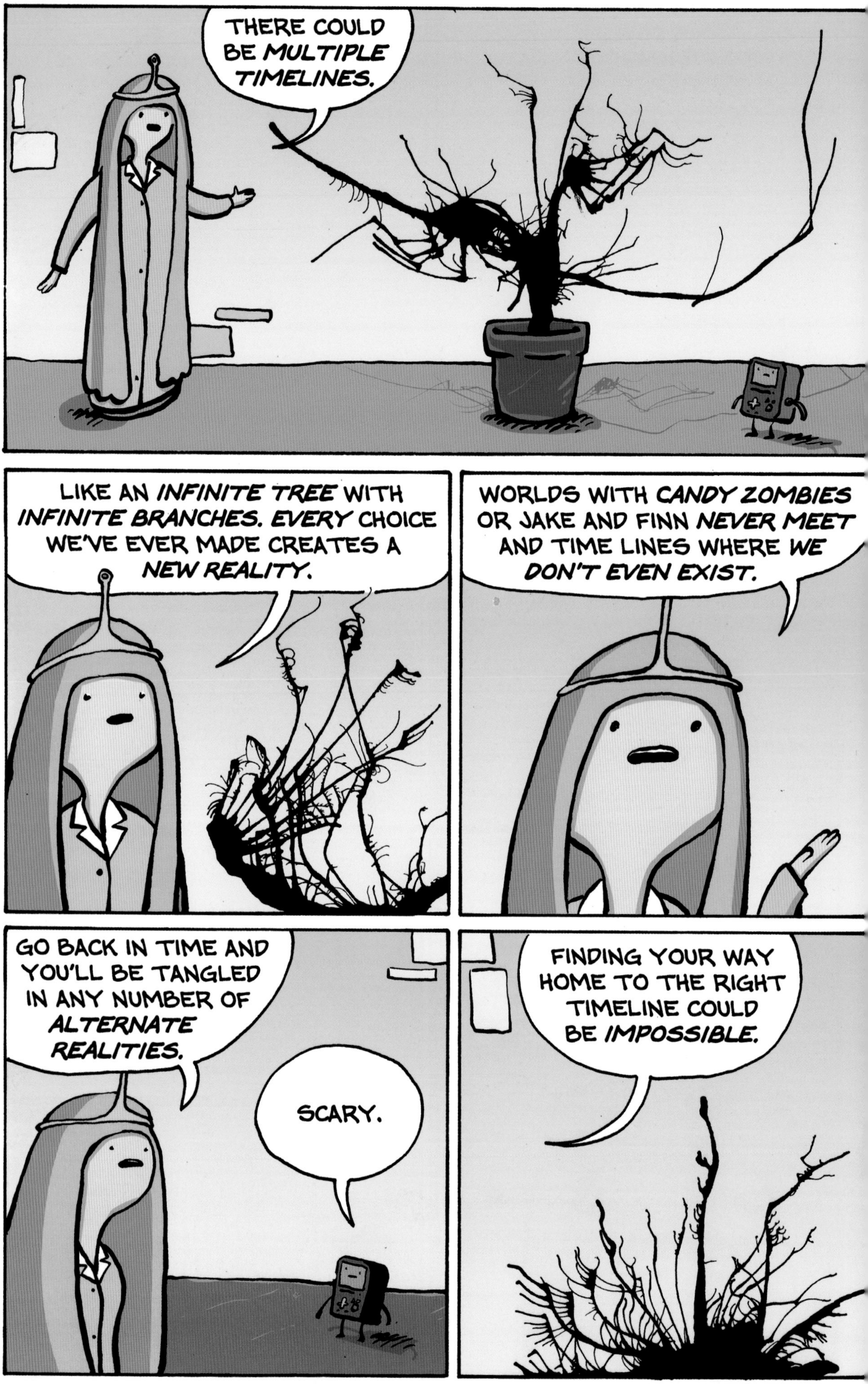
THERE COULD BE *MULTIPLE TIMELINES.*
LIKE AN *INFINITE TREE* WITH *INFINITE BRANCHES. EVERY* CHOICE WE'VE EVER MADE CREATES A *NEW REALITY.*
WORLDS WITH *CANDY ZOMBIES* OR JAKE AND FINN *NEVER MEET* AND TIME LINES WHERE *WE DON'T EVEN EXIST.*
GO BACK IN TIME AND YOU'LL BE TANGLED IN ANY NUMBER OF *ALTERNATE REALITIES.*
SCARY.
FINDING YOUR WAY HOME TO THE RIGHT TIMELINE COULD BE *IMPOSSIBLE.*

APOLOGIES TO LARRY NIVEN

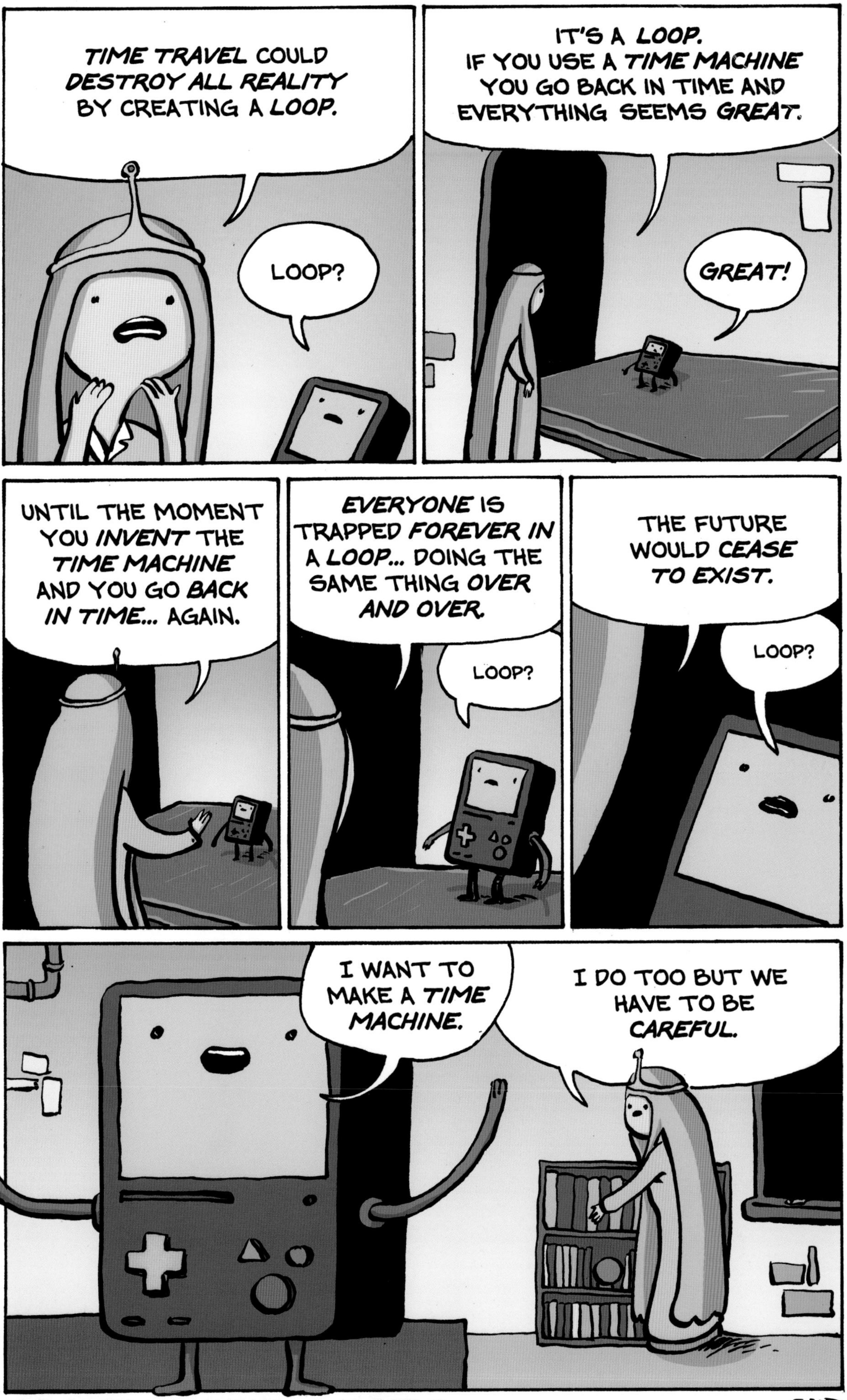
TIME TRAVEL COULD DESTROY ALL REALITY BY CREATING A LOOP.
LOOP?
IT'S A LOOP. IF YOU USE A TIME MACHINE YOU GO BACK IN TIME AND EVERYTHING SEEMS GREAT.
GREAT!
UNTIL THE MOMENT YOU INVENT THE TIME MACHINE AND YOU GO BACK IN TIME... AGAIN.
EVERYONE IS TRAPPED FOREVER IN A LOOP... DOING THE SAME THING OVER AND OVER.
LOOP?
THE FUTURE WOULD CEASE TO EXIST.
LOOP?
I WANT TO MAKE A TIME MACHINE.
I DO TOO BUT WE HAVE TO BE CAREFUL.

APOLOGIES TO MICHAEL T. GILBERT

END

LUMPY SPACE DRAMA

ISSUE TEN, COVER C
VICTORIA MADERNA

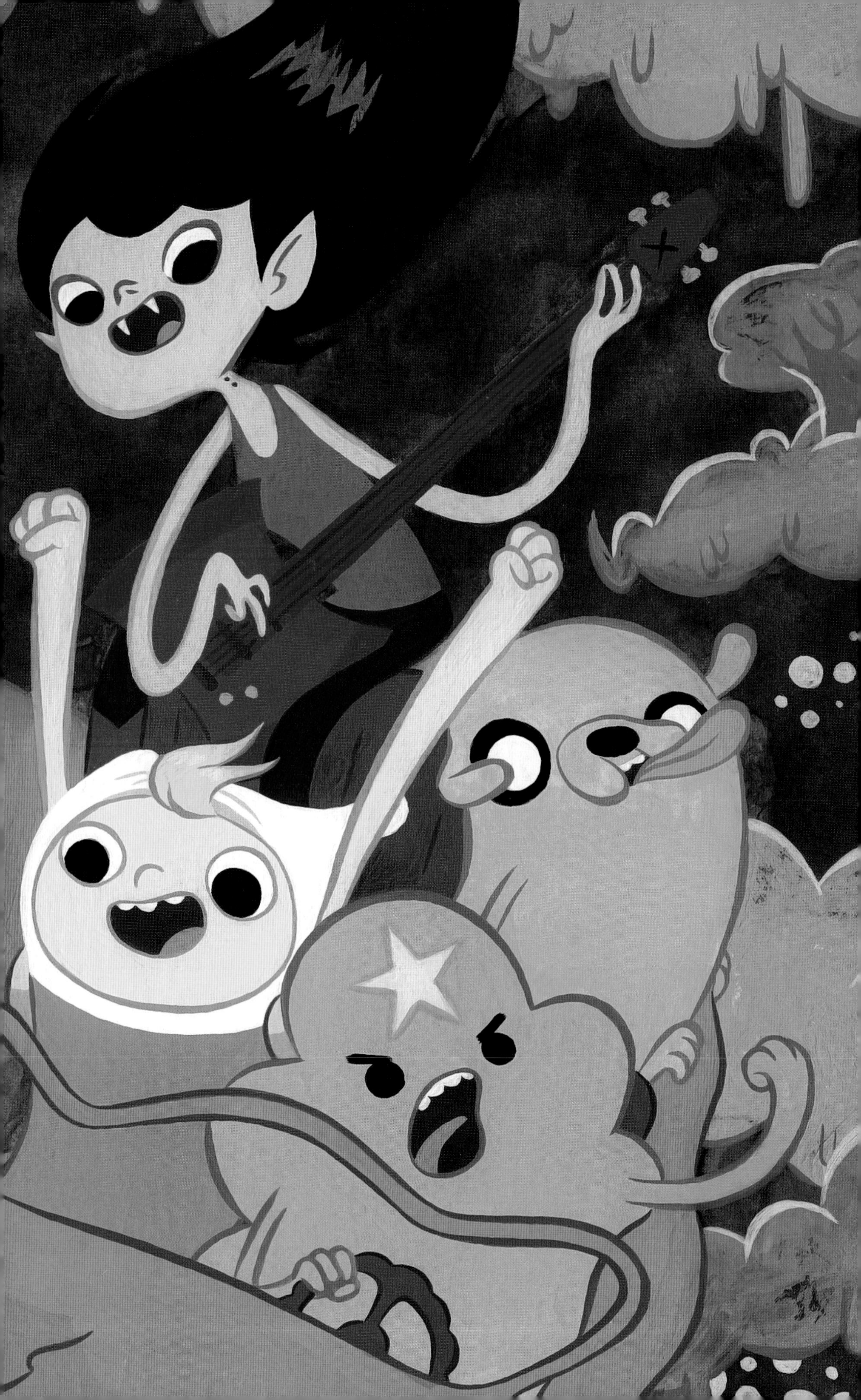

LUMPY SPACE DRAMA

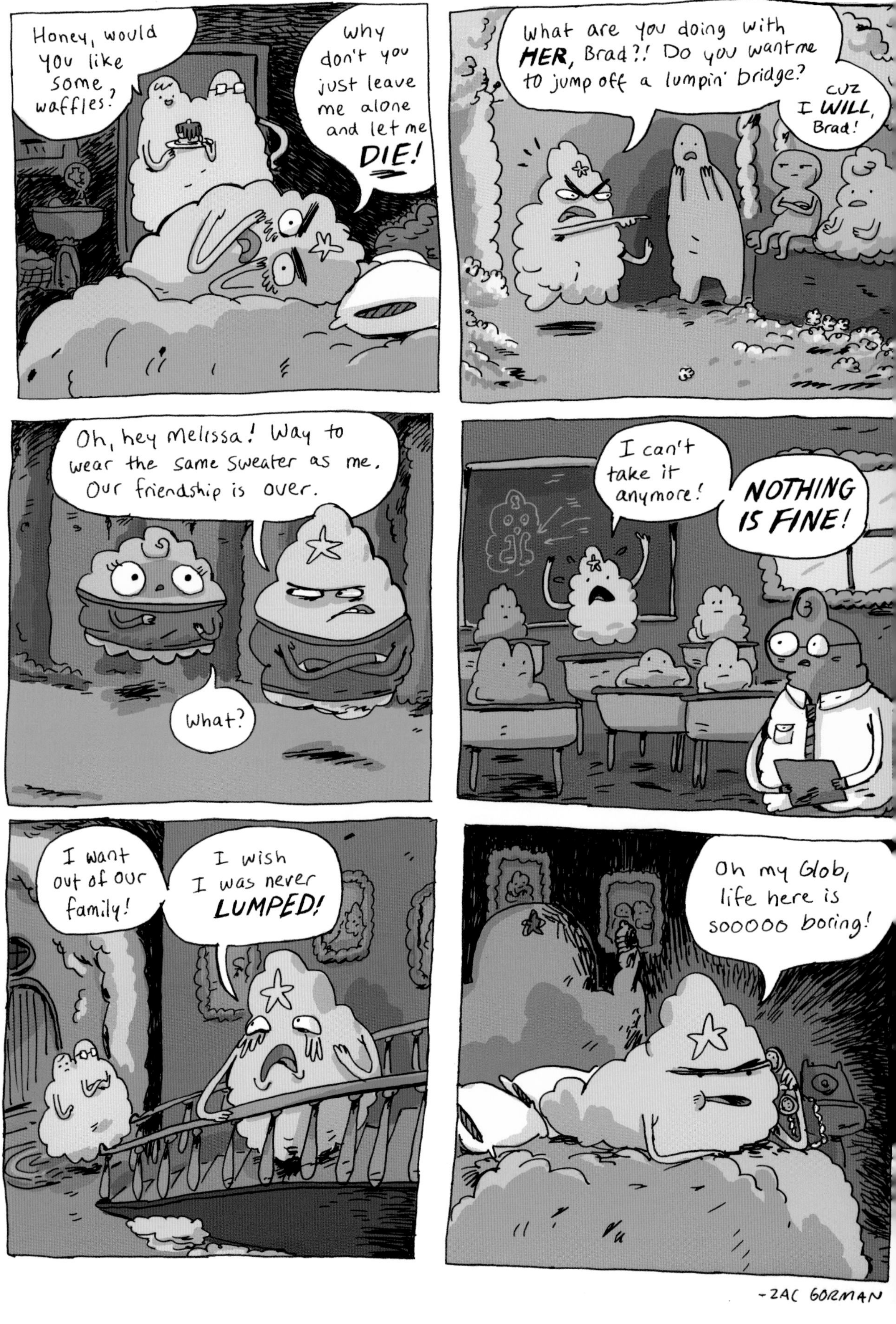
Honey, would you like some waffles?
Why don't you just leave me alone and let me DIE!
What are you doing with HER, Brad?! Do you want me to jump off a lumpin' bridge?
CUZ I WILL, Brad!
Oh, hey Melissa! Way to wear the same sweater as me. Our friendship is over.
What?
I can't take it anymore!
NOTHING IS FINE!
I want out of our family!
I wish I was never LUMPED!
Oh my Glob, life here is sooooo boring!

-ZAC GORMAN

HAPPY BIRTHDAY
HOT DOG PRINCESS

ISSUE EIGHT, COVER D
PHIL MCANDREW

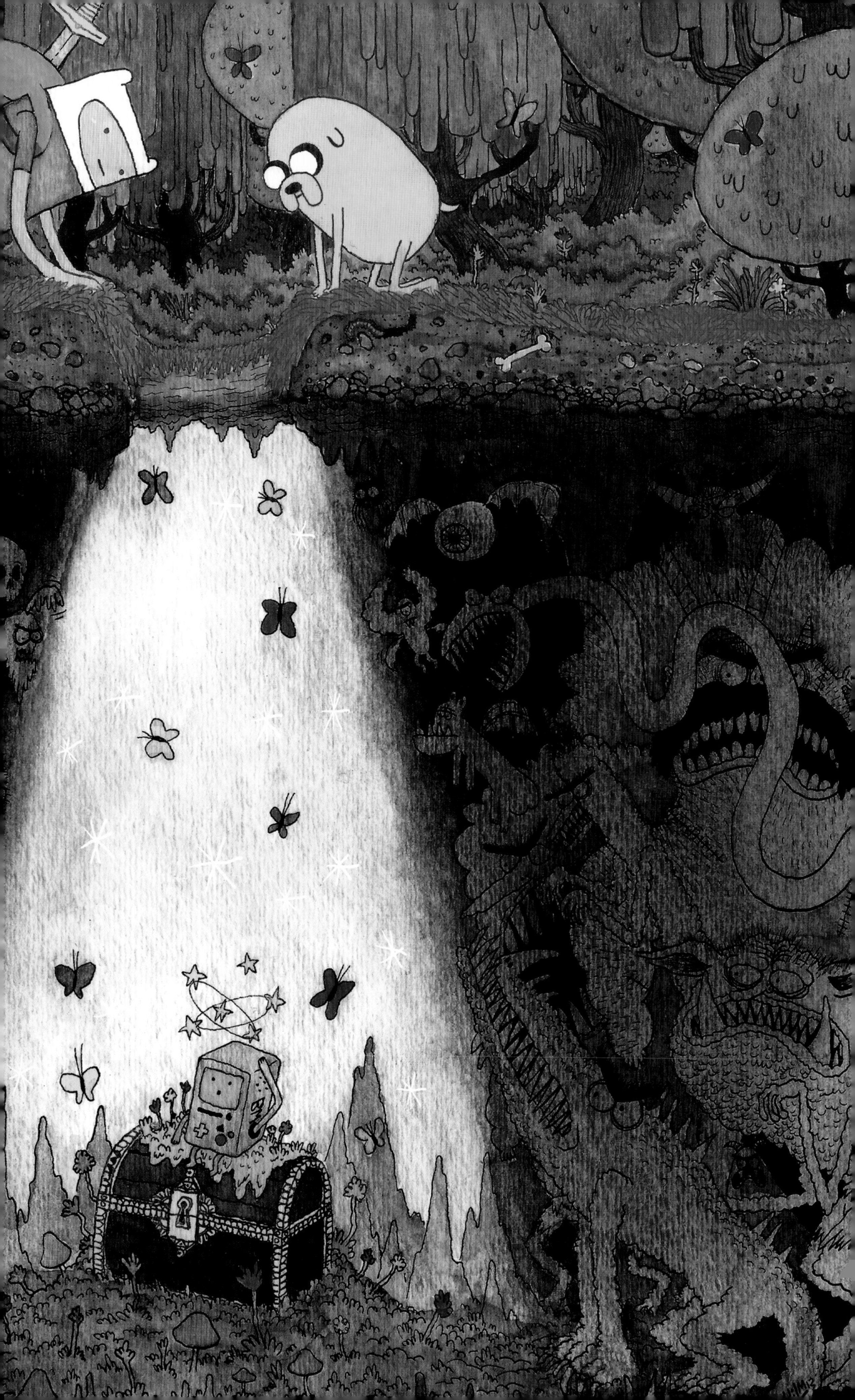

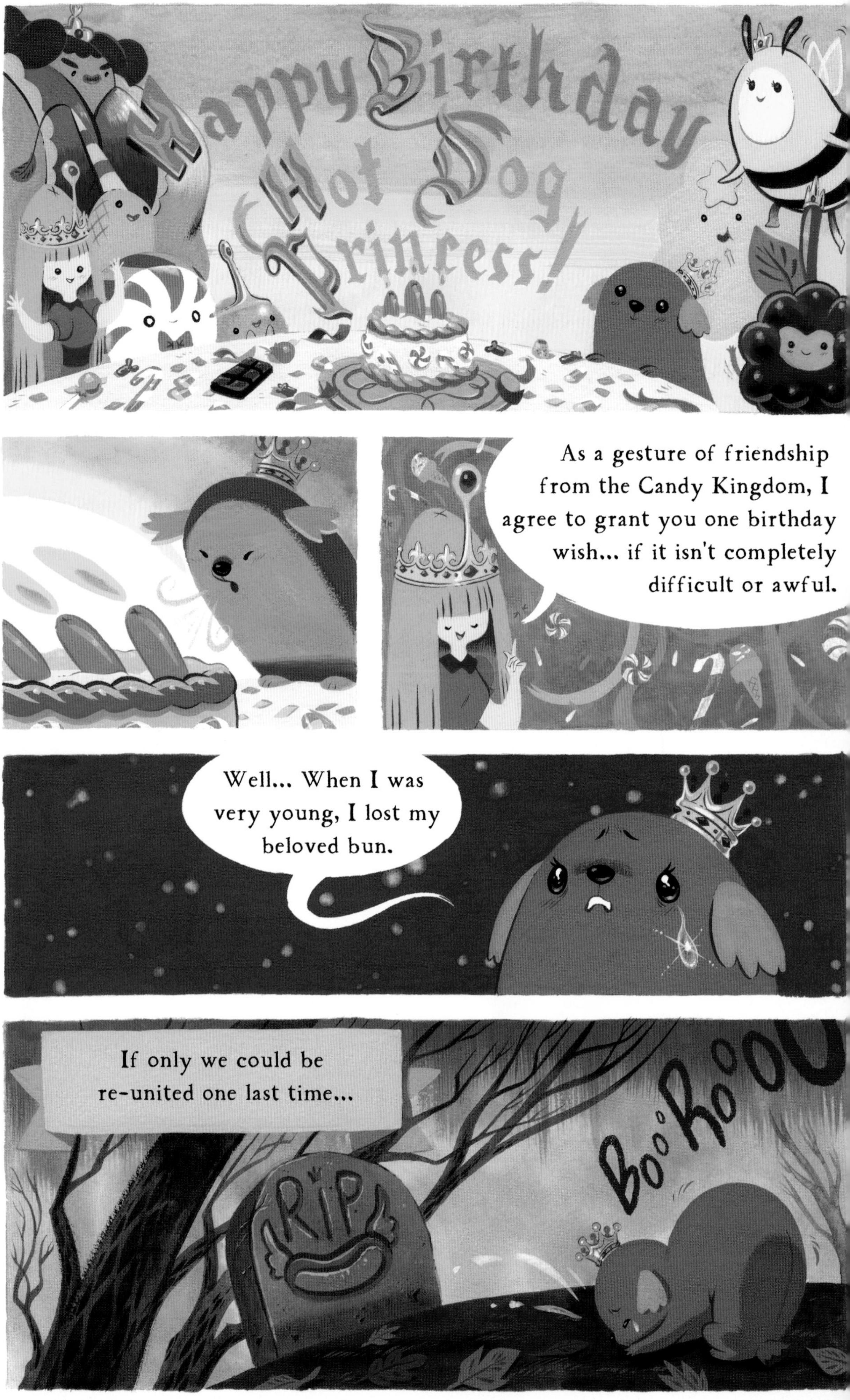
Happy Birthday Hot Dog Princess!
As a gesture of friendship from the Candy Kingdom, I agree to grant you one birthday wish... if it isn't completely difficult or awful.
Well... When I was very young, I lost my beloved bun.
If only we could be re-united one last time...
BooRooO
RIP

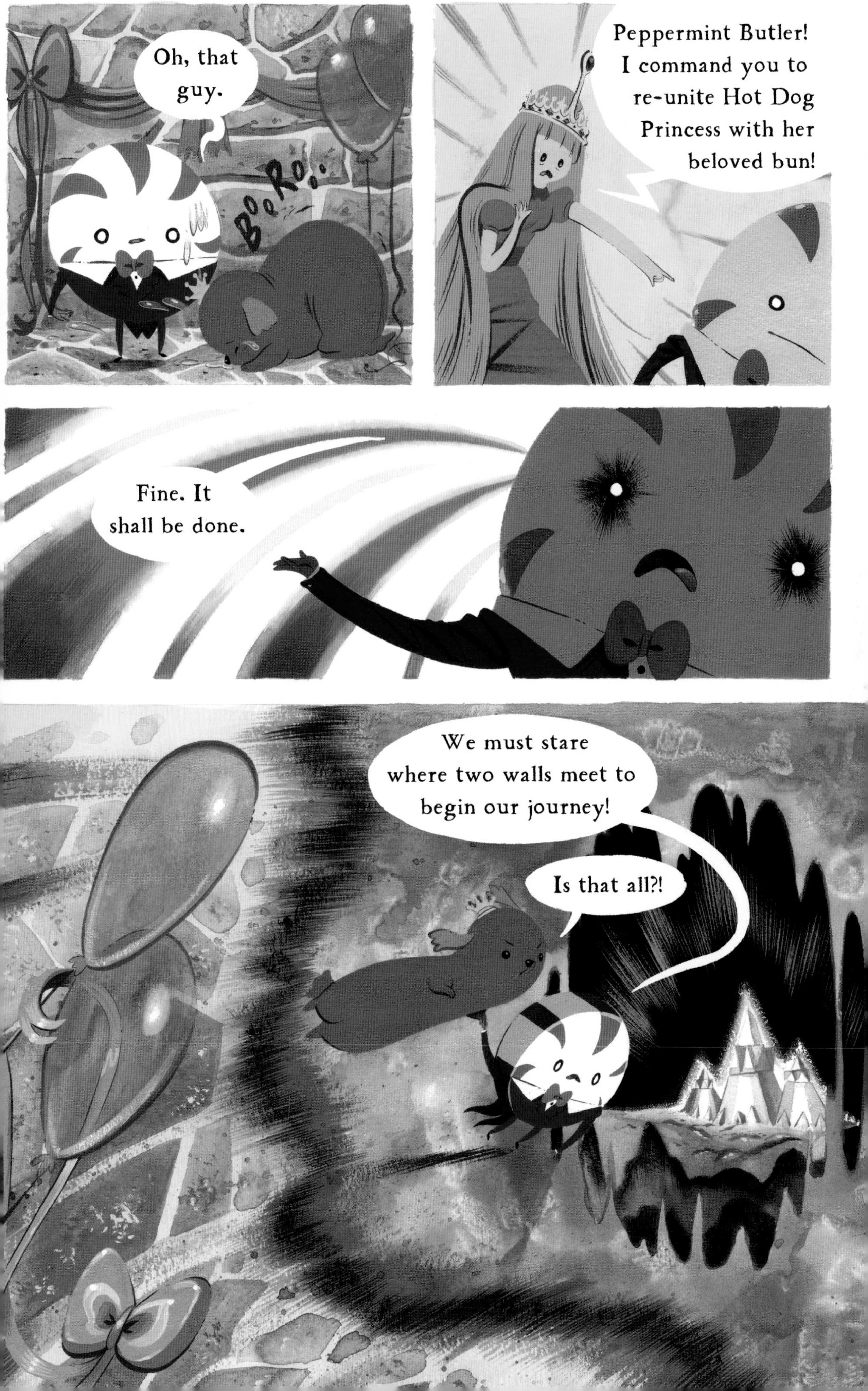
Oh, that guy.
BOOROOO
Peppermint Butler! I command you to re-unite Hot Dog Princess with her beloved bun!
Fine. It shall be done.
We must stare where two walls meet to begin our journey!
Is that all?!

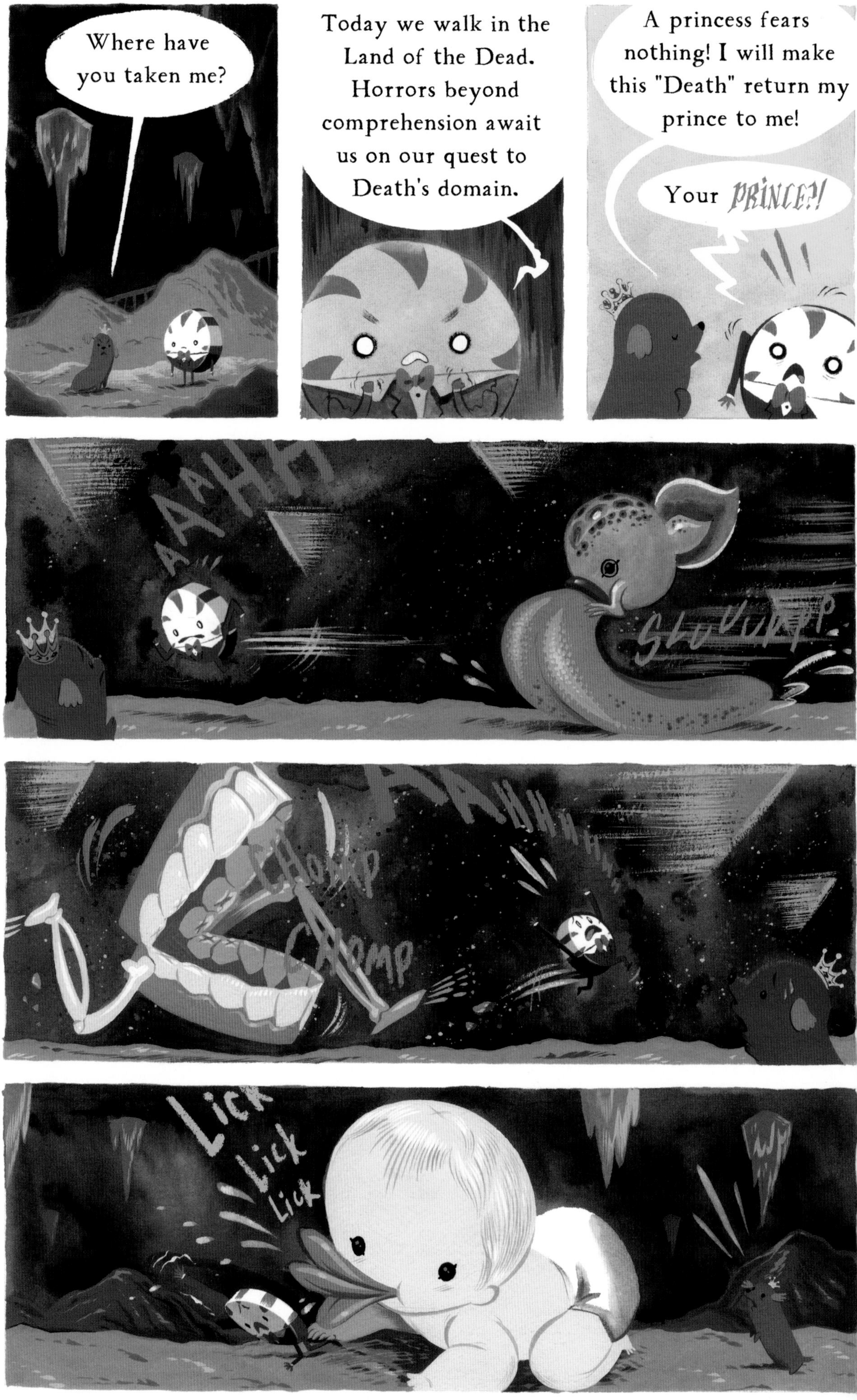
Where have you taken me?
Today we walk in the Land of the Dead. Horrors beyond comprehension await us on our quest to Death's domain.
A princess fears nothing! I will make this "Death" return my prince to me!
Your PRINCE?!
CHOMP
CHOMP
Lick
Lick
Lick

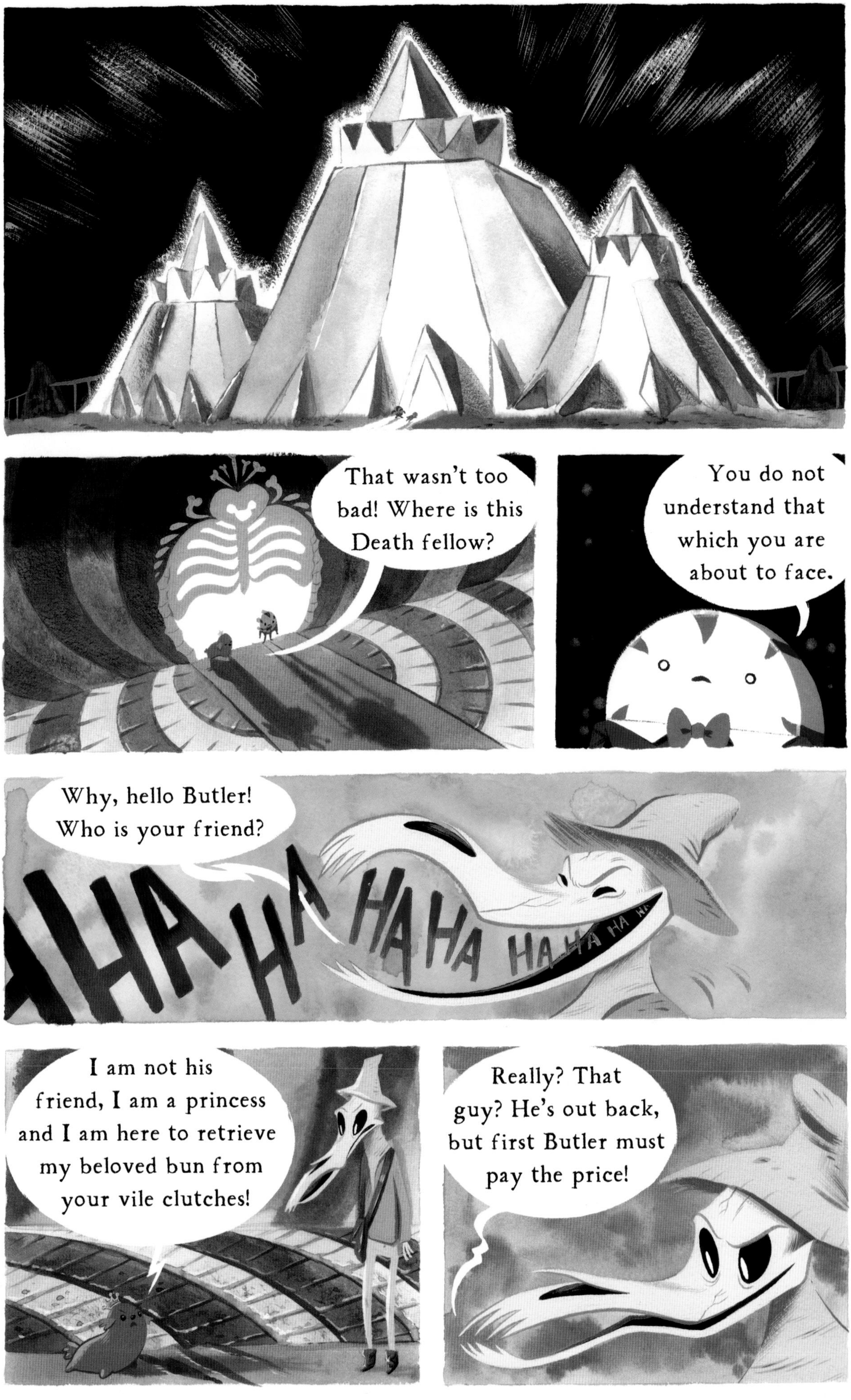
That wasn't too bad! Where is this Death fellow?
You do not understand that which you are about to face.
Why, hello Butler! Who is your friend?
HAHAHAHAHAHAHAHAHA
I am not his friend, I am a princess and I am here to retrieve my beloved bun from your vile clutches!
Really? That guy? He's out back, but first Butler must pay the price!

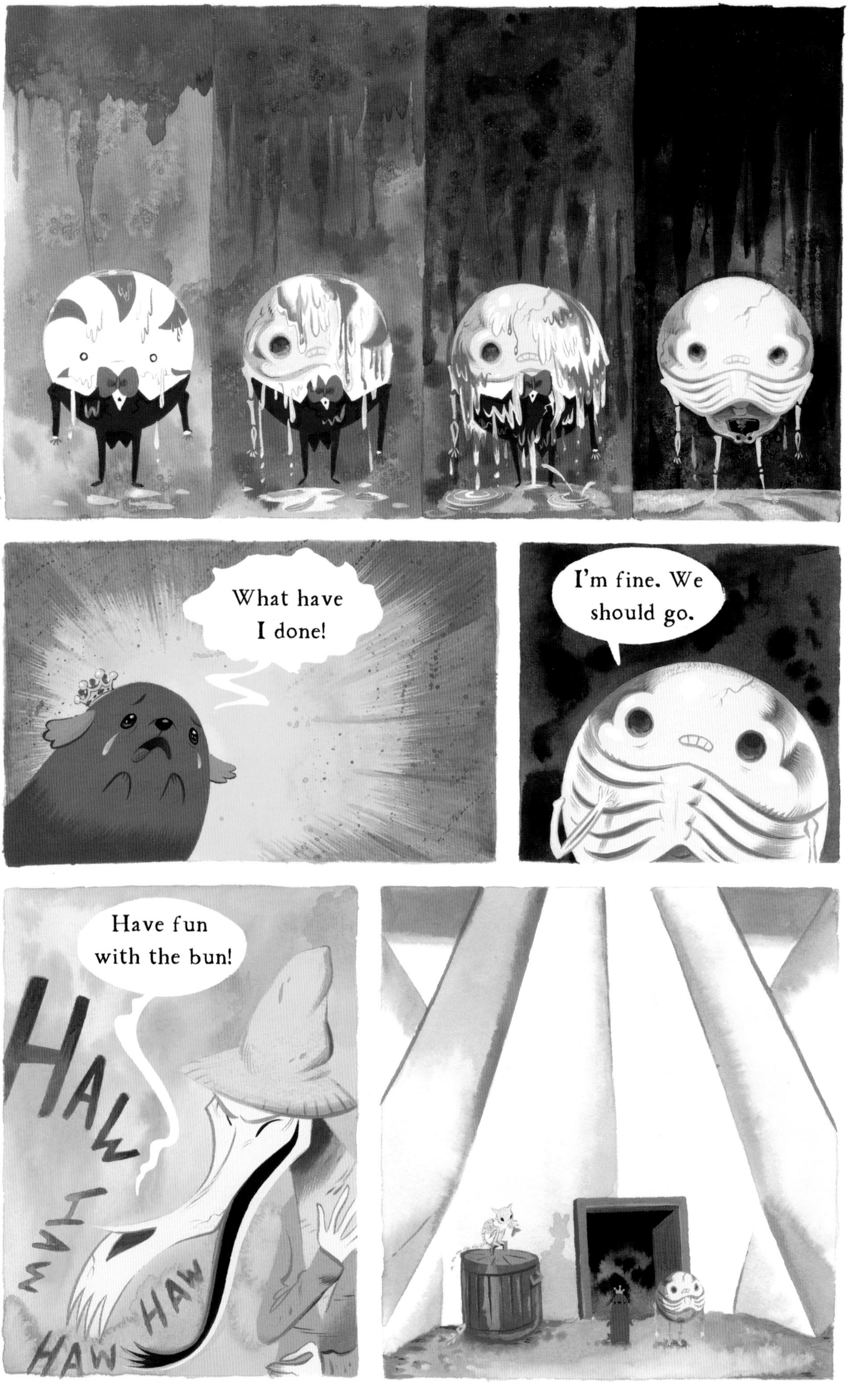
What have I done!
I'm fine. We should go.
Have fun with the bun!
HAW
HAW
HAW
HAW

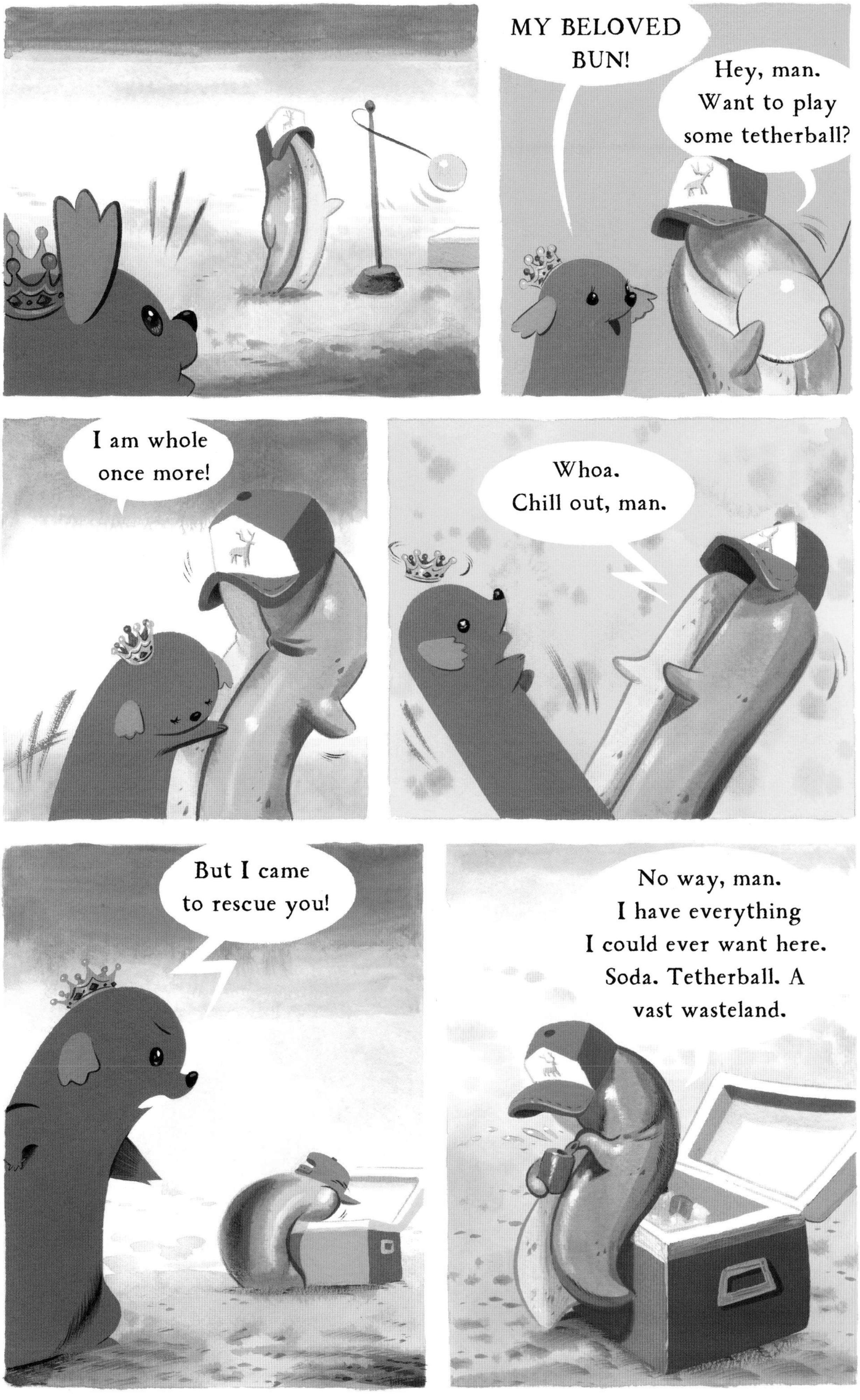
MY BELOVED BUN!
Hey, man. Want to play some tetherball?
I am whole once more!
Whoa. Chill out, man.
But I came to rescue you!
No way, man. I have everything I could ever want here. Soda. Tetherball. A vast wasteland.

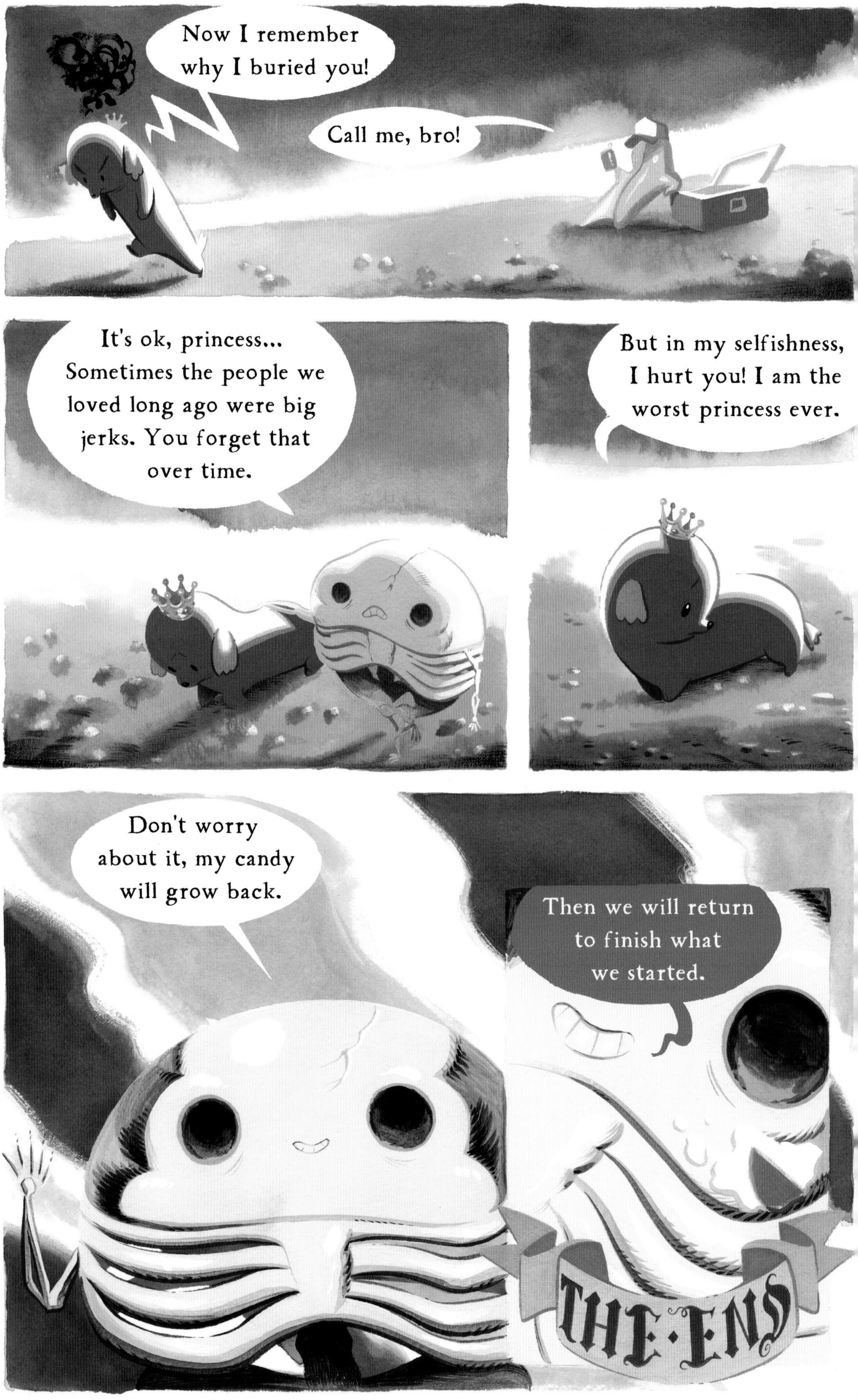
Now I remember why I buried you!
Call me, bro!
It's ok, princess... Sometimes the people we loved long ago were big jerks. You forget that over time.
But in my selfishness, I hurt you! I am the worst princess ever.
Don't worry about it, my candy will grow back.
Then we will return to finish what we started.
THE END

FISHLING

ISSUE NINE, COVER D
JON VERMILYEA

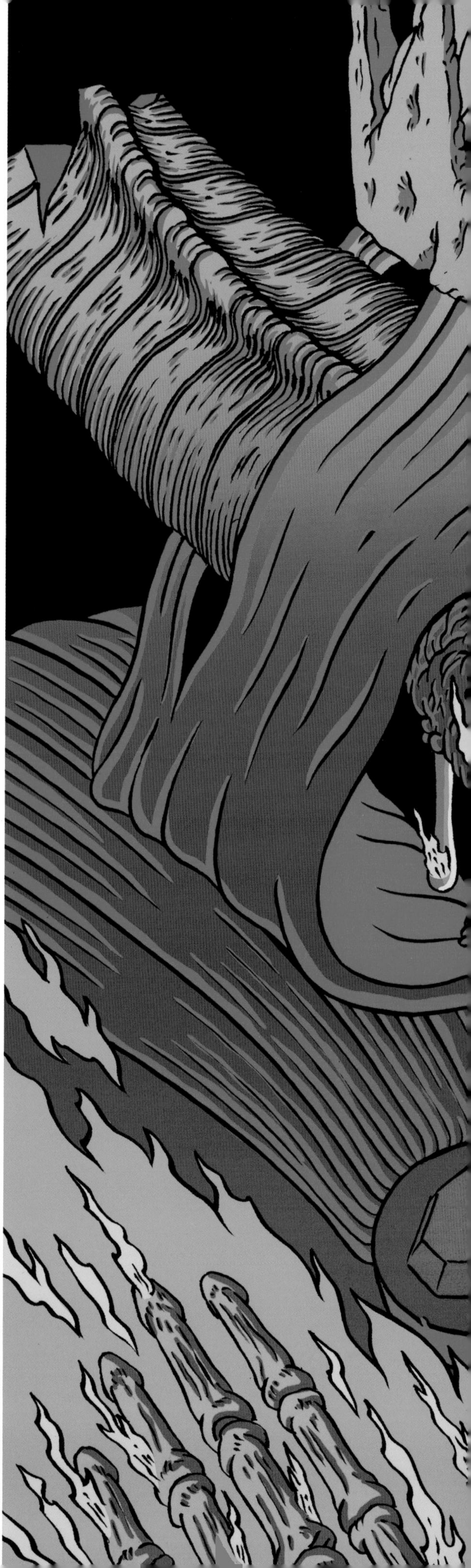

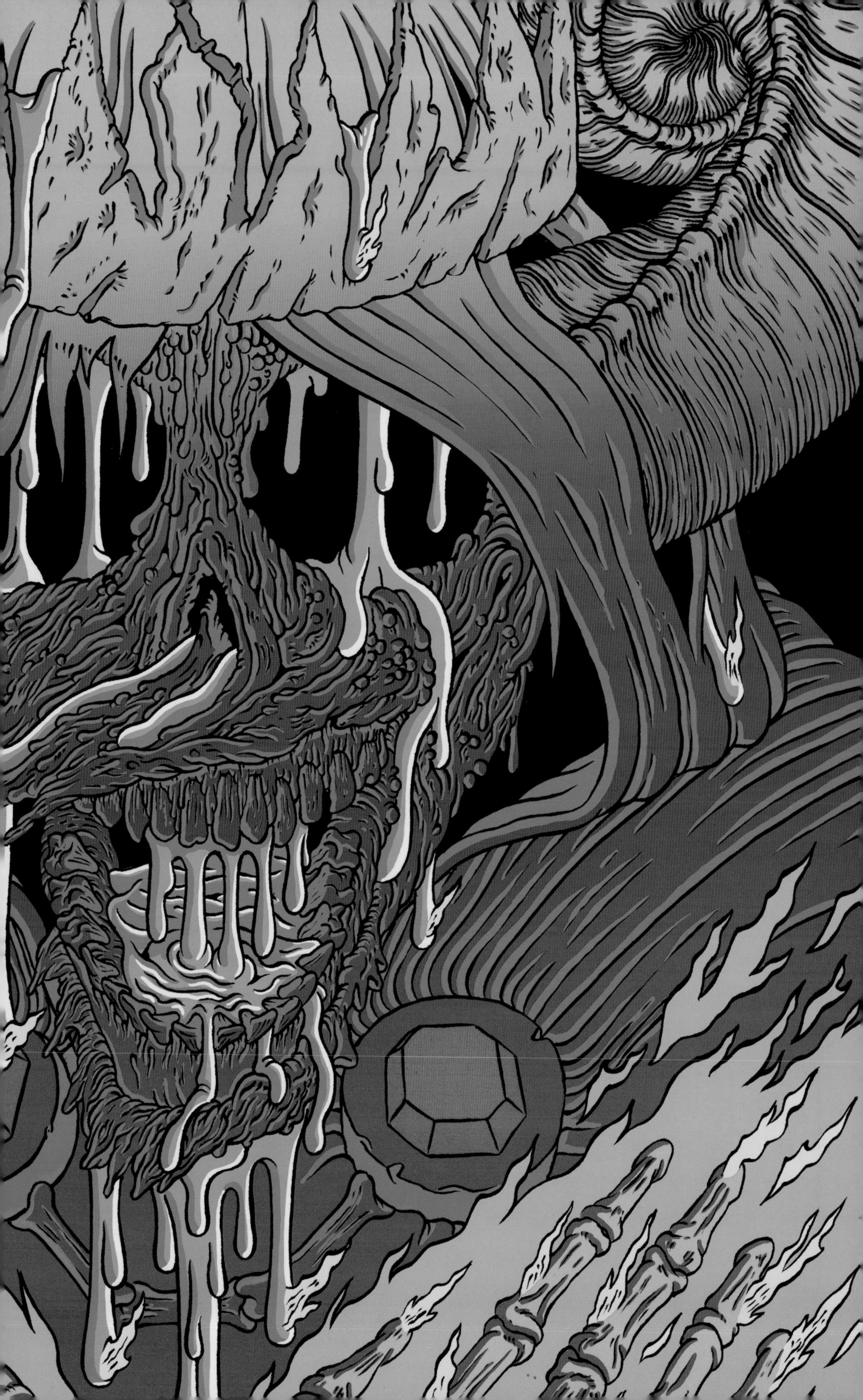

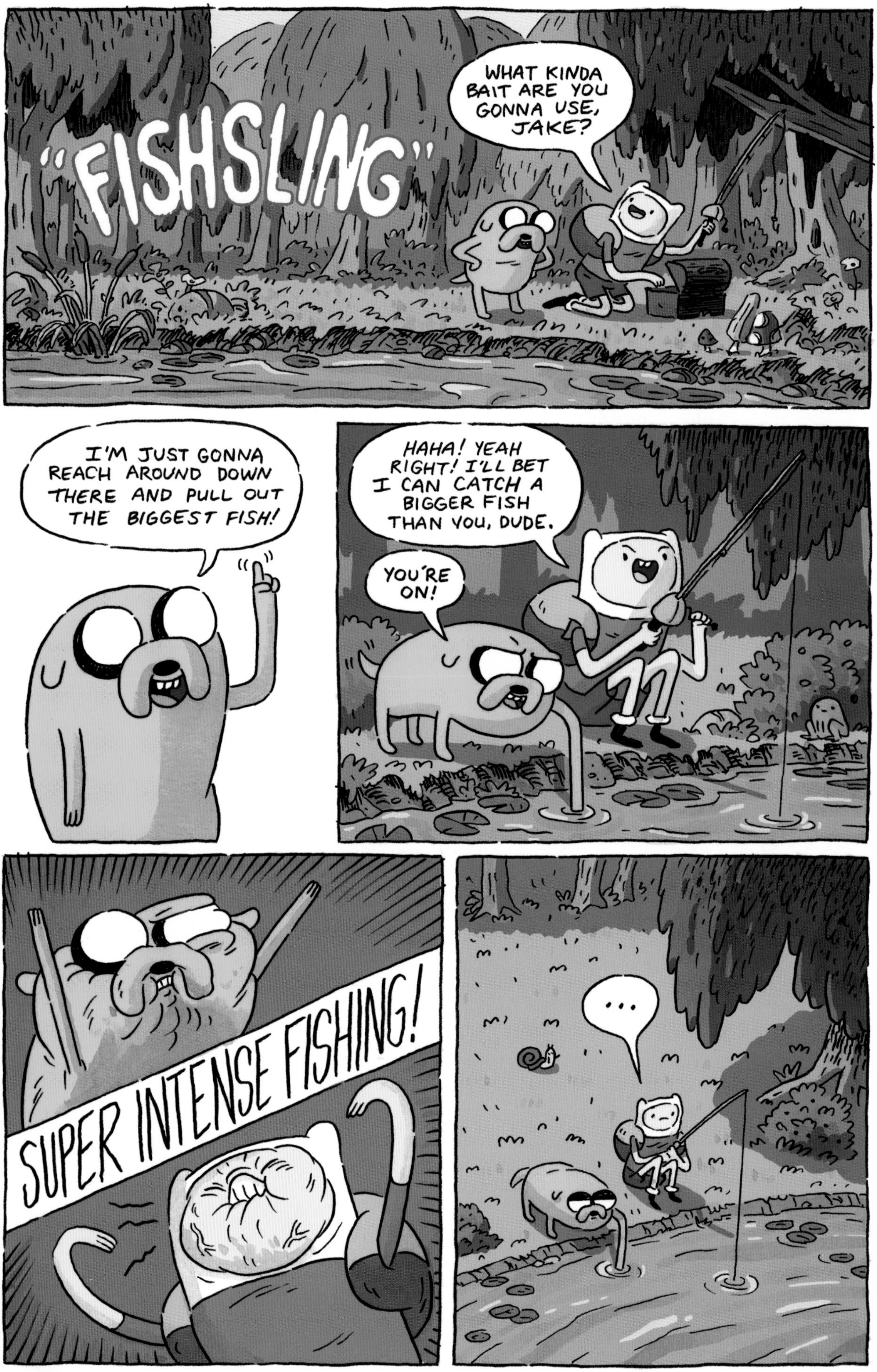
"FISHSLING"
WHAT KINDA BAIT ARE YOU GONNA USE, JAKE?
I'M JUST GONNA REACH AROUND DOWN THERE AND PULL OUT THE BIGGEST FISH!
HAHA! YEAH RIGHT! I'LL BET I CAN CATCH A BIGGER FISH THAN YOU, DUDE.
YOU'RE ON!
SUPER INTENSE FISHING!
...

WRITTEN BY: SHANE HOUGHTON DRAWN BY: CHRIS HOUGHTON COLORED BY: JOSH ULRICH

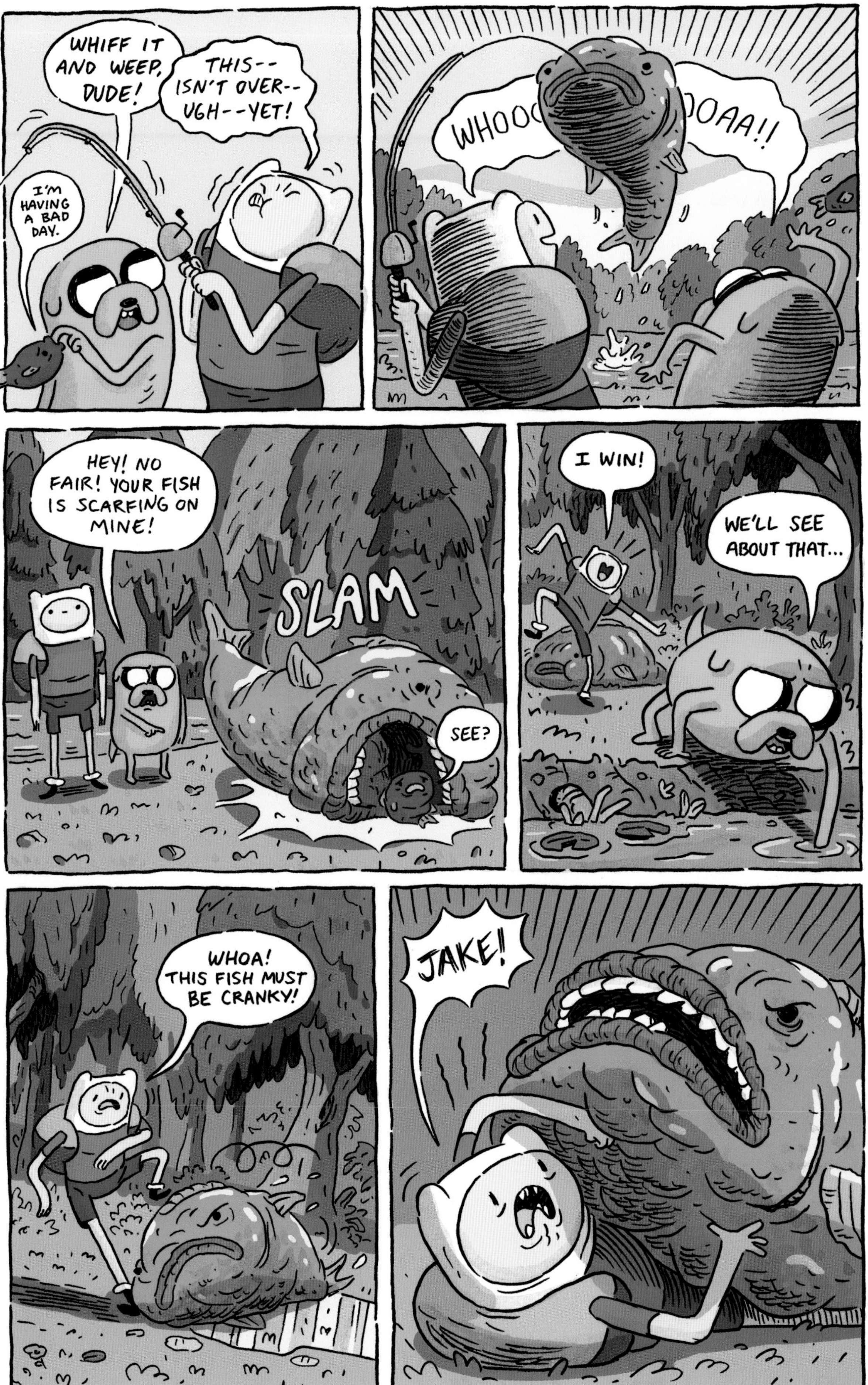
WHIFF IT AND WEEP, DUDE!
THIS-- ISN'T OVER-- UGH--YET!
I'M HAVING A BAD DAY.
WHOOOOOOAA!!
HEY! NO FAIR! YOUR FISH IS SCARFING ON MINE!
SLAM
SEE?
I WIN!
WE'LL SEE ABOUT THAT...
WHOA! THIS FISH MUST BE CRANKY!
JAKE!

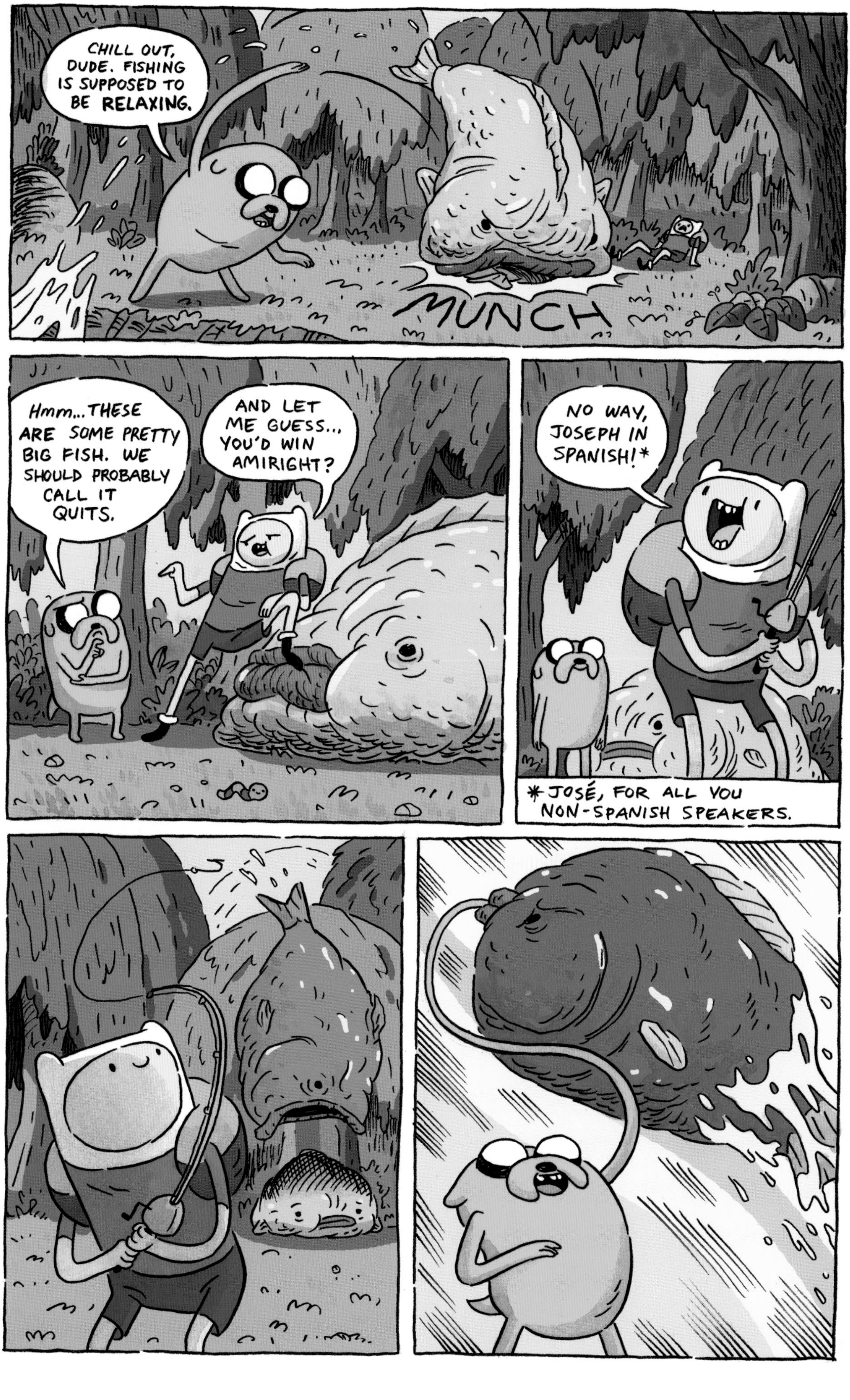

CHILL OUT, DUDE. FISHING IS SUPPOSED TO BE RELAXING.
MUNCH
Hmm... THESE ARE SOME PRETTY BIG FISH. WE SHOULD PROBABLY CALL IT QUITS.
AND LET ME GUESS... YOU'D WIN AMIRIGHT?
NO WAY, JOSEPH IN SPANISH!*
*JOSÉ, FOR ALL YOU NON-SPANISH SPEAKERS.

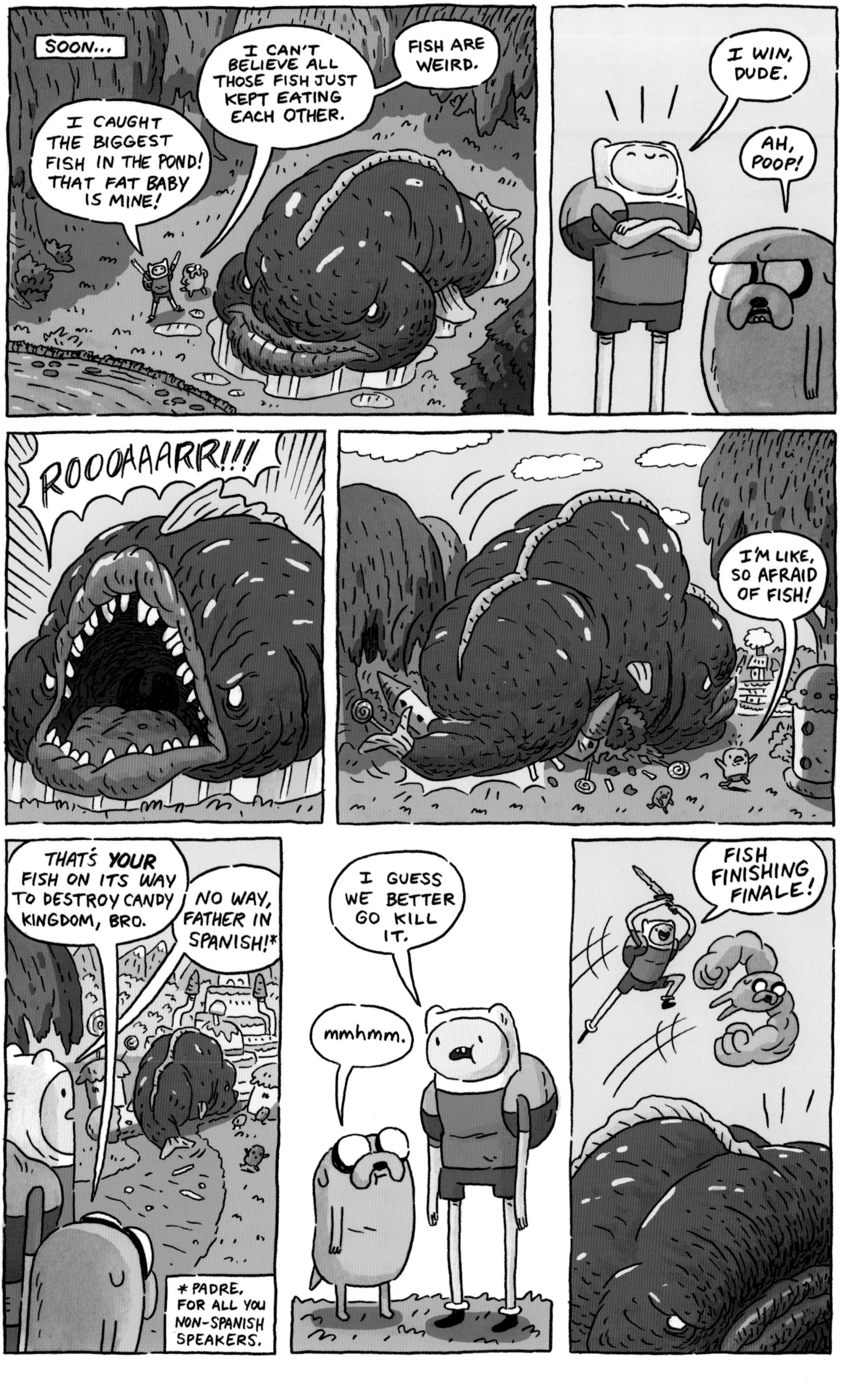
SOON...
I CAUGHT THE BIGGEST FISH IN THE POND! THAT FAT BABY IS MINE!
I CAN'T BELIEVE ALL THOSE FISH JUST KEPT EATING EACH OTHER.
FISH ARE WEIRD.
I WIN, DUDE.
AH, POOP!
ROOOAAARR!!!
I'M LIKE, SO AFRAID OF FISH!
THAT'S YOUR FISH ON ITS WAY TO DESTROY CANDY KINGDOM, BRO.
NO WAY, FATHER IN SPANISH!*
*PADRE, FOR ALL YOU NON-SPANISH SPEAKERS.
I GUESS WE BETTER GO KILL IT.
mmhmm.
FISH FINISHING FINALE!

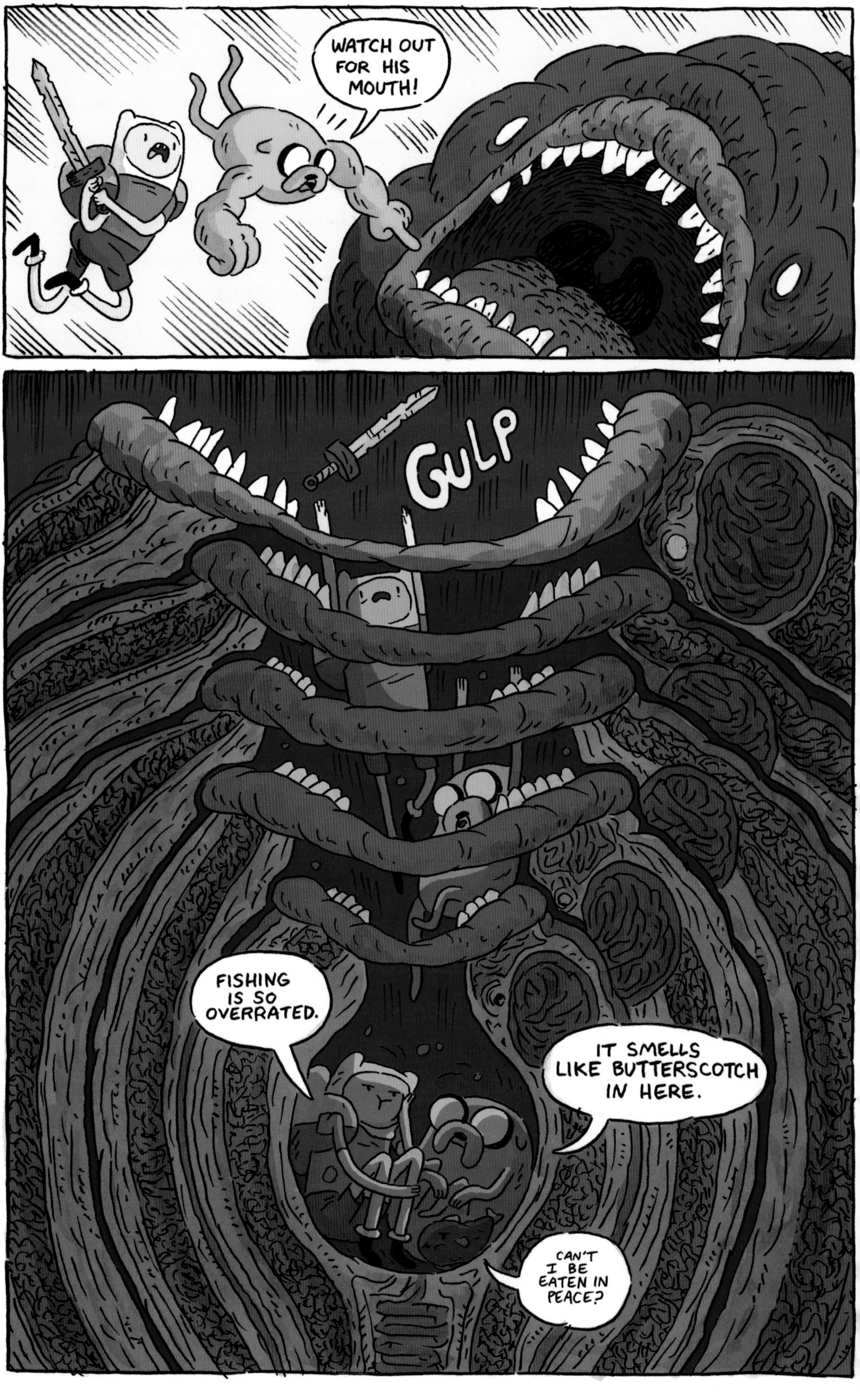
WATCH OUT FOR HIS MOUTH!
GULP
FISHING IS SO OVERRATED.
IT SMELLS LIKE BUTTERSCOTCH IN HERE.
CAN'T I BE EATEN IN PEACE?

DUDE.

ON THE ACCOUNT OF BEING EATEN AND EVERY-THING, I THINK WE SHOULD CALL THE CONTEST A DRAW.

TOTES. WE'RE BOTH PRETTY DOPE FISHER-FOLKS.

LET'S GET OUT OF HERE. I LIKE EATING FISH BETTER THAN BEING EATEN BY FISH.

I'LL BE THE LINE, YOU BE THE BAIT.

I'LL TAKE OFF MY SHOES 'CAUSE FISH LOVE TOESIES.

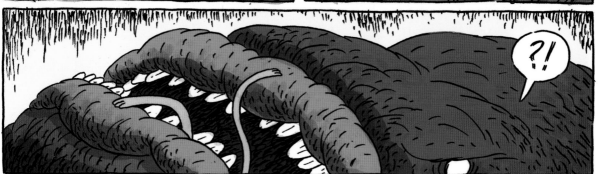

?!

WAHOO!

SHOULDN'T I HAVE SUFFOCATED BY NOW?

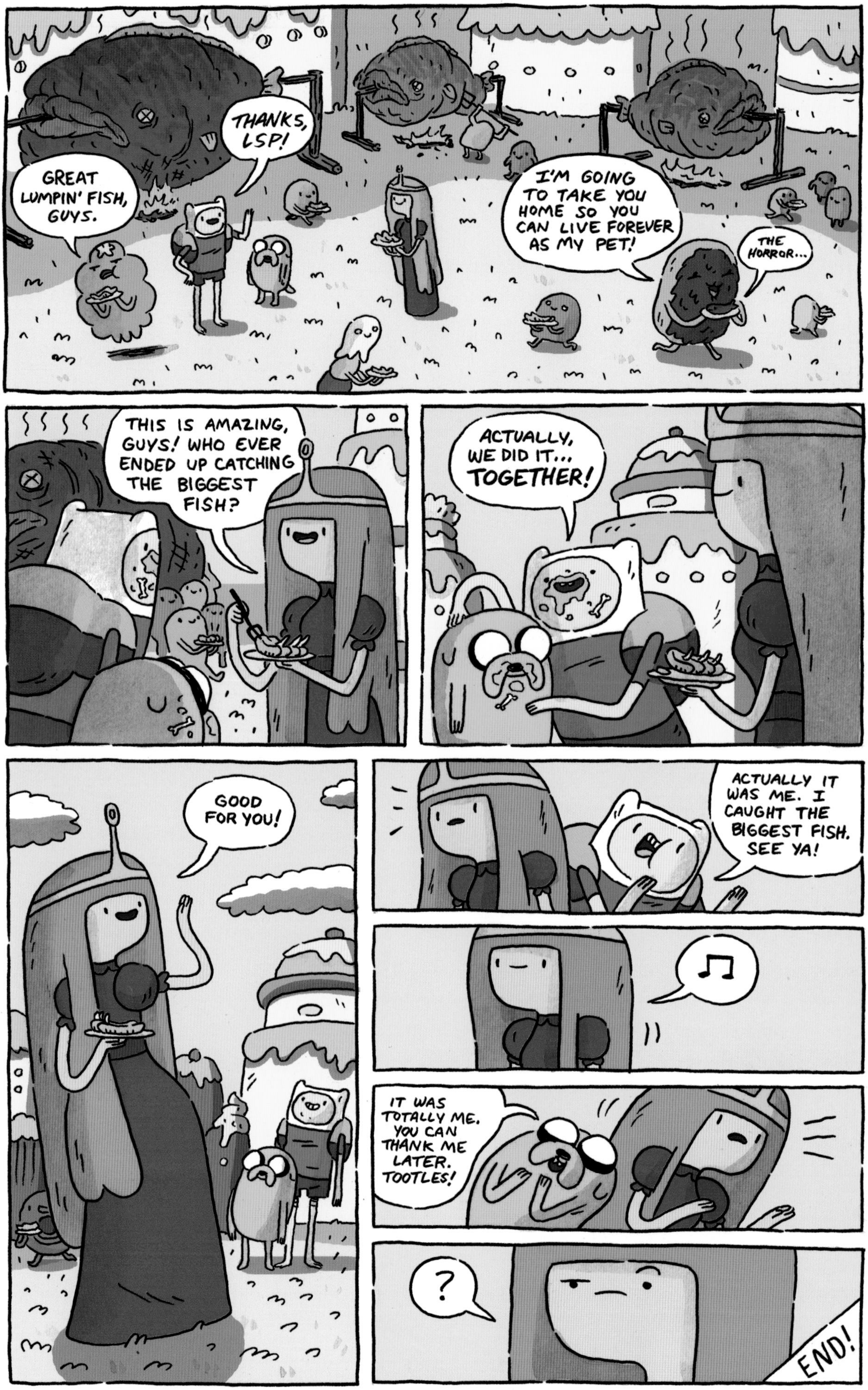
THANKS, LSP!
GREAT LUMPIN' FISH, GUYS.
I'M GOING TO TAKE YOU HOME SO YOU CAN LIVE FOREVER AS MY PET!
THE HORROR...
THIS IS AMAZING, GUYS! WHO EVER ENDED UP CATCHING THE BIGGEST FISH?
ACTUALLY, WE DID IT... TOGETHER!
GOOD FOR YOU!
ACTUALLY IT WAS ME. I CAUGHT THE BIGGEST FISH. SEE YA!
♫
IT WAS TOTALLY ME. YOU CAN THANK ME LATER. TOOTLES!
?
END!

HOT DEALS IN ICE KINGDOM

ISSUE TEN, COVER B
TYSON HESSE

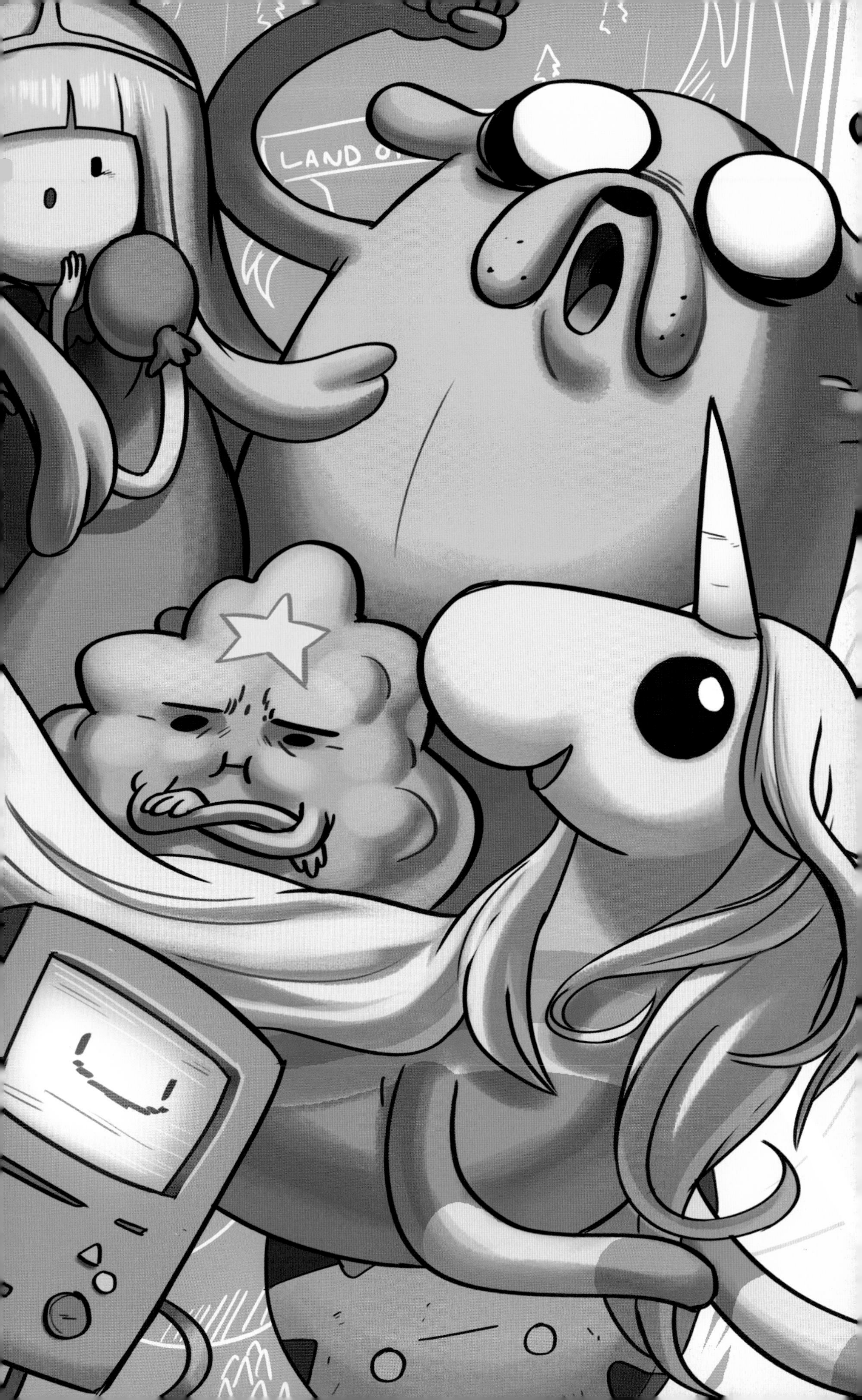
LAND O

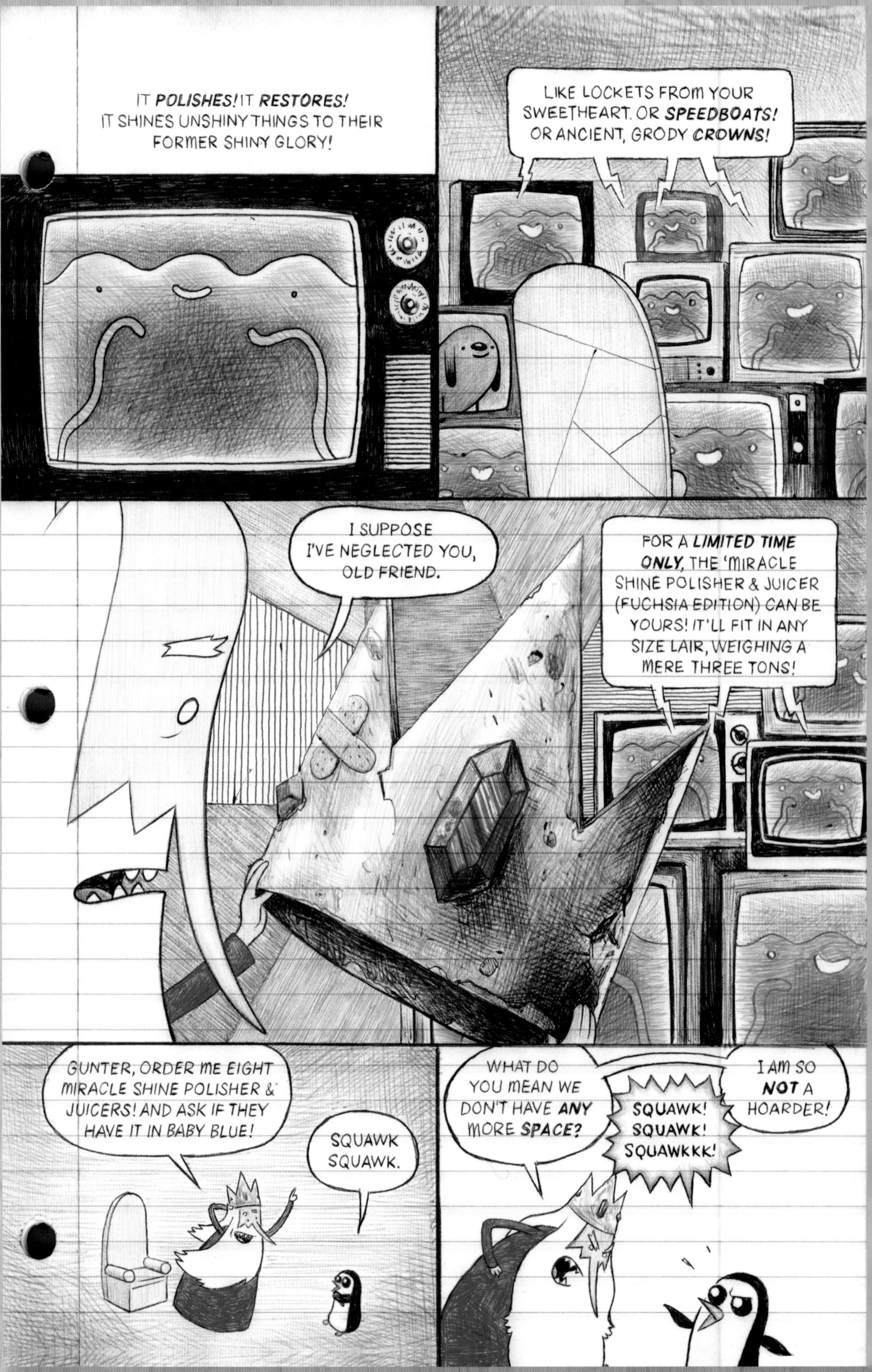

IT POLISHES! IT RESTORES! IT SHINES UNSHINY THINGS TO THEIR FORMER SHINY GLORY!
LIKE LOCKETS FROM YOUR SWEETHEART. OR SPEEDBOATS! OR ANCIENT, GRODY CROWNS!
I SUPPOSE I'VE NEGLECTED YOU, OLD FRIEND.
FOR A LIMITED TIME ONLY, THE 'MIRACLE SHINE POLISHER & JUICER (FUCHSIA EDITION) CAN BE YOURS! IT'LL FIT IN ANY SIZE LAIR, WEIGHING A MERE THREE TONS!
GUNTER, ORDER ME EIGHT MIRACLE SHINE POLISHER & JUICERS! AND ASK IF THEY HAVE IT IN BABY BLUE!
SQUAWK SQUAWK.
WHAT DO YOU MEAN WE DON'T HAVE ANY MORE SPACE?
SQUAWK! SQUAWK! SQUAWKKK!
I AM SO NOT A HOARDER!

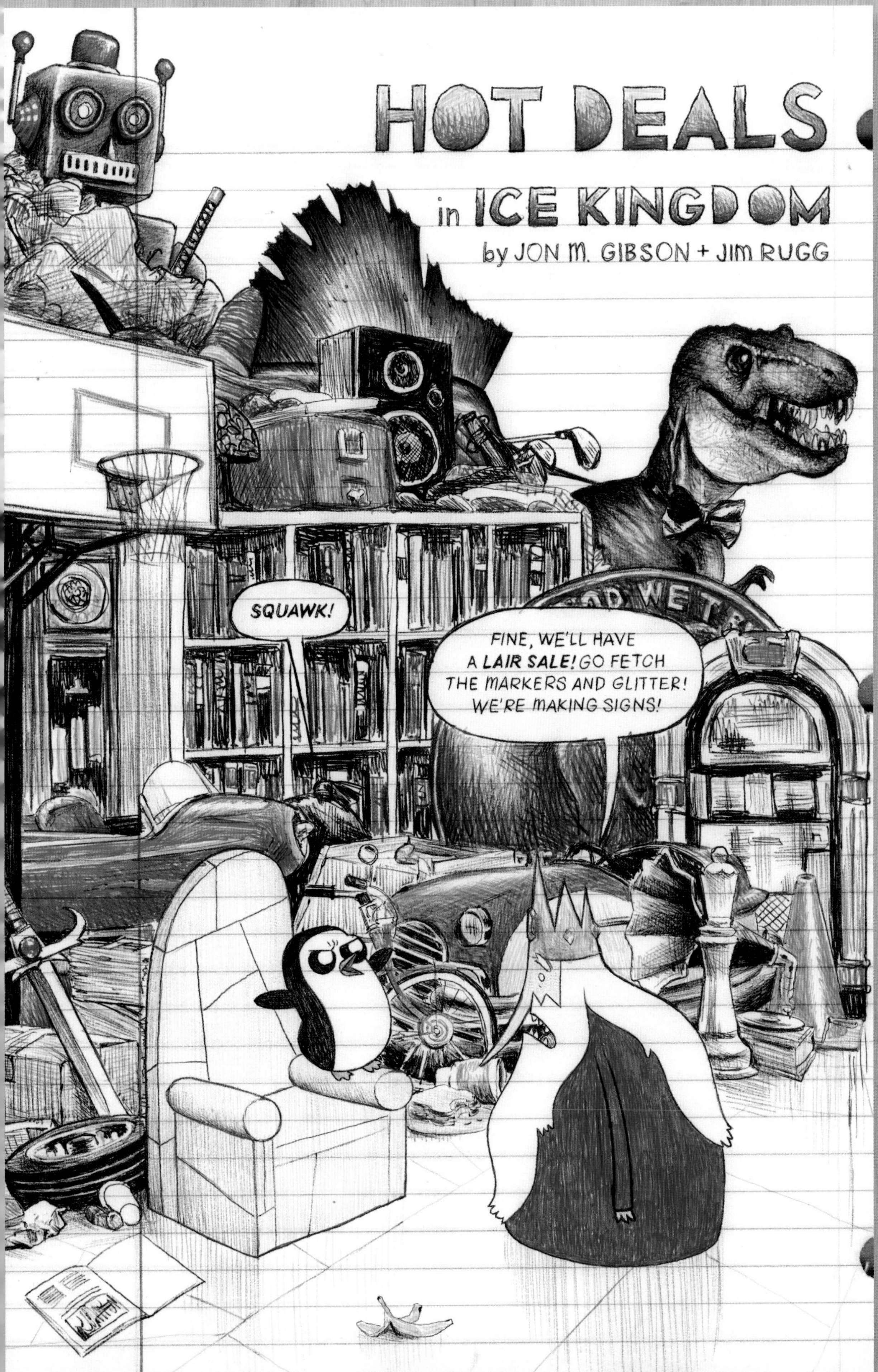
HOT DEALS
in ICE KINGDOM
by JON M. GIBSON + JIM RUGG
SQUAWK!
FINE, WE'LL HAVE A LAIR SALE! GO FETCH THE MARKERS AND GLITTER! WE'RE MAKING SIGNS!

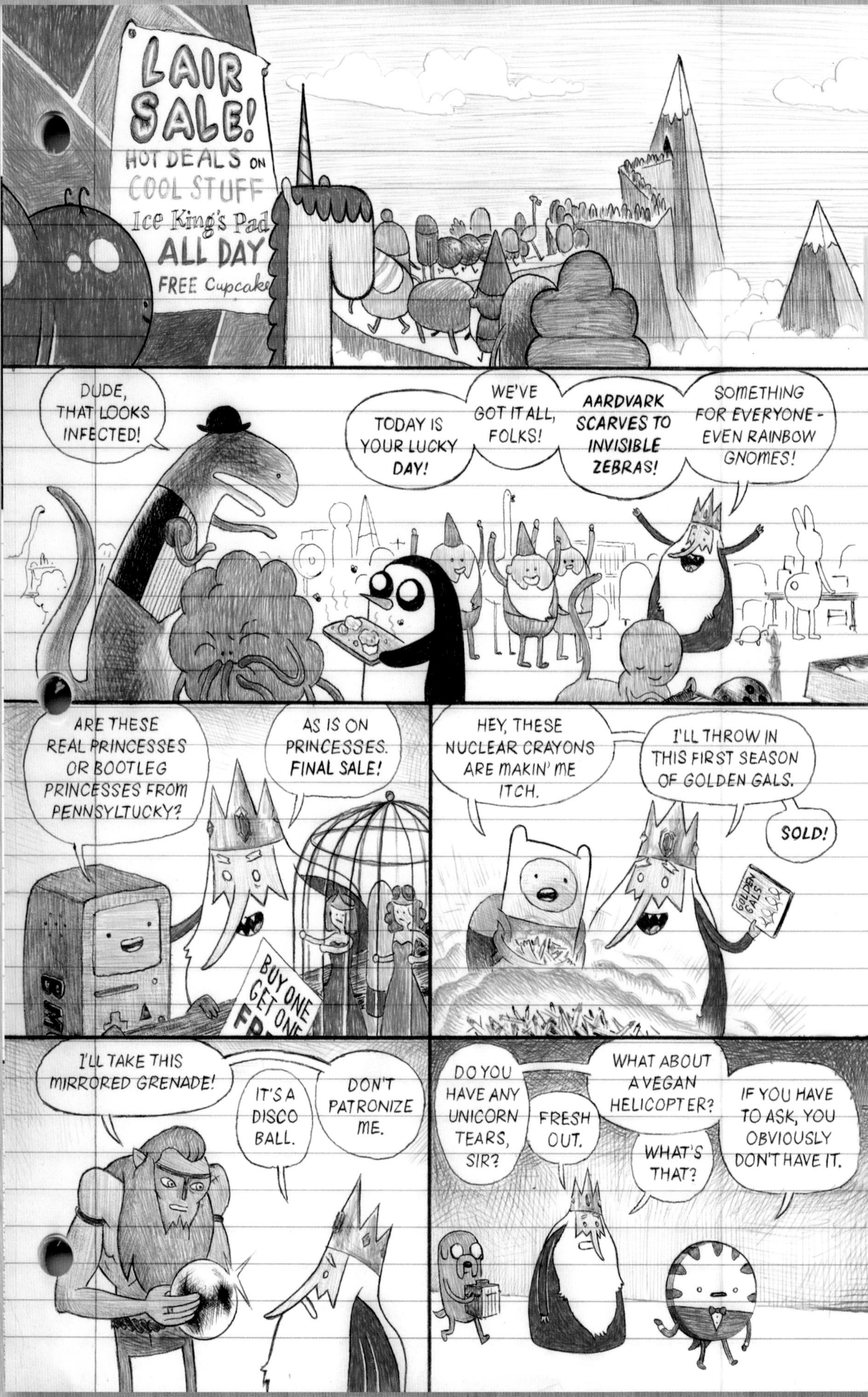
LAIR SALE!
HOT DEALS ON COOL STUFF
Ice King's Pad
ALL DAY
FREE Cupcake
DUDE, THAT LOOKS INFECTED!
TODAY IS YOUR LUCKY DAY!
WE'VE GOT IT ALL, FOLKS!
AARDVARK SCARVES TO INVISIBLE ZEBRAS!
SOMETHING FOR EVERYONE - EVEN RAINBOW GNOMES!
ARE THESE REAL PRINCESSES OR BOOTLEG PRINCESSES FROM PENNSYLTUCKY?
AS IS ON PRINCESSES. FINAL SALE!
BUY ONE GET ONE
HEY, THESE NUCLEAR CRAYONS ARE MAKIN' ME ITCH.
I'LL THROW IN THIS FIRST SEASON OF GOLDEN GALS.
SOLD!
GOLDEN GALS
I'LL TAKE THIS MIRRORED GRENADE!
IT'S A DISCO BALL.
DON'T PATRONIZE ME.
DO YOU HAVE ANY UNICORN TEARS, SIR?
FRESH OUT.
WHAT ABOUT A VEGAN HELICOPTER?
WHAT'S THAT?
IF YOU HAVE TO ASK, YOU OBVIOUSLY DON'T HAVE IT.

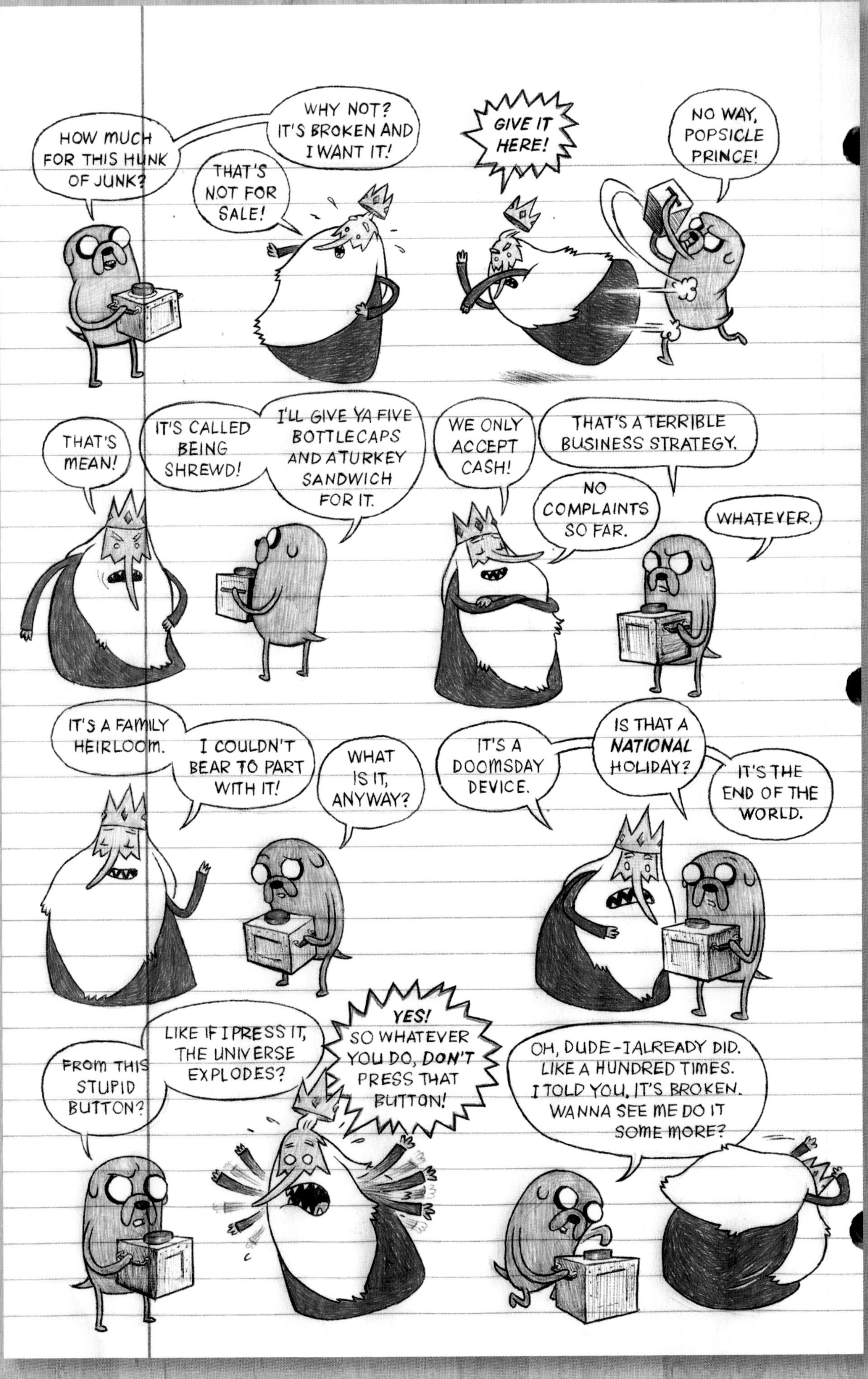
HOW MUCH FOR THIS HUNK OF JUNK?
THAT'S NOT FOR SALE!
WHY NOT? IT'S BROKEN AND I WANT IT!
GIVE IT HERE!
NO WAY, POPSICLE PRINCE!
THAT'S MEAN!
IT'S CALLED BEING SHREWD!
I'LL GIVE YA FIVE BOTTLECAPS AND A TURKEY SANDWICH FOR IT.
WE ONLY ACCEPT CASH!
THAT'S A TERRIBLE BUSINESS STRATEGY.
NO COMPLAINTS SO FAR.
WHATEVER.
IT'S A FAMILY HEIRLOOM.
I COULDN'T BEAR TO PART WITH IT!
WHAT IS IT, ANYWAY?
IT'S A DOOMSDAY DEVICE.
IS THAT A NATIONAL HOLIDAY?
IT'S THE END OF THE WORLD.
FROM THIS STUPID BUTTON?
LIKE IF I PRESS IT, THE UNIVERSE EXPLODES?
YES! SO WHATEVER YOU DO, DON'T PRESS THAT BUTTON!
OH, DUDE-I ALREADY DID. LIKE A HUNDRED TIMES. I TOLD YOU, IT'S BROKEN. WANNA SEE ME DO IT SOME MORE?

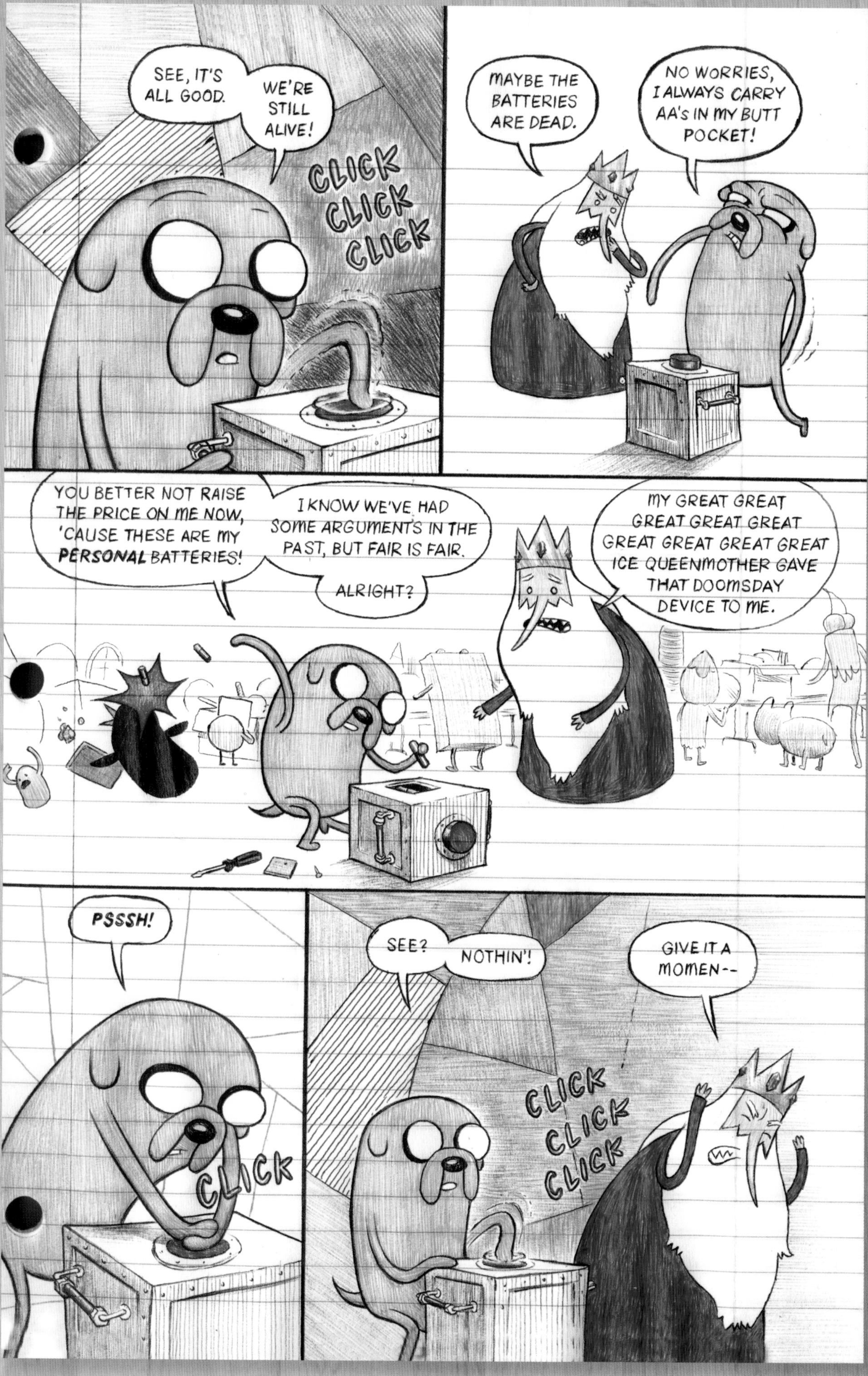
SEE, IT'S ALL GOOD.
WE'RE STILL ALIVE!
CLICK CLICK CLICK
MAYBE THE BATTERIES ARE DEAD.
NO WORRIES, I ALWAYS CARRY AA's IN MY BUTT POCKET!
YOU BETTER NOT RAISE THE PRICE ON ME NOW, 'CAUSE THESE ARE MY PERSONAL BATTERIES!
I KNOW WE'VE HAD SOME ARGUMENTS IN THE PAST, BUT FAIR IS FAIR.
ALRIGHT?
MY GREAT GREAT GREAT GREAT GREAT GREAT GREAT GREAT ICE QUEENMOTHER GAVE THAT DOOMSDAY DEVICE TO ME.
PSSSH!
CLICK
SEE?
NOTHIN'!
GIVE IT A MOMEN--
CLICK CLICK CLICK

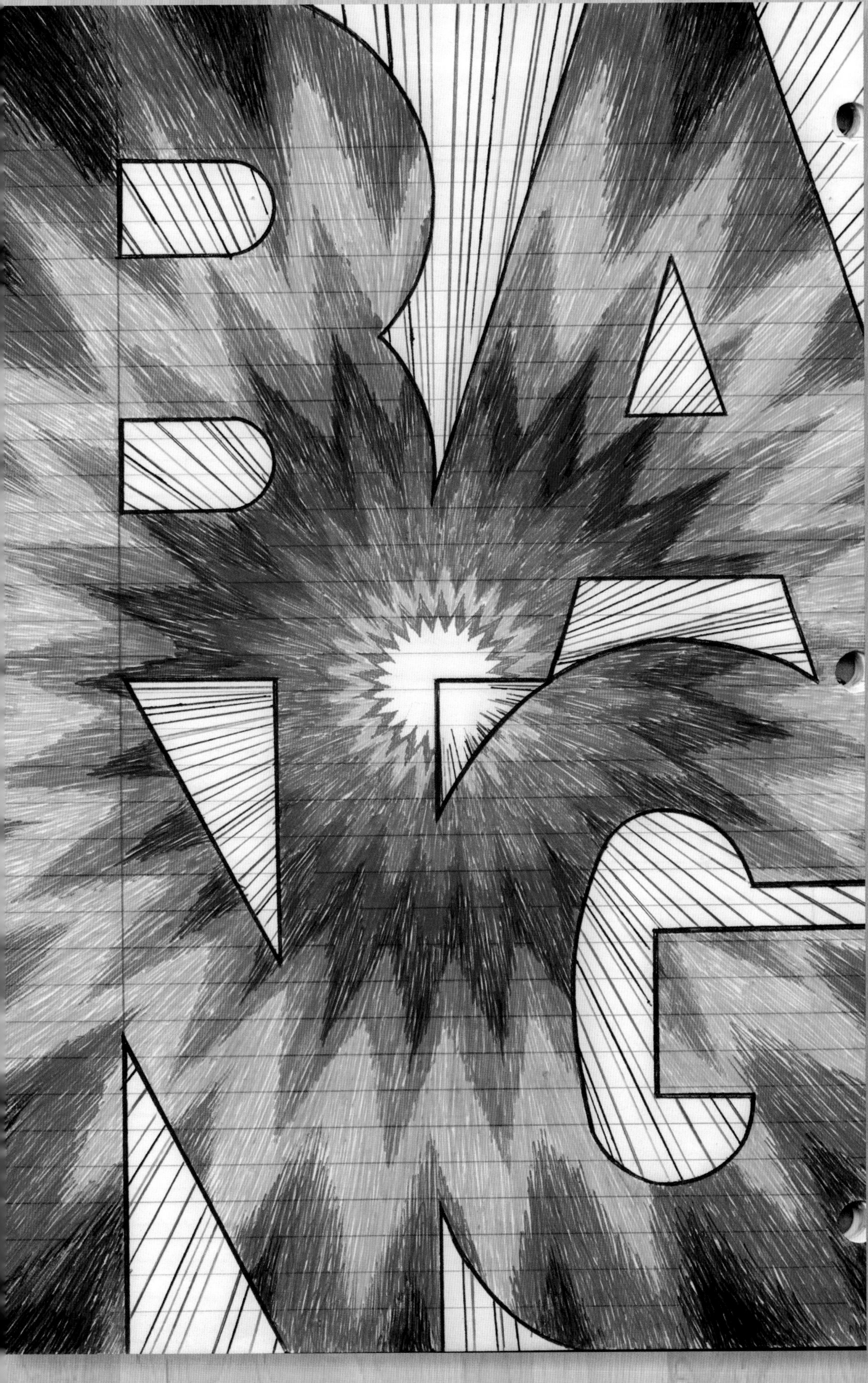

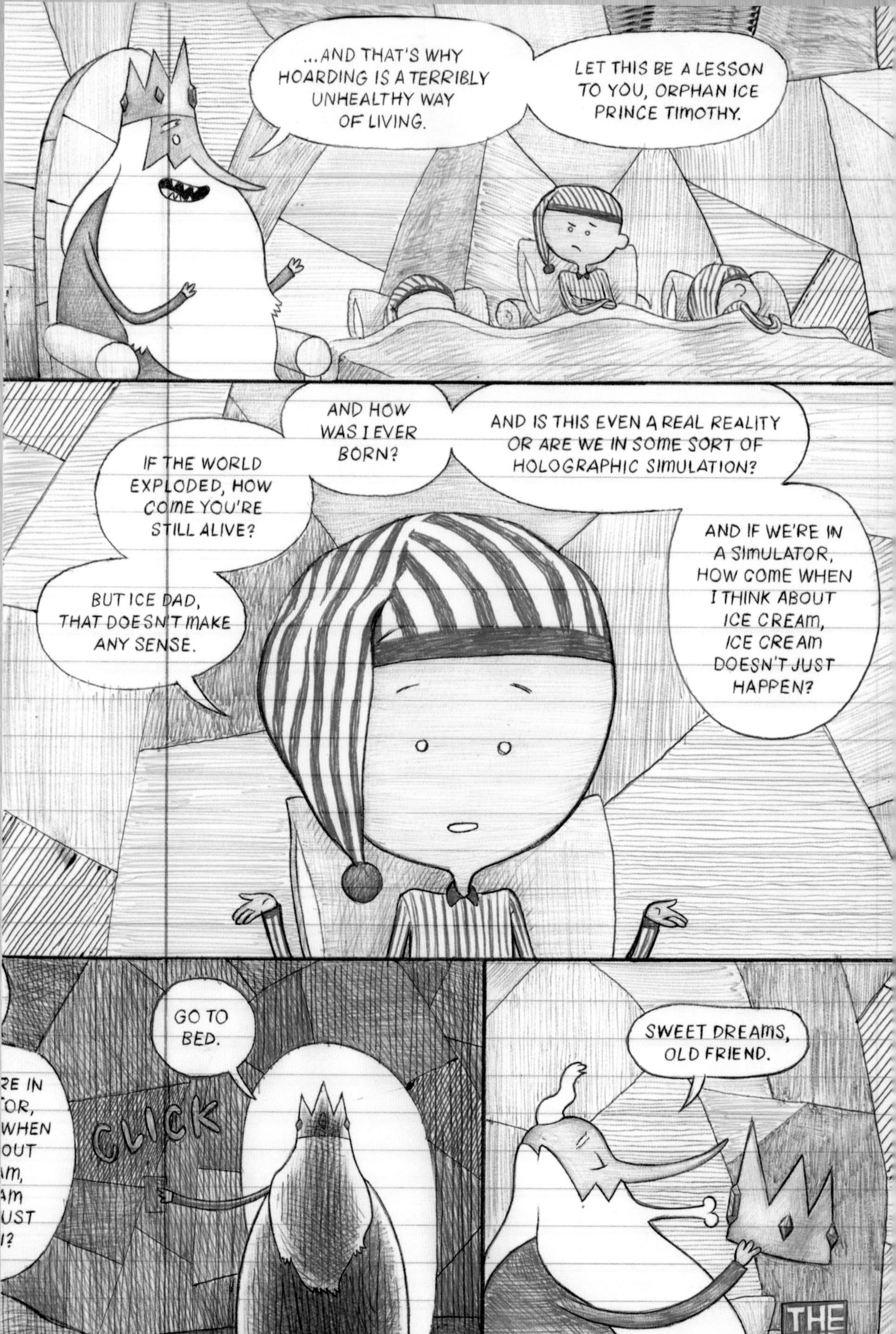
...AND THAT'S WHY HOARDING IS A TERRIBLY UNHEALTHY WAY OF LIVING.
LET THIS BE A LESSON TO YOU, ORPHAN ICE PRINCE TIMOTHY.
BUT ICE DAD, THAT DOESN'T MAKE ANY SENSE.
IF THE WORLD EXPLODED, HOW COME YOU'RE STILL ALIVE?
AND HOW WAS I EVER BORN?
AND IS THIS EVEN A REAL REALITY OR ARE WE IN SOME SORT OF HOLOGRAPHIC SIMULATION?
AND IF WE'RE IN A SIMULATOR, HOW COME WHEN I THINK ABOUT ICE CREAM, ICE CREAM DOESN'T JUST HAPPEN?
GO TO BED.
CLICK
SWEET DREAMS, OLD FRIEND.
THE END

THE MEANING OF BRAVERY

ISSUE ELEVEN, COVER B
KEVIN WADA

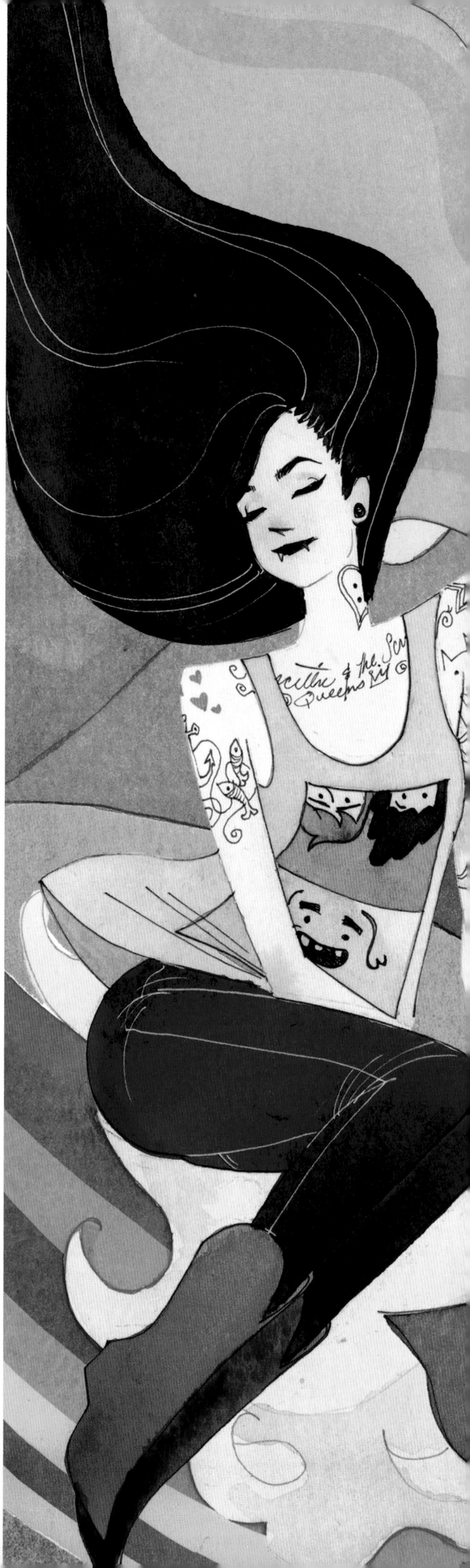

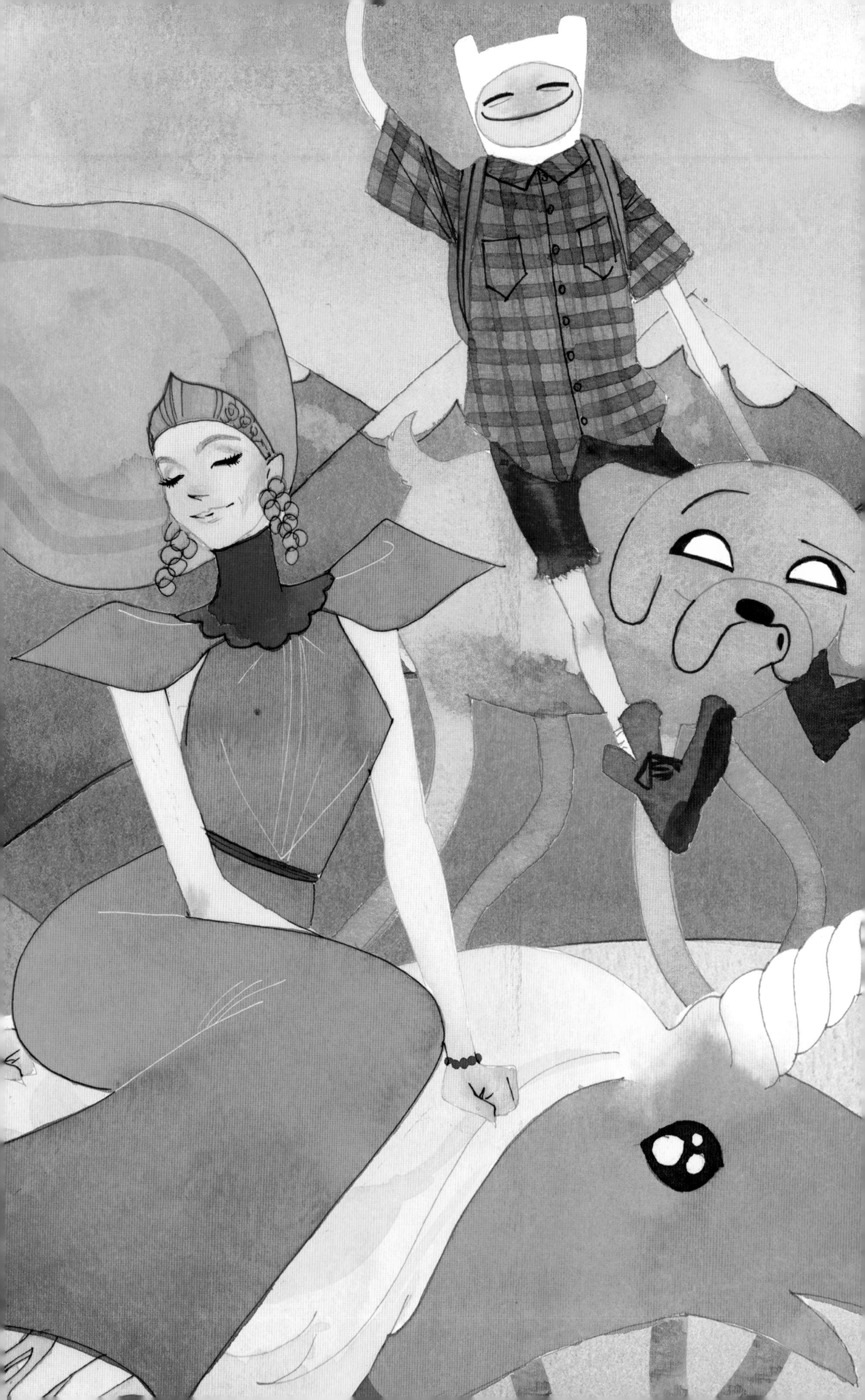

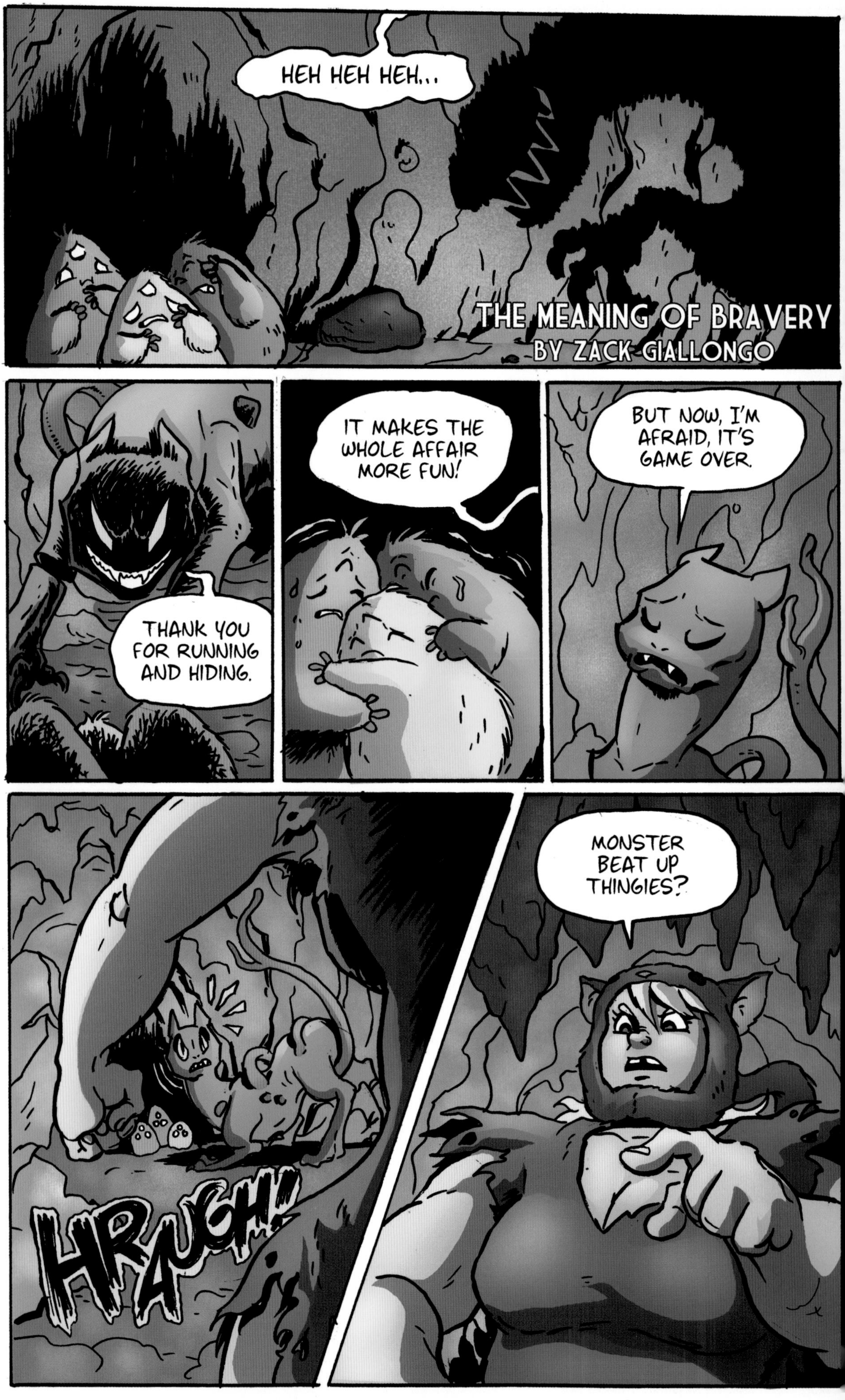
HEH HEH HEH...
THE MEANING OF BRAVERY
BY ZACK GIALLONGO
THANK YOU FOR RUNNING AND HIDING.
IT MAKES THE WHOLE AFFAIR MORE FUN!
BUT NOW, I'M AFRAID, IT'S GAME OVER.
HRAUGH!!
MONSTER BEAT UP THINGIES?

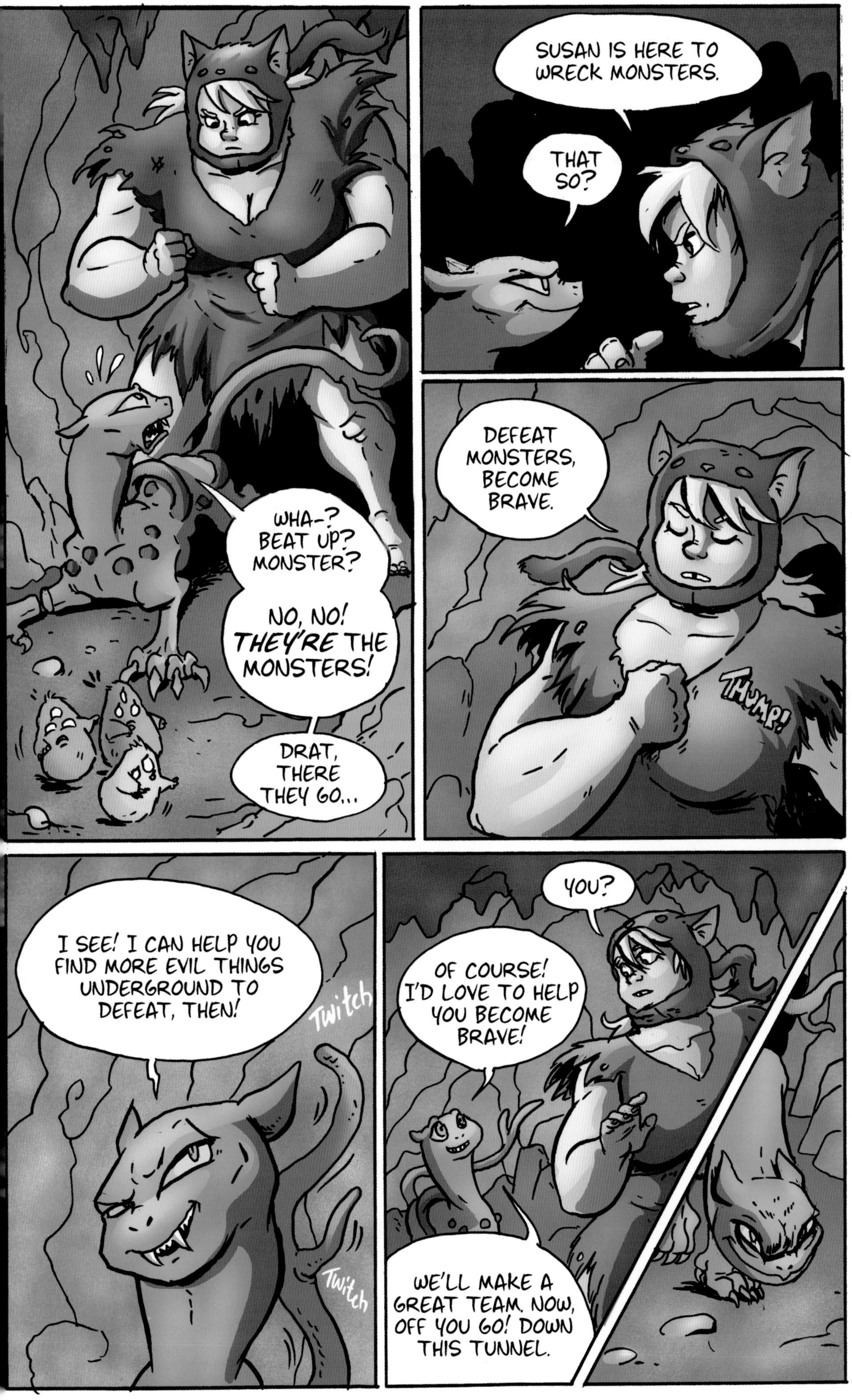

WHA-? BEAT UP? MONSTER?
NO, NO! *THEY'RE* THE MONSTERS!
DRAT, THERE THEY GO...
SUSAN IS HERE TO WRECK MONSTERS.
THAT SO?
DEFEAT MONSTERS, BECOME BRAVE.
THUMP!
I SEE! I CAN HELP YOU FIND MORE EVIL THINGS UNDERGROUND TO DEFEAT, THEN!
Twitch
Twitch
YOU?
OF COURSE! I'D LOVE TO HELP YOU BECOME BRAVE!
WE'LL MAKE A GREAT TEAM. NOW, OFF YOU GO! DOWN THIS TUNNEL.

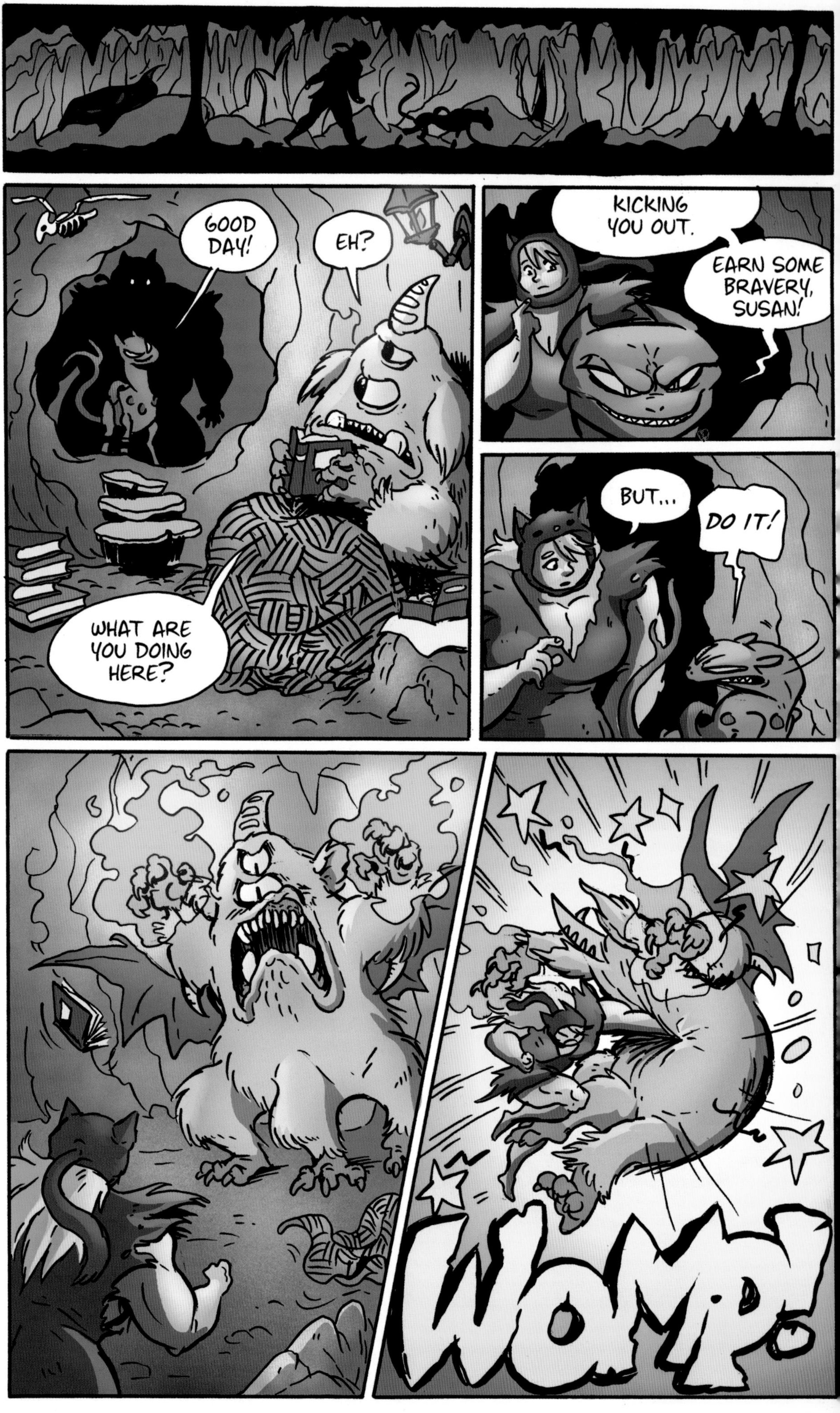
GOOD DAY!
EH?
WHAT ARE YOU DOING HERE?
KICKING YOU OUT.
EARN SOME BRAVERY, SUSAN!
BUT...
DO IT!
WOMP!

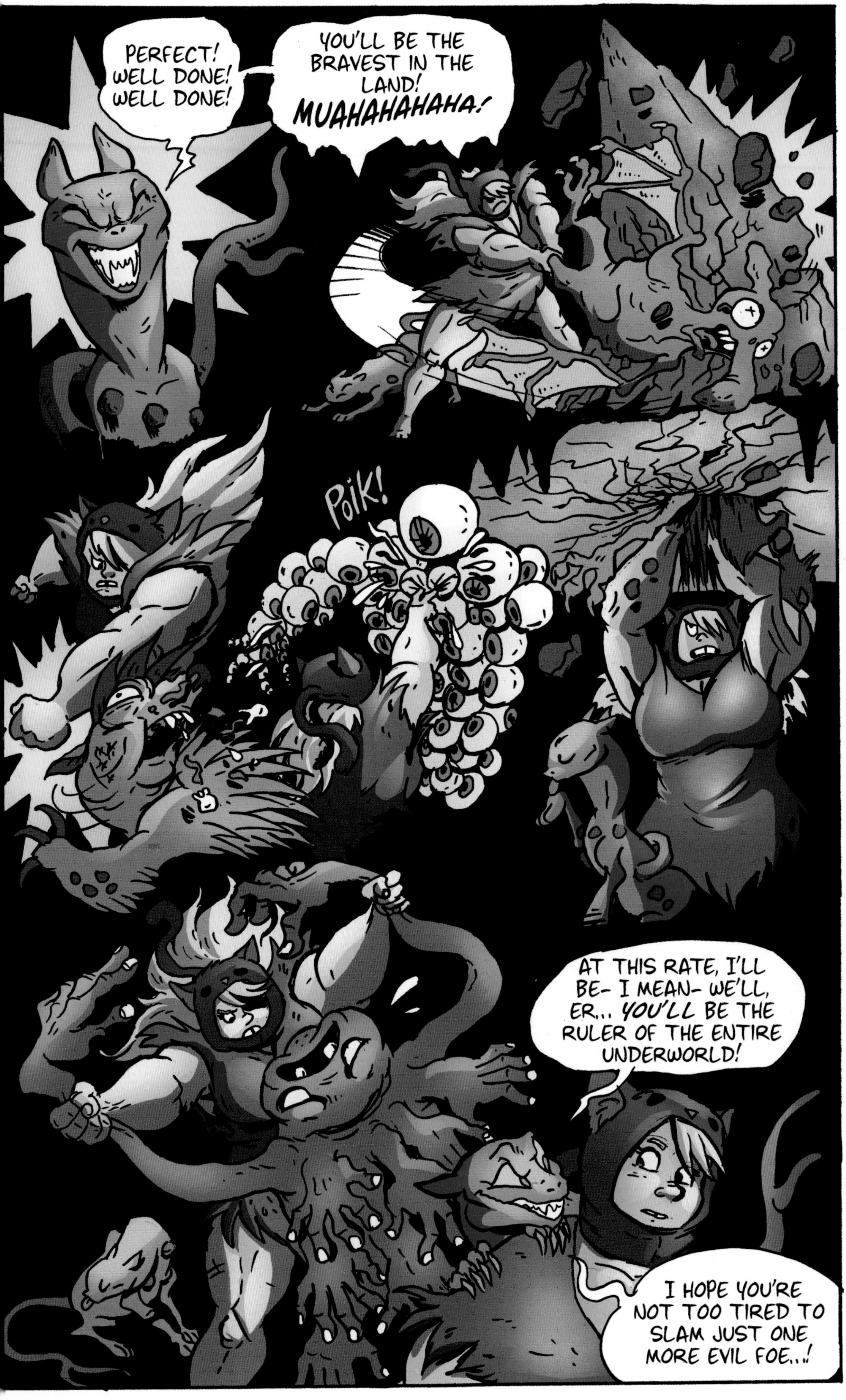
PERFECT! WELL DONE! WELL DONE!
YOU'LL BE THE BRAVEST IN THE LAND! MUAHAHAHAHA!
POIK!
AT THIS RATE, I'LL BE- I MEAN- WE'LL, ER... YOU'LL BE THE RULER OF THE ENTIRE UNDERWORLD!
I HOPE YOU'RE NOT TOO TIRED TO SLAM JUST ONE MORE EVIL FOE...!

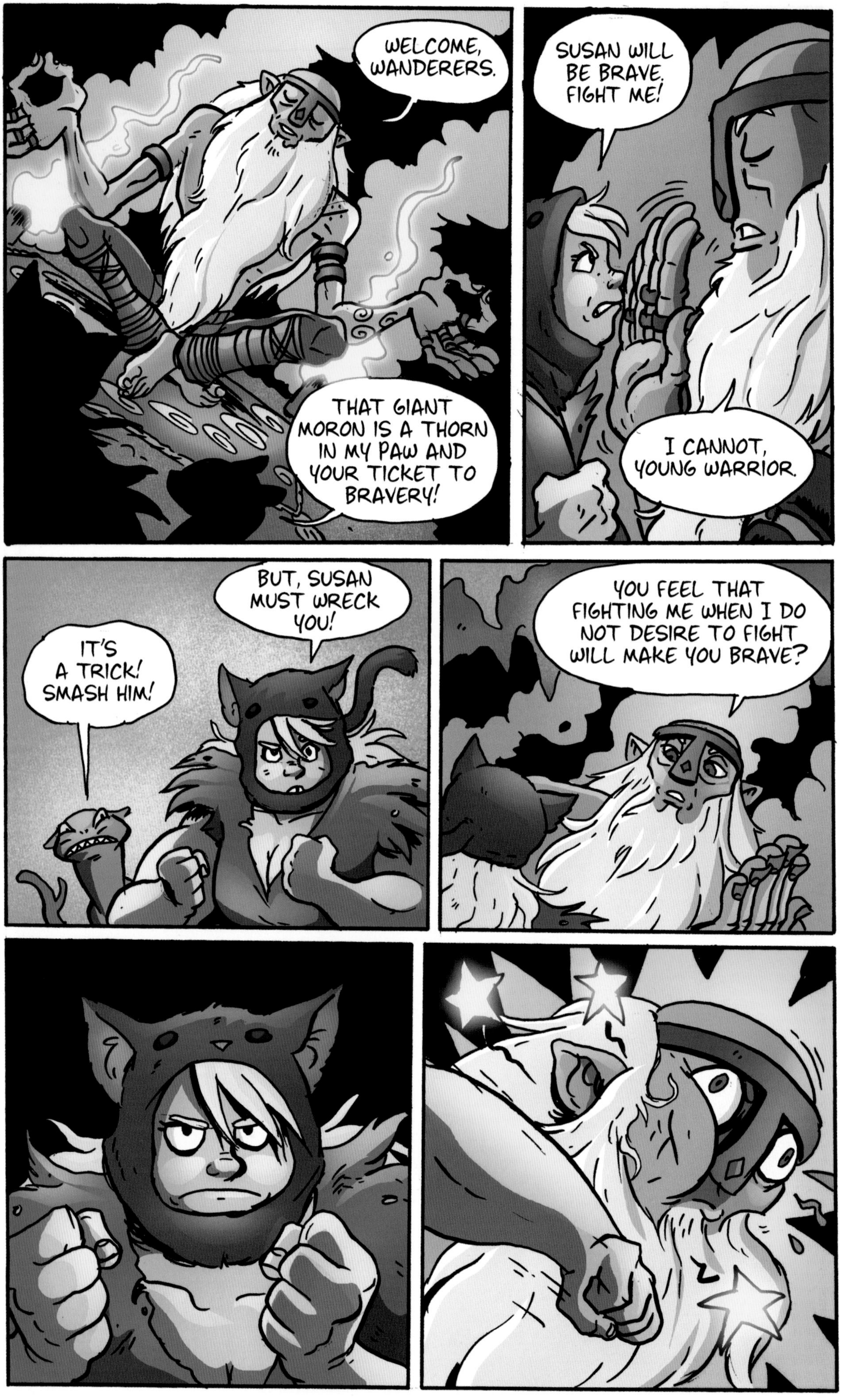
WELCOME, WANDERERS.
THAT GIANT MORON IS A THORN IN MY PAW AND YOUR TICKET TO BRAVERY!
SUSAN WILL BE BRAVE, FIGHT ME!
I CANNOT, YOUNG WARRIOR.
BUT, SUSAN MUST WRECK YOU!
IT'S A TRICK! SMASH HIM!
YOU FEEL THAT FIGHTING ME WHEN I DO NOT DESIRE TO FIGHT WILL MAKE YOU BRAVE?

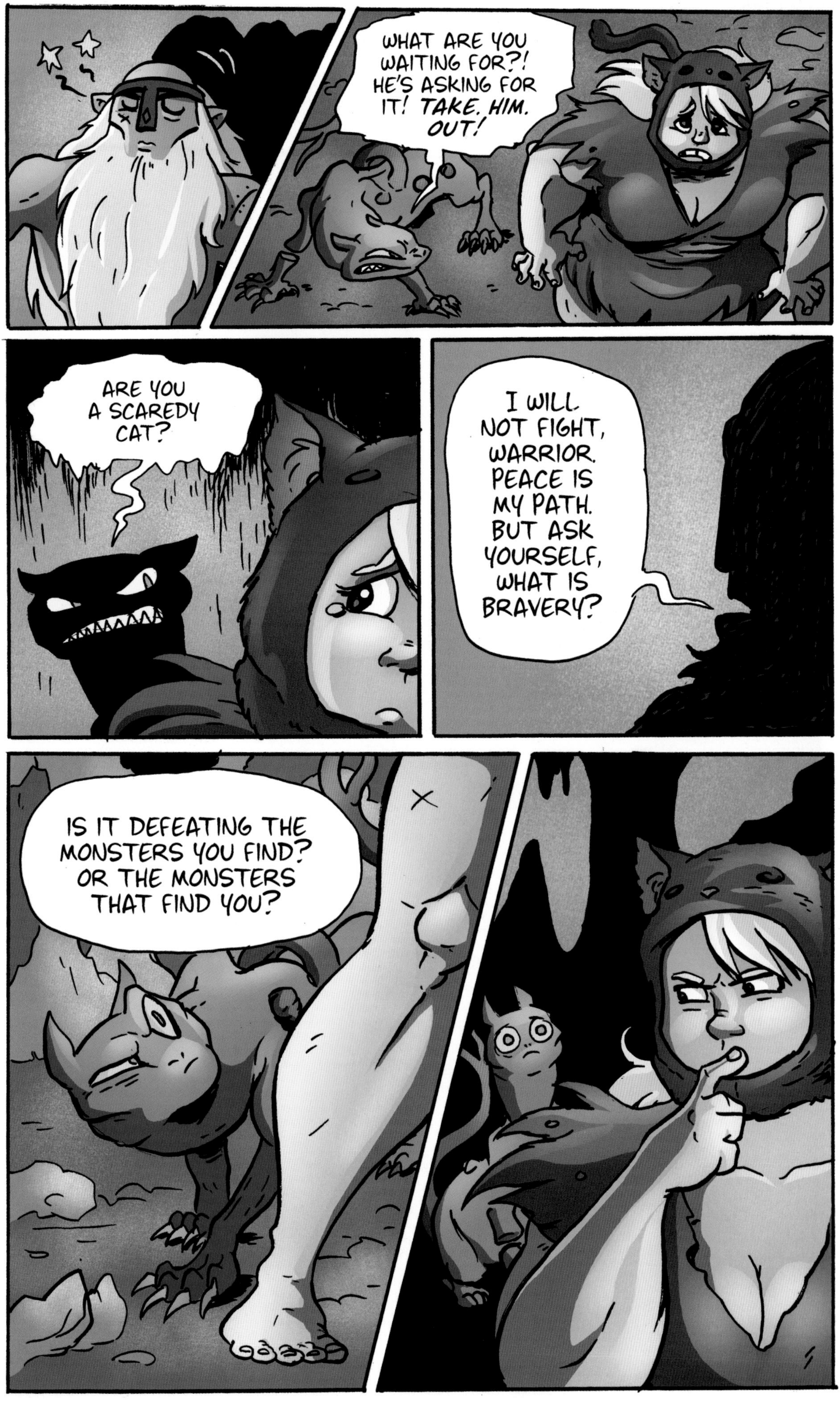
WHAT ARE YOU WAITING FOR?! HE'S ASKING FOR IT! TAKE. HIM. OUT!
ARE YOU A SCAREDY CAT?
I WILL NOT FIGHT, WARRIOR. PEACE IS MY PATH. BUT ASK YOURSELF, WHAT IS BRAVERY?
IS IT DEFEATING THE MONSTERS YOU FIND? OR THE MONSTERS THAT FIND YOU?

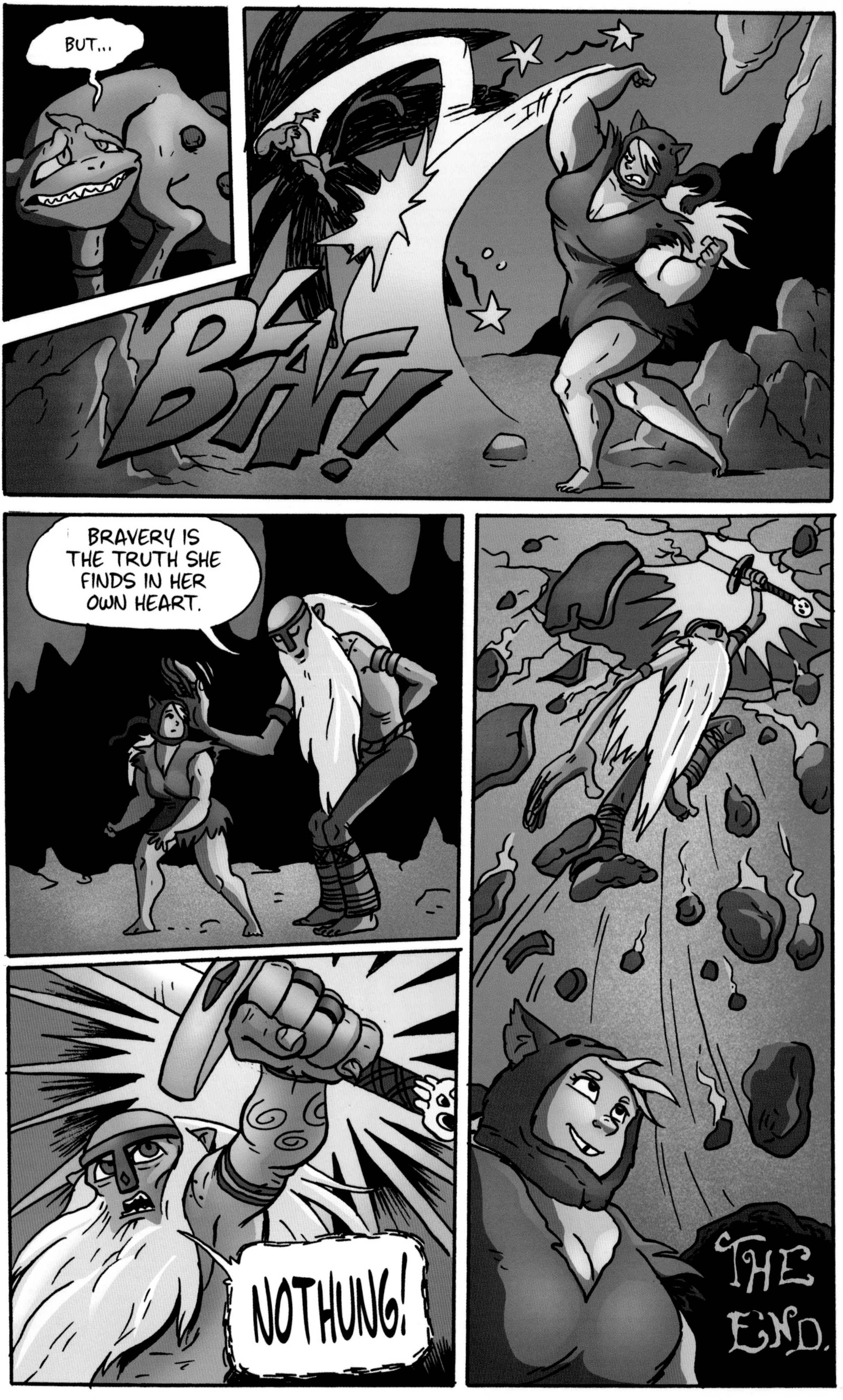

BUT...
BAFT!
BRAVERY IS THE TRUTH SHE FINDS IN HER OWN HEART.
NOTHUNG!
THE END.

THE ICE KING & HIS MAGICAL
MATCHMAKING MINI-COMIC

ISSUE TWELVE, COVER C
LILLI CARRÉ

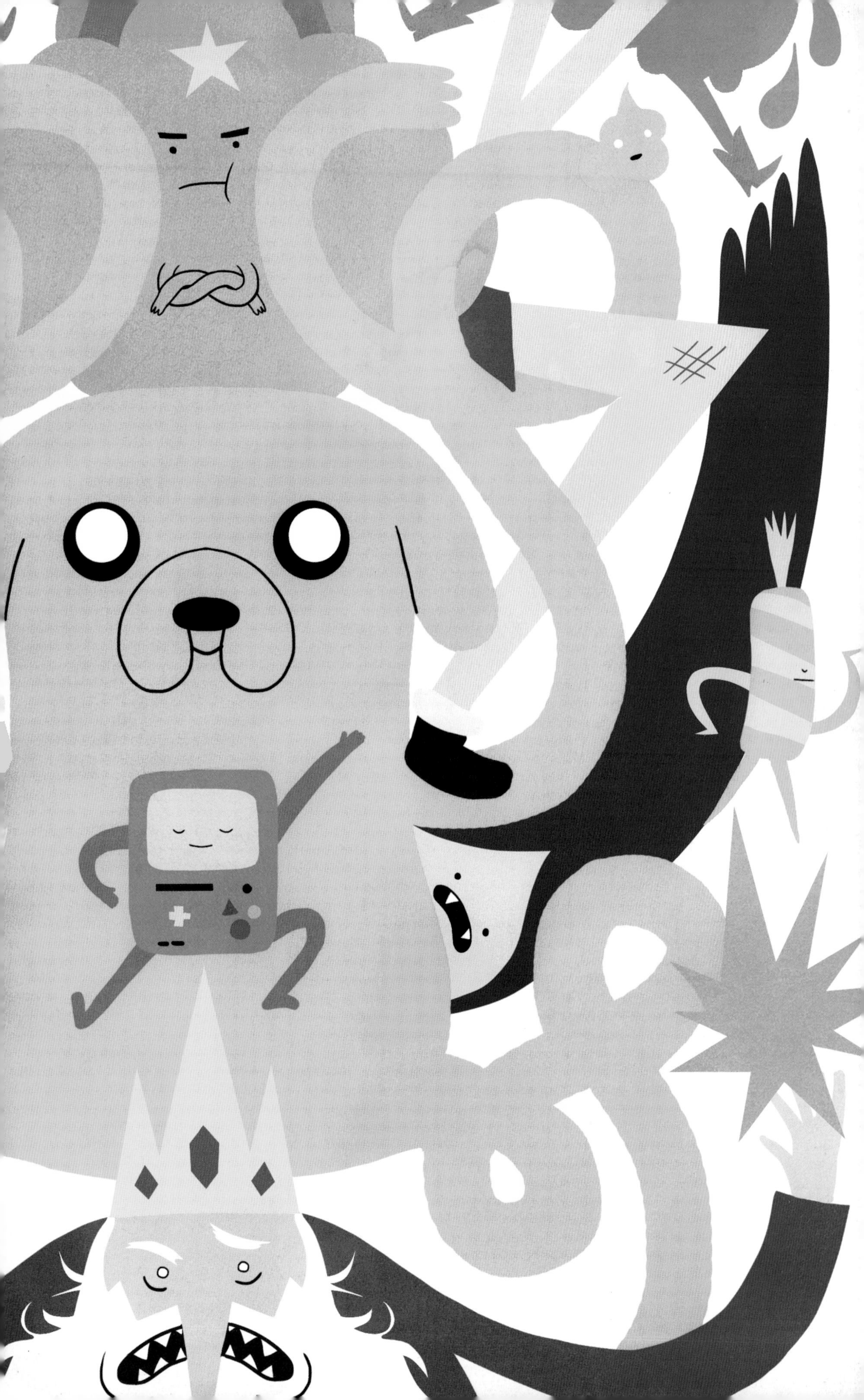

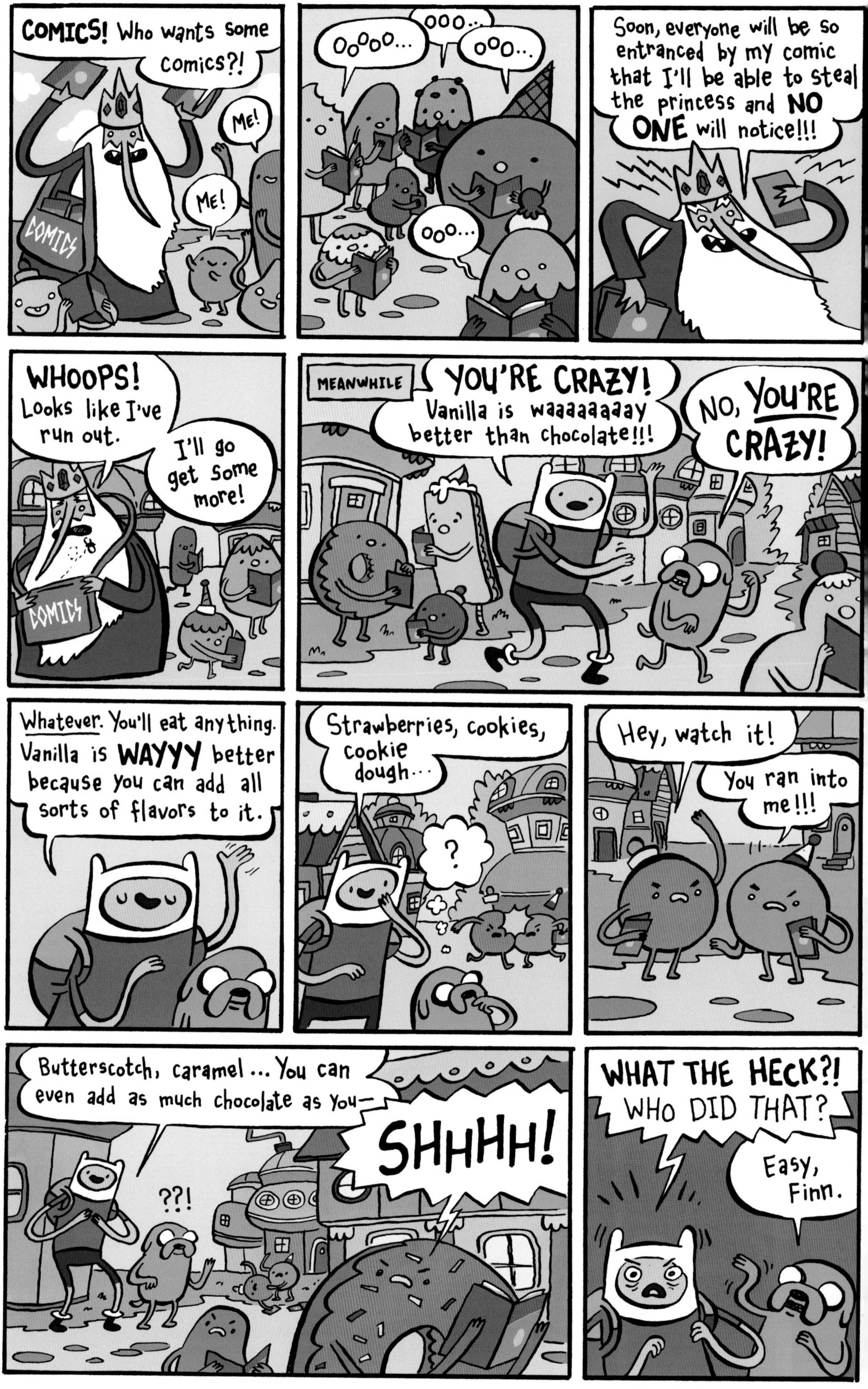
COMICS! Who wants some comics?!
Me!
ME!
OoOoO...
OOO...
OOO...
OOO...
Soon, everyone will be so entranced by my comic that I'll be able to steal the princess and NO ONE will notice!!!
WHOOPS! Looks like I've run out.
I'll go get some more!
COMICS
MEANWHILE
YOU'RE CRAZY! Vanilla is waaaaaaaay better than chocolate!!!
NO, YOU'RE CRAZY!
Whatever. You'll eat anything. Vanilla is WAYYY better because you can add all sorts of flavors to it.
Strawberries, cookies, cookie dough...
?
Hey, watch it!
You ran into me!!!
Butterscotch, caramel... You can even add as much chocolate as you—
SHHHH!
??!
WHAT THE HECK?! WHO DID THAT?
Easy, Finn.

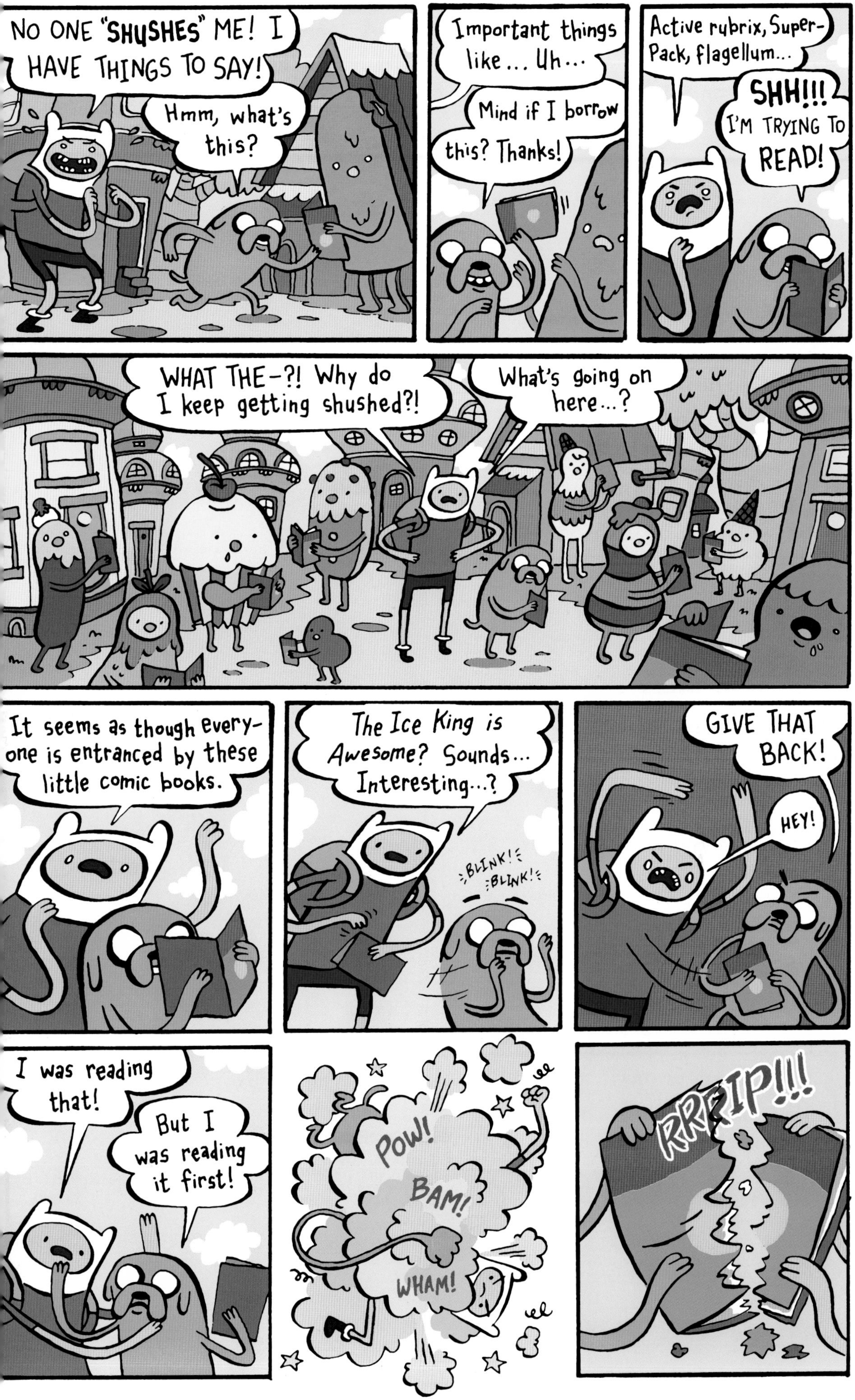
NO ONE "SHUSHES" ME! I HAVE THINGS TO SAY!
Hmm, what's this?
Important things like... Uh...
Mind if I borrow this? Thanks!
Active rubrix, Super-Pack, flagellum...
SHH!!! I'M TRYING TO READ!
WHAT THE-?! Why do I keep getting shushed?!
What's going on here...?
It seems as though every-one is entranced by these little comic books.
The Ice King is Awesome? Sounds... Interesting...?
BLINK! BLINK!
GIVE THAT BACK!
HEY!
I was reading that!
But I was reading it first!
POW!
BAM!
WHAM!
RRRIP!!!

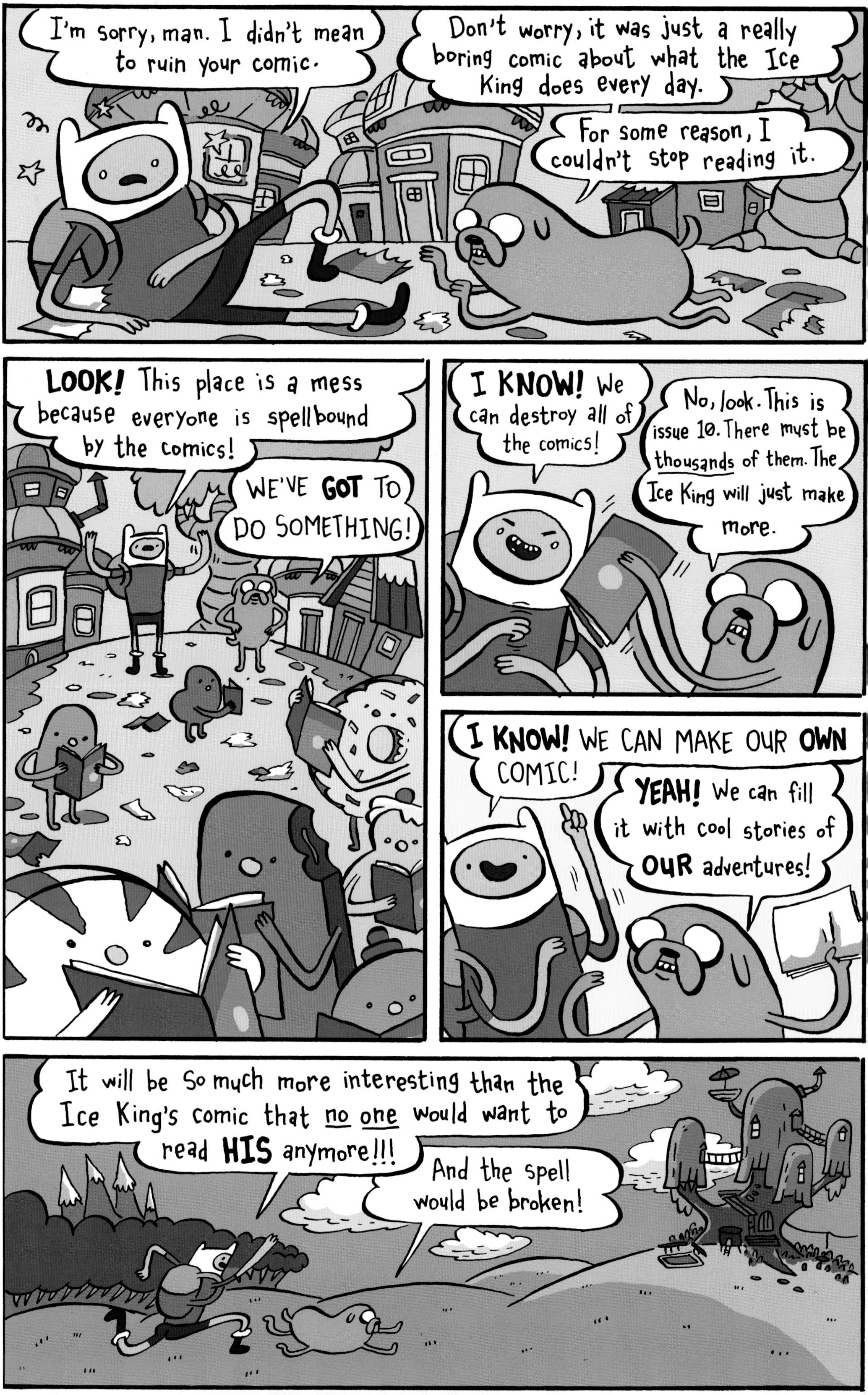
I'm sorry, man. I didn't mean to ruin your comic.
Don't worry, it was just a really boring comic about what the Ice King does every day.
For some reason, I couldn't stop reading it.
LOOK! This place is a mess because everyone is spellbound by the comics!
WE'VE GOT TO DO SOMETHING!
I KNOW! We can destroy all of the comics!
No, look. This is issue 10. There must be thousands of them. The Ice King will just make more.
I KNOW! WE CAN MAKE OUR OWN COMIC!
YEAH! We can fill it with cool stories of OUR adventures!
It will be so much more interesting than the Ice King's comic that no one would want to read HIS anymore!!!
And the spell would be broken!

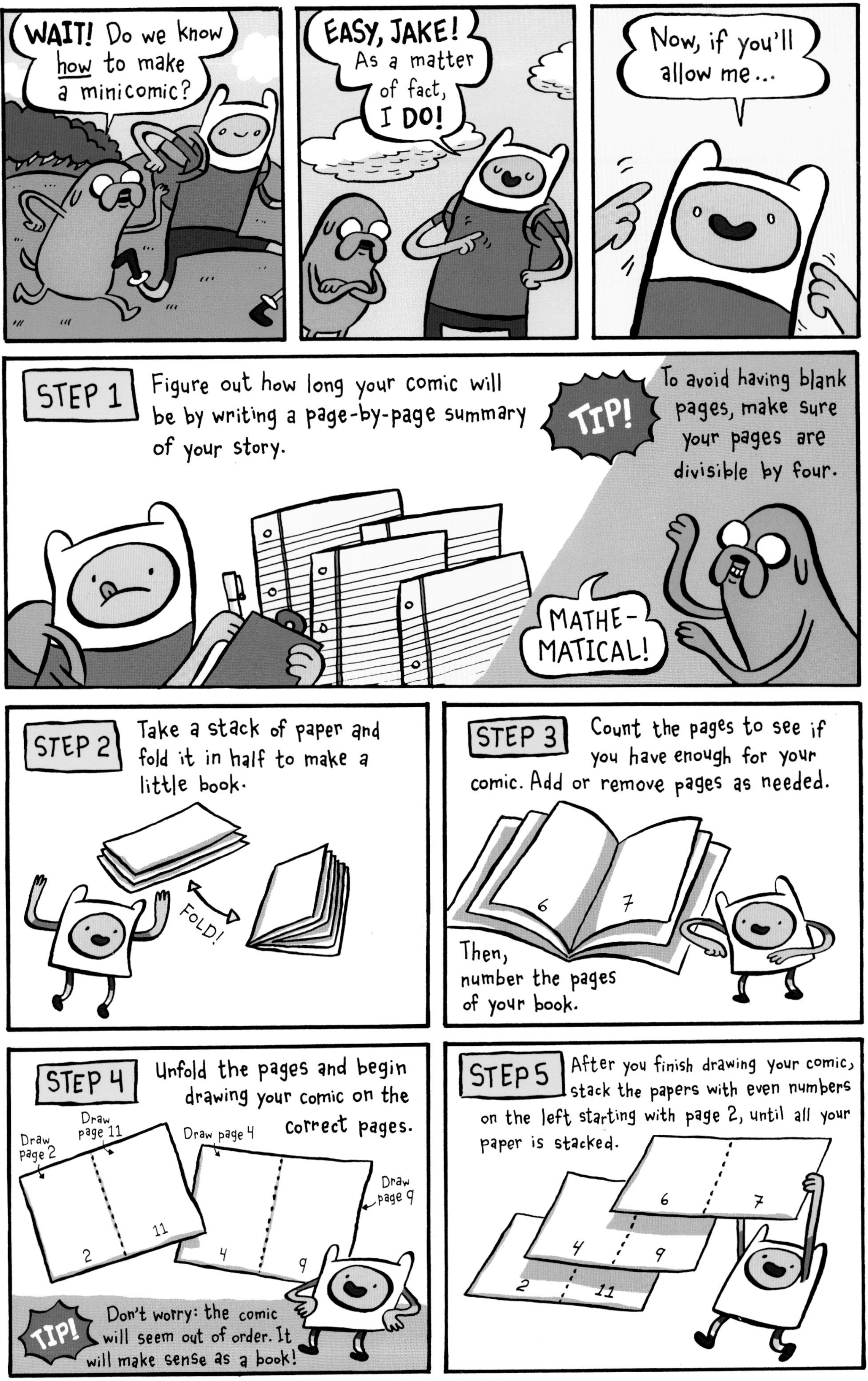

WAIT! Do we know how to make a minicomic?
EASY, JAKE! As a matter of fact, I DO!
Now, if you'll allow me...
STEP 1
Figure out how long your comic will be by writing a page-by-page summary of your story.
TIP!
To avoid having blank pages, make sure your pages are divisible by four.
MATHE-MATICAL!
STEP 2
Take a stack of paper and fold it in half to make a little book.
FOLD!
STEP 3
Count the pages to see if you have enough for your comic. Add or remove pages as needed.
6
7
Then, number the pages of your book.
STEP 4
Unfold the pages and begin drawing your comic on the correct pages.
Draw page 2
Draw page 11
Draw page 4
Draw page 9
2
11
4
9
TIP!
Don't worry: the comic will seem out of order. It will make sense as a book!
STEP 5
After you finish drawing your comic, stack the papers with even numbers on the left starting with page 2, until all your paper is stacked.
6
7
4
9
2
11

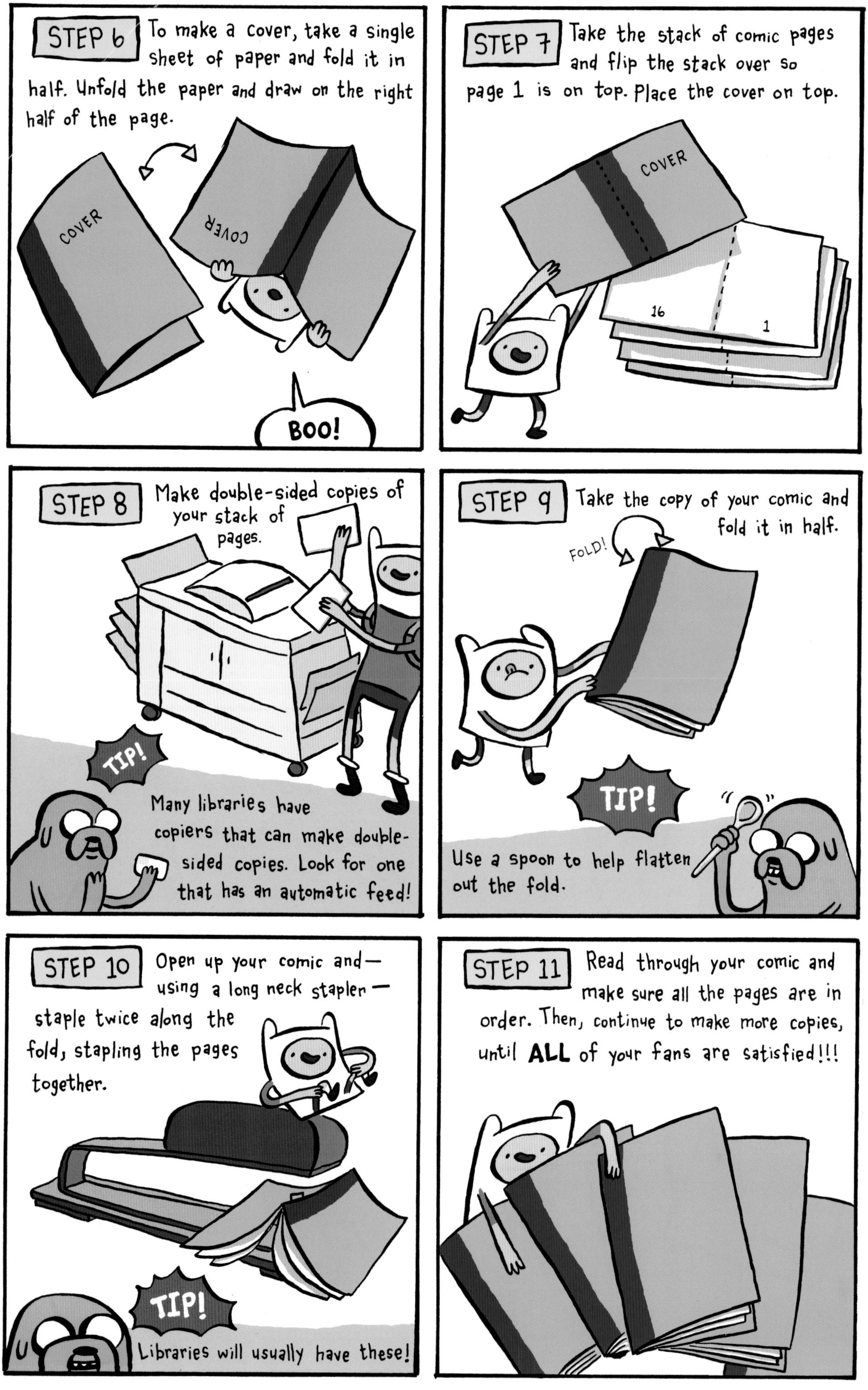
STEP 6
To make a cover, take a single sheet of paper and fold it in half. Unfold the paper and draw on the right half of the page.
COVER
COVER
BOO!
STEP 7
Take the stack of comic pages and flip the stack over so page 1 is on top. Place the cover on top.
COVER
16
1
STEP 8
Make double-sided copies of your stack of pages.
TIP!
Many libraries have copiers that can make double-sided copies. Look for one that has an automatic feed!
STEP 9
Take the copy of your comic and fold it in half.
FOLD!
TIP!
Use a spoon to help flatten out the fold.
STEP 10
Open up your comic and—using a long neck stapler—staple twice along the fold, stapling the pages together.
TIP!
Libraries will usually have these!
STEP 11
Read through your comic and make sure all the pages are in order. Then, continue to make more copies, until ALL of your fans are satisfied!!!

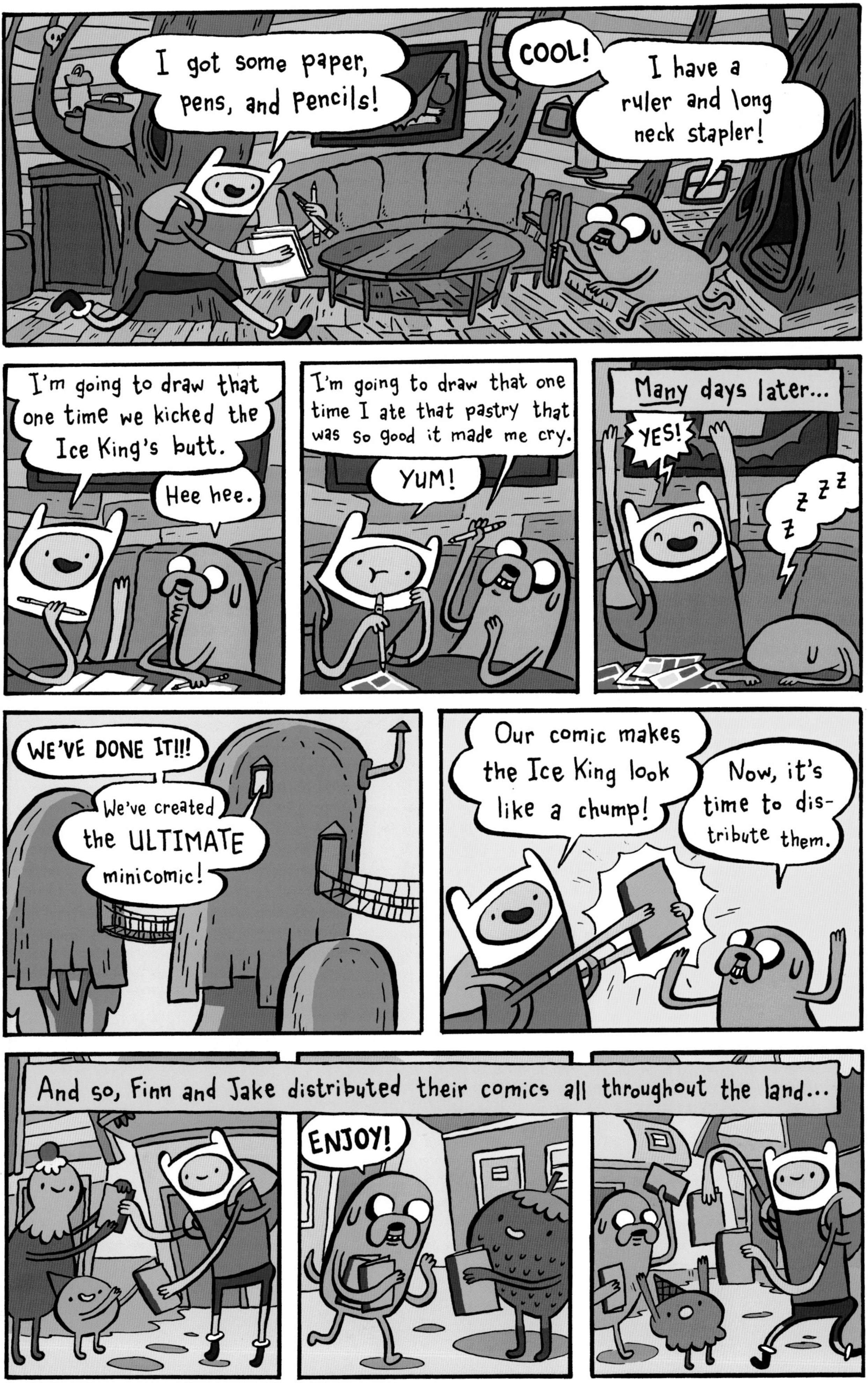
I got some paper, pens, and pencils!
COOL!
I have a ruler and long neck stapler!
I'm going to draw that one time we kicked the Ice King's butt.
Hee hee.
I'm going to draw that one time I ate that pastry that was so good it made me cry.
YUM!
Many days later...
YES!
Z Z Z Z
WE'VE DONE IT!!!
We've created the ULTIMATE minicomic!
Our comic makes the Ice King look like a chump!
Now, it's time to distribute them.
And so, Finn and Jake distributed their comics all throughout the land...
ENJOY!

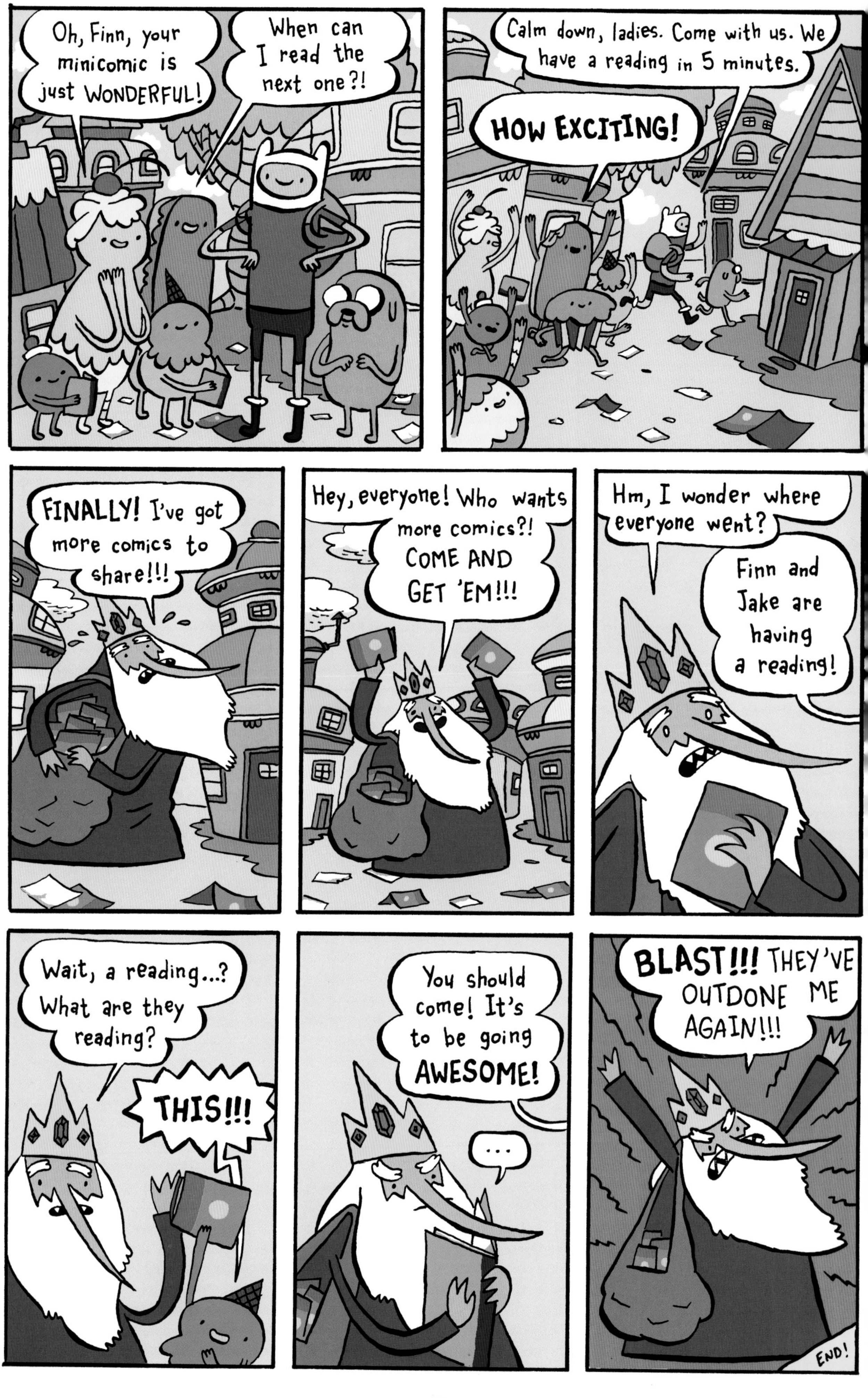
Oh, Finn, your minicomic is just WONDERFUL!
When can I read the next one?!
Calm down, ladies. Come with us. We have a reading in 5 minutes.
HOW EXCITING!
FINALLY! I've got more comics to share!!!
Hey, everyone! Who wants more comics?! COME AND GET 'EM!!!
Hm, I wonder where everyone went?
Finn and Jake are having a reading!
Wait, a reading...? What are they reading?
THIS!!!
You should come! It's to be going AWESOME!
...
BLAST!!! THEY'VE OUTDONE ME AGAIN!!!
END!

THE DEVILISH DEVOURER OF DELICIOUS DELICACIES

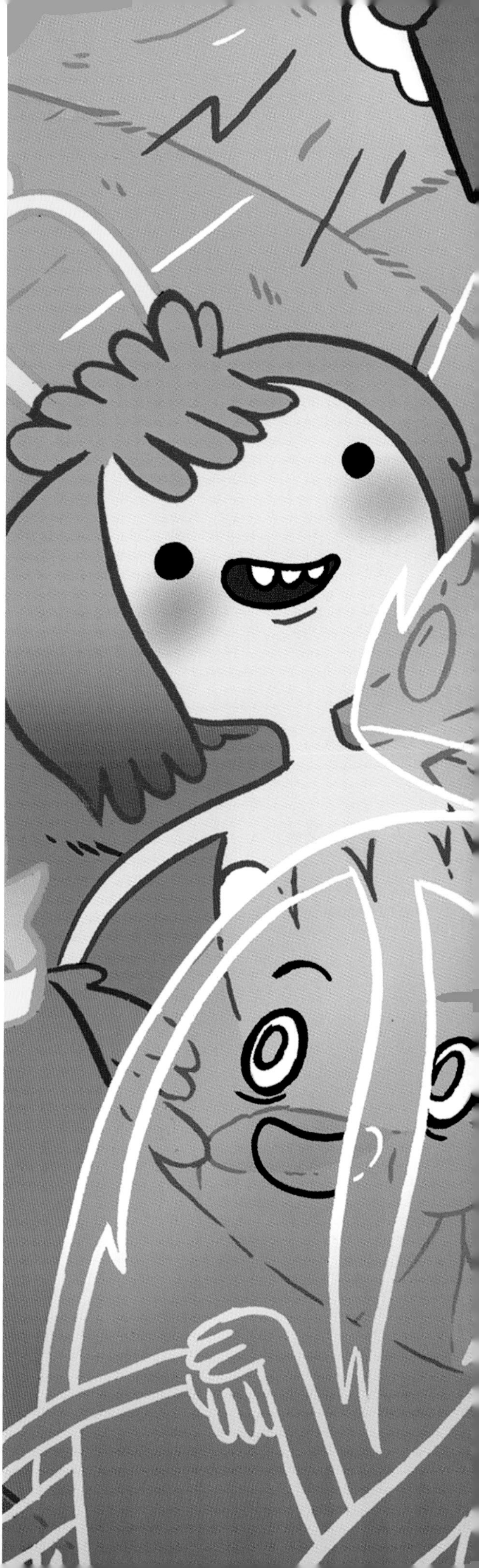

ISSUE THIRTEEN COVER D

MIKE BERTINO

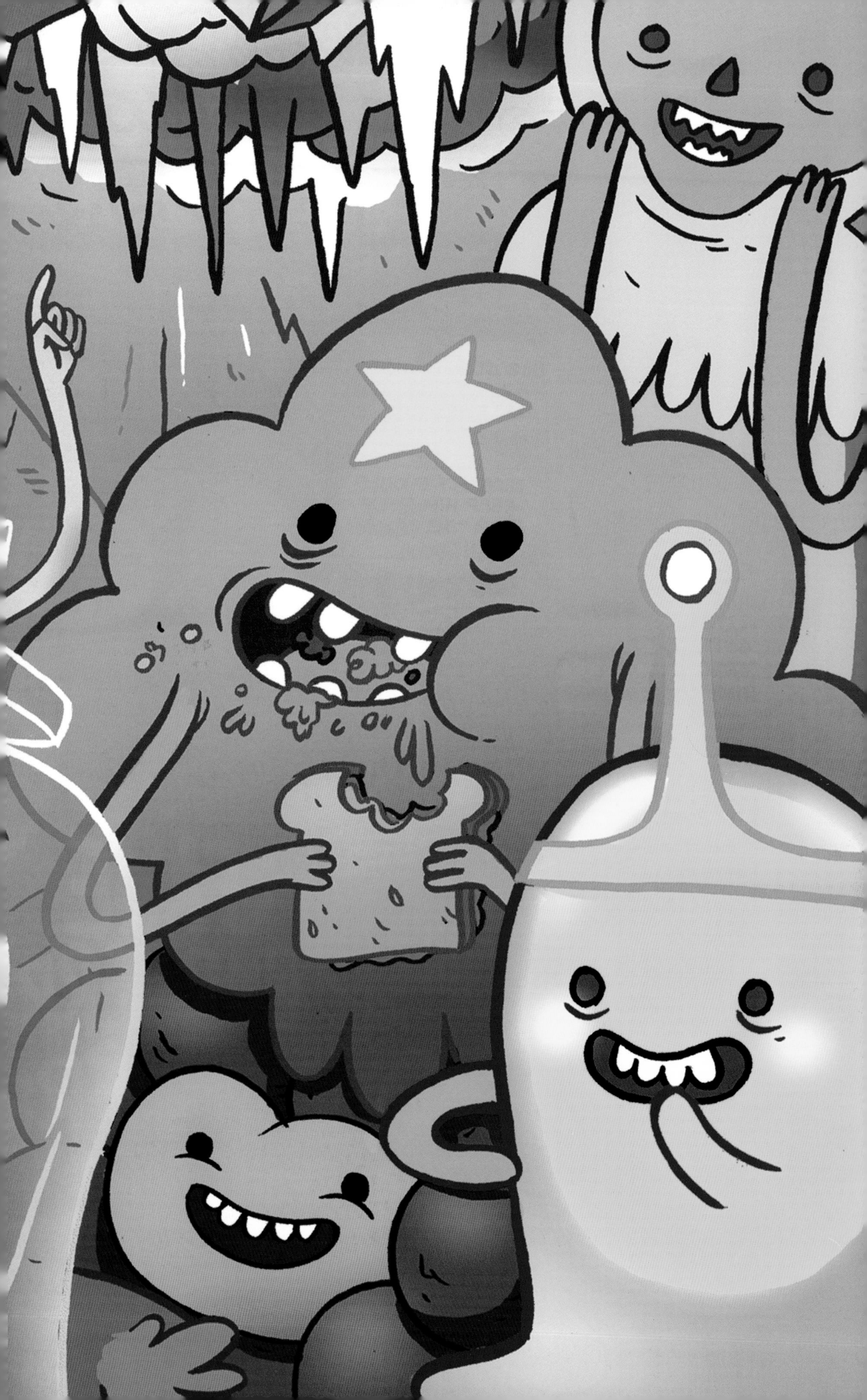

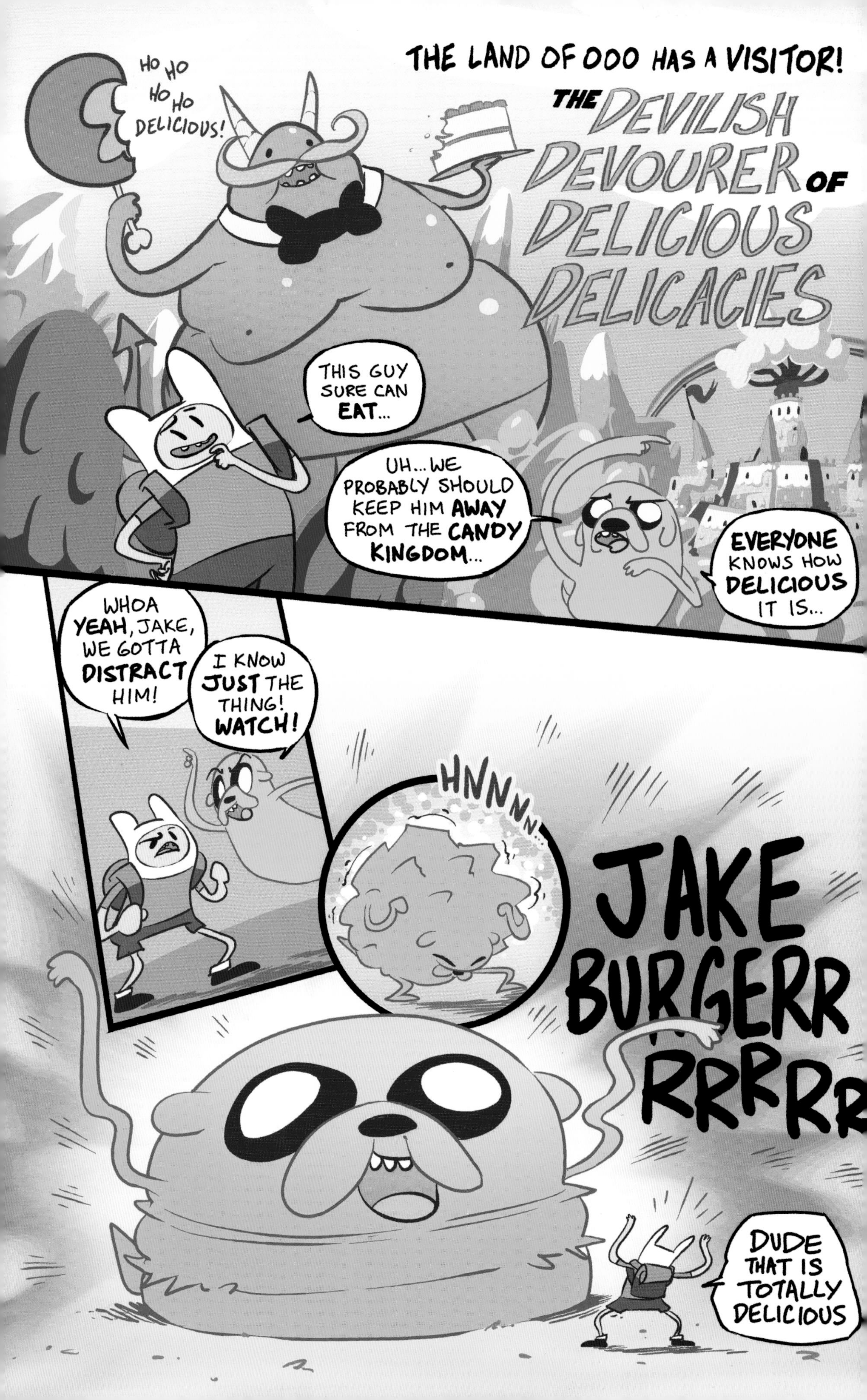
THE LAND OF OOO HAS A VISITOR!
THE DEVILISH DEVOURER OF DELICIOUS DELICACIES
HO HO HO HO DELICIOUS!
THIS GUY SURE CAN EAT...
UH... WE PROBABLY SHOULD KEEP HIM AWAY FROM THE CANDY KINGDOM...
EVERYONE KNOWS HOW DELICIOUS IT IS...
WHOA YEAH, JAKE, WE GOTTA DISTRACT HIM!
I KNOW JUST THE THING! WATCH!
HNNNN...
JAKE BURGERRRRRRR
DUDE THAT IS TOTALLY DELICIOUS

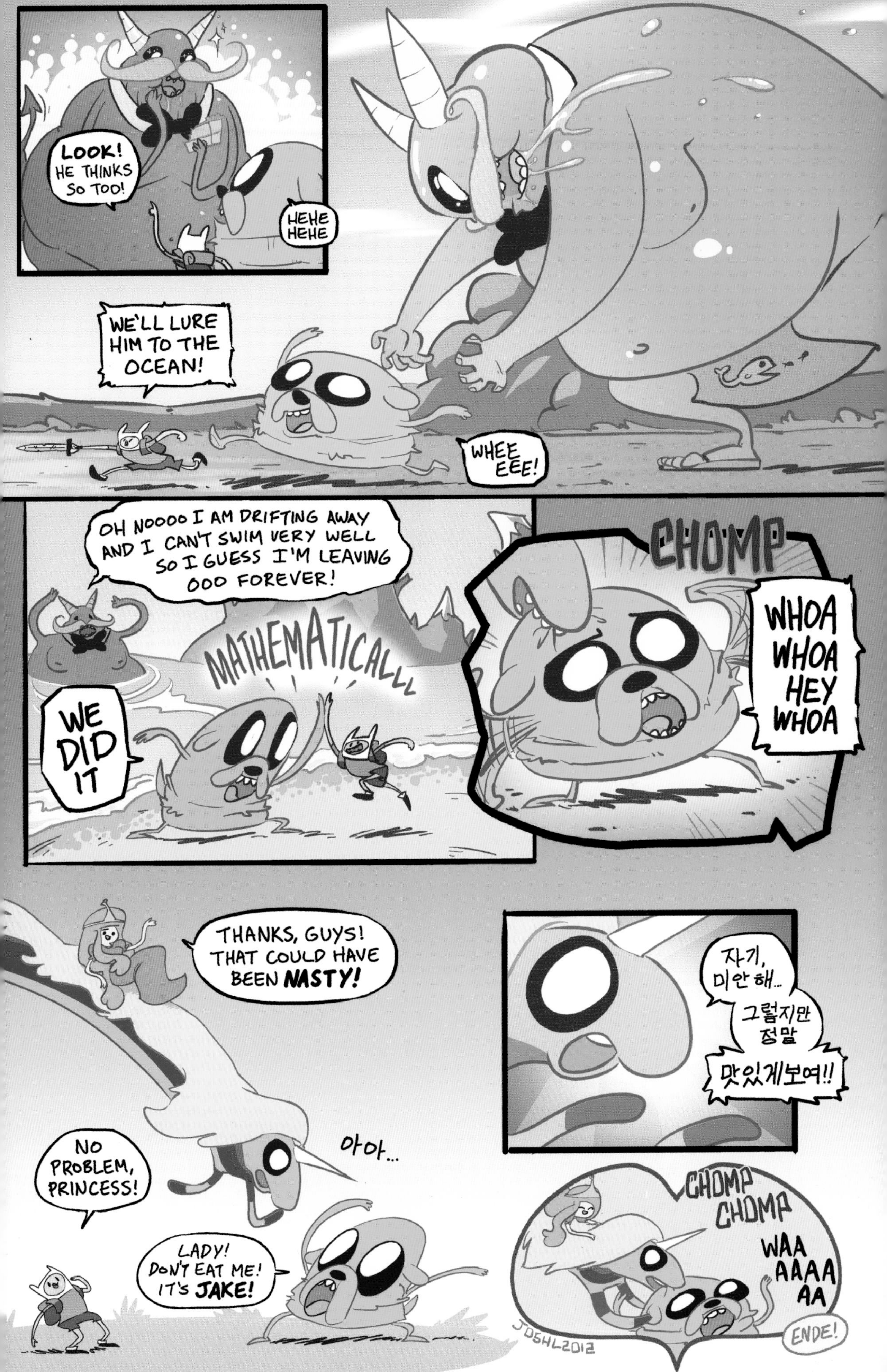
LOOK! HE THINKS SO TOO!
HEHE HEHE
WE'LL LURE HIM TO THE OCEAN!
WHEE EEE!
OH NOOOO I AM DRIFTING AWAY AND I CAN'T SWIM VERY WELL SO I GUESS I'M LEAVING OOO FOREVER!
MATHEMATICALLL
WE DID IT
CHOMP
WHOA WHOA HEY WHOA
THANKS, GUYS! THAT COULD HAVE BEEN NASTY!
NO PROBLEM, PRINCESS!
아아...
LADY! DON'T EAT ME! IT'S JAKE!
자기, 미안 해..
그렇지만 정말
맛있게보여!!
CHOMP CHOMP
WAA AAAA AA
ENDE!
JOSHL2012

THE PRINCESS OF RAD HATS

ISSUE FOURTEEN, COVER D
MING DOYLE

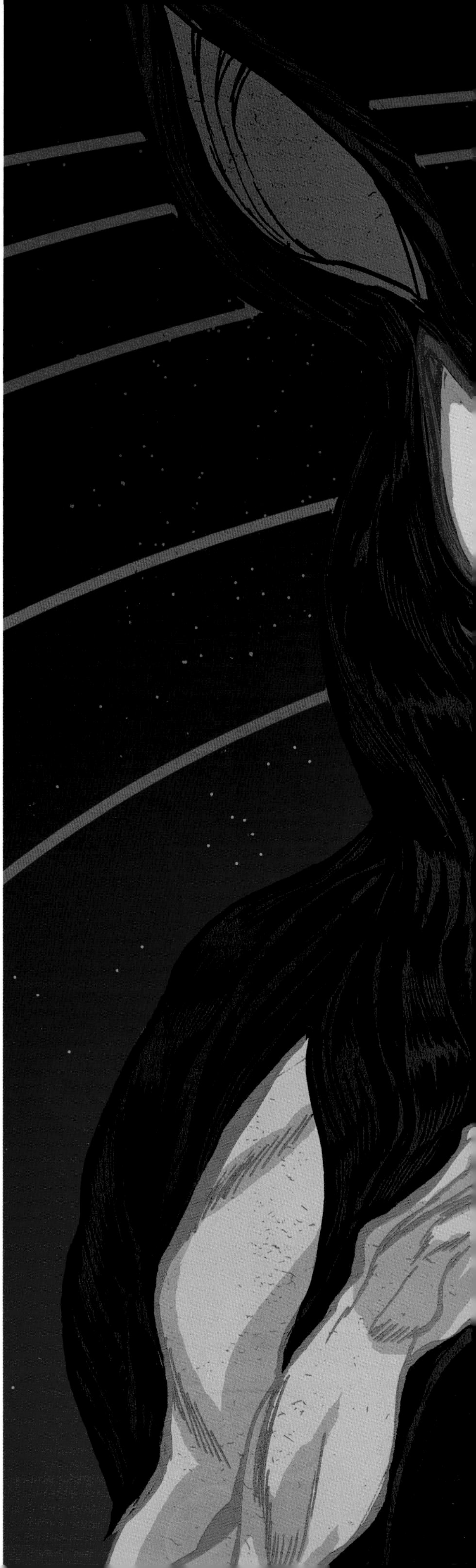

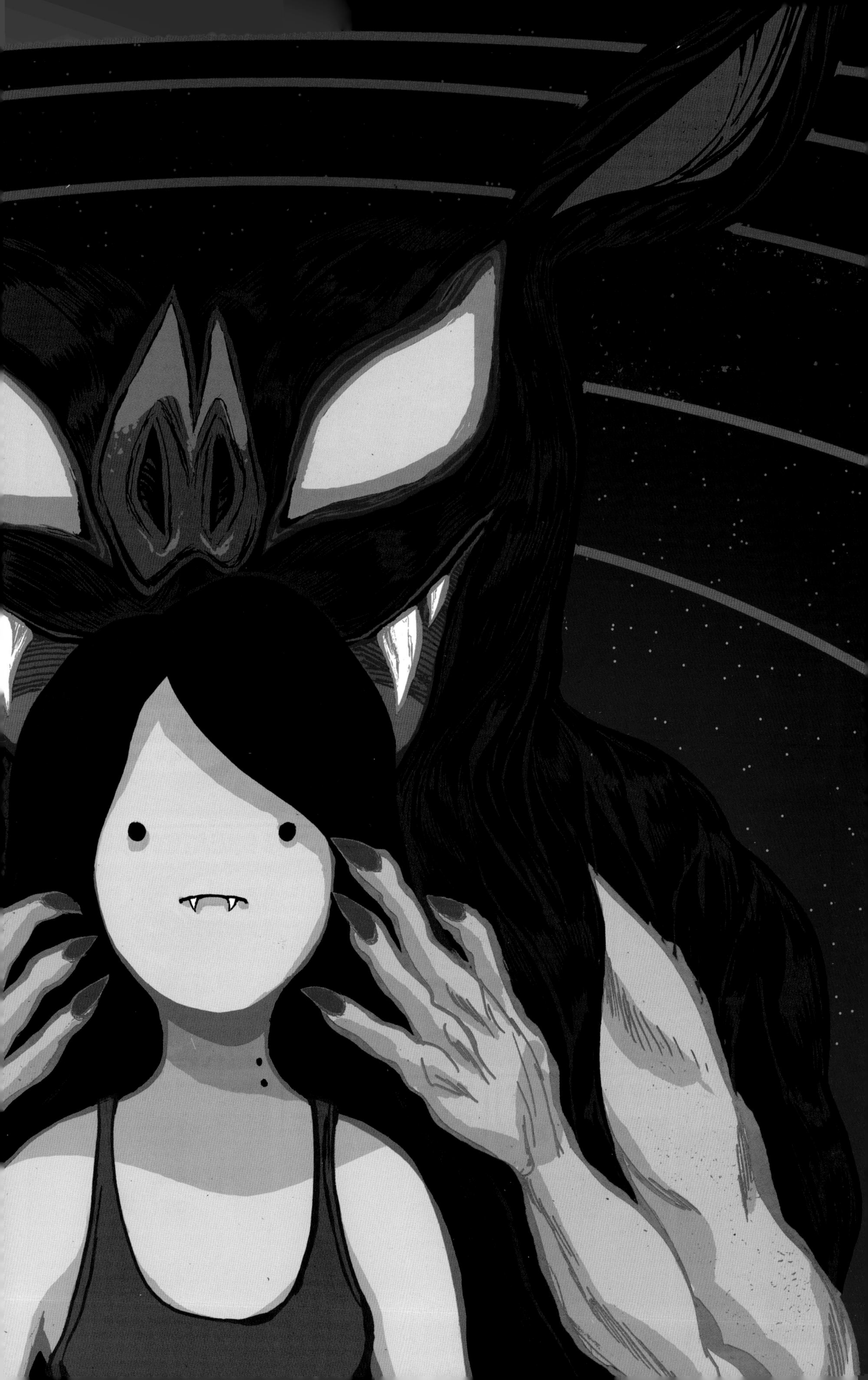

FINN & JAKE

"THE PRINCESS OF RAD HATS"

PART ONE

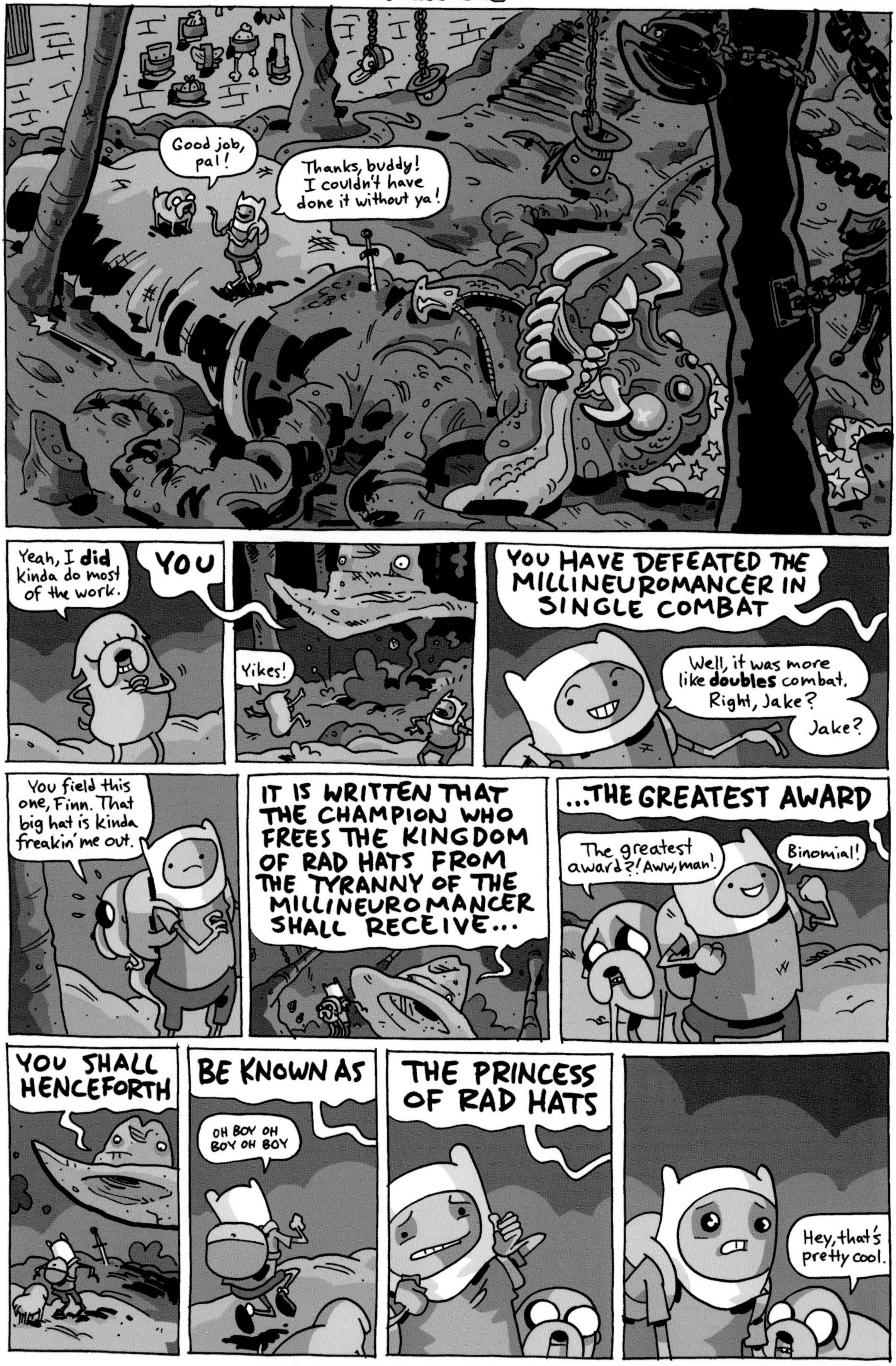
Good job, pal!
Thanks, buddy! I couldn't have done it without ya!
Yeah, I **did** kinda do most of the work.
YOU
Yikes!
YOU HAVE DEFEATED THE MILLINEUROMANCER IN SINGLE COMBAT
Well, it was more like **doubles** combat. Right, Jake?
Jake?
You field this one, Finn. That big hat is kinda freakin' me out.
IT IS WRITTEN THAT THE CHAMPION WHO FREES THE KINGDOM OF RAD HATS FROM THE TYRANNY OF THE MILLINEUROMANCER SHALL RECEIVE...
...THE GREATEST AWARD
The greatest award?! Aww, man!
Binomial!
YOU SHALL HENCEFORTH
BE KNOWN AS
OH BOY OH BOY OH BOY
THE PRINCESS OF RAD HATS
Hey, that's pretty cool.

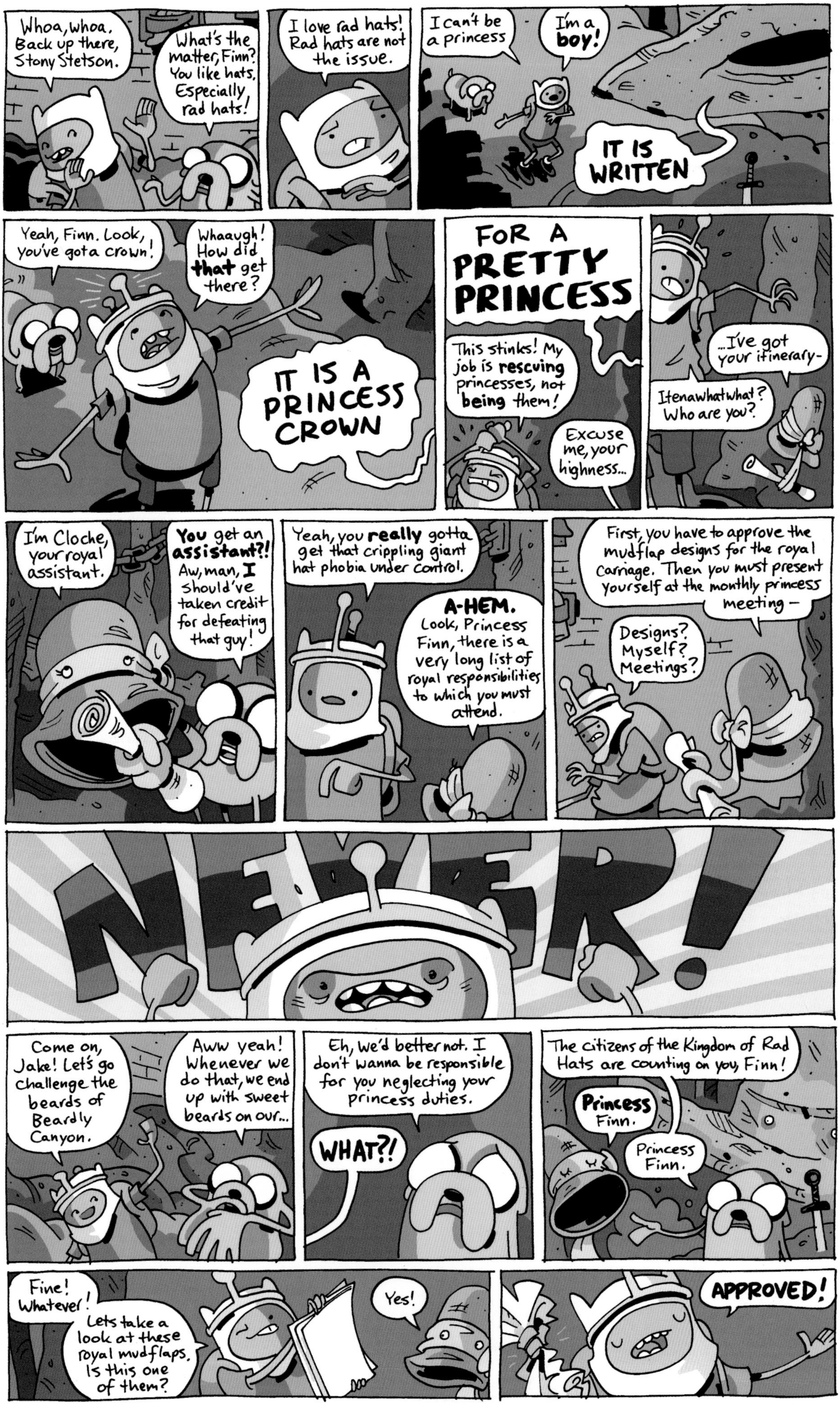

Whoa, whoa. Back up there, Stony Stetson.
What's the matter, Finn? You like hats. Especially rad hats!
I love rad hats! Rad hats are not the issue.
I can't be a princess
I'm a boy!
IT IS WRITTEN
Yeah, Finn. Look, you've got a crown!
Whaaugh! How did that get there?
IT IS A PRINCESS CROWN
FOR A PRETTY PRINCESS
This stinks! My job is rescuing princesses, not being them!
Excuse me, your highness...
...I've got your itinerary-
Itenawhatwhat? Who are you?
I'm Cloche, your royal assistant.
You get an assistant?! Aw, man, I should've taken credit for defeating that guy!
Yeah, you really gotta get that crippling giant hat phobia under control.
A-HEM. Look, Princess Finn, there is a very long list of royal responsibilities to which you must attend.
First, you have to approve the mudflap designs for the royal carriage. Then you must present yourself at the monthly princess meeting –
Designs? Myself? Meetings?
NEVER!
Come on, Jake! Let's go challenge the beards of Beardly Canyon.
Aww yeah! Whenever we do that, we end up with sweet beards on our...
Eh, we'd better not. I don't wanna be responsible for you neglecting your princess duties.
WHAT?!
The citizens of the Kingdom of Rad Hats are counting on you, Finn!
Princess Finn.
Princess Finn.
Fine! Whatever!
Lets take a look at these royal mudflaps. Is this one of them?
Yes!
APPROVED!

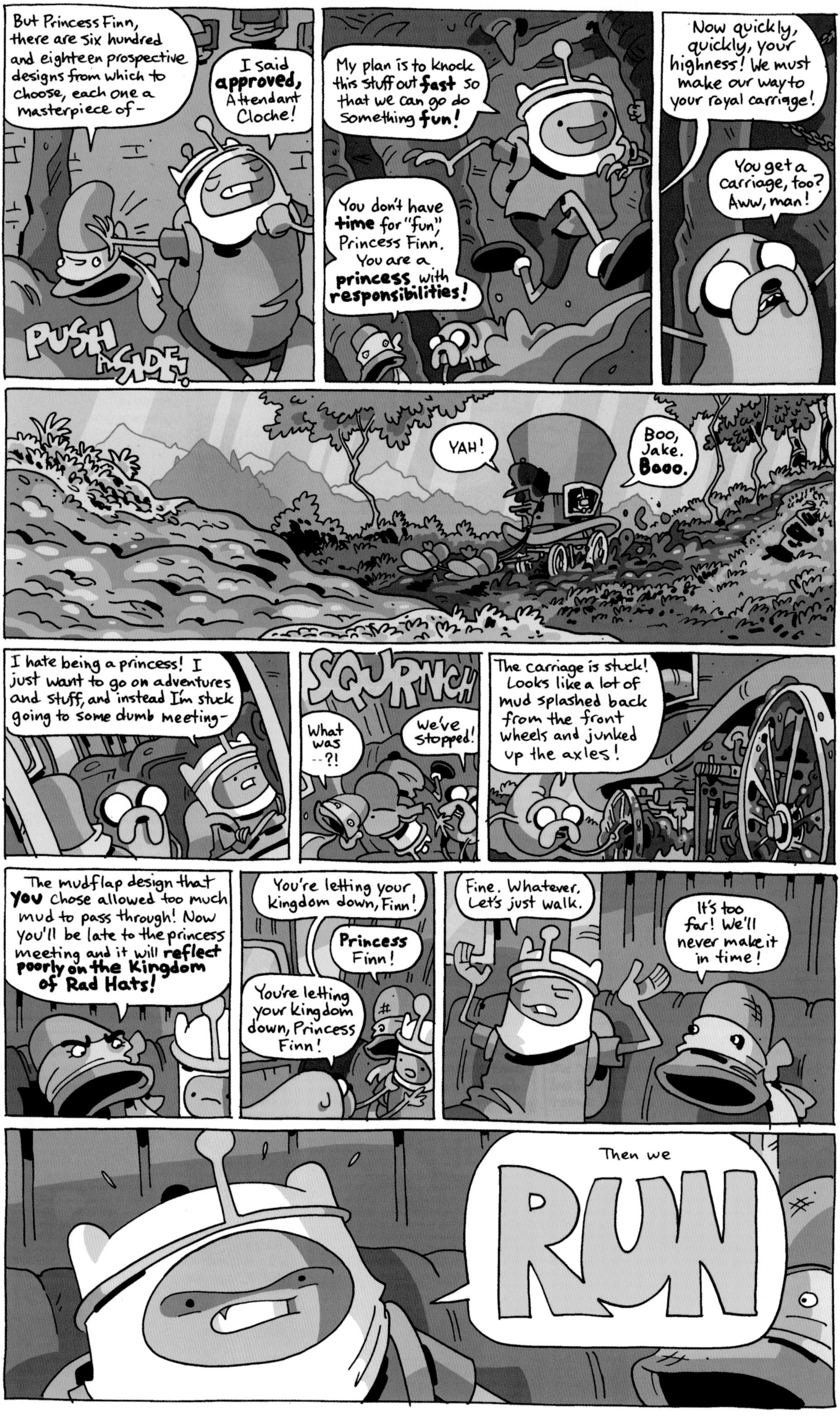

But Princess Finn, there are six hundred and eighteen prospective designs from which to choose, each one a masterpiece of-
I said **approved,** Attendant Cloche!
PUSH ASIDE.
My plan is to knock this stuff out **fast** so that we can go do something **fun!**
You don't have **time** for "fun," Princess Finn. You are a **princess** with **responsibilities!**
Now quickly, quickly, your highness! We must make our way to your royal carriage!
You get a carriage, too? Aww, man!
YAH!
Boo, Jake. **Booo.**
I hate being a princess! I just want to go on adventures and stuff, and instead I'm stuck going to some dumb meeting-
SQURNCH
What was --?!
We've stopped!
The carriage is stuck! Looks like a lot of mud splashed back from the front wheels and junked up the axles!
The mudflap design that **you** chose allowed too much mud to pass through! Now you'll be late to the princess meeting and it will **reflect poorly on the Kingdom of Rad Hats!**
You're letting your kingdom down, Finn!
Princess Finn!
You're letting your kingdom down, Princess Finn!
Fine. Whatever. Let's just walk.
It's too far! We'll never make it in time!
Then we RUN

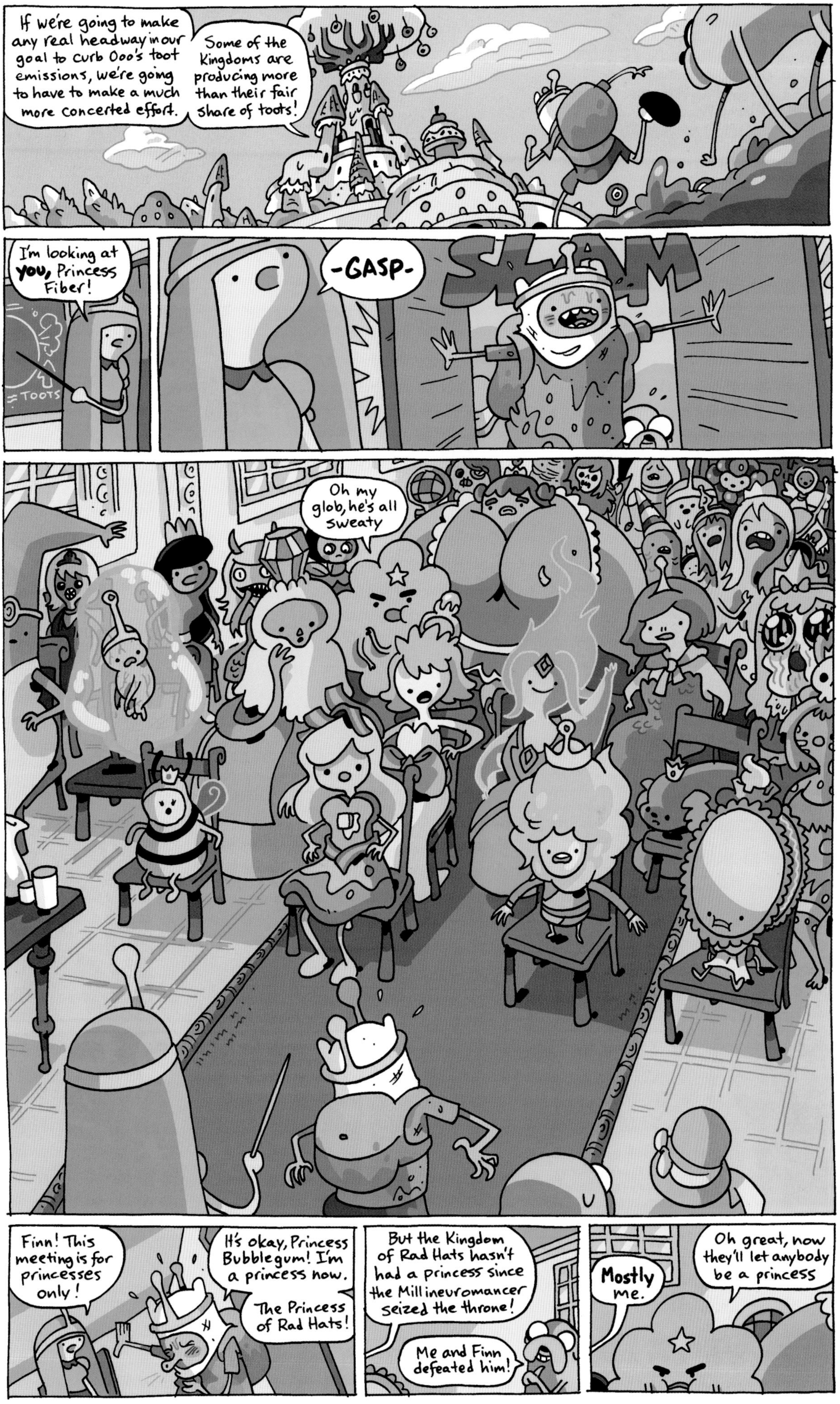
If we're going to make any real headway in our goal to curb Ooo's toot emissions, we're going to have to make a much more concerted effort.
Some of the Kingdoms are producing more than their fair share of toots!
I'm looking at **YOU,** Princess Fiber!
TOOTS
-GASP-
SLAM
Oh my glob, he's all sweaty
Finn! This meeting is for princesses only!
It's okay, Princess Bubblegum! I'm a princess now.
The Princess of Rad Hats!
But the Kingdom of Rad Hats hasn't had a princess since the Millineuromancer seized the throne!
Me and Finn defeated him!
Mostly me.
Oh great, now they'll let anybody be a princess

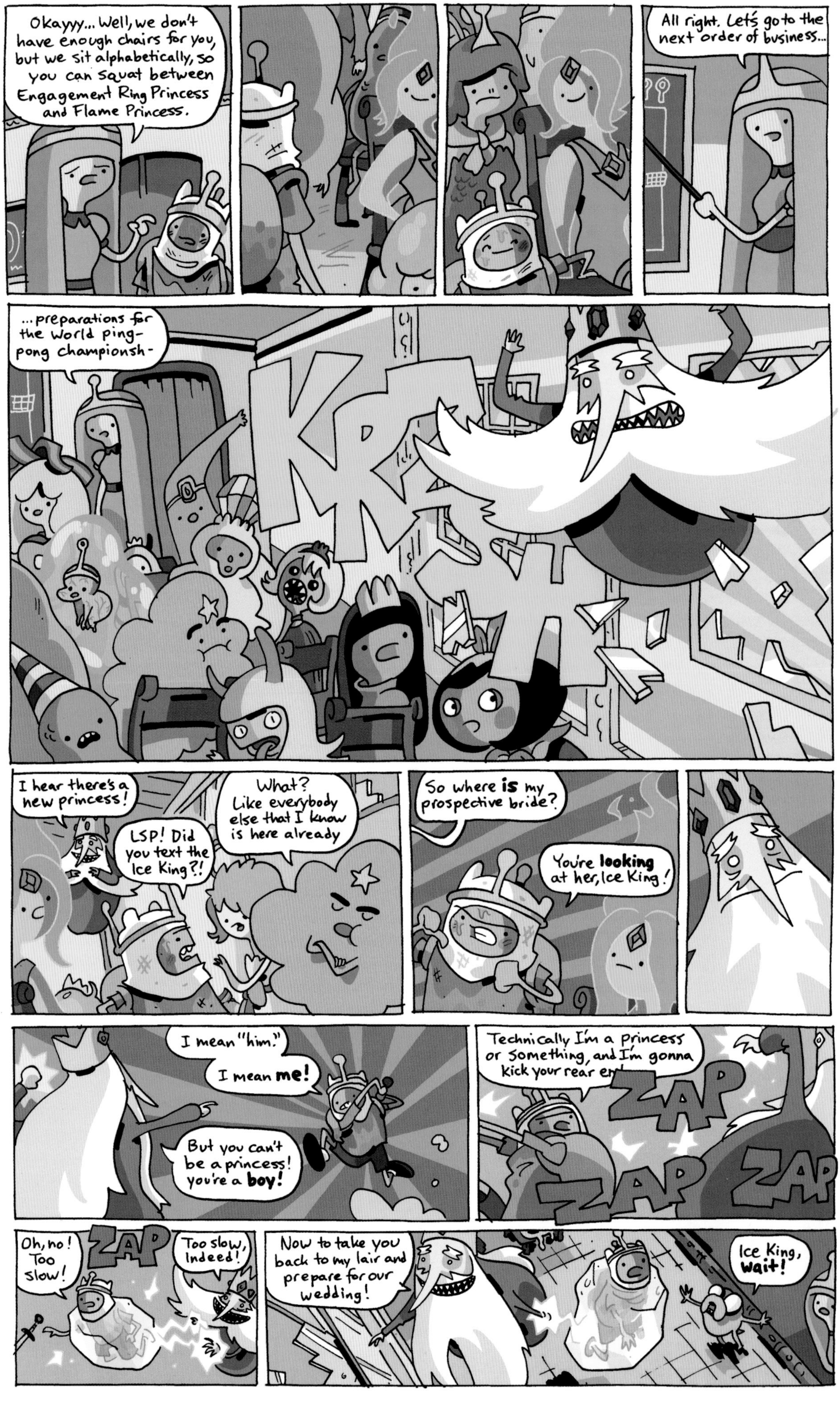

Okayyy... Well, we don't have enough chairs for you, but we sit alphabetically, so you can squat between Engagement Ring Princess and Flame Princess.
All right. Let's go to the next order of business...
...preparations for the World ping-pong championsh-
KRASH
I hear there's a new princess!
LSP! Did you text the Ice King?!
What? Like everybody else that I know is here already
So where **is** my prospective bride?
You're **looking** at her, Ice King!
I mean "him."
I mean **me!**
But you can't be a princess! you're a **boy!**
Technically I'm a princess or something, and I'm gonna kick your rear en-
ZAP
ZAP
ZAP
Oh, no! Too slow!
ZAP
Too slow, indeed!
Now to take you back to my lair and prepare for our wedding!
Ice King, **wait!**

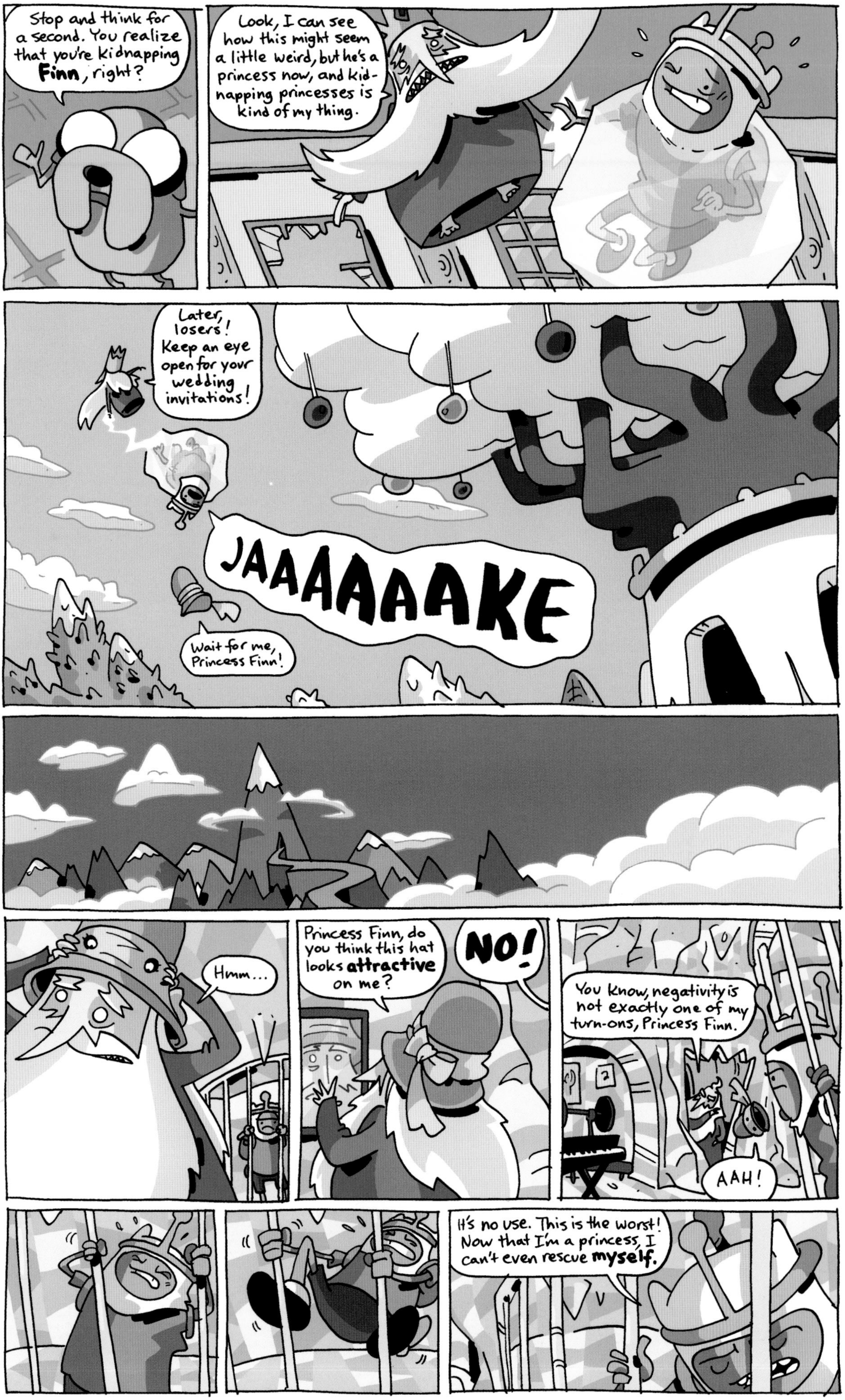

Stop and think for a second. You realize that you're kidnapping **Finn**, right?
Look, I can see how this might seem a little weird, but he's a princess now, and kid-napping princesses is kind of my thing.
Later, losers! Keep an eye open for your wedding invitations!
JAAAAAAKE
Wait for me, Princess Finn!
Hmm...
Princess Finn, do you think this hat looks **attractive** on me?
NO!
You know, negativity is not exactly one of my turn-ons, Princess Finn.
AAH!
It's no use. This is the worst! Now that I'm a princess, I can't even rescue **myself.**

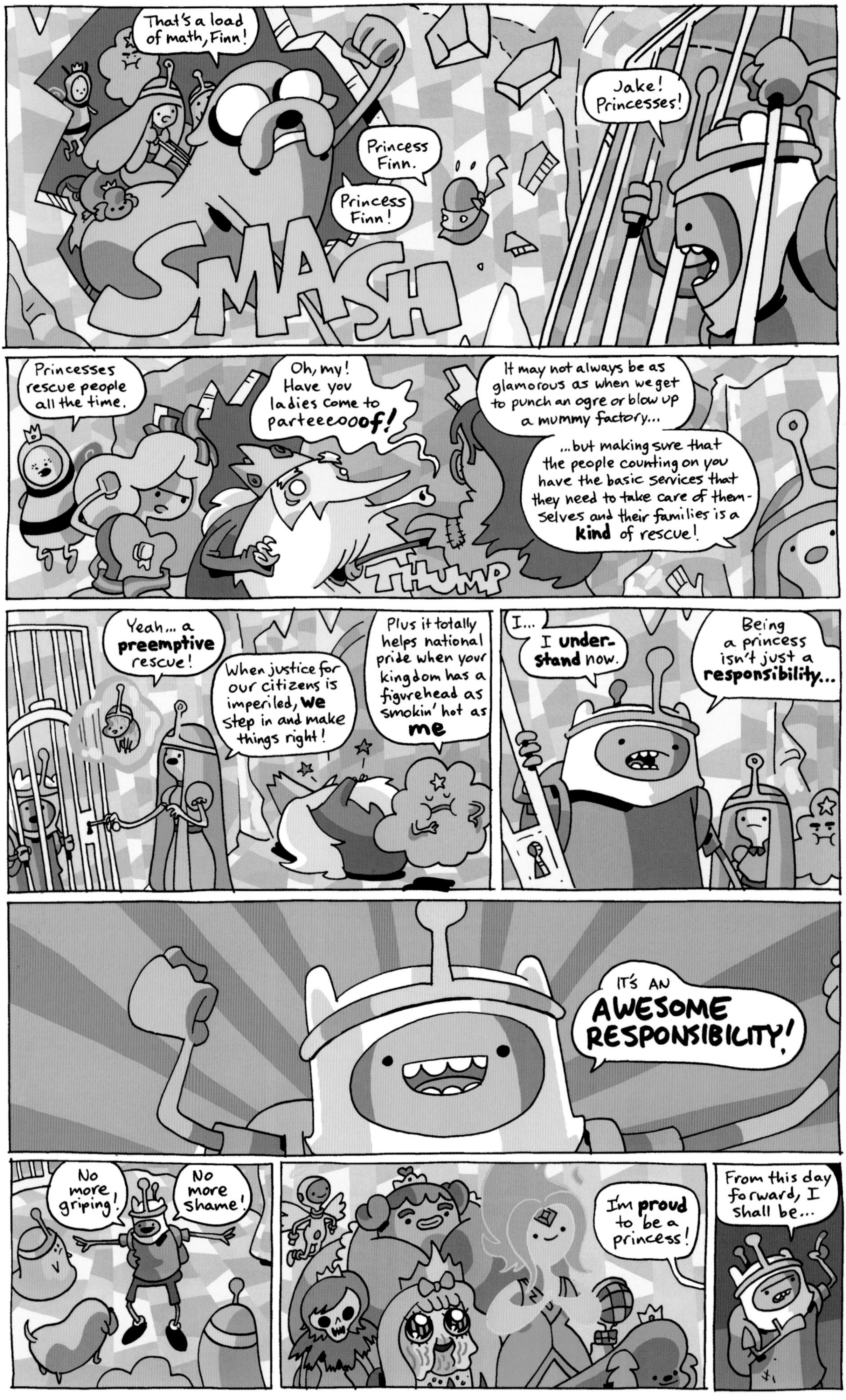

That's a load of math, Finn!
Jake! Princesses!
Princess Finn.
Princess Finn!
SMASH
Princesses rescue people all the time.
Oh, my! Have you ladies come to parteeeooof!
It may not always be as glamorous as when we get to punch an ogre or blow up a mummy factory...
...but making sure that the people counting on you have the basic services that they need to take care of themselves and their families is a **kind** of rescue!
THUMP
Yeah... a **preemptive** rescue!
When justice for our citizens is imperiled, **we** step in and make things right!
Plus it totally helps national pride when your kingdom has a figurehead as smokin' hot as **me**
I... I **understand** now.
Being a princess isn't just a **responsibility...**
IT'S AN AWESOME RESPONSIBILITY!
No more griping!
No more shame!
I'm **proud** to be a princess!
From this day forward, I shall be...

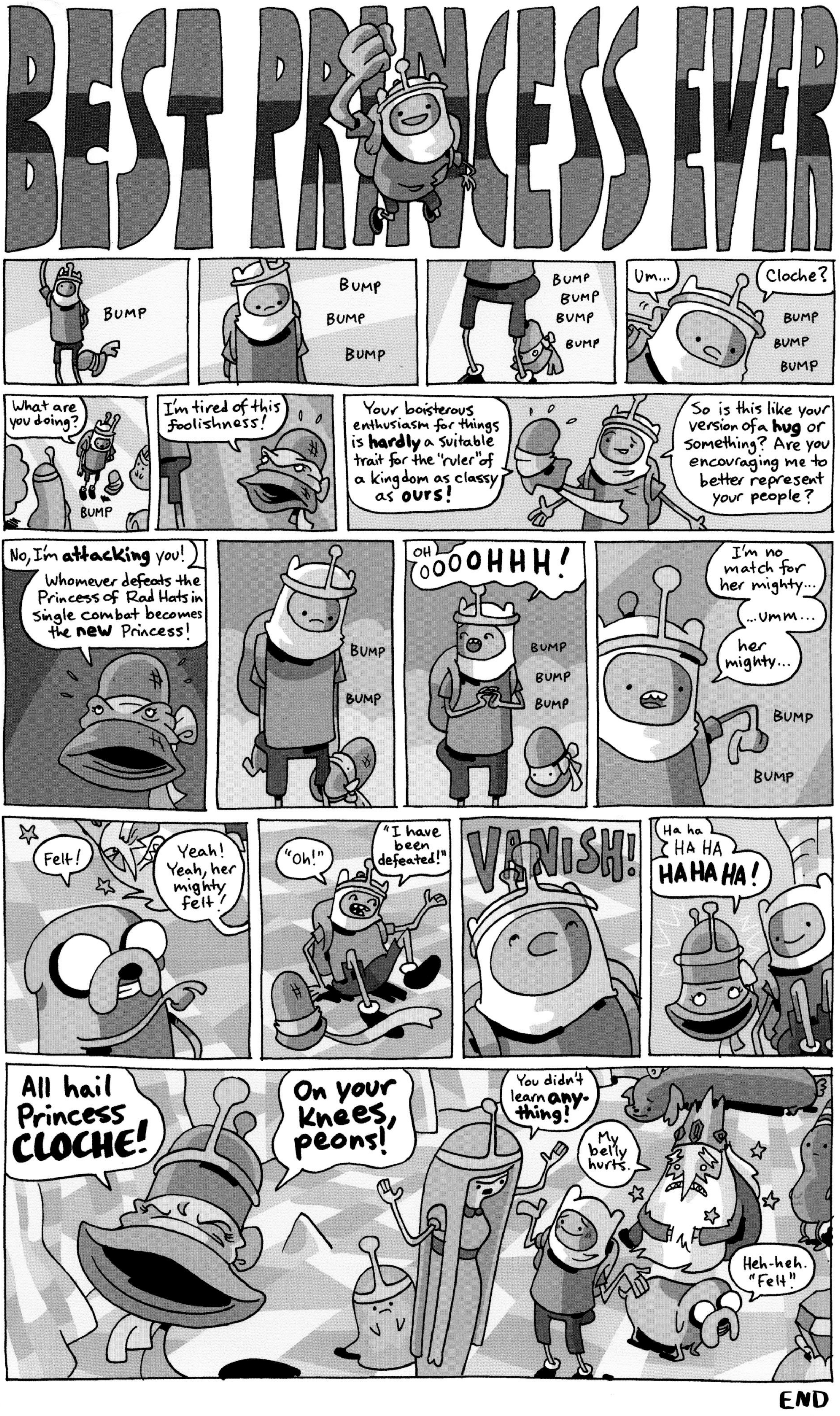
BEST PRINCESS EVER
BUMP
BUMP
BUMP
BUMP
BUMP
BUMP
BUMP
BUMP
Um...
Cloche?
BUMP
BUMP
BUMP
What are you doing?
BUMP
I'm tired of this foolishness!
Your boisterous enthusiasm for things is hardly a suitable trait for the "ruler" of a kingdom as classy as ours!
So is this like your version of a hug or something? Are you encouraging me to better represent your people?
No, I'm attacking you!
Whomever defeats the Princess of Rad Hats in single combat becomes the new Princess!
BUMP
BUMP
OH OOOOHHH!
BUMP
BUMP
BUMP
I'm no match for her mighty...
...umm...
her mighty...
BUMP
BUMP
Felt!
Yeah! Yeah, her mighty felt!
"Oh!"
"I have been defeated!"
VANISH!
Ha ha
HA HA
HAHAHA!
All hail Princess CLOCHE!
On your knees, peons!
You didn't learn any-thing!
My belly hurts.
Heh-heh. "Felt."
END

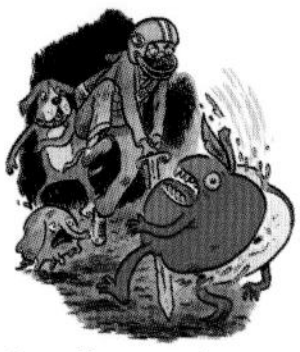

http://aaronrenier.com

"MY CIDER THE MOUNTAIN"
Written and Illustrated by Aaron Renier

Aaron lives in Chicago with his best friend Beluga. Most days they can be seen running around the park scaring ducks. Aaron has two graphic novels you can read if you want, the first one is called SPIRAL-BOUND, and the second is THE UNSINKABLE WALKER BEAN. Both are a little weird, but they're fun.

"LAUNDROMARCELINE"
Written and Illustrated by Lucy Knisley

Lucy Knisley is a comic artist and author. She is 27 and lives in New York. Her newest book is called RELISH. Learn way more than you ever wanted to about Lucy at www.lucyknisley.com.

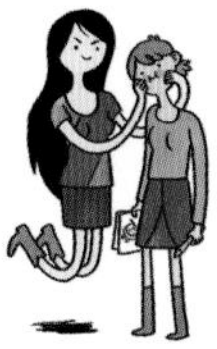

http://lucyknisley.com

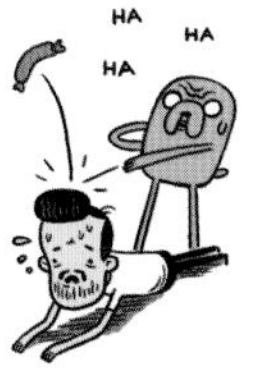
HA
HA
HA

http://kingtrash.com

"BACON FIELDS"
Written and Illustrated by Michael DeForge

Michael lives in Toronto, Ontario and works as a prop and effects designer on ADVENTURE TIME. He also draws comics on the side! He spends his time alternating between eating pizza, ordering pizza and thinking about ordering pizza, depending on the time of day. He is trying out a moustache.

"ULTIMATE PARTY DIP"
Written and Illustrated by Chris "Elio" Eliopoulos

Chris is a cartoonist from Chicago, IL. He loves drawing comics all day long. Check out his recent graphic novels, OKIE DOKIE DONUTS, GABBA BALL!, and MONSTER PARTY.

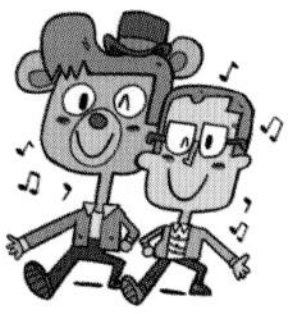

www.eliohouse.com

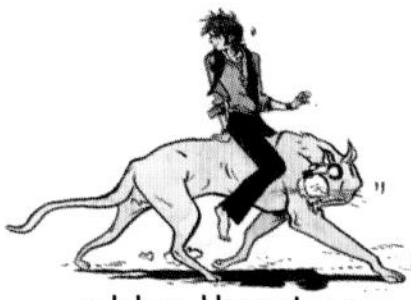

pulphope.blogspot.com

"EMIT ERUTNEVDA"
Written and Illustrated by Paul Pope

Paul Pope is an artist living and working in New York City, USA. His current project, a graphic novel called BATTLING BOY, will be out next year from First Second Books. His nephews, Ben and Alexander, are huge ADVENTURE TIME fans (hi guys!).

"LEVEL 99"
Written and Illustrated by Anthony Clark

Anthony lives in Indianapolis and draws cartoons about a half-bear/half-potato. You can read those and more at www.nedroid.com, if you are brave enough.

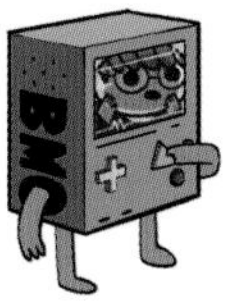
BMO

http://nedroid.com

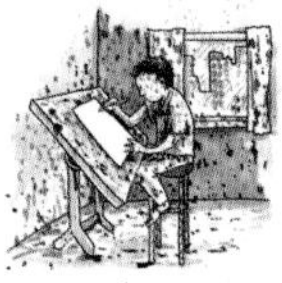

http://tmcm.com

"TIME WAITS FOR NO ONE"
Written and Illustrated by Shannon Wheeler

Shannon Wheeler is the Eisner Award–winning creator of TOO MUCH COFFEE MAN. He has contributed to a variety of publications that include The Onion newspaper and The New Yorker magazine. Wheeler currently lives with his cats, chickens, bees, girlfriend and children. His weekly comic strip is published in various alternative weeklies and online at tmcm.com.

"HAPPY BIRTHDAY HOT DOG PRINCESS!"
Written and Illustrated by Frank Gibson & Becky Dreistadt

Becky and Frank have been together for 7 years and have been making comics for almost as long! They love cartoons, cats, travel and old things. They make a hand-painted webcomic called TINY KITTEN TEETH and recently finished "Capture Creatures," a year-long 151 painting project.

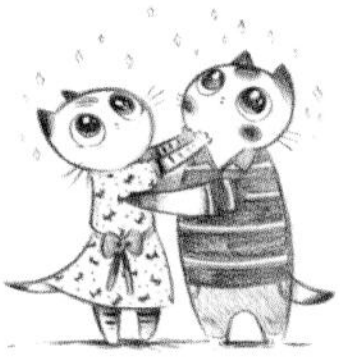

http://tinykittenteeth.com

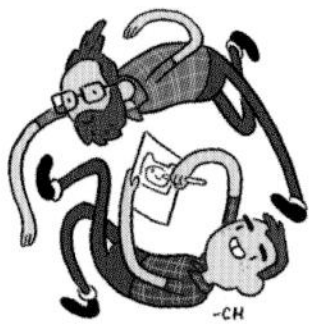
-CH

http://www.reedgunther.com

"FISHLING"
Written by Shane Houghton
Illustrated by Chris Houghton

Brothers Shane and Chris Houghton are the dynamic duo behind the Image comic book series REED GUNTHER. They have also worked on comics for THE SIMPSONS, PEANUTS, and more!

"HOT DEALS IN ICE KINGDOM"

Written by Jon M. Gibson
Illustrated by Jim Rugg

Jim Rugg is the co-creator of AFRODISIAC, THE PLAIN JANES, STREET ANGEL, and USAPE. He is also the co-host of TELL ME SOMETHING I DON'T KNOW. Jon M. Gibson is a writer/director who has done a bunch of seemingly random things with his life: scripts for animated cartoons, lots of articles for the few surviving print magazines, and founded a company called iam8bit, where he makes lots of fun stuff with his great pal, Amanda.

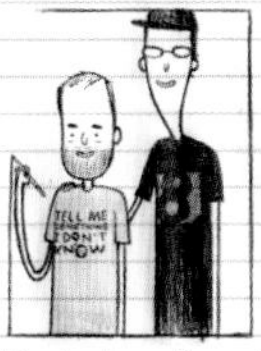

http://facebook.com/jonmgibson
http://jimrugg.com

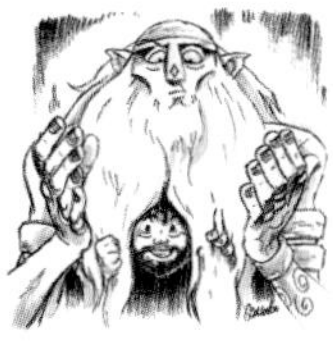

http://.zackgiallongo.com

"THE MEANING OF BRAVERY"

Written and Illustrated by Zack Giallongo

Zack Giallongo is a typical bearded cartoonist who plays the banjo and loves animals, both on and off the table. He just released his first graphic novel, BROXO, about teenage barbarians and zombies which somehow made it onto the New York Times Bestseller list.

"THE ICE KING & HIS MAGICAL MATCHMAKING MINI-COMIC"

Written by Alexis Frederick-Frost
Illustrated by Andrew Arnold

Andrew Arnold and Alexis Frederick-Frost are two heads of the 3-headed cartooning monster responsible for creating the ADVENTURES IN CARTOONING graphic novels from First Second Books. Alexis' other works include writing and drawing a series about the exploits of a worldly wise cat and ever-eager dog in Oxford, UK and creating numerous self-published mini-comics. Andrew's work has appeared in several publications from Roaring Brook Press, Cambridge University Press, and Nickelodeon Magazine, to name a few. He currently lives in New York City and works in publishing.

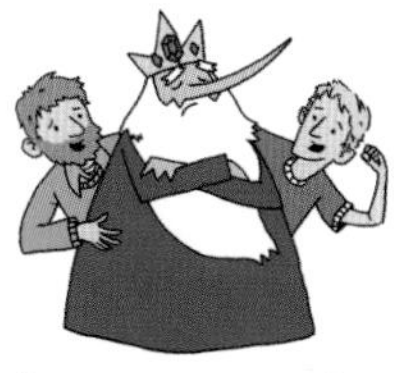

http://www.cartoonstudies.org/arnold/comics.html
http://www.cartoonstudies.org/frederickfrost/

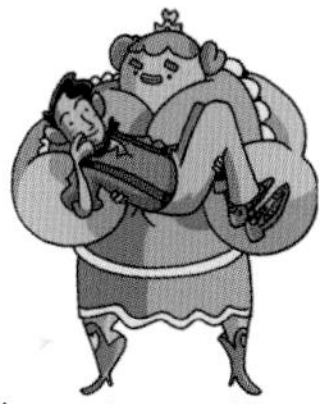

http://croganadventures.blogspot.com

"PRINCESS OF RAD HATS"

Written and Illustrated by Chris Schweizer

Chris Schweizer is the author of THE CROGAN ADVENTURES, a historical adventure graphic novel series full of pirates, ninjas, cowboys, and all the things that you probably never got to spend any time on in history class. He also does other stuff, like teach college, and be a dad.

"AFTER THE SHOW", "THE RIDE OF SIR SLICER" & "LUMPY SPACE DRAMA"

Written and Illustrated by Zac Gorman

Zac Gorman writes the webcomic MAGICAL GAME TIME, designs poster art, and has recently been dipping his toe into character design and other such jobs involving video games, comics and cartoons that are, "seriously, so freakin' awesome to be getting paid to do." His words, not mine. He lives in Chicago.

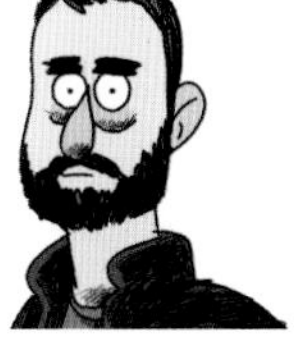

http://zacgorman.com

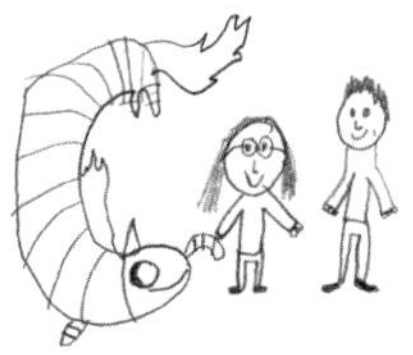

"ICE KINGDUMB"

Written by Georgia & Chris Roberson

Chris Roberson can type very fast (he writes comics like EDISON REX and THE MYSTERIOUS STRANGERS), but Georgia Roberson never lets him forget that she can draw better than he can. When Georgia isn't busy making up stories and drawing, she attends Buckman Arts Focus Elementary in Portland, Oregon.

"THE DEVILISH DEVOURER OF DELICIOUS DELICACIES"

Written and Illustrated by Josh Lesnick

Josh is an artist from Minneapolis who has drawn comics on the internet since 1951. He has much sympathy for the Ice King, because he is also quite fond of princesses, and his friends are all worried about him.

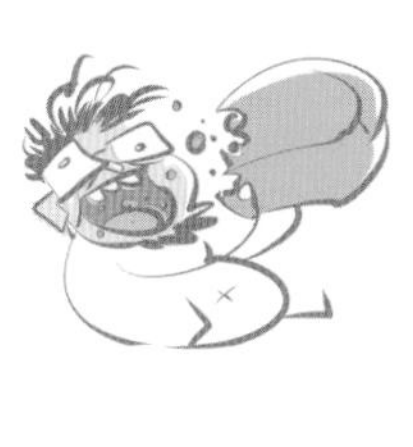

SUGARY SHORTS
Volume Two

COMING 2014

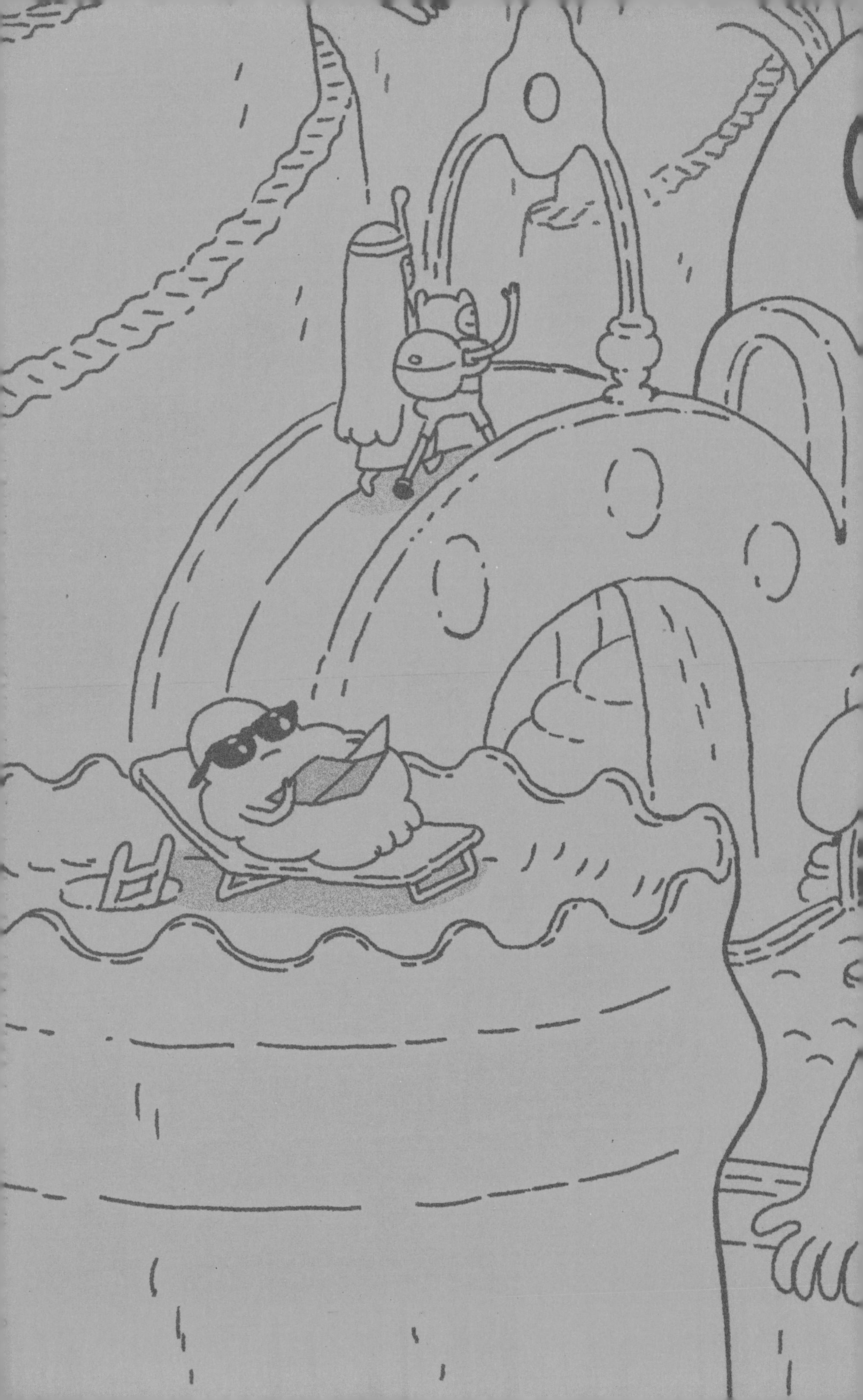